THE PIED PIPER

Also by Ridley Pearson

Beyond Recognition
Chain of Evidence
No Witnesses
The Angel Maker
Hard Fall
Probable Cause
Undercurrents
Hidden Charges
Blood of the Albatross
Never Look Back

RIDLEY PEARSON
THE PIED PIPER

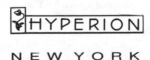

HYPERION

NEW YORK

Library of Congress Cataloging-in-Publication Data

Pearson, Ridley.
The pied piper / Ridley Pearson. — 1st ed.
p.   cm.
ISBN 0-7868-6300-5
I. Title.
PS3566.E234P54   1998
813'.54—dc21   97-49709
                          CIP

Designed by Nicholas A. Bernini

FIRST EDITION

2   4   6   8   10   9   7   5   3   1

For Paige and Marcelle
(Will miracles never cease?)

The author wishes to thank the following for their help and time in providing background information for *The Pied Piper*:

Sergeant Donald Cameron—Seattle Police Department, Crimes Against Persons

Mr. Ralph Stroup, Director—Society for the Relief of Destitute Orphan Boys, The Waldo Burton Home, New Orleans, LA

Ms. Claudine Wilkerson—Society for the Relief of Destitute Orphan Boys

Mr. J. Thomas Lewis—Monroe & Lemann, New Orleans, LA

Mr. Thomas B. Lemann—Monroe & Lemann, New Orleans, LA

Ms. Diana Lewis—New Orleans, LA

Lexis-Nexis—Dayton, OH

Dr. Donald Reay—King County Medical Examiner, Seattle, WA

Mr. Steven Garman—Mt. Medical & Security, Ketchum, ID

C. J. Snow

Editors:

Mr. Albert Zuckerman

Mr. Brian DeFiore

Office:

Mrs. Mary K. Peterson

Ms. Nancy Litzinger

This year marked the passing of three men instrumental to my work habits and my being published. No words of thanks or praise could ring loudly enough to acknowledge all that they gave to me, both as professionals in their fields and as dear and trusted friends and advisers. There is no greater argument for the importance of mentoring. Separately, these men took hold of my hand and led me, editorially, into the creative life of writing and publishing fiction, for which I am eternally grateful.

Gentlemen, you are here, on every page. You always will be.

IN MEMORY

J. Bradbury Thompson
Franklin Heller
Ken McCormick

THE PIED PIPER

CHAPTER

The train left the station headed for nowhere, its destination also its point of embarkation, its purpose not to transport its passengers, but to feed them.

By early March, western Washington neared the end of the rinse cycle, a nearly perpetual curtain of ocean rain that blanketed the region for the winter months, unleashing in its wake a promise of summer. Dark, saturated clouds hung low on the eastern horizon. Well to the west, where the sun retreated in a violent display, a glimpse of blue cracked the marbled gray, as welcome to the residents of Seattle as any sight alive.

Arrival at the dinner train surprised Doris Shotz. She had thought her husband Paul was taking her to Ivar's, one of Seattle's more popular fish-house chains. A simple dinner date had presented her with a test of sorts, being that it was her first evening leaving her four-month-old baby girl, Rhonda, with a sitter. She'd finally decided she could handle an hour or two a few blocks away from home. But an entire evening stuck on a train in the woods was unimaginable, unthinkable!

"Surprised?" he asked, displaying the tickets proudly.

On the verge of total panic, Doris reminded herself that Julie was an experienced sitter, having taken care of Henry for the last year, as responsible a fifteen-year-old as one could ask for. Better to give Paul his moment than to start a fight.

They'd been talking about the dinner train for years. And Doris had to concede that over the last nine months, Paul had been a saint. She owed him.

"I can't believe it!" she said truthfully.

"I know. You didn't guess, did you?"

"Not for an instant. I promise: It's a complete surprise."

"Good." He reached down and took her hand and squeezed. She felt flushed. She wanted to be home with the kids.

"All aboard," he said.

The train lurched. Doris Shotz shifted to avoid spilling the cheap champagne that Paul had ordered. Although she didn't want to drink while nursing, she knew Paul would consider it an act of defiance to say no to any part of the celebration, and given that she had already gone this far to please her husband, she wasn't going to let one glass of champagne ruin the evening. When the train turned east, the frosted mountains flooded crimson with the sunset, Paul said with obvious satisfaction, "This is a long way from the backside of a computer."

Paul repaired PCs for Micro System Workshop, a name his employer had invented because it could be reduced to MS Workshop, and in an area dominated by Microsoft those two initials meant dollars. Paul drove a blue MS Workshop van around the city, crisis to crisis, fire to fire: hard drives, networks, IRQ ports—Doris had heard all the buzzwords enough times to think she might be capable of a repair or two herself.

Paul provided for them adequately. He loved her in his own way. She loved him too, though differently than she once had. Now the children absorbed most of her time and much of her love, too. She wasn't sure exactly how to categorize her love for Paul; she simply knew that she would always be at his side, would attempt to put up with his moods. But the truth was that she lived for her children, Rhonda and Henry. She had never before known such a complete feeling. It warmed her just thinking about it.

She politely refused a refill of champagne as she watched her husband's cheeks redden behind the alcohol's effects. Clearly carried away with happiness and the light buzz that came from the champagne, he talked at her, but she didn't hear. Boys and trains, she thought.

"Do you think I should call home?" she asked him.

"Call?"

She motioned to the rear of the train car. "There's a pay phone. Cellular. I could call them."

"You know how much those things cost? Fifteen minutes, Doro," he pointed out, checking his Casio and saying sarcastically, "we've been gone a whole fifteen minutes!" He leaned closer and she could smell the sweet alcohol on his breath, a smell that reminded her of the occasional drunken violence that Paul had sometimes brought with him to their bed. "They're fine. Julie's perfectly capable."

"You're right," she said, offering him a fragile smile. He nodded and stared out the window. She felt sick with anxiety.

It occurred to her that in a few minutes she could excuse herself to go to the bathroom and use the phone. Paul would probably never know. The champagne bottle's white plastic cork rolled noisily at his feet. The train clattered past condominiums that reminded her of a Monopoly board. A few of the couples had dressed for the occasion, though most wore jeans and sweatshirts. It wasn't exactly the Orient Express.

It soon became clear that Paul's romance was with the train rather than her. Flushed cheeks pressed to the glass, his right foot tapping quickly as it always did when he drank in excess, her husband disappeared into the alcohol and she retreated into thoughts about her children.

Ten minutes passed with minimal conversation. Doris excused herself and made the call home. It rang and rang, but there was no answer.

Wrong number, she decided. At those prices—$3.95 for the first minute, $.99 each portion of a minute thereafter—Paul was certain to catch the charge on the credit card bill. But so what? She pressed NEW CALL. She redialed, again suffering under the weight of its endless ringing. She could envision Julie busy with a diaper, or in the middle of feeding. It didn't necessarily mean trouble. . . .

A fire, she thought. Paul's home entertainment center—a sports center was more like it—crowded the outlets with far too many wires. What would Julie do in a fire?

The knot in her stomach twisted more tightly. Her fingers went cold and numb. Julie might be in the bathroom. Nothing more than that.

But her imagination wouldn't let it go. Perhaps Julie had a boyfriend with her in the house. In that case, she wouldn't be paying attention to either the kids or the phone. Doris stole a look around the corner and down the shifting train car's center aisle to the back of her husband's head. She had already been gone a few minutes, and it would ruin everything if he caught her at the pay phone. She had promised him she would wait to call until after dinner.

She hung up the receiver, deciding to slip into the washroom and then try again when she came out. But she emerged only to find someone else using the phone, ironically a mother happily talking to her children.

When the woman hung up, Doris tried again. This time the phone's endless ringing seemed a kind of punishment for trying at all. She glanced up the aisle at Paul, but now all she could think about was that there was something terrible going on. She decided to call her neighbor Tina, who answered on the second ring.

Doris concentrated on removing any panic from her voice. "Tina, it's Doris. I have a really weird favor to ask of you. . . ."

In her mother's heart she knew: Something was dreadfully wrong.

CHAPTER

2

Hope sprang eternal. For Lou Boldt, who lived in a world of innocent or guilty, alive or dead, where the patrol officers drove cars painted black and white, hope rarely surfaced though always lingered, teasing and enticing.

A woman's rail-thin body lay in the hospital bed before him, dressed not in the familiar hospital gown but in the pink seersucker he had brought her two weeks before their fifteenth anniversary. Beneath that gown, as well as on the exposed skin, not a single hair. The chemotherapy had claimed the body fat, the hair, even any expression of joy from her sunken eyes. Her alien looks signified either a preparation for death, or a rebirth. The vomiting and complete lack of energy left Boldt with the impression of a woman half-dead. Despite his hope.

He placed a DO NOT ENTER—OXYGEN IN USE sign on the door to the room, a door that he shut tightly before jamming a white towel up against the crack at its base. He briefly caught sight of himself in the bathroom's mirror: a tired forty-two, thinner than he'd been since college, tough in the face, but kind in the eyes. Even dressed in his ubiquitous khakis and blue blazer, he no longer looked professorial but more like retired military—"a dog trainer," one friend had laid on him. The cop shop lived for such insults. Approaching his wife's roommate, a woman who liked afternoon tabloid television, Boldt knocked on the bed stand before pulling back the privacy curtain. "Medication time," he announced.

Stark and clinical, the room felt like a place to stockpile auto parts, not heal the sick—stainless steel, electric cable, faux grain vinyl veneer, bleach-white sheets—the room's only warm color came from the patches of pale human skin that escaped the bedding.

"Count me in," declared the roommate, Roberta, who was undergoing chemo for stage-four leukemia, her life expectancy, thirty to ninety days.

Elizabeth was battling lymphoma, life expectancy, three to six months. This lodged in Boldt's throat like a stuck bone.

The two windows looked out on a parking lot filled with the cars of visitors to the "C ward"—sad people carrying flowers on the way in, burdened by tears on the way out. Boldt parked out there among them. He opened both windows.

"Compliments of Bear," he explained to his wife, producing a perfectly rolled joint. Bear Berenson, a friend of twenty years, owned the comedy club Joke's On You, over on 45th near Stoneway.

Liz smirked. "A twenty-four-year veteran, a Homicide cop, pushing drugs."

"Medication," he corrected. "And I'm not Homicide any longer."

"Intelligence," she said. "There's an oxymoron."

He stood on a chair unsteadily and slipped a glassine bag, normally used for evidence collection, over the smoke alarm. His advancement to lieutenant had necessitated a transfer from Homicide; in a year or so he'd be back, and at a higher rank, better pay, better benefits, all made necessary by the mounting bills and loss of her banker's income. Change—Boldt's nemesis. Homicide was home; this woman was home. Home was changing.

"Disabling the lavatory smoke alarm can get you thrown off

the flight, you know?" Roberta had been an Alaska Airlines flight attendant for eleven years.

Boldt put the finishing touches on his effort and climbed down.

Liz grinned widely—a moment Boldt lived for. She put the joint between her lips, saying, "Times like this I miss the Jefferson Airplane." Boldt lit it for her and sat between the two beds passing the joint back and forth between the two women. Roberta smoked greedily and coughed loudly, bellowing smoke into the room, worrying Boldt that he too might get high.

"I don't know why we ever gave this up," Liz said, her eyes bloodshot, a wry smile forming. "God, I feel good."

"We had children," Roberta answered, and both women laughed hysterically, although Boldt missed the humor.

"Music," Liz requested, snuffing out the roach and eating it. She chased it with a glass of water and smacked her lips. "Some good old rock and roll."

Boldt tuned in a local TV channel that used an oldies FM station as its background music. Creedence Clearwater. Liz asked for more volume.

"Not until all the smoke is out," Boldt answered.

"Use the flower spray in the bathroom," Roberta suggested, cranking up the volume from her remote.

Boldt sprayed the room with an aerosol labeled Fields of Dreams. It smelled chemical, not floral. He removed the plastic bag as the two women began to sing along with John Fogerty, their transformation nothing short of miraculous.

"Pizza!" Liz hollered over the music.

"Pizza!" Roberta echoed, followed by a roar of laughter.

Boldt felt gratified by their request. He'd succeeded. He told Liz that he would head off for the pizza if she would prep herself for the kids.

"You mean the wig?" the bald woman asked. "I'm already wigged out." Both women erupted yet again. "Okay, okay, okay," his wife added, seeing the frustration on her husband's face. "I'm all eyebrows and hair. You get the pizza!"

Boldt drove into the heart of the U-District to Angelo's and bought a medium sausage and mushroom, a milk and a Pepsi. Pot smoking and pizza purchases—he felt transported back to college.

His concept of time had evolved from an internal clock predictable to within a matter of minutes, to where days now stretched on endlessly, driven by a doctor's prediction of a shortened life span and a husband's prayers for miracles.

He returned to the C ward to find Liz and Roberta in hysterics. Liz had drawn a pair of "wire rim" glasses around her eyes with eyebrow pencil, as well as a Marilyn Monroe birthmark mole on her cheek. Boldt made no comment; he simply served them the pizza. While Liz ate, her husband erased her spectacles with a face cloth and made an attempt at adding eyebrows to the hairless skin. Liz was well into her third slice by the time he offered her a hand mirror.

Chewing, she nodded approval.

He then placed her wig on in reverse, which caused Roberta to spit out some pizza in laughter.

"How much time?" Liz asked, sobering slightly, realizing that the arrival of her children was imminent.

"Ten minutes," he answered.

"Well, I'll say one thing: At least the pot allows me to smile. I want my kids to see me smiling."

Roberta struggled with her own hairpiece. Boldt offered to help, but she declined. "I've seen your work," she teased.

Liz hooked a finger into her husband's belt and pulled him in for a kiss.

A knock sounded. Boldt expected the pizza aroma to cover any evidence of the pot—ever the policeman.

He rose and answered it, thinking that nurses and doctors rarely knocked.

John LaMoia stood an inch over six feet, with sunken cheeks and a full mustache. He dressed like someone in a Calvin Klein ad.

LaMoia said, "Your pager and cell phone must be off."

"I'm on private time here," Boldt reminded. LaMoia had been on his Homicide squad for the last seven years; he had taken the sergeant's post Boldt had vacated. "Intelligence doesn't do on-call."

"John?" Liz called out.

LaMoia stepped in and said hello to both women by name, the room no stranger to him. He and Liz Boldt were gin rummy opponents.

"We got the call," LaMoia said, meeting Boldt's eyes seriously. "I tried calling you."

Judging by LaMoia's tone of voice, Boldt knew which call he meant. Boldt reminded, "I don't handle fieldwork." The words stung him. He missed it badly; LaMoia had come to exploit that.

"As a favor then," LaMoia suggested, appealing to Liz to help with Lou. She was the one in the hospital, but it was her husband who had lost forty pounds and the glint in his eye. The desk job was killing him.

"Go on, love—humor him," Liz encouraged. "What kind of case is it, John?"

LaMoia started to mumble but did not answer. No wife and mother would want her husband, the father of her children, on such a case.

"Wait for me downstairs," Boldt told his former detective. "I'll wait with you until Marina and the kids arrive," he told his wife after LaMoia had left.

"No need." All humor had left the room. "Go," she said. But Boldt stayed.

Five minutes passed in relative silence before Liz sat up sharply and Boldt recognized the sound of his son's voice approaching.

"You all set?" Boldt asked.

She nodded faintly, squeezed her husband's arm and mouthed the words, "I love you."

Boldt leaned over and kissed her on the cheek. "Likewise," he whispered.

Her cheek felt inhumanly cold.

CHAPTER

3

John LaMoia double-parked his red 1974 Ca-
maro in front of 2351 51st North and set its wide taillights flashing amid a veritable light show of emergency vehicles. He sat
behind the wheel for a moment gathering his strength. Any apparent kidnapping automatically evolved into an enormous investigation, requiring tact and diligence on the part of the lead
investigator, and he'd been named lead. Tact was not necessarily
LaMoia's long suit, and he knew it. His fellow officers called him
Floorshow, what with his creased blue jeans, steel gray ostrich
boots and rock star hair. Because of the Big-A attitude. LaMoia
knew he wore an attitude, but to hell with it: He was good at
what he did. People talked about talking the talk, but John LaMoia
talked it. He'd been the same cocky son-of-a-bitch since junior
high; he wasn't about to change now.

Boldt's beat-up department-issue Chevy slipped in behind him
and parked.

This particular kidnapping—of a white infant—would stir not
only the city's conscience but, quite likely, the nation's. Before
even stepping out of the car at the crime scene, LaMoia already

had a few suspicions about how it had happened, but for the moment he pushed them away. Not for anyone, including his ambitious Crimes Against Persons captain Sheila Hill, would LaMoia guess at a crime's solution before he could gather the necessary evidence, witnesses and facts.

"It's my job to make the call," he told Boldt. "Either I group it with the others, or it stands alone." Domestics and gang killings had occupied his past few months—*grounders* for the most part. A serial kidnapping case with national importance? He tried not to think of himself as Lou Boldt's replacement, even though others saw his promotion that way.

"So why drag me along?" Boldt asked.

"Maybe I'm insecure."

"Yeah, right. And it's going to be sunny tomorrow."

They ducked under the police tape onto the lawn. Officer Jonny Filgrim said to LaMoia, "Bad Guy used the back door, Detec—, Sergeant," he corrected himself. "It's him, right?"

"Keep the vultures back, Jonny," LaMoia said, indicating the press. "They want an interview, it's Hill, not me."

"Mulwright's here. Back door."

"Already?" LaMoia asked. He and Boldt met eyes in the flashing blues and reds of the emergency lights.

Boldt questioned, "Mulwright at a crime scene early?"

"Any of his boys?" LaMoia asked the uniformed officer.

"Special Ops?"

"Yeah, any of Mulwright's guys," LaMoia answered. Some of the patrolmen were thick as bricks.

"Ain't seen none," Filgrim answered.

"There was a woman watching the child," Boldt said.

Filgrim nodded, though seemed bewildered that Boldt already knew this. "The sitter? Yeah? Knocked out cold."

"Where'd they take her?"

"University Hospital."

Boldt offered LaMoia a look; they had passed an arriving ambulance on their way out of the hospital.

LaMoia ordered, "Get someone over to the hospital," as he took in the chaotic scene of the reporters and cameras at the edge of the property. "And make sure SID gets room to park their van close by."

"You got it."

Boldt caught him by the arm. "The baby sitter was unconscious?"

"Like I said, out cold on the kitchen floor. It's gotta be him. Right, Floorshow?" Filgrim said excitedly. "A kid, right? I mean, we've been expecting this, right?"

"The parents?" Boldt asked, releasing the man.

"Mulwright spoke to a neighbor lady. She'd heard from the parents, which is how come she was here. She got the other kid."

"Other kid?"

"A little boy. She took him home with her."

Boldt nodded.

"Go!" LaMoia ordered.

Filgrim hurried off at a run, grabbing his gun to keep it from beating his side.

LaMoia tongued his mustache nervously and said softly, "I'll tell ya, I am not calling it until we can rule out a copycat or a coincidence." He looked to Boldt for help but was met with the blank face of a teacher waiting out his pupil. "I suppose it is him. Baby sitter unconscious? The kid's age is right. Both parents out of the house."

"Even so," Boldt cautioned.

"I know. I know," LaMoia said nervously. "Where the hell is SID?" He checked his watch. Once the lab techs controlled a crime scene, the Feds would have a hell of a time trying to take over. No one in the Seattle Police Department wanted to play second fiddle to the Feds. An investigation's power remained with whoever controlled the evidence.

LaMoia studied the house, trying for a moment of calm. He then said to Boldt, "You're thinking the baby sitter is, by definition, also a victim." Boldt maintained that a victim, dead or alive, could tell an investigator more than a dozen witnesses. But the true victim had been taken from the crime scene.

"The sitter won't remember much," Boldt cautioned. "None of the others have."

"So I've got shit to go on."

"You've got a crime scene and the chance for physical evidence, a missing victim, a hospitalized victim. You've got neighbors, the possibility of unfamiliar vehicles in the neighborhood—maybe Neighborhood Watch," Boldt listed for the man.

"That's what I'm saying: We've got shit," LaMoia repeated.

Another patrolman approached. Name tag read Rodriguez. These guys were all over him at a crime scene, working for brownie points, hoping their names would be mentioned to someone, that they'd get a shot at something better than driving the streets. The advancement to sergeant had made LaMoia painfully aware of just how servile these guys could be. The female uniforms were a lot less so. Too bad.

He raised his index finger to stop Rodriguez from interrupting his thoughts. He spoke to Boldt. "Some asshole comes here to lift a toddler. He's got it all planned out, right? Use the back door, where no one's gonna see him. Whack the baby sitter, heist the little thumb-sucker and make tracks. So . . . is he alone, or does he have company?"

"He'd have a wheel man, I guess," Rodriguez answered.

"Not you!" LaMoia chided. "I'm asking the lieutenant."

"Let him answer," Boldt said. "You don't need me." The two exchanged a look, teacher to student.

Rodriguez waited until LaMoia nodded approval for him to speak. "Wheel man? Parked out front, where the neighbors can see him?" LaMoia wanted the man to think.

"Keeps moving, maybe. Driving around, you know, until the doer needs him."

"And if there's a sudden problem with their little visit?" LaMoia asked. "What's the Bad Guy gonna do, make a phone call, stand on the curb with his thumb in the air? Think!"

The patrolman paled.

"How would *you* do it?" LaMoia asked, as Boldt had asked of him dozens of times. "That's what a detective asks himself, Rodriguez: *How would I do it?*"

"I gotta get me inside the house. I come on as a plumber or something."

LaMoia looked back toward the house, nodding. "Yeah. A plumber, a fireman, a cop. He's played them all, if he's who we think he is."

"No shit?"

"No child," Boldt supplied.

"I zap the sitter in the kitchen and grab the kid out of the crib," Rodriguez said, getting into it. "Wrap it up in something, I suppose. I don't know."

"She's not an 'it,' " Boldt corrected harshly. "She's a four-month-old baby girl who has been abducted from her home." Boldt had kids of his own; kids LaMoia thought of as his own niece and nephew.

LaMoia patted the uniformed officer on the cheek. "You're excused."

They found Mulwright on the back stoop smoking a nonfilter cigarette. He looked about sixty. He was forty-one. Part Native American Indian, part Irish with a liver to prove it. Teeth that looked like a rotted picket fence hit by a truck. Skin that made enough oil for a refinery. Black hair and unibrow and five o'clock shadow. One eye green, the other nearly brown, like a junkyard dog. He held the constant expression of a person who didn't feel well.

"Lieutenant," Boldt said from a distance.

"Well, look what the fucking dog drug in." Mulwright's resentment of LaMoia's assignment to lead the task force was public knowledge. The task force itself was the source of much politicking because it had been formed *ahead* of any kidnapping, effectively limiting the FBI's powers by assuming that power for itself. It was the brainchild of Sheila Hill, captain of Crimes Against Persons, who now commanded the task force she had created. Mulwright was next in line seniority-wise, but as lieutenant of Special Operations he was more accustomed to surveillance and busting down doors than conducting an evidence-driven investigation. For that reason, Hill had chosen LaMoia, whose experience was mainly as a homicide detective, as lead investigator, which left Mulwright with an ambiguous job assignment until and unless they had surveillance to conduct.

To make matters worse, Mulwright blamed Boldt for ending his twenty-seven-year drinking spree, which had culminated in suspension and treatment programs. Rumor had it that the latter had not worked. The thick cone of cigarette smoke he blew into the air fairly reeked of resentment.

"Who called you to the scene, Lieutenant?" Boldt asked.

"I got a scanner in the kitchen. You? You got no business being here. You ain't got nothing to do with this task force."

"Adviser," Boldt reminded. As a division, Intelligence intimidated some detectives, especially those like Mulwright who got themselves into trouble. "I'm one of the task force links to the Bureau." It occurred to Boldt that Mulwright should not have arrived on the scene until *after* a call from LaMoia. "I'm also supposed to prevent press leaks."

"Is that right?"

LaMoia said, "The *National Insider* is offering two grand for task force information."

"Don't know nothing about it."

"So who called it in?" Boldt asked.

"I don't have to answer to you."

"No, you don't." Boldt waited along with the man through several long seconds of silence.

"A neighbor lady." Mulwright had no fondness for women, other than as the objects of obscene humor. "Name of Wasserman. Tina. Down the street." He checked his notes—every detective carried a notebook, even Mulwright. "Fifty-three hundred, Fifty-first North. Was asked to check on the place by the mother when the baby sitter failed to answer the phone. You ever heard of a dinner train takes off from Renton?"

"Sure," LaMoia answered.

"Yeah? Well, I hadn't. The parents are still stuck on the train. Due back any minute."

Boldt asked, "Does the press know about this neighbor?"

"How the fuck should I know?"

"Do we have someone meeting the parents?"

"I put someone with the neighbor. That redhead with the big tits. You know her? Motor patrol?"

"McKinney," LaMoia supplied.

"McKinney's with her."

"And who's meeting the parents at the station?" Boldt asked, checking his watch.

"Don't know," Mulwright answered.

LaMoia said, "You did or did not assign someone to pick up the parents?"

"This isn't my scene," Mulwright reminded.

"You're senior officer present," LaMoia countered. "Are the parents covered or not?"

Boldt turned to LaMoia, "What are the chances our kidnapper has someone watching the parents to make sure they don't return unexpectedly?"

LaMoia judged the question, hesitated, then nodded. "I can see that."

"He'd be on the fucking dinner train," Mulwright answered, tossing his cigarette into the grass. Boldt took note of where it landed; the cigarette had contaminated the crime scene.

Mulwright's eyes awakened, his face expanding. "We should have both the train station and the parents under surveillance."

"Can we handle that?" LaMoia asked, as innocent-sounding as possible. He agreed with Boldt's attempt to lead Mulwright away from the crime scene. Few officers, despite all the training, understood the delicate nature of a crime scene. LaMoia realized that if Mulwright had read the advance briefing papers he would have known the FBI had all but ruled out surveillance by the kidnapper—he was believed to be a solo operator.

"Got it," Mulwright announced, standing. "We'll watch the station and the train for strays. We'll work out a way to notify the parents we're with them. We'll make sure they head straight to the neighbors." He asked, "ID? How do we ID them?"

"Wait here a moment," Boldt said, leaning his weight against a sapling and slipping on a pair of paper shoe covers. He donned a pair of latex gloves and entered the kitchen, stepping carefully. Mulwright or the first officer on the scene had used blue painter's tape to indicate the position of the baby sitter's body on the floor. Boldt stayed clear of what looked like red confetti and the medical litter the paramedics had left behind. He located a family photo hanging to the side of the kitchen sink. It reminded him of his four favorite photos of Liz and the kids—three at home, one at the office. He suddenly wished that he had more photos of Liz in the prime of her health—he thought of her this way: her face full of color, her limbs lean but strong.

He removed the photo from the wall feeling pained—he hated to disturb any evidence no matter its apparent insignificance.

He renegotiated his way out of the house and handed the framed photo to Mulwright. "If you spot a suspect," he said, "he's better followed than confronted."

"I know the drill, Boldt. I've worked a hell of a lot more hostage situations than you."

LaMoia believed that Boldt could probably recite the names of each of those hostages for Mulwright if pushed. But it wasn't Boldt's way to throw around his knowledge; he hid himself from all but the most intimate friends.

"What time's that train arrive?" Boldt asked, checking his watch.

Mulwright hurried off, calling back to them, "Tell Hill we're on it."

LaMoia watched him go and said with admiration, "You knew he'd take the bait, knew he hadn't read the briefings."

"Mulwright is Special Ops—translated, he's a thrill seeker and likes working from the seat of his pants. He needs credibility to shore up support after this drinking thing. He stays around here, he looks bad. He goes off on surveillance, he's on familiar ground."

"You hosed him."

Pocketing Mulwright's discarded cigarette butt, Boldt said, "I offered him what he wanted: a dignified way out. The meet and greet with the parents is important; he wants to feel important. Daphne plays those head games every day. Maybe she's rubbing off on me."

"I wouldn't mind if she rubbed off on me," LaMoia said.

"Spare me."

Daphne Matthews, the department's resident psychologist, was good-looking to a fault. As an interrogation team, few were better than Boldt and Matthews.

LaMoia and Boldt stood just inside the kitchen door studying the litter of the discarded gauze left behind by the medics and the unusual red confetti sprinkled across the floor. LaMoia snapped his gloves in place.

"What's with the red shit?" LaMoia asked.

"AFIDs," Boldt answered.

"An air TASER, not a stun gun?" Air TASERs fired a projectile carrying a pair of probes that delivered the device's electrical charge via thin wires—a stun stick capable of being fired from a distance. When the projectile cartridge fired, the weapon released confettilike ID tags called AFIDs. "First I've heard of it."

"We can assume it's Need to Know," Boldt suggested. In repeat offenses, law enforcement never revealed every piece of evidence, so as to separate out copycat crimes. Near the litter was a tangle of thin wire and the probes.

"Yeah? Well, I Need to Know if I'm going to make the call that it's task force jurisdiction."

"Flemming knows more about these kidnappings than we do. He's got ten children and six months on us. If their guys beat us to the evidence, if Flemming takes control, it won't be the worst thing."

"Tell that to Hill," LaMoia said.

"Thankfully, I don't have to. That's your job."

"That's what I'm saying." LaMoia added, "And don't forget: You end up with Shoswitz's desk and you'll be reporting to her as well."

"One day at a time," Boldt said.

To invoke task force jurisdiction was to invite national attention, internal power struggles and regular four o'clock meetings with the Feds. It was all laid out. Mulwright, by showing up, had already made the call.

LaMoia sketched the kitchen indicating the litter and the AFIDs. "She meets him at the back door, makes it about five steps and he zaps her."

Boldt said nothing. He orbited the spot where the girl had fallen.

LaMoia wrote meaning into Boldt's silence. He studied the blue tape outline and reconsidered his opinion. "Of course it depends if he fried her from the back or the front."

"Yes, it does."

"If from the back, yeah: She makes it a couple steps and goes down. But if he's over here when he hits her—" he said, moving across the room.

Boldt finished for him. "She may have let him inside without panicking."

"The girl gets the door shut, guy takes a minute to make sure they're alone, and then he zaps her. She goes down."

Boldt stood to the side allowing his former detective to think it through.

LaMoia continued, "The doer starts his search for the infant— providing he doesn't already know which room." He looked to Boldt for support. "You're doing a pretty good imitation of Marcel Marceau over there."

"You don't need me for this, John. I tried to tell you that."

"So you came along to humor me."

"No, to compare what I've read in the briefing papers with what I might see at the actual scene. Analysis, comparison. What the Bureau has or hasn't included in their briefing material not only tells me about the suspect, but about what the Bureau wants us to know, how a guy like Flemming operates." He added, "Where's the little boy all this time?"

"Glued to a TV?"

"Maybe," Boldt allowed.

"Hiding in the corner?"

"More likely."

They moved as a pair through the house slowly and carefully as they had at dozens of other crime scenes. "Thing about a death investigation," LaMoia said, "it's over and done with. I mean, there's urgency, sure. But not like this. Nine kids."

"Ten now," Boldt corrected.

"Where the hell is SID?" LaMoia moaned.

They walked single file through the living room, checked the first bedroom for a crib, but found it in the second.

Approaching the crib, Boldt remaining in the doorway, LaMoia felt a crunch under his shoe. "Hold it!" he exclaimed, stepping back and away, fearing he had destroyed possible evidence. He dug into the carpet, his gloved fingers moving through the nap slowly and carefully, and came up with a piece of thick glass the size of a small pearl. He held it up toward the ceiling light so that Boldt could see it as well. "Thick. Square cut. Bluish tint maybe."

"How thick?"

"Lead crystal maybe, or one of those Mexican drinking glasses—the blue ones. It's not window glass, not kitchenware." He elected to bag it, which he did—marking the glassine bag with the date and location found—but wondered if he would have done so without Boldt looking over his shoulder. "Probably nothing," he said. "Parents will know if it belongs." He realized he worked a crime scene differently with Boldt in the room and wondered silently if that was why he had wanted so badly for the man to accompany him. "You coming in?" he asked.

"Better if I don't. Keep traffic down until Bernie arrives."

LaMoia pocketed the glass and leaned over the crib, catching sight of an object lying where little Rhonda Shotz should have been. He felt an ache in the center of this chest beneath his ribs. "Sarge?"

"The yellow smudge?" Boldt asked. "I can see it from here— about *knee height*. We'll want Bernie to sample it for the lab."

"No, in the crib," LaMoia said, leaning back and seeing the smudge of a fine yellow powder on the crib's frame. "It's a penny flute I think. One of those dime-store-variety penny flutes."

"Well, at least that explains how they named him," Boldt said. "Another convenient detail the Feds neglected to share."

"A fucking calling card? We wouldn't have shared it either, John." He added, "You know, just because Hill feels competition with the Bureau—"

"Doesn't mean I have to," LaMoia completed. "I know that. It gets a little contagious though."

"Daphne can help you with the penny flute. His leaving a calling card presents an entirely different profile. Baiting. Taunting. It helps explain some of Flemming's reticence to share: the AFIDs and the penny flute. If they're this guy's signatures, they're certainly the angles he's working."

"I'd wondered how they came up with that handle," LaMoia said, again referring to the FBI's nickname. His job to make the call, LaMoia spoke the words that would set into motion one of the highest profile cases in the city's history, involving three states and nine missing babies. Ten, LaMoia corrected himself, staring back into the crib. The words came out of his throat stubbornly. "It's the Pied Piper," he said.

"If I'm not mistaken," Boldt advised, "we have visitors."

Captain Sheila Hill's yelling at the media filtered through the walls. LaMoia confirmed her presence through the window.

Over the long haul, police work typically hardened many of its women—language toughened, even a woman's walk became more angular, less gracious. But Sheila Hill was the exception. At forty-two she looked thirty-five. She wore her blonde hair shoulder length, and today wore a navy blue sport jacket, khaki shirt and a pair of brown corduroy pants. Her Italian loafers gleamed.

Divorced with an eight-year-old son named Tommy, Sheila Hill still managed to work twelve-hour days, six, sometimes seven, days a week. No one on the force, including LaMoia, expected her to stop at captain.

She carried a knowing self-importance in her posture, transforming her five feet six inches into a much taller figure. Her voice, strident and defiant, carried through the walls as she addressed the press. "We have confirmed an apparent kidnapping, a missing infant by the name of Rhonda Shotz. The relation of this crime to the nine earlier kidnappings in California and Oregon, currently being investigated by the FBI, is *not known at this time*, so please spare me any such questions; you're wasting your breath. You can help the parents of this girl, and all of us in law enforcement, by getting an image or a description of that child in front of the public just as quickly as possible. We should have an image for you shortly. Beyond that, it's far too early to comment. Please, allow us the room to do our jobs efficiently, and I promise you a full press conference in the next six to nine hours. That's all, people. Thank you."

She walked away from the shouting as if unable to hear it, sensuous and fluid, right toward LaMoia.

"Sergeant." She looked LaMoia up and down.

"Captain." He locked eyes with her.

"Lou," she addressed Boldt, while continuing to look at LaMoia.

"I asked the lieutenant to join me, Captain."

"We paged you," Hill reminded Boldt, as if it had been her idea, not LaMoia's, to include Boldt. Ever the politician.

"I was on private time," he explained. One of the luxuries of Intelligence was its lack of being on-call. "John chased me down."

"I see," she said, weighing Boldt's presence. As long as Boldt was around, LaMoia would listen to him, regardless of assignments, and Hill wanted full control. "You heard me just now," she said. "How much of what I just told that horde is bullshit?"

LaMoia knew that Boldt would leave it to him to answer. "The Bureau withheld a couple signatures. From all of us," he added.

She glanced at Boldt—Intelligence was expected to know everything about anything, even FBI investigations. "We can assume they've withheld some of those crime scene reports to protect the Need to Know. Not all of them," he cautioned, "but some of them." He reminded, "We would have done the same."

"If the FBI had asked?" she countered. "No, we wouldn't have. It's a one-way street, Lieutenant. We both know that." She pursed her lips. LaMoia considered them full and luscious lips—kissable lips surprisingly void of any age lines.

"AFIDs," LaMoia said. "An air TASER, not a stun stick." He carried his own stun stick under the Camaro's front seat. "And a penny flute left behind in the crib."

"He's leaving a calling card?" she exclaimed. "He's proud of these kidnappings? What kind of creature are we dealing with?"

"Matthews can help there," Boldt contributed.

"One of those dime-store flutes," LaMoia said.

Perplexed, Hill asked incredulously, "He *wants* us to connect these kidnappings? What the hell is that about?" She nodded, thinking to herself, her expression grim. "Shit," she mumbled.

LaMoia explained, "We'll get the parents' permission to trap-and-trace the phone. Get Tech Services over here to put a tape recorder on the line. Until Flemming confirms the signatures we'll still hope it's not him and that there might be a ransom call." The Pied Piper had yet to request a ransom. The suspicions ranged from a child molester to an illegal adoption ring.

Glancing at her watch, Hill said, "How long has he had?"

"Two-hour lead," LaMoia answered.

"That's an eternity." Her ice blue eyes flickered with worry.

LaMoia reminded, "Dispatch has already notified the airlines, rail and bus carriers. Canadian Immigration. Sheriff's Department. The ferries—"

"Two hours? Shit." She filled her chest with a deep breath and exhaled slowly, shaking her head. "Shit." She glanced around as if the press might be overhearing them. She ordered LaMoia, "Get in that house and find me a picture I can use. If we don't fax that image around, we haven't got a chance of saving this baby."

LaMoia returned inside and searched. In the living room he found a stack of photos showing a tiny baby in the arms and on the breast of her mother. Any of three close-ups in the pile would fax well enough: a tiny glowing face with bulging cheeks and clear blue eyes. He suddenly felt unbearably cold.

As he rejoined Boldt and Hill, SID's black panel truck pulled up into the space cleared for them. Hill took the packet of photos from LaMoia and leafed through them. She said, "God, I hate this job sometimes."

As a group, the three caught up to Bernie Lofgrin heading toward them. The Scientific Identification Division's director, a small man with a beer belly, wore thick glasses that grossly enlarged his eyes. He walked quickly with stiff legs, carrying a large red toolbox at his side that weighed him down and tilted him to his right. As a group they spun around and matched pace with him.

"We need it quick but we need it right, Bernie," she told him.

"This time of night and you hit me with clichés? Tell me something new, Captain," Lofgrin quipped. "I was in the middle of dinner."

"I stepped on this," LaMoia interrupted, reaching out to hand Lofgrin the evidence bag. "May be nothing."

Hill snatched it up for herself, held it up closely to her eyes and passed it on to Lofgrin. "I didn't hear about this," she complained.

Lofgrin stopped, as did LaMoia, Boldt and Hill. His team of technicians raced past the four of them.

"AFIDs where the body fell," Boldt added, "and a calling card in the—"

The cry of tire squelches cut him off as a Town Car and a black van blocked the narrow residential street. Boldt had seen the FBI's evidence van enough times to recognize it. The Town Car produced two men and a woman.

"Get your people to work, Bernie," Hill ordered. "I've got this," she announced, peeling away and cutting to intercept the Feds.

As LaMoia followed Hill with his eyes he saw beyond her to a set of six balloons waving in the wind up the street.

Lofgrin asked, "You coming, John?"

"Flemming, Hale and Kalidja," Boldt told his former detective. At Hill's request, Boldt had done background checks on all three. "This is the wrong place, the wrong situation for me," he said. "Hill is going to squirrel the moment. I need to be able to work with these people. We'll talk later, John."

"Sure," LaMoia confirmed, still intrigued with what he saw across the street. "Later," he called out to Lofgrin, who hurried on.

Boldt headed to his car. He stopped and shook hands with the FBI agents on his way.

LaMoia followed, but steered clear of Hill and the FBI agents. As he approached the officers responsible for crowd control, they all noticed him; another of those effects of being a sergeant that bothered him. As a detective, the uniforms had rarely noticed. Two of the officers, anticipating him, lifted the yellow police tape and cleared a hole in the gawkers—neighbors and police-scanner junkies who had nothing better to do—and helped him through. LaMoia walked straight to those balloons, and their ribbons stretched tight. The small metal realtor sign flapped lightly in the breeze: *Represented by Sherry Daech—McCann, Daech, Fenton.* The sergeant tugged on the balloons. Tight. Fresh helium. *Open House Tonite!* it read on a smaller sign. If the open house had been the day before, the balloons would have sagged by now. It meant that the open house had been this same evening.

Out came his notepad.

If the realtor had kept track of her visitors, then the police had possible witnesses coming and going throughout the evening. On occasion potential buyers even took photos. LaMoia finished writing this down, closed his eyes and whispered, "Please."

Behind him, Hill and the FBI agents were marching in lockstep toward the Shotz house.

CHAPTER

LaMoia toed the cracks in the sidewalk in front of
the Wasserman home, tracing them like veins beneath the skin.
He felt in no particular hurry to get inside.

A steady cool breeze blew east out of the Olympics and up into
the heart of the city.

Daphne Matthews arrived in her red Honda. She deftly parallel
parked behind LaMoia's Camaro. As staff psychologist, Matthews
was an anomaly within the department. She operated on a cere-
bral plane, erudite, always choosing her words carefully. LaMoia
guessed that her dark, brooding beauty had forced her as a young
woman to erect a wall that as an adult she now found difficult to
dismantle; he found her remote. Whatever the case, her controlled
distance and unavailability attracted him just as it did so many
others. Her close friendship with Boldt was a matter of departmental history: The two had collaborated successfully on several
major investigations. Other rumors surrounded them as well, but
LaMoia discounted these.

Matthews approached him with her game face firmly in place.
She held a leather briefcase, her wrist laden in bracelets that rattled like dull bells.

"Who's in there?" she asked, all business.

LaMoia answered, "Father, Paul; mother, Doris. Their little boy, Henry. The neighbors, the Wassermans. She's Tina. Don't know his name. They've got kids, I think. McKinney's inside."

She wanted full control of the environment. "We'll lose McKinney for the time being. Let's try to get Henry moved upstairs with the neighbors. I doubt the mother will let him out of her sight, but ultimately we want only the Shotzes downstairs with us. Once we're settled, we offer our sympathies. We try to avoid letting them find out that neither of us has kids, because we lose rapport there. We give them a little background about the task force, try to build up their hope, their faith in us. All this before we ask a single question. I'll handle it. When we reach question time, you'll take the wheel. Start all your questions with your eyes toward the floor," she acted this out as she explained, "lifting them slowly as you work into the question, punctuated by eye contact as the question is completed. Soft voice. And something new for you, John: humility.

"There are things you should know," she continued. "For a parent, a kidnapping is more difficult to endure than a death. We can expect some guilt, maybe blame between them. They may even blame us. They are desperate. Vulnerable. They'll turn to anything, anyone that they believe might return their child to them: psychics, private investigators, clergy, you name it. Part of our job is to protect them from this. We want their faith in us. This is, more than likely, their first contact with SPD beyond a traffic cop. This first impression will carry lots of weight as to how much cooperation we get. You like to fly by the seat of your pants. Fine. You're great in the Box because of that. But this is not an interrogation. Keep reminding yourself of that. They are convinced they know nothing that could help us. TV, movies, novels, make them expect miracles. So we go easy with reality for now. We soften them up. If we do our jobs properly tonight—we go slowly—by tomorrow they'll be feeding us information even they didn't know they knew. We step on the gas too hard," she said, adjusting to his language, "and we'll flood it, and it won't restart."

"I'm with you, Lieutenant." She knew that her senior rank

bothered LaMoia. Most psychologists would have been on the civilian payroll. She had done the academy, carried a weapon and a shield believing one could not consult and advise cops without knowing everything there was to know.

She said, "For the record, we're going to get her back, John. Never mind that the other cities failed. That doesn't have to affect us. If we start discouraged we'll never overcome it." Looking toward the house she said, "These people have information for us. We both know that. They doubt it. The clock is running. If everyone does their job—and we're part of that—then by morning that child is back in her crib." She glanced over at him. "Believe it."

"Save the cheerleader routine for them, Lieutenant. They're the ones who need it."

The woman—the mother, Daphne thought—looked a wreck. The father was drunk and had been for some time. Daphne introduced LaMoia and herself twice but knew the only thing that registered was their occupation: police.

The mother clung to her three-year-old son like life itself. Daphne offered her sympathies and the husband burst into tears, mumbling apologies to his wife, who clearly did not want to hear them.

The parents had been briefed by Mulwright concerning the baby sitter's ordeal as the victim of a stun gun and that she had been transferred to the hospital. Daphne drew this out of the mother, regretting she had not had the opportunity to tell them herself and gauge their reactions. Doris Shotz then rambled on about asking her neighbor to check the house for her, and the neighbor's discovery of the unconscious sitter and little Henry, who had been found safe hiding in a corner of the kitchen. The neighbor had rescued Henry, phoned the police and had called back the train car's cellular pay phone connecting with Doris—which, according to the husband, "was when all hell broke loose."

LaMoia mentioned the string of kidnappings that had swept up the West Coast and that the Feds attributed the abductions to a man they had dubbed "the Pied Piper."

Doris Shotz said she'd heard about the kidnappings, but her next words were absorbed in her sobs and lost to both police officers.

Together, Daphne and LaMoia then filled in the blanks: the FBI's involvement in the investigation, the task force headed by SPD. Determining that the husband had purchased the dinner-train tickets, LaMoia directed to him, "Do you remember who you told about the dinner train?"

"No one," he said, numbly.

"A co-worker, a secretary, a neighbor?"

"No one. It was a surprise. Doro thought we were going to Ivar's."

Doris Shotz nodded.

"You made the arrangements yourself?" LaMoia inquired.

"Yeah, yeah. Had the tickets mailed to the shop."

LaMoia checked his pad. "Micro System Workshop."

"Doro," the husband chastised his wife, "are you listening? These other kidnappings? They have not gotten one of these kids back." He asked LaMoia, "Isn't that right?"

LaMoia avoided an answer, directing himself to the wife. "Can you explain some pieces of broken glass found in front of your daughter's crib? A drinking glass, maybe—a mirror?"

"There was nothing like that when we left," the wife replied. "I cleaned the room just this morning."

"Vacuumed?" Daphne asked softly, doubting the woman could focus on anything but her missing child.

LaMoia sat forward on the edge of his chair, the detective in him smelling hard evidence: the Pied Piper's shoes, his pants cuffs, his pockets. . . .

Doris Shotz mumbled nearly incoherently, "There's never been any broken glass in Rhonda's room. That carpet was laid a month before she was born—"

"That's true," the husband responded, reaching for his wife's hand. "If there's glass in that carpet, this bastard brought it with him."

"My baby," Doris Shotz pleaded.

"We're going to bring her home," Daphne declared. She met eyes with the mother: Doris Shotz did not believe.

CHAPTER

No one knew better than a homicide cop the ability of the human mind to forget.

Not only was LaMoia required to locate and interview any potential witness, but on occasion such a witness had the potential to blow a case wide open. A realtor—whose job requirements included sizing up potential clients—seemed a decent place to invest his energies. The door-to-door work, conducted by a combination of task force detectives, FBI and SPD alike, had produced little of value. If Sherry Daech had seen anything—suspicious or not—the night before, LaMoia needed to interview her immediately. Memories deteriorated quickly.

He feared that any attempt to bring her downtown would send the wrong message. He did not want attorneys involved. A quiet chat in her office seemed more the thing.

But when his first two attempts to make an appointment failed, he placed his third call as a prospective buyer, and this time he scored, convincing him that Sherry Daech wanted nothing to do with the police, good citizen or not.

"Something in the high threes, low fours, on Mercer Island. If you have anything that fits." A secretary returned a call less than thirty minutes later. Daech would meet him out on Mercer in an hour if he had the time. LaMoia scribbled down an address.

The house was off an unbearably steep lane that serviced three others and led to a private dock on Lake Washington. LaMoia squeezed the red whale through a gauntlet of stone walls that would have sheared a fender off without thinking anything of it, and swung a hard left into the tight driveway. Daffodils, blooming in regimented rows like little suns, lit the front of the house and cut a hole through the interminable gray of Seattle.

Daech presented herself perched on a low garden wall, wearing a red Mexican skirt, a flouncy blouse marked by enormous breasts and the wide warm smile of a woman who knew her business. She wore a lot of silver and turquoise on her ears, neck and wrists. She had blonde hair, and if it was dyed it was a pro job—no dark roots; it looked like the hair of a surfer girl in her twenties. She had smooth, unwrinkled skin, and if the product of a tuck or two, it was again the work of one hell of a razor man, as LaMoia referred to surgeons. She straightened up as the detective swaggered toward her. He knew he had a good walk; women had been telling him that since junior high.

"That your ride parked up there?" he asked. "The Hummer?"

"Business has been good," she said, not breaking the practiced smile.

"Hell of a set of wheels," he said, lowering his eyes to her chest and then back to the emerald green that sat beneath the warm arcs of darkly penciled—or were they dyed?—eyebrows. He smiled back for the first time. "John," he said, offering his hand and squeezing hers so that she understood his strength. He liked to get things straight right off the top. "Gulf War, right? The Hummer?"

"Yes."

"Hell of a set of wheels," he repeated, knowing the car cost over two years of pay for him.

"It makes a statement," she said honestly. He liked that. Standing, smoothing her blouse and skirt until she approved of the contours, she added, "Some people respond to that. You don't, do you?"

"Not in terms of a person's ride," he replied. "Other things I respond to. Sure."

"Nice boots," she stabbed, quickly and efficiently. Calling his number. "Some kind of endangered snake or something?" Leading the way toward the front door, she let him have two very active cheeks. She was no stranger to the Stairmaster. The woman was a prepared, well-conceived package. He warned himself to watch out; he'd have his checkbook out in a minute if he wasn't careful.

She keyed the front door. "Owners are overseas. Microsoft. Paris. They have it priced at five-fifteen. They bought high, a couple years back. Comps would put it closer to four and a half. I don't represent them—only you—so I can tell you all this."

He realized his mistake then and he chastised himself. Sometimes he was too flip, too impressed by his own genius to step back and look at what he was doing. Boldt was forever on his case: "Lose just a little of the attitude, John, and maybe there's no one better at what you do."

He had picked the wrong house. He should have manipulated her into the house across the street from the Shotzes. The visual environment was a great stimulus to memory. He tuned her out briefly while debating how to pull the switch on her. He could claim poverty. The one across from Shotz had to be in the twos, if that.

"If someone puts a chain saw to those four pines down there, then the lake view might justify the low fives," she said, pointing down the hill. She wore fire-engine red nail polish. It worked with the Mexican skirt. "It's a killer view, I'm sure, but those trees are our bargaining chip." She moved well. Knew her body. She did a slight spin and faced him, her skirt still following. "You single . . . or married?" she added as an afterthought.

"They're ostrich."

"They're *expensive*, don't you mean?" She played her game

right to the edge. "The Hummer is eighty-K *before* the extras. That's what you want to know. Am I right?"

The expression—"Am I right?"—was one his lieutenant, Shoswitz, used all the time. It sounded funny coming from a pair of moist red lips. "Single," he said.

She bit the corner of her lip, lowered her head demurely and looked out the tops of her eyes at him—her little girl look. Convincing, too. "We're going to do some business here, John." Allowing a full grin, she asked, "Do you get that feeling?"

"I got all sorts of feelings going at the moment," he answered.

She barked a small laugh of surprise. Maybe he had scored one on her. She whisked past him, close enough for her skirt to drag on his jeans and make a whispering sound. "Let me show you the rest."

"I'd like that," he added so quickly it sounded as if he'd expected the line.

She stopped at the bottom of the stairs. "Yes, you will. It's dreamy. Everything you're looking for, and more."

"Is it built to take it?" he asked, following her up. "A single guy can kind of put a place to the test."

"Oh, I think it can handle a guy like you, John. I think we've got a good match, here."

It was a little too much fun for him to want to spoil things. He enjoyed this kind of sparring. Didn't find much of it anymore. Maybe he'd been pursuing women too young, he thought.

"How about you?" he asked, reaching the top landing. "All those rings, a guy can't tell if you're married or not."

She held up her left hand and examined the assortment of jewelry. "Is that right?" she said. "Well, you'd never make much of a detective, would you? Do you see a wedding band anywhere here?" She held out the hand for him, pulled it into a fist and motioned with her index finger for him to follow. She walked him to the end of the hall and the splendid elevated view of the lake. "Rings come off, you know." She threw open the door. It was to the master bedroom. "Now this," she said, returning to her saleswoman voice. "This is a room you can really sink your teeth into."

"Do tell," LaMoia said, wondering if he dare follow her inside.

The bathroom was marble and large enough to park the Camaro. She was wearing a good scent, warm and suggestive. In the close confines it grew stronger. "What do I call you?" LaMoia asked. "Sherry? I keep thinking of the wine."

"You can call me anything you like, sweetheart. I answer to Sherry, but I can get used to change real quickly. In my line of work, you learn to adapt."

"Even four and a half is steep for me. And to be honest, it's more house than I need. I'm kind of a bedroom and kitchen guy. My needs are small."

"Don't underrate yourself."

"And I hadn't considered the bridge traffic, which was stupid. I'm thinking maybe I should be looking north of town. Above Forty-fifth. Didn't I see a sign of yours on Fifty-second, Fifty-first?"

"Fifty-first." She sounded disappointed. He had just cut her commission in half.

"What's that one going for?"

"Asking two-thirty. I think they'll probably get it."

"Could we see it? Take a look?"

"This is a steal at four-fifty. It's worth the offer." The spark went out of her eye, as if he had pointed out the mole on her neck below her ear, which did bother him. When he failed to reply to her suggestion, she said, "Sure thing. Today?"

"If you have the time."

"Well you're the client, sweetheart," she said, her engines running again. "What works for you works for me."

LaMoia felt awkward turning his back on the Shotz residence as he walked up the short front path to the house. A white van belonging to KOMO News was parked out front topped with all kinds of antennae. The Shotzes had yet to grant interviews. Thank God for small favors, he thought.

Sherry Daech's backside kept his attention as she climbed the short steps to the front door. "You know that kidnapping yesterday?" she asked as she worked with the realtor's combination box to get the key. "Happened right there."

She turned around to point, but saw LaMoia's badge first and it registered with shock.

LaMoia flipped the badge wallet closed and slipped it into his pants pocket. "It's Detective Sergeant. Crimes Against Persons division. Homicide. You had an open house last night."

She stammered, "The house on Mercer?"

"I tried to make an appointment through your receptionist."

"You little shit." She looked him over. "You come on to me hoping for an interrogation? I ought to file a complaint!"

"I came on to you because you came on to me."

"Is that so?"

"Because you're an attractive woman," he said, hoping to annul some of the damage. "You know how to talk the talk. I like that."

"Is that so?" she replied, in a more approving tone, a finger nervously hooking some of the blonde hair and stashing it behind her left ear.

"The open house was during the time we believe the baby was kidnapped."

"*Was* it the Pied Piper?"

"Chances are you may have seen something. A car? A man?"

"So you *tricked* me? Is that how you do it?"

"Every hour that baby is missing means we're less likely to return her to her parents. There are over thirty of us on this case. Not one of us has slept in the past seventeen hours."

"I didn't see anything." She glanced at the key in her hand. "You don't want to see this house," she realized. "You little shit! God, I can't believe this. *This* is my tax dollars at work? Are you the best we've got, Detective?"

"Sergeant," he corrected, thinking that Boldt was the best they had, feeling inferior suddenly. "I'd like to go inside, please."

"Shit," she said, keying the door for him. "Why didn't you just ask—" But she caught herself, realizing he had. "Cops. You guys are a different species."

LaMoia followed her inside, saying, "I want you to stand right here for a minute." He took her shoulders gently and turned her toward the Shotz residence. "How many times you must have opened this door last night." He left his hands on her shoulders, which were warm to the touch. It was dangerous ground, she could file a complaint about his misleading her, and the physical contact, if mentioned, would be difficult to justify to a review board. LaMoia had a history with the review board, and it wasn't all rosy. "How many people came by to look at the house?"

She stood at an angle facing the Shotz residence, down the street. He could sense her searching her memory.

He asked, "Can you remember standing here?" She gave him a faint nod. "Can you glance over the shoulder of those people and see the street beyond?"

"I've never done anything like this."

"That's okay," he coached. "Are my hands bothering you?"

"No, not at all."

"You can close your eyes. It helps sometimes."

He leaned around her to steal a peek; her eyes were pinched tightly shut.

"The house was all lit up over there. I remember that."

Remember more, he silently encouraged. The baby sitter had confirmed the lights. She had turned on as many as she could find. She hadn't remembered much else: a man wearing goggles at the back door—an exterminator.

Daech pointed, "An old-model Wagoneer, a white minivan, a black STS, my Hummer, an ancient pickup, kinda blue-gray. Driveway. Blue Toyota Camry. The STS and the Camry were mine—the open house."

"You know your rides," he said, somewhat disbelieving. They could check her recollections against vehicles owned by the residents of the other houses.

"Honestly? Listen, this may sound crude, sweetheart, but you are what you drive. When I see someone pull up to an open house, first thing I do is look at the car. You can judge one hell of a lot by that." She added, "A couple getting out of a foreign car? That's got good strong legs for me. I pay attention. The STS fits that: Cadillac, you know. A guy, alone, climbing out of something American and a couple years old: probably just killing time. Free glass of wine and someone to talk to. I get a lot of that. Maybe he's got enough for the down, but I'm not betting on it. If it's during a weekday, and it's a woman, maybe a young kid or two in tow, a Volvo, an Audi, out-of-state plates, I'm thinking the wife is out shopping for a home while the hubby's at the office."

"You check the tags?"

"I'm telling you, out-of-state plates means they're in a hurry—they're looking to buy. Usually a little less concerned about price, more concerned about contents. Kitchen, if it's a woman. Men are interested in the living room and the master bedroom. Women think about closets and tubs."

The pickup truck or the minivan made sense to him for a person posing as an exterminator. "A minivan or a panel van?" La-Moia asked, trying to keep excitement out of his voice. The woman clearly studied her clients and applied her own skewed science to what she observed. She was a good witness—someone a jury would find believable. He couldn't help but jump ahead. Hope was a detective's only fuel.

"White minivan. A mommy-mobile. You know. Pretty new. Might have been something printed on the driver's door."

"What? A name? A business?" LaMoia encouraged.

"Listen, I'm not sure about any of this."

"Parked where?" He didn't want to lose her.

"Just down the street there." She pointed again, though this time hesitantly. "Maybe two cars ahead of where you're parked. I was just about where you are."

"But not in front of the house, the Shotz house," he clarified.

She grimaced. "Pretty damn close. Parking wasn't easy last night. A lot easier this time of day."

LaMoia took notes. "The driver?"

"Was the driver the kidnapper?" she blurted out quickly. "I don't know about any of this."

He removed his hands from her shoulders. "Take your time."

She turned around and faced him. "Maybe it wasn't last night. Hell, I see a lot of cars, you know?"

"The driver. You were watching to see who got out," he reminded.

"A worker bee. I wasn't interested."

"Worker bee?"

"Overalls. Coveralls. You know? A worker bee. He wasn't there for me. I tuned him out."

LaMoia told her. "Can you describe him?"

"I tuned him out," she repeated, seeming confused whether to answer or not. "I don't know," she said, searching his face for the right answer. "Maybe that wasn't last night." A quick retreat. LaMoia had seen it dozens of times, almost always in the suburbs. People tended to be excited at first by the idea of having witnessed a crime; they felt important, listened to, wanted. Then it slowly dawned on them that, like jury duty, police involvement meant a commitment of time and energy.

LaMoia decided to try an end run, to play on her apparent tendency to make a show of herself. "Listen, if it's the publicity you're worried about: the TV, the papers—they're likely to swarm a possible witness—there are precautions we can take. We can keep you off the front page." He left it hanging there as a carrot.

Her face brightened. Her finger wormed that curl of hair again. "No, no . . . it isn't *that*."

"You sounded as if you weren't sure about the minivan."

"Oh, no," she corrected. "I'm pretty damn sure about that minivan, Detective."

"And the driver?"

"Just a worker bee in overalls."

"Overalls," LaMoia repeated, jotting it down. "Color? Description?"

Shaking her head, she confessed, "I don't know. He pulled up over there, and I was thinking housewife until he climbed out. Then I was thinking what did I care because he was a worker bee, and no worker bee is going to pay over two for a home. Not in my experience. One-eighty's the ceiling in that market and I don't even list that stuff. The only people I'm interested in at an open

house are the ones with that glint in their eyes. You know. Someone shopping? Someone in a buying mood?" She looked at La-
Moia. "You were shopping when I saw you. But it wasn't for a
house, am I right? I understand that now. But at the time, I saw
that car all buffed out like that, the boots, that hunger in your
eyes, and I thought I had a live one."

"The minivan? Windows, or a panel truck?" He thought of
little Rhonda Shotz in the back of that minivan, and felt sick.

"Windows?" she winced. She wasn't sure. "Listen, it was
white. Windows? No clue about the windows." Looking around
nervously she said, "Tell me about the TV people. Who do we
contact about that?"

CHAPTER

6

Since the birth of her son Hayes, six months earlier, Trish Weinstein had felt out of synch, as if a week or a month had been stolen from her and she had never made up that loss. At twenty-seven she was feeling tired and old. Her body had not come back the way she had hoped; her stomach still looked like a five-day-old balloon; she still couldn't get into her favorite jeans— the standard by which she measured her progress. Life as a mother was not what she'd expected, not always the maternally blissful state of joy everyone made it out to be.

Thursdays were her haven, a day she eagerly anticipated all week.

On these days, her mother-in-law, Phyllis Weinstein, arrived right on time, shortly after lunch. Same schedule every week.

"Hello, dearie," Phyllis called out in that slightly condescending tone of hers, letting herself in through the back door without knocking first. Overbearing and protective of her son, Phyllis Weinstein seemed to view Trish as little more than a baby factory for furthering the diluted family line. As a gentile, Trish was never going to win the woman's full affections; she felt tolerated—in the worst way—but her son Hayes had gained her some unexpected points.

"Hi, Phyllis," Trish responded belatedly, a bit wearily.

"Where's my little Hayes?" Phyllis asked, pushing past her daughter-in-law without any further attempts at niceties. She moved about the small house, Trish following. The woman just couldn't stand still, stop talking or avoid mentioning bowel movements.

"Just waking up," Trish explained. No matter her own relationship with Phyllis, it was good for all to have a grandmother around.

In a voice that grated like bad brakes, Phyllis admonished, "Don't forget some shower scrub, will you? Sidney says the shower is growing into a rain forest."

Phyllis then turned in time to watch Trish blush scarlet at the idea that her husband was reporting her housecleaning abilities to his mother.

"It's the climate," Trish explained with the knowingness of a transplanted Californian. "Hang out a fresh towel, it's damp by evening."

"Which, though it's bad for a lot of things, is good for the skin. You know, Trish, you could use a little moisturizer around the eyes." She winked. A little harder and the entire fake lash would have fallen off.

Trish reminded, "I'm at the gym 'til two, then the market."

"Same as always," the older woman said. "I'm not stupid, you know."

"Home at three," she reminded, heading to the back door, glad to be out of there.

Throughout the crunches, the leg lifts, the treadmill, the Northwest News Station carried updates on the Pied Piper kidnapping. A blonde—it had to be dyed—realtor was said to be a possible eyewitness that police and FBI were questioning. An adorable picture of the missing child was repeatedly shown and an 800 number superimposed on the screen. Trish felt God-awful for the poor parents. The TV reporter said something about thirty thousand children going missing each year, though most were over six years old. But for Trish and the rest of Seattle, it was only one child that mattered right now, and that was Rhonda Shotz.

She didn't know what she would do if she ever lost Hayes. The kidnapper had overcome some teenage baby sitter. Thank God for Phyllis, she thought, in a rare moment of appreciation. She pitied the man who crossed Phyllis.

CHAPTER

7

On Friday morning, March 13, two days after the Shotz kidnapping, Boldt pulled a chair into his former office cubicle, now occupied by LaMoia. "A lesson," he said, opening a file. "Flemming's people loaned us a look at their report on the AFIDs found at the various crime scenes."

"Stolen," LaMoia guessed.

"But of course," Boldt answered. "An entire shipment of the replacement cartridges for the air TASER went missing when an eighteen-wheeler was hijacked west of Chicago two years ago. Until the first child was kidnapped in San Diego, the FBI had lost track of it. The ATF had not. Three dozen of the cartridges were bought out of Las Vegas seven months ago using a counterfeit card—"

"Surprise."

"At a gun shop that dealt black-market goods. These militia boys love untraceable hardware. The ATF did some good work. The owner of the card was under surveillance by the FBI for three weeks before any questions were asked. This cardholder lives in Kansas City, runs a commercial air-conditioning company—wife, kids, the whole number. When they get around to questioning him, he says that only the one errant charge was ever made—six hundred and change—and this is supported by his formal complaint to the card company. But as you and I know, it's not how a stolen card is typically used, so the Bureau takes a handoff from ATF and grinds this one in with their toes. They ran every possible lead—tracked this guy's movements for a two-year period, his wife's, their phone records, even UPS and FedEx histories. Clean bill of health—he's not connected."

"Too bad," LaMoia said.

"But they have the Las Vegas connection, so they pursue it—maybe they bust the rest of the cartridges and plea bargain information on the three dozen sold. Together they had two dozen agents on it, including a half dozen undercover."

"But did they find the cartridges?" LaMoia asked. Hill's dislike of the federal agencies had infected LaMoia.

"No. They chased some information—it's all in here—conducted maybe twenty interrogations, but the cartridges were long gone and not one of the gun dealers was saying to where. The Bureau now believes that maybe a third of the original shipment made Las Vegas. Trail went cold. But keep in mind: The AFIDs found at each of the ten crime scenes are for cartridges part of that original shipment."

"So, cold or not, it's still a trail to follow," LaMoia suggested.

"Exactly. The Bureau followed the evidence."

"But—" LaMoia said sharply, all too familiar with Boldt's inflection. He considered where Boldt might take this and said, "You would pursue the victim."

"Yes."

"And the only real victim in sight is this credit card holder." LaMoia thought a moment and said, "They considered him a suspect but never made the jump back to victim. They chased the cartridges instead—the evidence."

"For which no one can fault them."

"But whoever used this guy's credit card number had to get it somehow. A discarded carbon—"

"Telephone mail order . . . ," Boldt contributed.

"A waiter at a restaurant, any number of cashiers, Ticket-Master."

Boldt nodded and said, "Random or not, they got hold of this guy's card number. The Pied Piper made contact, directly or indirectly."

"He could have bought it off any of hundreds of counterfeiters who knew the number was valid."

"Maybe," Boldt agreed, "but there's still a bridge there between the kidnapper and that cardholder."

"And you want me to pursue it," LaMoia added sarcastically, "because I've got nothing better to do."

"Intelligence doesn't investigate," Boldt reminded. "We collect and analyze."

LaMoia mimicked the man, making faces and mouthing his words. His pager vibrated at his side. He held it into the light: Its message screen carried a string of ten numbers.

Boldt tapped the file and picked it up. "If you need any specifics, I've got this. Happy to help." He stood and left before La-Moia could think of a way to beg some investigative work from him. He looked back at the pager.

The time of day told him as much as the page itself: an hour before lunch. He dialed the first seven numbers. An operator's voice answered, "Mayflower Hotel." He hung up. Fancy digs, he thought.

He had logged nearly fifteen hours of O.T. since Wednesday night. One thing about a major crime: It made you rich. But he had traded sleep for the O.T. and knew that despite his surface energy he would pay. Lack of sleep seemed to galvanize him, at least for the first three days. After that, it was all downhill. He was in a holding pattern, awaiting results from the lab on the broken glass—the penny flute had come up clean. Boldt had pointed him toward a good chase, the credit card.

Doris Shotz, mother of the abducted child, maintained a vigil on the oak bench out in the hallway, her young son at her side. To pass by her out there made LaMoia sick to his stomach. His offers of coffee or pop went refused, attempts to communicate went unreciprocated; she sat there, an icon to the task force's incompetence, which in turn reminded him of the four o'clock meeting the day before.

Thursday's four o'clock task force meeting, the first of its kind, had run about as smoothly as an elementary school play. With the FBI and SPD in the same room, both believing themselves in control, the meeting had ended in a confrontation.

Sheila Hill lorded over the head of the table, passing judgment with her stern facial expressions.

Homicide's situation room, a glorified conference room wrapped around a large oval table that sat twelve, doubled as task force headquarters. At the near end, behind Hill, a white board held scribbled notes in colorful markers. To Hill's right, a well-worn cork bulletin board adorned with crime scene photographs carried family photos not only of the Shotz residence and child but of nine other small and smiling faces.

Matthews and Mulwright looked up as a sharp rap on the door announced the entrance of two gray suits and a gray skirt that was occupied by a long and slender pair of dark legs. As Special Agent in Charge, Gary Flemming headed the FBI's investigation and had done so since the first kidnapping in San Diego. He had arrived in Seattle expecting that he and his team would control any and all kidnapping investigations, an opportunity removed by SPD's advance formation of the task force and Sheila Hill's appointment as its commander. Flemming had lost the upper hand. Hill had warned all her subordinates to expect Flemming to do everything in his power to regain it.

A substantial man with ebony skin and a head nearly shaved clean to hide encroaching baldness, Flemming had a worried-looking face and bloodshot eyes. He sat in the chair immediately to Hill's left and spoke in a deeply rich voice. He made no apology for his late arrival; nor did Hill for starting without him. Flemming's reputation preceded him: meticulous, ambitious, firm, demanding. He got results. An astute politician and negotiator, Flemming not only understood law enforcement politics but had overseen six hostage/kidnapping investigations and had never lost a victim. He held the highest clearance rate for kidnappings in the Bureau's history. One listened carefully to his words and looked for hidden content.

"We're coming up on forty-eight hours," he cautioned. "He and his victim are long gone from the city by now. We'd like to help with the glass samples you recovered," he informed LaMoia, who stared back stunned by the man's information and his arrogance. "You have some pollen as well, as I understand it." He referred to the yellow smudge Boldt had noticed on the crib. LaMoia didn't know where he got his information, but earlier that day the department's lab had IDed the yellow powder as pollen, genus unknown. Flemming continued, "This pollen was found on the child's crib, as well as on some carpet fibers your lab obtained from the crime scene." He editorialized sarcastically, "Of course, I know you were going to share this with us, but as I understand it, the fibers came off a floor mat from last year's Taurus—which, according to color schemes, should make it a champagne-brown exterior, I believe." LaMoia understood then that Flemming's people had already interrogated the Shotzes and had made inquiries at the lab, all with no one the wiser. Strangely, he did not dislike Flemming for this, but found himself admiring him. Flemming continued, "Our lab people would like to review the pollen as well as the Taurus fibers ASAP. We'd also like to conduct our own interview with this realtor, Daech. Quite frankly, Captain," he said, addressing Sheila Hill, "we're a little disappointed we weren't included in the first round with Daech."

"I have a decent relationship established with Daech," LaMoia informed him.

"I'm sure you do," Flemming returned, staring him down.

"Cop to witness," LaMoia explained, his admiration melting away.

"From what we know of your reputation," the linebacker, Dunkin Hale, contributed, "that would be something of a first."

Only Mulwright laughed.

Hill cautioned the FBI man, "That's enough of that! She's LaMoia's witness, and she's assisting this investigation."

"For the sake of the investigation," Hale questioned, "or for the publicity?"

Hill decided, "You're welcome to the sergeant's notes. Let's leave the witness to him, shall we? You gang-bang her and we'll lose her."

"The notes will do fine," Flemming acknowledged, having never taken his eyes off LaMoia. "And perhaps the sergeant will allow us to add a few questions to his script for their next session." Flemming hesitated, holding the attention of everyone in the room. He said, "Let me be perfectly candid, shall I? This is my investigation. Has been since San Diego and that first kidnapping. Task Force, Special Crimes Unit—dress it up however you want, make all the claims of ownership you want, it's not going to affect me. Sticks and stones, as far as I'm concerned. It's these kids I'm worried about, not the name tags or the stripes on the sleeves—the kids. And it's mine. Not yours," he said to Hill, "or yours," he said to LaMoia, "mine. You play games with me—concealing evidence, delaying reports—and you'll regret it. That's about as clear as I can make it to you. And why will you regret it? Because I don't give a shit about you or your careers. I'll walk right over you if necessary."

Looking at Hill he added, "Destroy you, if necessary. Any one of you. All of you. Any of my people as well, and they know this about me." Hale and Kalidja did not so much as blink. "They know it's about the kids, and only the kids. It's about catching this guy and doing whatever it takes to find those kids. Rant, rave, scream, bitch, kick—complain to whomever you wish. Washington D.C.—I don't care. It won't do you a bit of good. Why? Because it's mine to win or lose, and lose is not an option. Remember this, and remember it clearly: You are working for me. You are working for these kids, and I am their guardian angel. I am bringing them home. And the first person to get in my way, the first person to slow me down even a step, is going to wish they'd never seen this thing, wish they'd never heard of it." He met eyes with each person, sighed deeply and said, "Ah. Feels good to get that off my chest."

Daphne Matthews spoke in a near whisper, thereby commanding everyone's attention. As if reviewing the fundamentals, she said, "A task force is assembled to facilitate an open-minded exchange. The FBI can run an investigation without us—as we can without them. The point, the intention, of such a task force is to bring us all under one tent," she looked at Flemming, "so that we don't double up the lab work," to LaMoia, "so we don't monopolize a witness. The daily four o'clock is our chance as a team to share our progress and our hurdles, to communicate, to facilitate a more efficient investigation."

Mulwright interrupted, "They withheld critical information."

"The AFIDs, the penny flute," LaMoia said, "we would have withheld those as well."

The lack of team support angered Mulwright. True to form, he had not heard a word of what Matthews had to say.

Flemming said, "I think I've made my position perfectly clear. Or are there questions?"

Dunkin Hale, a thirty-five-year-old red-headed jock with an attitude, chewed gum violently and wore a thick gold wedding ring on his left hand. They didn't make ties to fit necks like his; the silk knot stood out like a large thumb protruding from his Adam's apple. His attention remained primarily on Flemming, a dog awaiting a scrap, his loyalty unmistakable.

Flemming informed them, "We are looking for this Taurus."

He nodded to Hale, who said, "We're running rental car contracts—all contracts made here in the past four days compared against all rentals contracted in the week prior to the Portland and San Francisco kidnappings. Credit card comparison, model requests. It's slow going, but maybe it kicks a match."

"Who informed the press of the hundred-thousand-dollar reward?" Mulwright challenged. "The phone number in that release was the task force hot line, not an FBI number I noticed, which means it's us getting a couple hundred calls *an hour*, all of which have to be followed up, meaning we're out chasing ghost stories while you guys are working real leads. Is that cooperation?"

"Lieutenant!" Hill chided. "Although we were in fact blindsided by the reward and the flood of calls it caused, let none of us forget that the task force phone number was our idea. We asked for this.''

Flemming spoke in his low, warm voice, ''Special Agent Kalidja is our research expert and our fact-finder.'' Delegate the problems: what every bureaucrat learns early on.

Kay Kalidja's parents had immigrated from the Caribbean. She had lighter skin than Flemming and widely set, Asian eyes. Bone thin, she looked more like a runway model than an FBI agent. She wore a starched white shirt and crisp gray suit. Her tobacco-colored hair was done in corn rows with terra-cotta beads that clicked if she shook her head quickly. She kept her attention on Flemming like a benched athlete watching her coach, and took her cue.

Her voice was musical, her accent vaguely British. The moment she spoke, she captivated everyone. ''The press release was our doing, it is true. We have case history to support that an informed public, an alert public, a motivated public, can and does lead to arrests. Also, although there is no apparent *direct* link between widespread publicity and the abrupt end to the kidnappings in the prior cities, its influence cannot be discounted. In each case, the louder the cry of the press, the quicker the kidnapper moved on.''

Daphne Matthews objected, ''Moved on, yes. But that's all.''

Flemming reminded, ''It's to our benefit if we keep this guy on the run.''

Daphne Matthews contested, ''The penny flutes indicate a person intent on making a statement. We put him between twenty-five and forty. High school graduate at least. Organized—he knows what the hell he's doing; what comes next. Most likely scenario: He never met his father, mother died before he was fifteen. He's never known any family. If he's using the children sexually, then he will have been arrested on similar though lesser offenses—he may or may not have served time. If he's selling the children, then we can be fairly certain he was an only child, and that his mother either sexually abused, physically mistreated or abandoned him. We have a disturbed but rational individual who suffers no remorse. The children are either a form of company—we call it the Boo Radley Syndrome; a source of physical pleasure for him—a diddler; or a means to financial enrichment. He's a con artist—"

"Now wait just a minute!" Flemming said, cutting her off. "This is where you and five of this agency's best criminal behaviorists happen to disagree, Ms. Matthews."

"Lieutenant," she corrected.

It won a grin from Flemming, an act that seemed foreign to his face. "Irrespective of your profile, our people give great weight to the influence of publicity on the perpetrator's behavior."

"He's monitoring the press," Daphne confirmed. "I have no argument there. But allowing it to dictate his actions? He's an organized personality, a control freak. He's not going to let the news services, the FBI or the police run his show. There is no consistent thread linking news reporting and his abandoning a city. To the contrary, the decision seems random—designed to keep law enforcement off guard." She paused, the silence in the room suffocating. "How thoroughly have you investigated known confidence men?"

"Con men?" Dunkin Hale asked, chiding her. "These are kidnappers."

Flemming focused on Daphne, clearly interested.

"Our man is an actor," she explained. "He enjoys playing roles. It's the one consistent element to every kidnapping. A person doesn't develop such abilities overnight. Only a con man has such talents."

"Forget it," Hale said rudely, his wide neck florid and bulging like a blowfish.

"What we will do," Flemming answered her calmly, ignoring Hale and nodding toward Kalidja, "is check for releases from correctional facilities, six months and prior. The Club Feds, and state minimum security facilities." Kalidja copied all this down.

Sheila Hill spoke up for the first time in several minutes. "We're crossing the forty-eight-hour mark, a mark none of us wanted to see. Some of us are preciously low on sleep. We need to pull together if we're going to be an effective task force. Judging by his history, we have another five to fifteen days before he's back for another one. If we're not going to work as a task force then let's drop the charade right now, issue a joint press release and go to our corners. S-A-C Flemming?" she said, knowing that with the evidence controlled by SPD, Flemming had little choice.

Flemming looked up and said, "We're in."

LaMoia reviewed all this as he left the office, scrawling LUNCH onto the scheduling board between the numbers 12 and 1. He took the stairs, not the elevator, an act that had nothing to do with fitness and everything with impatience. He had never been a person to wait. His motto was, This Ain't No Dress Rehearsal, and he lived accordingly.

The air, heavy with fog, delivered a bone-cutting chill. Every person's face advertised their eagerness for spring. LaMoia charged through this malaise like a beam of light through darkness, grinning to himself, his long legs stretching out before him in defiant strides. To hell with those poor slobs—you either swam with them or against them, and LaMoia had made his choice a long time ago.

He jumped a bus and rode it eight blocks and walked the rest of the way to the Mayflower, a corner hotel with a lot of class. The last three digits on his pager referred to the room number. Codes. Little games. He'd been doing this for months. An unfamiliar feeling blossomed in the heart of a cynic formerly confused by easy sex and his own silver tongue. Attracting women had never been a problem for LaMoia, only staying interested in them. He rode them hard, put them away wet, and rarely returned. The first attempt at hand holding or sweet talking and LaMoia launched into his litany of excuses, only to find himself in a bar or the gym or a coffee shop working his magic all over again.

The bounce in his step had little to do with the promise of a nooner, and everything to do with a light flutter in his chest. He didn't tire of this new woman in his life, didn't look for ways out of their next encounter. As unlikely a match as he might have ever imagined, he nonetheless felt an attachment, a profound desire, a need, to spend increasing amounts of time with her. The hotel rendezvous was getting old; he wanted to share a bed, a sunrise, a shower, a cup of coffee. He wanted to test himself, to see how real or unreal these feelings actually were. He believed he wanted a relationship with her—an unthinkable thought given his history. He felt terrified to mention this change in himself, partly because she remained always at an arm's length. He hoped like hell that wasn't part of his attraction.

He rode the elevator to the seventh floor wondering if he was in control or on a leash, light headed and slightly afraid. The idea of sleeping with the teacher had always appealed to him—he had done so more than once—but his current arrangement threatened his career, not just an A in math.

He knocked sharply, already aroused by expectation. The door cracked open, and by the time he stepped inside, she was nothing more than a terry cloth robe walking away toward the bed. Then the robe fell away as LaMoia helped the door shut and threw the security bar in place. He turned to face a black teddy overflowing out the top with soft flesh, and tight and bulging where her legs met.

He hurried out of his crisply pressed jeans. Every square inch of her was darkly tanned, no bikini line whatsoever as she unsnapped the teddy in three short pops.

"Leave it," he said. She enjoyed instruction.

"Come and get it," she offered, "though not necessarily in that order." She grinned behind eyes flashing with excitement.

In the bedroom, Sheila Hill put rank aside and willingly took orders.

The resulting forty minutes of athletics left the thick scent of woman in the air and a sheen on their skin, the bedding off the mattress and Sheila Hill still on all fours, her hands holding loosely to the headboard, her glistening back heaving from her panting.

"Oh, God," she said deliciously, "you're going to kill me if we keep this up."

"It would be more fun if we didn't have to leave," he risked saying. "If we could wake up at three in the morning and go again."

"Not this lifetime," she quipped. "I like my job. Besides," she added, "my bed never would have made it through that." She let go the headboard and slouched down so that her head found the pillow but her buttocks remained hoisted high in the air.

With her he found himself in a nearly constant state of arousal. He felt seventeen again.

She lowered herself and stretched out, and he wished she would have stayed like that a little longer.

"They can't dictate what we do in our off hours," he reminded.

"One of us would be off the task force in a heartbeat. Flemming would see to that. Count on it. It would look wrong, and it would damage both of us. We've been over this. *God . . . ,*" she moaned. "Get me a cigarette, would you?"

He obeyed, though he wondered why. No woman had ever ordered him about.

"And the lighter," she reminded.

He didn't like the smoking, but he never said anything. He climbed off the bed and found her purse and delivered the cigarettes and lighter. She rolled over, her upper-chest rash red and shiny with sweat, lit the cigarette and inhaled deeply. "Okay, fun is fun, and that was fun! But we've got work to do." She worked the cigarette down hungrily, arched her back and lifted her pelvis. "God, you're something," she whispered through the smoke.

"A dinner over at your place, early to bed but not to sleep. Who's going to know?"

"We start that, and it won't stop."

"So?" he complained. "What's wrong with that?"

She said soberly, "We agreed up front about all this, John."

"Things change."

"This hasn't. We're attracted to each other. We enjoy each other's company. The sex is out of this world—and I mean that. But we're both Crimes Against Persons, we're both on the task force; that's conflict of interest. That's a no-no. We are not taking this to the next step. Not so long as the present situation exists."

LaMoia felt a tightening in his throat and chest, and felt almost obliged to break something. "Bernie says the glass chips are automotive."

She rolled up onto an elbow and cast a knee forward. She looked like a model to him despite a few extra pounds. He would never get tired of looking at her. He had tired so quickly of the others. She smiled coyly, "You got this *when*?"

He gave her the answer required of him, "This morning, Captain." She knew immediately that he had received the information ahead of yesterday's four o'clock.

"Well, you little shit." She grinned widely. "I love the way you operate, you rogue son-of-a-bitch. Have I told you that?"

He wanted a different statement of love from her, and the comment stung him in a way she wouldn't understand.

"The glass is from a side window, not the windshield. They picked up some tiny lettering on one of the chips. Ironically, the Bureau may be able to help us trace the manufacturer."

"Ford Taurus?"

"No."

"Anything else I should know?"

"The pollen has been passed along to the botany department at the university for analysis. If Flemming finds out and grabs the sample, there's not much we can do. The university needs federal money. The Bureau can make up all kinds of shit to justify taking the samples."

"Flemming doesn't need any justification. He's going to do what he likes." A seagull cried outside the window. LaMoia looked up to see a gray and white blur. A second echoing cry, farther away. He wondered about the Shotz baby and if she was crying too.

"Yeah, Flemming's little speech," she said to herself. "Got to respect him, though. Did you know that he worked that CEO in New Jersey found buried alive? Intelligence dug this up," she said, meaning Boldt.

LaMoia could feel her nervousness. He didn't want to operate in Flemming's shadow any more than she did.

"Consulted Hale from the start of this—from San Diego on.

They'd worked other kidnappings together. Didn't bring Hale or Kalidja on until Portland, after he'd cleaned house a few times." She added softly, "He meant what he said about walking right over us. But then again, he doesn't know us."

LaMoia had not seen her like this—Flemming had knocked the wind out of her, not an easy thing to do. "Hale bothers me," he confessed. "He's Flemming's hit man. He's the one that's going to do the damage, if any's done. Flemming keeps himself squeaky clean. Knows what he's doing. Fraternity types were never my favorites."

"Hale is ambitious. Tough. He's married—the only one of the three of them who's married. Three kids. He must feel these kidnappings as much as Boldt and I do. Yet Flemming's the one who's all passionate about the kids. Protecting his rank is more like it."

"That's not how it felt to me. He meant that shit."

"Hale made a name for himself with the Bureau down in Texas by solving some border kidnappings—kids—Mexican fathers taking their kids away from Mom and back across the border. I agree that Hale's the wild card. We keep an eye on him."

"And Kalidja?" he asked, appreciating the information.

"Boldt couldn't dig much up. Came out of the Washington Metropolitan Field Office. Background in analysis is about all that Boldt did find. That would imply she's Flemming's fact-checker. But she may be more than that: With her ties to Washington, Flemming buys himself a field agent with good contacts at headquarters. He gets a spy; a liaison. With the kind of heat he must be taking—"

"That would be invaluable."

"Exactly." She stubbed out the cigarette in a water glass.

He said, "We gotta do something for the mother—Doris Shotz. Counseling? I don't know. She sits outside the fifth-floor door all day long. Barely moves. Just sits there."

"We find her kid. The rest will take care of itself. We're not in the baby sitting business. She shouldn't be spending so much time with us. It doesn't help anyone."

"You're a mother," he reminded. "Where would you spend your time?"

She rolled onto her back and put her knees up. "You want to hear something strange?" she asked rhetorically. "That child went missing, and I had an incredible urge to have another baby. You'd think just the opposite, you know? But not me. I wanted a child."

"I could arrange that," he said.

"Oh no, you don't. You keep those things on."

"I mean a family, a child of our own."

She didn't say anything for a long, long time.

A nude in a Rubens oil, he thought. Round in all the right ways. She cast her hair off her face and behind her ear, exaggerating her graceful neck. "Spare me. Your reputation precedes you, pal."

"People change."

"People maybe, but not men," she said. "Believe me, I have a divorce to prove it." She said, "We shouldn't be talking about kids. Not with Rhonda Shotz out there somewhere. Probably shouldn't be here at all, although I work better when I'm relaxed. And you *do* relax me. You want the shower first?"

"No," LaMoia said, edging closer to her. "I want something else first." He ran his hand lightly from her ankle to her pubis and watched her hair stand on end under his touch.

"Oh, Jesus. I'm going to be late for my one-thirty." She sighed.

"You want me to stop?" he asked, his fingers gently massaging her.

"What do you think?" she asked, separating her legs for him.

"I think you're going to be late for your one-thirty," he answered. He no longer cared about nights with her, another half hour would have to do.

"That's absolutely perfect," she said, leaning her head deeply back into the pillow with a warm smile of satisfaction curling her lips. "Absolutely perfect." She arched her back higher and sighed.

Music to his ears.

CHAPTER

Accustomed to his wife's bald head and lack of
eyebrows, Boldt decided she looked wise, like a Buddhist monk,
not sick like a cancer patient. He hated the smell of hospitals.

"It's early," she said.

"Priorities."

"Progress?"

The adjacent bed lay empty and made, its surrounding tables
neat and cleared of anything personal. In a ward where people
went missing for good, the void pulled at Boldt. Had Rhonda
Shotz gone missing for good as well?

Distracted, Boldt answered, "Five days now. Precious little to
go on. We've lost her for the time being. Worse, we know he'll
strike again in the next few days."

"What's he doing with them?"

He shrugged. "Speculation."

"You're in a sick business."

"With sick people. LaMoia calls the kidnapped children
thumb-suckers. One of the Feds, a guy named Hale, he calls them
'milk cartons,' because their pictures used to be on the sides." He

saw a dying mother, not a sick woman—this happened occasionally. "You don't need to hear this."

"You could use some sleep," she said kindly.

He couldn't take sympathy coming from her.

She needed the sleep, not him, the insomnia having come with
the bed rest, the bed rest with the treatment, the treatment with
the disease. She refused the pills. She gladly accepted his reading
to her, if and when his schedule allowed, which depended on
Marina's schedule. Lately, everything depended on something.
Nothing stood alone: Even the grandest of trees anchored itself in
the earth.

"Did you see the kids at all today?" she asked in a tone that
bordered on accusation.

He answered with silence, for he would never lie to her. He
devoted every spare minute to his two children, but to a mother
in a hospital room this would seem like too little.

She suggested, "Maybe if you drove them to day care instead
of Marina."

"I'll bring them by to see you tomorrow night after dinner." He
drove them to day care three days a week. Argument had no place
here. He and his wife had fallen deeply in love again. If only he
might be given a second chance. . . .

"Can I read to you?" he asked.

"Please."

He dug around on her cluttered end table looking for the Mah-
fouz novel she had been reading.

"Not there. Here." She strained to her right, fingers searching.
Her nightgown fell open and he saw the broad freckled skin of
her back. Her ribs showed. He didn't know that back. It belonged
to a different woman.

He subscribed to the belief that two could solve their individual
problems better than one person alone. He felt terrified by the
thought he might lose her.

"Read this," Liz said, handing him a leather-bound Bible that
Boldt had never seen. Numbered metal tabs marked sections.
"Start at seven. The text is marked in chalk."

Sight of the Bible sent a shiver through him. Did she sense

the end? Had she spoken with her doctor? Panic flooded through him.

"Anything you want to tell me?" he asked, his voice breaking, the Bible shaking slightly in his hands.

"Number seven," she said. "It's marked."

He fumbled with the book. He had ridden this roller coaster for months; he wasn't sure how much longer he could endure it.

He cleared his throat and read aloud, his voice warm and resonant. She loved his reading voice.

Liz closed her eyes and smiled.

Some things were worth the wait.

CHAPTER

9

The Town Car stuck out, black and gleaming, showroom fresh. It was parked out front of Boldt's home, beneath a street light, ostentatious and isolated, as if none of the other neighborhood cars, unwaxed and dull from a winter of rain, wanted to socialize with it. Boldt slowed the Chevy as he drove past, turned into his drive and pulled to a stop.

Gary Flemming sat at the kitchen table with Miles on his lap, speaking Spanish to Marina who was doing dishes. Sarah, in an outrigger high chair, had a cherub face smeared in pulverized pears. Caught in the midst of a euphoric laugh, Marina glanced toward Boldt, registering disappointment as if he'd spoiled the party.

Flemming put down Sarah's baby spoon—it was Boldt's joy to feed his daughter in the evenings—and met eyes with Boldt, who immediately felt uncomfortable in his own home. He wished Miles would get off the man's lap. Sensing this, Flemming eased the boy down to the floor. Miles ran for Boldt's leg and attached himself. Flemming wiped Sarah's chin with her bib.

"Mr. Flemming with FBI," Marina explained, eyes to the dishwater.

"Yes, we've met," Boldt said.

"A handshake at a crime scene is hardly what I would call an introduction," Flemming said. "You'll pardon my intrusion, but I've seen nothing but hotel rooms and offices for the past six months. I thought we should meet."

Boldt motioned reluctantly toward the living room. There was something not right about Flemming coming here. Marina stole another glance toward her employer. Miles clawed to be held. Boldt hoisted him into his arms, stopped at the high chair and took Sarah as well.

Standing, Flemming made the chair look small and the kitchen table like something from a kid's set. The two men sat across from each other, Boldt on a couch. Miles bailed out and went running back to the kitchen. Boldt held Sarah in his arms and cleaned her up with his handkerchief.

Flemming's voice resonated in the small space. "You know, when we looked toward Seattle, we were quite convinced that you would be behind the wheel of this one."

"It's good to be wrong once in a while."

"I've offended you by coming into your home. I apologize. Your housekeeper offered. I shouldn't have accepted. As I said, the hotels. . . ."

"Surprised is all."

"Fresh start?"

"Sure," Boldt agreed, but he didn't like the individual attention. He didn't like this man being in his house at all.

"Ten kids, six months and few leads. You've worked some big cases here. Worked them successfully, I might add. That's why we were so convinced this would be yours."

"But it's not."

"On paper at least."

"It's not my case."

"An intelligence officer at crime scenes?"

"I was asked to have a look around, that's all."

"My point exactly," Flemming said. "And I like to know the players."

"Am I a player?" Boldt asked rhetorically, finishing with

Sarah's hands. "I suppose so. But on the bench. I doubt I'm worth your time."

"In the bullpen is more like it," Flemming corrected. "Third base coach, maybe. I can see you standing out there waving La-Moia toward home."

"He's good. You'll find that out if you give him a chance."

"You see me as a control freak."

"You *are* a control freak," Boldt corrected. "You made that point at the four o'clock, from what I'm told."

"As Intelligence officer, you've run background checks on me and Hale and Kalidja. Anything I can clarify?"

"As Intelligence officer, I've waited for crime scene reports that have never arrived. Interviews with the parents. Local cop reports. You want to do this alone, in a vacuum, that's your business, Special Agent. You want to look down your nose at us, that's your business. A pitcher can't win a game all by himself."

"Then you like baseball."

"Hate it. But my CAP lieutenant loved the game. Lived for it. Softball. PAL league, some city intramural stuff. The analogies kind of wear off on you."

"It's a great game. And your point is taken. I have no intention of fighting this battle alone." He hesitated before saying, "I just like to make it clear where I stand."

"And that is where? In the corner? At the head of the table? Where?"

"I had hoped that you would be lead. The Cross Killer, that product tampering thing—you know this kind of pressure. There's a difference that you and I understand between being a good cop and doing good work under unusual circumstances. Between a real-time case and working a dead body."

Boldt didn't want to be grouped with Flemming. The man was far too sure of himself, far too in control for someone with ten kids on his mind. He said, "Maybe you're good with that kind of pressure, but it crushes the life out of me. Makes me crazy. Honestly it does. I can't sit around with that kind of pressure on me, so I act. That's just the way it works with me."

"And me." Flemming said, "If you had connected a kidnapping here to one in a small town in the middle of the state, what would you have said at the four o'clock?"

Boldt nodded. "Yeah, but I wouldn't stonewall reports. If the catcher isn't sending the pitcher signals, he can't expect to catch every pitch."

Flemming smiled. Huge white teeth. Dark black skin with peach-colored lips. It was slightly too friendly for Boldt, an unwanted intimacy. "Stonewalling? You think?"

"I think. And I have to wonder why. We know about the penny flute now. The AFIDs. What's to hide?"

He nodded. "Let me talk to Kay Kalidja." He smiled again. "You see, you *are* a part of this one. I took that for granted, LaMoia having been on your squad all those years. You have much more influence on this case than you give yourself credit for. Will you support me?"

Sarah arched her back and struggled for a new position. Boldt held her facing out. He leaned and kissed the top of her head. He loved the smell of the very top of her head. She kicked, enjoying the kiss. He gave her another.

"I understand you," Boldt said, "perhaps better than the others. I understand that kind of pressure. And I don't envy it."

Flemming stared at him.

Boldt said, "You came for my advice, I think."

Flemming grinned.

"And my advice is to avoid Mulwright, work with LaMoia and trust that we want this as badly as you do. Sheila Hill will be consumed with whose collar it is. Maybe you are too, for all I know, but I doubt it. And they don't know that about you. They think that by trying to control it all, you want it all for yourself, rather than understanding you just want it done right."

"Perhaps you could explain that to them," Flemming said. This was what he had come for—Boldt's support in the trenches.

"It wouldn't do any good. You'll have to convince them, not me. We don't have to love each other; we just have to work together. What you may not know is that this is not some town in the middle of the state. This is a good team you've got to work with. What you do with it is your decision."

Flemming pulled his substantial weight out of the couch. "They should have made you lead in spite of your transfer."

"I'm okay with the way things are," Boldt said, hugging Sarah a little tighter.

"Sorry about your wife," Flemming said. "Hope she's better."

"She is," Boldt said.

He watched the Town Car pull away from the curb and drive off. He wanted to see it for himself. Wanted to make sure Flemming was gone. He checked the kitchen for bugs. Checked the phone as well. He trusted Gary Flemming about as far as he could throw him.

CHAPTER

10

Trish Weinstein had been in the car only fifteen minutes when she felt the first cramps. With the initial nauseating wave, she knew the gym time was out. Some months hit her hard. She didn't even feel like shopping. More than anything, she wanted a Midol and a hot-water bottle.

She drove faster than usual, eager to be home, the nausea worsening. A bath. Maybe Phyllis would stay and let her get a short nap in herself.

In an act impossible for her to later understand or explain, Trish Weinstein headed to the front door, not the back. The door immediately bumped against something and caught. Trish looked down to see a pair of hairy boots—Uggs. Phyllis wore Uggs, she thought, not making the connection at first. She pushed harder against the door, only then realizing she was sliding her mother-in-law across the carpet. Her cry of terror caught in her throat with sight of the woman's foaming mouth and convulsions. A heart attack!

But a heart attack didn't explain the large cardboard box torn open in the living room. Nor did it explain the door to the nursery being open. It was then that her vision collapsed, her ears rang and darkness swarmed her. She tingled with cold and reached out to steady herself, for she had lost her balance. She missed the doorknob for which she was aiming and sagged to her knees, crawling toward the nursery. "H . . . a . . . y . . . e . . . s," she bellowed.

CHAPTER

On Thursday, March 19, a hysterical call was received by the Emergency Communications Center at 1:07 P.M. announcing that a child was missing and that an older woman needed immediate medical attention. An ambulance, dispatched from a local fire company, arrived at 1:21 P.M., followed less than ten minutes later by Daphne Matthews and John LaMoia, who intercepted the EMT crew as they loaded the stricken woman into the ambulance.

"Convulsions," the ambulance driver informed LaMoia as Daphne consoled the parents. "Seizure of some kind."

"Stun gun?"

"Could be, I suppose, but epilepsy more like. Been lying there the better part of an hour, I'd guess. She's lucky to be alive—*real* lucky."

"If it's epilepsy," LaMoia mumbled to himself, not believing it was.

A minute later the ambulance charged off.

"I'm going to follow them," Daphne announced. "What I got was that the wife was out for her regular aerobics class and grocery shop. Mother-in-law watching the kid. Wife started her period and felt lousy. Came home. Finds her baby boy, Hayes, gone, mother-in-law, down by the front door in convulsions."

LaMoia scribbled it down.

"I'll be in touch," she said, turning toward her car.

"Later," LaMoia called out after her. He pulled the front door shut behind him, only a few neighbors out on the sidewalk. He said to the first officer, the first uniform on the scene, "Nice job on keeping this low profile. Let's see if we can't keep it that way. Send the neighbors home nice and quiet—the woman had a medical problem. She's being taken care of. No mention of any kidnapping."

"Got it." The man hurried off.

The ECC had gotten it right, using landline telephones instead of contacting SPD dispatch over the radio, keeping it away from the media and the curious. Boldt had written the suggestion up as a memo after the Shotz kidnapping. The result, not a single reporter outside and LaMoia had some breathing room.

He sketched a rough look of the front door area in his notebook, including a large, empty cardboard box. As he did so, the crime scene came alive for him. With a patrolman shadowing him, he walked through the motions and explained, "Man arrives with a package. Large, heavy, by the look of it. Nearly empty, in fact. Convinces the mother-in-law to let him in to put it down. Does so. Turns around and zaps her with a TASER. It's all a ruse in case of neighbors. Inside the box is a smaller one—seen entering with one box, leaving with a different one. Inside the smaller is the kid. Climbs back into his delivery truck—a white minivan, I'm thinking, with some kind of delivery name on the side—and is gone, no one the wiser."

"You think?" the patrolman had the stupidity to voice.

"No!" LaMoia barked. "I'm telling stories here to entertain you. Go do something productive. There's some phone equipment in the briefcase. Set it up."

Hayes Weinstein might have been kidnapped by a copycat, someone who might attempt to ransom the child, unaware the Pied Piper never did so. The convulsing mother-in-law told him differently: the TASER had struck the diaphragm or too close to the heart, jarring her nervous system and sending her into the seizures. It was the Pied Piper. A sense of failure and guilt stole through him—as lead, it was his job to stop this bastard.

He made more sketches of the home's interior and wrote notes to later remind him of what he saw. A few minutes later, at the door to the empty nursery, he announced sharply, "Carpet patrol!"

He and the first officer took to their knees, picking at the rug, working a grid imposed by LaMoia and pictured in his notepad. He started too fast, too anxious, and had to settle himself before beginning again. They then moved with caution and no eye on the clock, carefully working deep into the nap: crumbs, pet hairs, thread, pebbles—collected into white paper sandwich bags and labeled with ink. This, before other shoes arrived contaminating the scene.

They spent fifteen minutes in the nursery and another ten near the front door. SID's crime scene van pulled up outside as La-Moia reached the front door's threshold. He carefully worked the carpet there, knowing that shoes flexed as they bridged the gap between the door's threshold and the carpet. As his fingers pinched a small, hard object, he released a grunt of excitement, his heart pounding. He lifted his find to the light beyond the uniformed officer on hands and knees and took in his prize.

A small but thick chunk of translucent blue glass.

Daphne used her badge and an implied sense of urgency to secure an empty office at the hospital. The hospital reminded her of Liz Boldt, who in turn reminded her of Lou, who in turn reminded her of her own lover, Owen Adler. Her hopes and fears cascaded over her as she awaited the Weinsteins. Her life pattern was to immerse herself alternately in work and then a lover, then work, then another lover. She could trace this history in the few tiny worry lines that insinuated themselves at the edges of her eyes, a history that had culminated over a year ago in her breaking off her engagement to Owen. And now he was back.

The flowers had never stopped, although the calls had. He had given her the time and space to think things out—to feel them out—but never let her fully forget him. Irises one week, lilies the next, daffodils, peonies, never roses, which were far too obvious for a man of Owen's subtleties. She had placed the first call, and the second. She had arranged a reunion dinner. For weeks now they had dated, and he had never once pushed it past a goodnight kiss, even though lately she had wanted him to. A self-made millionaire who haunted the fund-raiser circuit, Daphne had come to accept his money, his prestige, the public's seeking out his time and funds. She could do pearls and black velvet as easily as jeans and Birkenstocks.

Footsteps approached, and she called herself back to her work effortlessly, though did not entirely let go of Owen Adler, and this spoke volumes to her. Would he ask again, or would it be up to her?

While Phyllis Weinstein remained with doctors, Daphne spoke with the husband and wife, Sidney and Trish, emphasizing the importance of fresh memory to the recovery of their child.

Over the past two weeks, Daphne had studied more than fifteen child abductions in preparation for her appointment to the Pied Piper task force. Nine were attributed to the Pied Piper. The six others all involved illegal adoption, four overseas, two in the United States. Given such short notice, she felt as prepared as she could hope to be. As it turned out, nothing prepared her for Sidney Weinstein.

The small man had a predatory look about him. Average looking made older in appearance by a balding head, Weinstein sat hunched forward on the edge of his chair, his fingers laced together, his eyes wide, almost bulging, the vein in his forehead swollen and popped out like a long pulsing blister. Dressed in casual clothes, his button-down shirt was soaked through at the armpits, his throat and voice tight with venom.

His wife sat curled in on herself, as close to the fetal position as an adult could achieve. Paste white, her tearstained face carried blotches of pink, like hives. Her mouth hung open in a frozen state of disbelief, and she stared at Daphne with dead, unflinching eyes.

"Is it him?" Weinstein asked with difficulty, clearing his gravelly throat.

Daphne felt willing to allow in him some disdain for the police and for the FBI's failure to solve the case, but his hostility seemed more deep-seated. "What we know at this time, Mr. Weinstein, is that your son has gone missing, and that your mother—" she paused to make sure she had it correct, "has been assaulted, most likely during the abduction." She paused, expecting something back: anger, resentment, impatience. The wife remained in shock; the husband boiled internally. "By him, I assume you're referring to the Pied Piper." The wife lifted her head sharply, a sleeping animal startled.

"Damn right I am."

"That bears further investigation."

"Bullshit," the husband spit out.

"Sid!" the wife chided sharply.

"It isn't something we do, sir." Daphne explained, "We do not attribute a criminal act to any individual without due cause. We treat each crime uniquely, your son's included. To group his abduction with the other kidnappings would be premature and unfair to Hayes." To the wife she said, "I need you both to answer some questions. The sooner we get those answers, the better our chances of recovering Hayes."

"You know exactly who did this!" the father objected, erupting to his feet. "You let this man into our house! What good are you people?"

"Time," Daphne said, maintaining her calm and poise, "is working in our favor now. Every minute wasted, every minute lost diminishes those odds." Directing herself to the father, she said, "You want to make assumptions, Mr. Weinstein, I don't blame you. This could well be the work of the Pied Piper—"

"Of course it is, and you know it! I *told* you people!" he blurted.

"I beg your pardon," she said.

"Ten days ago, I told you people that someone was watching

our house, and you ignored me, gave me the runaround. Ignored me! Now our son is missing, and goddamn it, you are to blame! This did not have to happen!"

"Back up," Daphne said, her composure lost. "Ten days ago you told us what? Exactly what?"

"Go ask your nine-one-one operators, for God's sake. They're the ones that screwed me over."

"You actually saw the individual?"

"No, I didn't say that."

"What then?"

"I *felt* him."

"Oh."

"You know that feeling of being watched. Don't tell me you don't," Weinstein complained. "It's not like anything else." He glanced searchingly between his wife and Daphne for support, but found little.

"You never told me any of this," the wife complained.

"Sure I did."

"You told me some kidnapper was watching our house? I don't think so." A look of discovery swept the wife's face. "Is that what has been bugging you?" To Daphne she explained, "He's been acting like a nutcase for two weeks." Returning to her husband, she told him, "I thought you were having an affair, however unlikely that is." She returned her chin to between her knees.

Daphne said slowly, "Tell me how you knew you were being watched, Mr. Weinstein."

"First off, there were noises one night. I heard them, even if she didn't. . . . That's when I called you people. Right outside the house, they were. 'Someone out there,' I told the woman who answered. 'Send someone.' But did you? She wanted a full description. Can you imagine? I'm being burglarized and the person who answers wants a description of every sound. 'Oh, hang on a minute,' I say to her. 'I'll go get my tape recorder. It sounds like a burglar,' I tell her." He sought sympathy between them. Found none. "She told me a car would do the neighborhood, but did I ever see one?"

"Were you burglarized?" Daphne asked. "A patrol car may have in fact come by."

"That's a crock of shit, and we both know it."

"On any other occasions did you—"

"The next time I was in my car. *I* was driving the neighborhood, coming home from work. Two, three blocks north. I passed a guy getting into his van. You know, what do you call them? A bug sprayer—"

"An exterminator," Daphne answered, feeling weak in her stomach. This matched Daech's information.

"An exterminator!" Weinstein agreed. "And I swear he was watching me, even though he looked away. It may sound crazy to you but—"

"It doesn't," Daphne assured him. She appreciated witness testimonies and put more faith in them than her colleagues. Sometimes the content was off, but the littlest details right on target.

"And so I called again. Right? Same thing from you people: Was he on my property? Did he make a verbal threat? Was there any physical contact?" He shook his head disgustedly. "And now this . . . ," he mumbled.

"The vehicle?" Daphne asked, displaying no excitement in her voice. "A van, you said. What color van?"

"So now you care? Is that what you're saying? You people are too much, you know that?"

"The color of the van?" Daphne pressed.

"White."

"Tell me about the driver," she encouraged.

"What's to tell?" he asked. "Face was covered up. Goggles. One of those mouth things."

"A respirator," she supplied.

"Yeah. And what do I get from the cops? Questions. And here you are again, same thing. What's any of it matter to Hayes? A dollar short and a day late is what it is. I'm going to sue you people. Goddamn it, I'm going to sue you!"

The door was opened by a woman doctor wearing a white lab coat and a grim expression. She took in both Weinsteins with her sad eyes and slowly shook her head. "I'm sorry to have to tell you this—" she said.

CHAPTER

12

"Lou! We have a situation!" Daphne shouted frantically as she ran past his office door. Boldt knew her well enough not to question. He left his office at a run and followed her down the stairs, two at a time. The fifth floor, Crimes Against Persons—Homicide—remained his emotional home. His time with Intelligence, required for his advancement, felt more like a probationary sentence.

He guessed: two officers going at it; a suspect loose; a threatened suicide—police work did strange things to people.

They reached the entrance to Homicide and peered through the safety glass. "Who is that?" Boldt asked, seeing a man waving a police-issue 9mm at a semicircle of a dozen uniformed and plainclothes officers, all perfectly still.

"Sidney Weinstein. Father of the second child," she answered. "His mother is the homicide. We asked him down to view mug shots because he may have had a look at the Pied Piper." Her breath fogged the glass.

"This is not good," he said.

"You see who I see?" she asked.

"Wish I didn't."

Well behind Sidney Weinstein and just around the corner, Dunkin Hale and Gary Flemming, there for the four o'clock task force meeting, observed the chaos.

Boldt signaled the receptionist to admit them. Weinstein was shouting obscenities and complaints about the incompetence of the police. "My mother *and* my child!" he cried out.

The receptionist slowly lifted her arm and depressed the button that freed the secured door. Sidney Weinstein, hearing the electronic buzzing, waved the gun frantically, parting the semicircle. "No one comes in here!" he shouted.

"It's only me," Daphne announced, stepping inside. "I'm with Lieutenant Boldt. He's the one who has been looking into those nine-one-one calls. Your grudge is with them, Sidney, not any of these people."

Boldt stepped through behind her, knowing nothing of any 911 calls.

The heavy door closed with a thump, distracting Weinstein.

In that instant, Boldt caught a signal from Flemming, who pointed to the coffee lounge—the glass wall on which Weinstein was leaning. Formerly a copy room, the lounge had two doors around the corner from each other. Flemming intended to reach Weinstein through the lounge if Boldt could shift the man closer to the door that stood open to Weinstein's left.

Daphne continued to work with the man, Boldt blocking out her words, his attention riveted on Flemming, who gently twisted the doorknob and slipped into the lounge. Daphne ignored Flemming, her methods psychological, not physical. "Let's think about Hayes for a moment," she encouraged, winning back Weinstein's attention. She didn't want any mention of his deceased mother—there was still hope for Hayes. She stepped closer.

"You stay where you are!" he thundered, shaking the gun at her.

Daphne stopped short. "Okay . . . okay . . . let's think about this. Together. Sidney? Okay. You are an intelligent man, *not* a criminal. If you shoot one of us, where does that leave you? Where does that leave Hayes? You are going to be shot dead or locked up if you fire that weapon. That's what they'll do to you," she said, indicating the gathering of uniforms and detectives. "Where does that leave Hayes?"

"He's never coming back. Not one of those kids has been found."

"Are you giving up?" Daphne asked. "Do you want us to give up?"

Weinstein strained to make a decision. "My mother," he moaned.

"Put down the weapon, Sidney," Daphne advised. "Right now." The man continued to wave the gun. "What if Hayes, right this minute, has a weapon aimed at him, the same way you're aiming it at us? Are you going to condone that?"

The weapon bobbed in Weinstein's grip, his finger dangerously on the trigger. Daphne took another step forward.

"No," Boldt hissed at her.

She motioned Boldt away. She had spotted Flemming and wanted to prevent a violent solution.

Boldt knew that her ambitions could blind her. She carried an ugly scar on her neck from an encounter with the Cross Killer and wore turtlenecks and scarves to cover her mistake.

She asked Weinstein, "How do you think these people feel with a gun trained at them?"

Weinstein swept the crowd with the barrel of the weapon. To Boldt, he looked unpredictable and crazed.

Flemming, unseen on hands and knees, reappeared briefly at the door nearest Weinstein. He needed Boldt to move Weinstein closer.

Boldt edged right, threw his hands over his head, and said loudly, "Most of us in this room have children, Mr. Weinstein. I have two. Miles and Sarah."

Weinstein tracked Boldt with the gun and in the process shifted slightly closer to Flemming. "You stay where you are."

Daphne glared at Boldt, angry that he would assist a violent solution. "Yes," she said, "you stay where you are."

Keeping his hands over his head, Boldt continued to his right, maintaining Weinstein's attention.

"You see this man?" Daphne asked Weinstein, gesturing at Boldt. "He has been working around the clock on these kidnappings, and now here he is having to deal with you instead. Is that fair to Hayes, Sidney? Think about it. *Put the gun down!*"

Flemming, still on all fours, again appeared in the doorway to Weinstein's left. Everyone saw him but Weinstein, whose back remained pressed against the wall.

"You're incompetent! All of you!" the man shouted. "Stop!" he ordered Boldt, taking yet another step closer to the door.

Boldt moved with him, one final step. Weinstein tracked him, nervously pulled in the same direction. Flemming looked prepared to spring.

"Put the gun down!" Daphne begged, not wanting the risk of a physical intervention. "Please, Sidney. For Trish, for Hayes. Put . . . the gun . . . down . . . *now!*"

Weinstein's face bunched in grief and his shoulders shook. He could no longer support the weight of the weapon. Its barrel sagged toward the floor.

Flemming sprang like a cat, chopped the man's arm to the floor, dislodging the gun, yanked an arm back hard and threw a choke hold onto the man, all in one fluid movement. He kneed the back of the man's legs, dropped him to the floor face down and fell atop him. Boldt reached them, fished under Flemming and cuffed Weinstein's wrists. "Got him," Boldt announced.

"Check it," Flemming demanded, not letting up the pressure, charged with anger.

A uniformed cop toed the fallen weapon away and retrieved it.

Boldt tugged. "Okay. He's cuffed." He overheard Flemming whisper menacingly into Weinstein's ear, "You're a son-of-a-bitch. You know how hard these people are working for you?" Flemming smacked the man's forehead to the floor and then climbed off, panting.

As he stood, the room exploded into applause.

Weinstein was hauled off to booking, Daphne by his side.
Boldt, Hale and Flemming gathered in the coffee lounge. Hale
shook Flemming's hand like a player to the coach. Flemming's
black face shined bright with sweat as he met eyes with Boldt and
said, "You're thinking I was a little rough with him."

"I'm thinking you're fast for your size, and I'm grateful for it."

"He'd lost control of himself. That's something I abhor. Emotion and reason—it's a delicate balance. Got the better of me for
a moment."

"He'd flipped out," Hale said, eager to be part of the conversation.

"Not that I don't empathize," Flemming added. "I can imagine
the loss he's suffered, a parent's grief, the guilt. Who wants to sit
on the sidelines? I wouldn't. And given his history—having called
nine-one-one but to no good—one can hardly blame him for the
anger, the frustration. The rage."

Boldt said, "You don't settle it with a gun."

"You have children," Flemming said. "How would you feel if
the situation were reversed?"

"How I would feel, and what I would do about it are separate
matters," Boldt said.

"Are they? Only if you have reason and emotion balanced and
in check," Flemming explained. "Weinstein didn't. Once a person loses that balance, there's no telling what's going to happen,
what he'll do. I've seen it firsthand, maybe you have too. I even
feel that way myself sometimes," he said more quietly, "on the
edge like that."

"I've been there." Hale sounded proud of himself.

"We all have our breaking points," Boldt agreed. "Weinstein
certainly found his." Boldt realized he and Flemming had not
broken eye contact since the start of their conversation. Flemming
came off as an intense man; he took over without any apparent
effort on his part. "A born leader," men like Flemming were
called. "Thanks for what you did out there."

The two men shook hands again. "Thanks for moving him toward me. We made a pretty good team out there."

Boldt didn't want to think of himself as part of Flemming's team. He took the stairs back to his own floor, considering the line between emotion and reason, wondering what it had felt like inside Weinstein's mind at that moment of uncontrollable rage, and knowing it was not a place he ever wanted to be.

CHAPTER

13

A sympathetic judge prevented an overnight stay for Weinstein in city lockup, reducing the charge to reckless endangerment. His bail waived, Weinstein was released on his own recognizance and ordered to appear in two weeks' time.

Friday morning, March 20, arrived on the back of monsoon rains and wind gusts to fifty knots. Rain pellets struck Public Safety's fifth-floor windows sounding like handfuls of gravel, forcing those with adjacent desks to shout into their phones. Morale was low, moods sour. The task force team sagged: the further away from a kidnapping, the further away from the hope of recovering the victim.

John LaMoia slept three hours, showered, changed clothes and returned to Public Safety in a pair of unpressed blue jeans, making himself as noticeable as if he'd set himself afire. After three consecutive lattés he felt as if someone had sewn a string through his scalp and was tugging hard in poorly timed jerks. Two missing kids and a dead grandmother. The shit was well through the fan, and it was sticking to him. He had long since learned from Boldt that in police work one expected the unexpected. He thought he had had about all he could take. Again, he was proved wrong.

Detective Bobbie Gaynes marched stridently toward LaMoia's upholstered office cubicle, her shoulders arched forward as if fighting a wind or climbing a long hill. Small and strong, Gaynes had short brown hair and hands like a man. Homicide's first female detective—Boldt's protégée—Gaynes was known for thoroughness, punctuality and professionalism.

LaMoia had no desire to meet with her. He had assigned her an accidental death in Fremont, a case he wanted closed and out of the way, allowing him and his squad to focus on the Pied Piper. He had assigned her the case thinking she could clear it without his involvement. He had his own dead body now—he didn't want hers.

"I don't want this right now," he groaned, raising his hands like a traffic cop to stop her.

"Oh, yes you do," she informed him obstinately, coming to a breathless stop. Like LaMoia, Gaynes took the stairs most of the time, not the elevator. She was small-chested and firm, carrying twice the strength her looks suggested. "This will have you changing your shorts it's so good."

"From the mouths of babes . . ." He unwound the string from the paper button that sealed the heavy manila envelope she delivered and withdrew the contents. "A lab prelim?" he asked incredulously. "And I was hoping for eight-by-ten glossies of First Avenue strippers."

"This is better, believe me."

Tossing the folder aside, he said, "You want to give me the Cliff Notes?" He caught himself using a Boldt line and wondered how much of his job he did on autopilot, and how much was he himself.

"This so-called accidental death?" she reminded. "The belly flop in the tub with the crushed windpipe? Name of Anderson. White male, mid-forties. First officer's report had it down as an accident."

"Don't do this to me," LaMoia said. "Just clear the thing, would you?"

"So I do the scene, search the guy's crib, make the sketches, hit the neighbors. The usual dime tour. He's neat and tidy. A woman notices that. He's got a T-shirt folded up under his pillow for crying out loud. Everything in its place. He's found by a neighbor, face down in the tub. The idea is he's taking a shower, slips, and does the funky chicken: busted neck. It happens, sure—to eighty-year-olds. This guy's mid-forties?"

"It happens," LaMoia encouraged. "People slip in the tub."

"Thing is, Prince Charming is wearing a rug in the shower and that's not right."

"Could have been a bath. A quickie at that. Keeps his wig on. Pulls the plug, stands up and gets the Blue Meanies. Goes down hard. What's the big deal?"

"No, no, it's not like that. The shower was *running* when they found him. Didn't I say that? Neighbor in the next apartment got curious. It was a shower, not a bath. And if it's a shower, then he should have had the hairpiece on the little Styrofoam head over by the sink. That rug being up on the chrome dome does not make sense."

"Clear the case, Bobsie. You got nothing." He knew the nickname bothered her. He hoped it might rid him of her.

"I'm just warming up here," she announced. "You think I'd bother my *sergeant* with a toupee?" She crossed her arms. "Just be glad you sent a woman to this one."

"I'm thrilled, can't you see?" He forced a yawn.

"The stiff's clothes are in a messy pile on the floor—this anally neat guy, right? Worse, six pair of laced shoes in the closet, every single one with the laces untied. But the shoes found in the bath-room, the ones he was apparently wearing prior to his shower, the laces are found *tied*. Tugged off the foot. That goes straight to behavior. That can be taken to the bank."

"Shoelaces? Come on, Detective!"

"Listen, this is the circumstantial stuff. It just gets my juices going, right? Gets me looking around. The smoking gun is in the hamper where I find a pair of khakis stained yellow around the knees. Knee height, as in the Shotzes' crib." She leaned over him and tapped the lab report he had chosen not to read. "Yellow, as in pollen."

LaMoia shook his head to clear it and replayed her words inside his head. She spoke deliberately slowly. "The yellow smudge on the crib—pollen—was at knee height. The Taurus carpet fibers vacuumed from the nursery also contained pollen." She crossed her arms. "You still want me to clear this one, *Sergeant*?"

"Lay off." She wasn't the only one teasing him about his promotion. She had turned up a possible link to the Shotz kidnapping. He couldn't ignore it, even if he wanted to.

She explained, "Lofgrin worked the Shotz evidence. Samantha Hiller worked Anderson's. Two different techs, same result: yellow pollen. We've got to pursue it." Her eyes sparkled. LaMoia missed that feeling.

He pushed back his chair, faced her, and said reluctantly, "Who is he?"

She was pretty when she smiled. "He has a pretty long sheet: trespass, couple counts of invasion of privacy—tapping phone lines, snapping Polaroids."

"A private dick," LaMoia guessed.

"But without the license. I checked."

"Boldt might know," LaMoia suggested. Intelligence had files on everyone.

"I thought you weren't interested in Anderson," she crowed.

"Put a sock in it. We're going upstairs."

"He's a camera for hire," Boldt informed them, studying his computer screen. "Or he was. Low-rent surveillance: the husband doing the secretary, the wife doing the tennis pro. Maybe run some drug or gambling money if he's desperate for rent. Maybe use a baseball bat if the pay's good enough, and I'm not talking softball. He's small change. A troublemaker. A bottom feeder."

"Good riddance," LaMoia said.

"Is he, was he, the Pied Piper?" Gaynes inquired. "Is that possible?"

She had briefed Boldt on the pollen connection. He scowled. "He's trash, Bobbie. A sucker fish. A local. Room temperature IQ. He's not capable of something like this."

"The pollen is a coincidence?" Gaynes asked, knowing Boldt hated the word.

LaMoia tossed out, "What if the Pied Piper hires low-rent guys to do his legwork? Once it's done, he clips 'em."

The suggestion won Boldt's interest. "Not the actual abduction," Boldt protested. "Some of the advance work maybe. We've seen stranger things, I suppose."

Gaynes suggested, "They arrange a meeting and both come away carrying pollen. The Pied Piper carries it to the crib, Anderson leaves it in the hamper. Why not? Circumstantial, but it's still a direct link between the Shotz kidnapping and this vic. One of those coincidences my former sergeant told me never to accept." She glared at Boldt.

"And one we must pursue," Boldt agreed. "We need the source of that pollen," he reminded LaMoia. "A garden near the Shotzes? A commercial nursery? A rendezvous between the Pied Piper and Anderson, as Bobbie suggested? Maybe this pollen gives us the Piper's location." He continued, "No matter what, it's worth pursuing." He asked her, "Autopsy?"

"When they can get to it," she answered. "Several days at least."

"I'll push Dixie," Boldt said. Dr. Ronald Dixon was one of Boldt's few close friends. "You two have a minute to brainstorm this?" They nodded. "Okay. Bobbie's right about not taking the hairpiece into the shower—"

LaMoia jumped in. "So the doer smokes him, missed the hairpiece, strips him naked and leaves him in the tub for us to find."

Gaynes said, "In stripping him, he leaves the shoes tied. Doesn't notice that Anderson is the neat and tidy type. He leaves the clothes in a pile."

LaMoia spoke excitedly, "Let's say they didn't meet until Anderson's crib. It's Anderson with this pollen on him. The Piper does Anderson, gets the pollen all over himself, and the rule of mutual exchange leaves it on the crib and the floor mat of his Taurus."

Boldt cautioned, "Possible. But the pollen is on the knees of Anderson's pants in the hamper," he said, checking with Gaynes, who nodded, "and the smudge on the crib is at knee height. Could mutual exchange explain that? More likely Anderson and the Piper were in the same garden, or nursery, or field. But, no matter what, we—"

"—Need a second look at Anderson's apartment," Gaynes interrupted.

LaMoia didn't want Boldt running his investigation. Advice was one thing, taking control another. He spoke quickly. "Sarge checks his snitches for any word about Anderson on the street. You," he said to Gaynes, "sit in on Dixie's autopsy. Cause of death is critical here." LaMoia ignored her attempt to interrupt. "I chat up Bernie Lofgrin and ask for some comparison microscopy on the pollen, hoping pollen A matches pollen B. SID returns to Anderson's for a more thorough pass. You know why I love this shit, Sarge?" he asked Boldt rhetorically, not pausing. "We've got ourselves some lunch meat. A bag in the fridge. A toe-tagger. A good old naked stiff, hairpiece and all. A body!" He felt elated. "So shoot me," he said, catching Gaynes's disapproving expression. "I love dead bodies. I'll take a bloody crime scene over a missing baby any day of the week."

"You've still got two missing babies," Boldt reminded. "The dead body is Bobbie's. She's lead on it. And I happen to be free at the moment." He stood and offered Gaynes an expression that asked if she were ready to go. She nodded. "SID can do Anderson's again, but it needs a detective's eye first."

"Foul ball," LaMoia complained, searching for some support.

Boldt said slowly, "Your job is to deliver all this to the task force. Our job is to keep you from making a fool of yourself and make sure it's worth it."

"We'll get back to you," Gaynes said, proud as a peacock.

LaMoia grimaced at her. He felt as if his head were in a vice. He checked his watch: Hayes Weinstein had been missing for twenty-two hours. Rhonda Shotz, for ten days.

"Shit," LaMoia said.

CHAPTER

Anderson's apartment occupied the left half of a 1930s clapboard that had been converted to a duplex. Situated behind a video store, it shared space with a JC Penney catalog outlet. The potholed alley leading into it was partially buried in fast-food litter and soggy newsprint and smelled of cats.

Reaching the mouth of the alley, Boldt grabbed the elbow of Bobbie Gaynes and stopped her. He listened hard and then looked around, studying every crack and crevice. The sun would be up for another few hours, but wedged between two towering brick walls the alley was in the midst of an artificial twilight. Boldt looked around, his unease contagious.

"Okay," he said, though unsure. He'd been out of the field too long.

They walked on. Anderson's banged-up door had three keyholes at varying heights and a Day-Glo police sticker laid across the doorjamb, sealing it. They both donned latex gloves. Boldt felt a rush of satisfaction: a crime scene. At the same time, he experienced a pang for the two missing kids. If anything ever happened to Miles and Sarah . . . he didn't blame Weinstein for breaking. No one could.

Gaynes slit the police sticker and keyed the top and bottom locks as she told him, "It's a walk-up to the kitchen and living room. Another flight up to the bedroom and bath."

Boldt noticed the home security panel immediately. "You said the neighbor found him."

She shut the door behind them, locked one of the dead bolts and switched on the light. The walls needed paint, the stairs some new treads. A bare bulb hung high over the stairwell, too bright for the small space. It obscured the top of the stairs.

Climbing, she said, "Neighbor hears the shower running, pounds on the wall. Gives up. Goes to the front door."

"Locked?"

She stopped on the stairs and looked back at him quizzically, or maybe impressed. She turned and continued up. "Right."

"Tried the fire escape next," Boldt guessed.

"Right. Bathroom window. Saw him in the tub. Called nine-eleven."

There was another door at the top of the stairs that could be dead-bolted.

Anticipating him, she said, "This one was not locked when the first officer arrived."

"Front door was opened by?"

"The landlord tried it. The neighbor called him at the request of the nine-eleven operator," she explained. "Landlord couldn't get in. New locks, and more of them. Locksmith did the work."

"The security alarm?" Boldt asked, entering a small room that shared the kitchen.

Gaynes pushed past him. "Is there one? Hadn't noticed, to be truthful."

"And the bathroom shade?"

"Neighbor explained that one. It was pulled down. But with an eye to one edge, you can pick up a reflection of the tub in the mirror. I tried it. It's legit."

"But the alarm was off."

"I guess so. Must have been." She considered this as Boldt walked slowly around the crowded sitting room. Television, rack of electronics, desk, computer, telephone, printer, two yard-sale chairs, two metal file cabinets, different makes and colors. "But he was home."

Boldt studied the room's ceiling and walls. A motion sensor high in the far corner; shades and extra thick curtains on the windows; a heat alarm in the kitchen. "Installed the security stuff himself, I bet." He bent over and yanked up a cheap throw rug. Put it back down and pulled up another by the top of the stairs.

"What's that?" she asked, seeing what he had discovered.

"Pressure switch. You step on the rug and it trips the alarm, same as a motion detector." He moved on, checking the interior of a small pantry.

"What's up?" she asked.

He didn't answer. It wasn't what he was looking for. "An upstairs closet?" he asked.

"Yeah."

He stopped at the bottom of the stairway, which was a tight turn to the left. He stooped and eyed it carefully. Again the overhead stairway light was twice the wattage it needed to be. Again, it obscured one's vision of the top of the stairs. Another motion detector directly overhead. "The guy was careful," Boldt allowed. "A guy like this probably made more than a few people mad. Or broke. Or both. You think about it," he considered aloud, "no shortage of enemies."

"I know it doesn't help our case any," she said, discouraged.

"Pressure pads under his carpets. I tell you what, I arm that security system whenever I'm home. Anyone tries to sneak in on me, I know about it."

Boldt asked her to walk on the outer edges of the carpeted stairs. They ascended awkwardly.

The upstairs floor plan nearly mirrored the second story, the bathroom over the kitchen, the bedroom over the living room, the closet space stacked vertically. Boldt headed directly to the closet while Gaynes called out to him that the bathroom was the other room. He didn't answer. He opened the closet door and studied what he saw.

"What are you doing?" she asked.

"You checked this?"

"Sure."

"And what did you find?"

"A cedar-lined closet," she answered. "Clothes, shoes, sweaters."

"Telephone?"

"What are you talking about?"

He pushed some hanging clothes out of the way and pointed down the rear wall of the closet, showing her the phone.

"What the hell, Sarge?"

His promotion clearly didn't register with anyone but the book-keeper. None of those who had served under him were going to call him Lieutenant.

"You notice the closet door?" He pointed. "Two interior dead bolts, top and bottom. A telephone. Behind the cedar you'll find sheet metal at the very least, plate steel, if he had the bucks. And somewhere in here . . ." Boldt pushed the clothes around, but didn't see what he was looking for. He dropped to his knees and clawed at the carpet. The far corner came up. Beneath it, a piece of particleboard had been cut out of the subfloor. He hooked a finger into the joint and lifted.

"My God!" Gaynes said, on her knees alongside him.

Inside was a Glock 21 10mm and three loaded magazines, headlamp, batteries and a variety of ugly-looking grenades.

"Grenades?"

"Probably phosphorus and stun grenades. It's his safe room. A phone line to the outside, hardened walls, lots of weapons. A place to hide if the boogeyman shows up. We'll want to catalog it all, get it down to property."

"Sorry I missed this," she apologized.

Back in the bedroom, Boldt explained, "I know his type. That's why I say the security would have been armed once he was inside. He gave people trouble. At his level that could mean some vicious reprisals."

"The alarm should have been armed?"

"It was at some point."

"I don't get it."

"By the time we responded, the alarm was off," he reminded, testing her.

Her face knotted in concentration.

"Front door was found locked," Boldt added. With Gaynes as his shadow they moved over to the door to the bathroom and Boldt leaned his head in, not stepping inside. "The clothes you found on the floor here, did he have possessions in his pockets? Change? Pens? Wallet?"

"Yes." She spoke as a student to the teacher, "But we don't necessarily accept that the dead guy put them there."

"No we don't," Boldt agreed, still not venturing inside the small room. "Where's his stuff? Personal possessions?"

"The contents of his pants were bagged along with the clothes themselves."

"Keys?"

"I could call in," she offered. "Have somebody check for me."

"Call it in," Boldt advised. "Number of keys and make. Especially Yale. How many Yale keys?"

"What's up anyway?"

Boldt looked around the bathroom once more and then met eyes with Gaynes. "Mr. Anderson had a visitor. A very smart, very careful visitor."

Boldt ate a piece of cheddar cheese he found in Anderson's refrigerator. Was just going to go to waste. Dead man's cheese, eaten wearing latex gloves. He followed it with some Triscuits from an overhead cabinet and a warm 7-UP. He sat at the kitchen counter snacking while Gaynes watched him, her ear to the phone, awaiting an answer.

"You could use the weight," she said.

"Grief diet," he told her. That made him check his watch and think about his son, his daughter and his wife lying in that hospital bed.

The crackers helped ease the pain in his belly. He'd had ulcers. There wasn't anything new under the sun.

Gaynes mumbled thanks into the phone and hung up. "Eleven keys. Two were Yale."

"Two," Boldt stated. He nodded. "Okay, then that's it."

"Sarge, I don't mean to be—"

"The front door," he told her. "Just to make sure, you'd better check it." He grabbed another handful of Triscuits. "I'll finish my lunch, if you don't mind."

Gaynes maintained her curious expression. She had a pleasant, boyish face. They had built a history together. She had worked undercover for him on the Cross Killer case and had impressed him with her nerve and good instincts. She didn't demand the spotlight. She reminded him of himself: a cop who wanted the challenge of difficult work, the lure of Homicide. She headed back down to check the locks. When she returned, hurrying, she announced, "All three are Yale. Top of the stairs is an Omni. You caught that on the way in, didn't you?"

"Had to make sure," he said, and thanked her for the legwork. He put the crackers away, washed off his gloved fingers.

"So!" she announced loudly, nervously, after a long silence.

"So someone comes to the front door," Boldt said, moving from the kitchen toward the stairs. "Our boy checks it out." He walked over to the television remote, turned on the TV and began to surf the channels. Gaynes looked confused and anxious. After thirty-four channels he hit gray sparkles and continued on into the sixties, mumbling, "It's here somewhere. Got to be." He then keyed in 99. The TV screen showed a fish-eye black-and-white image of the area outside Anderson's door.

"No way," Gaynes groaned, impressed.

Boldt said, "He concealed it behind that row of mirrors over the front door. Did you catch those?"

"I feel like I should go back to the academy."

"Just lucky."

"Right," she replied sarcastically.

He continued with his theory. "Presumably he liked what he saw, approved of whomever was standing there." He asked her, "Do you know home electronics?"

"A little."

"Check that mess for an extra VCR. If I'm James Bond Anderson I run a twenty-four-hour video loop of all the action at my front door." She was on it immediately, checking the gear.

"Two VCRs," she confirmed, glancing back at him as if he were some kind of specter. "One's running."

"I'm telling you: just lucky. I know these guys."

"You're freaking me out here, Sarge."

"The tape's long erased itself by now. No use to us. But still, let's log it as evidence and you take it home with you and play with your fast forward button. Watch it all the way through, just to cover our bases."

She turned off the machine and popped the tape. She made a note in her spiral notebook, and Boldt signed alongside as a witness.

"He goes down to answer the door." Boldt walked down the stairs, followed by Gaynes close on his heels. "Turns off the security and greets the person at the door. He locks back up but does not arm the system, and the two go upstairs." He turned, and motioned Gaynes upstairs. "Guests first. He's not going to give anyone his back."

Gaynes preceded him up. In the sitting area, Boldt motioned her into a chair. He said, "Maybe this guy accepts the chair, maybe not. Probably they know each other well enough for Anderson to be relaxed. I wonder. Big mistake, as it turns out. What you look for when you and Dixie have got him on the butcher block is lividity consistent with some kind of choke hold or strangulation. Toxins. Poisons. And make sure Dixie works the earwax; that is extremely important."

"Earwax," she mumbled.

He turned his back on her. "At some point he made the mistake of offering his back."

She looked down at the floor as if seeing the body there. She returned to the carpeted stairs and squatted as Boldt had earlier. She said, "Dragged up the stairs. You can see it in the nap of the carpet."

"The visitor is strong enough to haul him up the stairs."

"If I hadn't worked with you before . . ."

"Hold the compliments. This is all smoke, no real proof."

"This is amazing is what it is," she said. "You saw that earlier," she said, pointing up the stairs. "The nap of the carpet."

"Yes, I did."

"I didn't even look."

He shrugged. "Victims talk if you listen."

"Undresses him, stages the shower . . ." She thought a minute. "I'll be damned!" she exclaimed, when she understood. "Takes one of the three keys off Anderson's key chain and locks the front door."

Boldt agreed, nodding. "Basic to the ruse. The place has to be locked up tight, and Anderson found alone, dead from a nasty slip. Who's going to investigate that?"

"But the security is not on. That's what tipped you." She showed Boldt to the clothes hamper. "This is where I found the pants. You'll want to see 'em. *Covered* in that yellow pollen, Sarge—at the knees, I'm talking about. They're lousy with the stuff."

He said, "It makes Anderson important to us. It's good work, Bobbie. We can only make an extremely circumstantial case. That's all. If we're right, then we're up against someone who's thinking. He assumed we would not check for the door key. He understood that the door being locked was crucial. That kind of guy scares me. We certainly have enough to investigate this. We need to bring in SID again, photograph everything. Maybe Bernie and his Boy Wonders can turn up something useful. Carpets. Phone records and finances if we find them. We give it a shake-down. Something falls out, we run with it." Boldt nodded, unan-swered questions all around him. A part of him hadn't felt this good in ages, but he ached for those missing babies, and their parents who had to endure another night without them.

CHAPTER

15

Several hours later, Boldt was paged by LaMoia while on his way to the University Hospital, making the visit with Liz brief but memorable. She had natural color in her cheeks, light in her eyes, and warm hands. She called him over to sit on her bed and announced proudly, "I'm coming home."

He felt a pang of hope. Tears. "You can go back to being an outpatient?"

"The doctors will tell you it's the drugs. But I know better." She looked over at the Bible, and next to it a copy of a religious textbook.

He gasped, "Liz—"

"Don't! Keep that comment to yourself until we have a chance to talk about it."

"The chemo took, that's all."

"That isn't all," she objected. "That isn't *any* of it. But don't do this now. Let's wait 'til I'm home, okay? Tomorrow, or Sunday at the latest."

He squeezed her hand, thrilled and troubled. "We need to talk about this."

"We will. Let me get home first."

He nodded. Then he saw a look he knew too well. "Dr. Woods approves, doesn't she? Of your going home." A resonating fear penetrated through him: She was giving up on treatment.

"Dr. Woods is somewhat baffled by my improvement, love. She would like to hold me for observation."

"Improvement?" he said skeptically.

"My count is down significantly. Katherine can't explain such a quick change, but I can. And I don't need observation, love, I need to go home. To you, the children. Home. The work that needs to be done is better done there."

"The work? You're scaring me."

Speaking like a Transylvanian, she mimicked, "It vill all be revealed to you in time." And then she smiled a smile that could have filled a stadium with light, or a cathedral with warmth, a smile that had nothing to do with illness, a smile that came from a Liz before their marriage, their children, their trials, a smile that convinced him that she knew what was best.

"I'll be damned," he whispered.

"No you won't," she said, a different, all-knowing smile taking its place.

LaMoia appeared disheveled and tense. "First hail, then rain. I'm getting a little sick of this."

Bobbie Gaynes, on the other hand, looked positively radiant.

"What did I miss?" Boldt asked. The fifth floor was near empty.

LaMoia said, "SID discovered a caller-ID box at Anderson's."

Gaynes declared enthusiastically, "The caller-ID unit kept a record of the last ninety-nine calls made to Anderson's apartment." She repeated, "Every incoming call."

"Technology is a beautiful thing," LaMoia said.

Gaynes handed Boldt a list of the calls. "These are the last thirty incoming calls. We're thinking maybe his visitor might have paid Anderson the courtesy of an advance phone call before com-

ing over. If so, it might be the Pied Piper, if the two had a relationship."

"And?" Boldt asked, handling the pages. "What do we have?"

LaMoia explained, "The guy had an obvious network going.
Look at all the pay phones: nine of the last thirty calls he got."

Both detectives looked up at Boldt simultaneously with wanting
expressions.

"Oh, I get it," Boldt said.

"It's your field, *Lieutenant,*" LaMoia fired back, with emphasis
on the rank.

"We'd like to talk to all the people who called Anderson. Including whoever used these pay phones," Gaynes said. "Maybe
we find out why both Anderson and the Shotz crime scene had
pollen all over them."

"No, no, no," Boldt cautioned.

"Sarge, it's a homicide," Gaynes pleaded. "A homicide that
ties directly to the Pied Piper investigation through that pollen
match."

"You want me to run the pay phone numbers for you," Boldt
said, scanning the list, "and see if Anderson was running any of
our snitches." A number jumped off the page at him as he said
this. He concealed his reaction by forcing a cough. The number
belonged to one of his more reliable snitches, the pay phone in a
tittie bar by the airport, The Air Strip. He tallied the number of
its appearances: three calls, all just prior to Anderson's demise.

"Sarge?" LaMoia asked.

"It's nothing," Boldt answered. Intelligence operated in its own
sphere. The squad worked autonomously, gathering its information, creating its files, running its snitches, from five-hundred-a-
night call girls to mayoral aides. Boldt had to protect the identity
of his snitches, even from his own detectives. "Let me work with
this," Boldt said.

"Sarge?" LaMoia inquired, noticing the change of voice.

"I'll run the phone numbers for you. Be thankful for small
favors."

"Sarge?" Gaynes asked in an equally accusatory tone. She exchanged looks with LaMoia, then back to Boldt. "We're on the same team here, right?"

"I'll run 'em for you," Boldt repeated a little more sternly, both excitement and concern competing inside him, along with the secrecy the moment required of him. "I'll handle it." LaMoia said something else, but Boldt didn't hear. He was thinking about his snitch, Raymond, and why the hell the man might repeatedly have been calling a chump like Anderson a few days before the man's murder.

CHAPTER

16

The Air Strip's facade glowed Pepto-Bismol pink with a metal awning that proclaimed in chipped lettering LIVE GIRLS—ALL NUDE. Boldt had never seen a sign advertising dead ones. He stepped inside, faced with a potbellied doorman wearing a tuxedo T-shirt, black leather Army boots, dark shades and a hoop earring. The doorman said to Boldt, "Five-buck cover. Two-drink minimum."

Boldt's first reaction was to offer his gold badge, but he owed it to Raymond to keep his identity as a cop hidden. He paid the five. Tina Turner blared from the enormous speakers about wanting his love. The doorman said, "Enjoy yourself." Boldt stepped in, overwhelmed by the smoke and smell of salty flesh.

There were fifteen or twenty men scattered among twice that many tables. Most wore business suits or sport coats, their ties loosened. The air held a low cloud of cigarette and cigar smoke. Salesmen, Boldt figured. Regulars, a couple nights a week, a couple nights a month. In the dark shadows to Boldt's right a pair of young women moved like painted horses on a carousel as they lap-danced for two sets of legs and two pair of hands that gripped the arms of the chairs like a strong wind was blowing. To Boldt's left a girl in her late teens stood with her hands on her hips, her young breasts bare, her crotch barely within a sequined G-string, rocking her pelvis in time to the pounding music, throwing her brown hair forward like a curtain of water. She hooked her thumbs into the G-string, intent to remove it, and Boldt looked straight ahead to the bored bartender and his gaggle of barflies.

Coming into Raymond's bar was a blatant violation of their agreement. The man—a darkly handsome Latino—sat at a stool at the far end, leaning against the wall. He wore mirrored sunglasses that fit his face like swimming goggles, trained onto Boldt as he closed the distance and perched on an aluminum stool next to the man. Boldt ordered a ginger ale, winning a snort from the bartender and a comment that the first two cost five bucks no matter what you ordered, and you had to order two. Boldt changed his order to a 7-UP.

"This is not cool, man," Raymond said in as much of a hush as he could manage over the music. "Very uncool."

"You think she's eighteen?" Boldt asked of the woman writhing against a vertical bar on stage.

"No clue, man. Nice jugs and trim. That's all the man cares about. You don't see no driver's license on her, do you?" Raymond enjoyed his own jokes. "What? You gonna pull her over for speeding up your ticker, man?" He lit a cigarette. "A guy your age, she probably gives you a woodie. Don't do nothing for me."

"How about we take it outside?" Boldt asked.

"Dude!" Raymond called out to the bartender, who glanced over, "We gonna party for a minute behind the curtains."

"Don't bother the girls, damn you."

Raymond led Boldt through a pair of velvet curtains, through a door, and into a brightly lit area where three bare-breasted women were in the process of applying too much makeup. Two shared a joint. The other chewed gum. They walked past the women, Boldt careful not to brush up against a bare back. All three seemed fascinated with Boldt's attempts not to look.

"Heat?" one of the youngest asked, eyeing Boldt.

Raymond said, "Get real. Like I'm gonna bring heat on you!

This here is my man. We gonna hang back in the coatrack for a minute or two.''

The coatrack was a wardrobe area: sequins, boas, spike heels, hats of every description and a variety of props including rubber snakes, dildoes, a saddle and stuffed animals. That smell of cigarettes and sour skin was concentrated here, like opening a leftover container kept too long in the refrigerator. Raymond found them both inverted milk crates and they sat down.

"This sucks, man."

"Had to happen. You didn't answer my page."

"One page. I was busy."

"So am I. It couldn't wait."

They entered a staring contest. Boldt won.

"This is bullshit."

"We've got a guy who slipped in his tub and ate his teeth."

"Probably didn't use one of those rubber mats, you know?" Raymond looked to be in his mid-twenties. He was thirty-nine. In another era he would have been called a dandy. He dressed sharp and greased back his hair into a ducktail so that his chocolate-brown eyes appeared to come right out of his face like a pair of dark olives. His teeth were too white to be real, and his smile approached an icy glee that warned of a stiletto or a piece hidden somewhere on his person. His pants were so tight that Boldt took them as explanation of the man's unusually constricted voice.

"You and I are supposed to have a warm rapport, Raymond." *Ray-moan.* "A nice fuzzy relationship free of surprises for either of us." Boldt allowed the comment to hang in the thick air. "Now I've got to wonder if I can still trust you, because if I can't, your name comes out of my book, and the cash stops coming your way. We get off the bus at the next corner. Know what I mean?"

"Wait one damn minute," Raymond protested. "What the hell you talking about?"

"The dead guy in the bathtub went by the name of Andy Anderson." Boldt watched for a response and won it.

"Never heard of him." Raymond knew to stay clear of a dead body.

"You called him three times in the past ten days and you never heard of him? I'm the one that never heard about him, and I'm not happy about that. Now he's in the fridge downtown wearing nothing but a string around his big toe, and my Homicide friends come and tell me you two were chummy right before he *slipped*."

"Hey, man, this the first I heard about him going down, swear to God."

"Way they're thinking—my friends in Homicide—maybe someone put a bar of soap under his feet, kind of helped things along. You know?"

"Don't look at me, man."

"I'm not looking, Raymond, but I am listening. I'm the guy keeping Homicide off your case for the time being."

"I'm sure."

"It's me or them. Your choice. Personally, I'd like to keep you as a source—we work well—but if you surface because of this, then our relationship's over."

It was warm in the small room, and Raymond's face shined with perspiration. He wouldn't like losing the occasional payoff. Whatever else Raymond did for money he managed to keep his name off the pink sheets, which made him all right with Boldt. "He's a pussy chaser," Raymond said, laconically. "A guy gets into some pussy he shouldn't and Anderson's the one rigging the motel room for Panavision and Dolby. Know what I mean? A little private screening for the wife. He's been in here a couple times asking questions. The girls here . . . some do more than dance. He pays well. We had a little business from time to time. No big deal."

"That's not answering my question."

The man grimaced. Sources did not like discussing their deals. Boldt understood this. He said, "Make an exception, Raymond. The man is dead."

"Yeah. But something got him that way," he said cautiously. "That shit gets contagious and I be a fucked-up dude."

"Work with me." Boldt zeroed in on the man's eyes and locked up good and tight. He was stoned or high on something. Boldt repeated, "Work with me."

"Anderson says the Fremont neighborhood gonna get hit.

Some heavy lifting, you know? It's too big an area to watch by himself—alone, he says—and that any news about such an activity would be appreciated. So I put out the word. You understand. And the only shit I hear about is some white dude about to get fried for using the wrong house for surveillance. Two to five o'clock in the morning some chemists are cooking meth in the basement of this vacant house, see? Three o'clock in the afternoon along comes this white boy who looks like he's snuffing termites. But no he ain't. He goes *inside* for a little hide-and-peek. Up on the second story. The chemists put it out on the street wanting to know if this is heat or just some stupid jackass. Not good business to whack heat. Which is how come my man hears about it, and how come I hear about it after him."

"And you told Anderson."

"Figured it might play. Could be his boy, you know? Watching for a house to hit."

"Did Anderson bite?"

"You know the drill. Paid me light until he checked it out. More on the back side if it proves good." He eyed Boldt.

"Did it prove out?" Had Anderson run smack into the Pied Piper scouting his kidnaps?

"He was gonna check it out. Get back to me."

"Sure he was."

"Damn right. And now you telling me he's tits up! Fucking guy has a fifty belongs to me. This be bullshit."

"Address of the vacant house?" Boldt asked. It was quintessential Raymond, just weird enough to ring of truth.

A huge grin overcame the man's face, reminding Boldt of the grille of a '47 Chrysler New Yorker. "I'm smelling that fifty," Raymond chortled.

If the drug lab existed and they busted it, they would have probable cause to turn the house upside down and shake. If something fell out pertinent to the Pied Piper then it would later be admissible in court. The Shotzes' baby sitter had mentioned an exterminator, as had Sherry Daech. The connection was enough to get a judge behind a warrant.

It was the first place Boldt started.

Busting a drug lab was second in risk only to defusing a known bomb. The "cookers" were typically heavily armed and sitting on a powder keg of volatile chemicals. The raid had to be sanctioned by Narcotics for warrants. Boldt processed it accordingly and got lucky: Narcotics had been after the roving lab for weeks. With the word of a reliable snitch behind it, authorization came down quickly. Behind it was the full force of Special Operations, and its elite Emergency Response Team—with an abundance of fire-power and expertise.

By 11:45 P.M. all necessary warrants had been walked through the system and the first of three neighboring families was quietly evacuated from its home adjacent to the suspected lab. Under instruction by telephone, the parents and their child simply drove out of their garage and were met downtown by a woman from City Services who housed them in the Westin. At 12:20 A.M., as the second of three surveillance units was established and the second home evacuated, a special listening device was sequestered onto one of four basement windows (all of which had been painted black from the inside), and it was established that the structure was empty. Working on a combination of collected in-formation, the third surveillance unit was in place by 12:50, be-lieved to be ahead of the arrival of the cookers.

Combat units followed.

The street cleaner that had broken down across from the target structure was receiving mechanical assistance from three under-cover Narco detectives.

The commercial Dumpster left on the street in front of the evacuated neighbor's house contained two ERT sharpshooters. With slits cut by acetylene torch, the Dumpster was one of SPD's cheapest and most easily disguised fortresses and had been dubbed the Trojan Horse.

One street to the south of the target residence was parked a tractor trailer—an Allied moving van—containing eight Special Ops officers, a six-foot battering ram and enough armament to start and finish a small war.

In the evacuated homes to either side, four ERT officers, all medal-winning sharpshooters, sat behind darkened windows at the ready, communications devices hissing in their ears.

Mulwright, his field dispatcher and a lieutenant of Narcotics manned the department's Mobile Command Vehicle, a confiscated steam-cleaning van, parked with a view of the vacant house.

Boldt technically was not involved, even though he had helped plan the operation. He waited impatiently in his car along with SID's Bernie Lofgrin, a handheld radio listening in on a Special Ops frequency.

There was no idle chatter.

Amet Amali Ustad, squad leader of Mulwright's Special Ops unit, waited inside the Allied moving van along with seven ERT officers. Egyptian and Indian by heritage, his parents had moved as children to the Northwest following World War II and had met in Seattle in the Eisenhower era. A fierce fighter tagged the Warrior by his fellow officers, Ustad was darkly handsome with unexpected green eyes. He wore a tight-fitting charcoal gray uniform that distinguished itself from ERT's all-black. Across the back of every Special Ops field agent the word POLICE was printed in bold yellow letters. Amet Ustad looked over his men, worried only for Devon Long, whose personal problems with an invalid mother made him more of a burden than an asset to the team. Ustad made it his business to hear about any problems with his officers; he had consulted Lou Boldt's Intelligence unit more than once about rumors concerning members of his elite team.

The radio traffic delivered no surprises. Three separate surveillance teams tracked any and all movement surrounding the target while six unmarked patrol cars worked the surrounding blocks alert for the arrival of the meth lab cookers.

"Stay loose," Ustad said, addressing Devon Long, worried about him. More than any other, his squad—"the ramrods"—worked with precision timing, striking a target with a fierce intensity and heavy firepower. There was no room for a straggler, no room for error.

The regular radio reporting of the various units rolled through predictably. There were good raids and bad raids, and Ustad expected the current one to fall in the latter category because it had been conceived hastily by a group of desk jockeys in desperate need of "warm ink"—favorable publicity to feed the media monster. He knew all the warning signs, multiple command being at the top. A woman captain and an admitted drunk were running this one. Ustad needed little more than this to fuel his concern. "Stay alert, people," he told his troops. "I think we've got a live fish." He pressed the earpiece farther into his ear and listened.

In proper order, each unit responded, Ustad taking his turn. His elite unit looked up at him as he spoke into the small microphone positioned by a flexible boom in front of his lips.

Besides the various shooters in the Trojan Horse and adjacent buildings, ERT had a six-man unit in a black panel van two blocks away, ready to strike within one minute of a summons. Ustad knew the ERT leader unit well and respected him. Together, their squads would constitute the advance strike. Ustad to the rear, the ERT boys at the front door. If all went well, a swarm of Narcotics officers would follow and actually lead the hit behind the protection of the two squads. The choreography and timing were rehearsed regularly in a police-confiscated warehouse on the south end of Boeing Field, inside of which stage sets of house and apartment interiors had been constructed. Amet Ustad was a believer in such mock exercises, and his team was so well trained that they were the advance unit of Washington State's elite Quick Response Police Squad. QueRPS, consisting of various units from a variety of state and city law enforcement agencies, traveled to crisis scenes—terrorism, hostage or armored drug raids—and put out the fire.

SURVEILLANCE 2: We've got Joy.

SURVEILLANCE 3: Tally-ho. I count four going in through the back door.

SURVEILLANCE 2: Roger that count.

OPERATIONS: We've got four birds, people. Vehicle's tag number does not check as the owner of the house. We've got a green light from the top.

SURVEILLANCE 3: Door is shut. They're inside.

OPERATIONS: This is it, people. Let's look alive and end up that way. Okay? Allied, it's your lead.

USTAD: Copy that. Our lead.

Ustad looked to each of his rangers—his nickname for them—and silently made contact. Each of his boys nodded in return. They knew the drill. They had heard the words "our lead," and understood it was time. Training had its rewards. Devon Long's eyes were dead, void of the fear his squad leader wanted to see there. If a person didn't find some form of terror in the prospect of ramming down a door and charging into a darkened house filled with bad guys, then Ustad didn't want him along. Ustad told him softly, "Long, you're doorman here."

The rest of the squad glanced at the man, knowing it meant he was being left behind, and obviously curious as to why. Long, for all his personal problems, was one of Ustad's two or three natural leaders.

"Yes, sir, Squad Leader," Long returned in a hushed voice in true spirit and form, although Ustad saw something else entirely in his eyes, something he didn't like.

Ustad told his team, "We go on three. I want this done smart. We've got a lot of firepower out there so watch what the hell you're doing, verify targets and don't shoot any yellow letters. We've got four birds in the roost," he said, lifting his right hand and holding up four fingers. "Four!" he repeated. "Give it back."

"FOUR in the roost, sir, Squad Leader!" the squad whispered in unison.

"On the count of?"

"THREE, sir, Squad Leader!"

"Radio check," he demanded.

Each of his men counted down into their headsets.

"Ram up," he ordered.

Four of the men took hold of the heavy device termed "the big dick" by his squad. It was a steel battering ram with rubber-padded handles on the side and a wedgelike tip carrying four one-

foot stripes of luminescent paint that sharpened to its point like
an arrow. It was scuffed and scarred from its many operations,
both practice and real-life. The four men on the handles had the
weight and size to deliver the big dick with the force of a small
truck. Ustad's squad was anything but dainty.

Officer Devon Long moved past Ustad to the back of the trailer
to take care of the trailer's large door.

Ustad turned around, away from his other men, and switched
off his mike at his belt. "You okay, son?" he asked Long.

"Roger that, sir," the boy answered in a hushed voice.

"Stay alert," Ustad ordered.

"Yes, sir."

Ustad switched on his radio and contacted operations. Blood
pulsed loudly in his ears as his remaining men came up off the
steel bench behind him. He counted down in rehearsed rhythm,
"One . . . two . . . three . . ."

Long threw the two halves of the trailer's reinforced doors open
and the squad disembarked as silently as a snake. Ustad took the
lead, followed by the big dick and then the remaining two rangers.
Ustad turned sharply left, having memorized the route: straight
down the driveway into an overgrown backyard, up the steps and
right through that door. No turns, no tricks. Surveillance reported
his squad's actions, the only other sound the uniform rhythmic
crunching of gravel beneath his team's feet. Halfway there and
closing, he lifted the shotgun he carried, silently reminding himself he had five rounds to use before abandoning it for his sidearm. He mentally rehearsed his every footstep as he gained on the
house ahead of him. Seconds to go.

He knew that the Trojan Horse and the snipers were prepared
to provide cover, to defend them if needed. One of his rangers
would let ERT in through the front door, Narcotics to follow his
own ERT unit. He brushed his thumb against the protective vest
just to assure himself he had remembered to wear it. Drug labs
were the absolute worst. If the small weapons fire didn't take you
out, the fire would.

He bounded silently to the platform of the back porch, his crew
coming to a halt below. He hand-signaled their surveillance tech-

nician forward. The man snaked a thin tube of fiber-optic wire beneath the crack in the door, viewed a small monitor strapped to his chest, withdrew the wire and pronounced a thumbs-up to his squad leader.

Ustad signaled the two trailing rangers to break formation. Armed with a bolt cutter, they would attempt an incursion through the locked storm cellar on the building's south side, but only in the event of weapons fire.

So far, so good. The back of the house was empty. The intelligence was proving sound. The lab was believed to be in the basement.

From that moment out, Ustad feared a shooting gallery. The key element missing was the floor plan. They had no idea of it, other than a generalized opinion that similar structures of a similar era accessed the basement from a door in or near the kitchen. That was the door they'd be looking for.

Ustad waved the big dick up the stairs. Leaving the device to two men, the two others readied their weapons. He held his five fingers out straight and folded them in, thumb first, one by one until his hand became a fist. As he began his count, the ram swung back once, forward once, back again and then blew the door, frame, hinges and all, right to the kitchen floor. The team flooded into the kitchen. Within seconds, Officer Randy Deschutes signaled that he had found the basement door.

The big dick rocked once, twice and smashed into the door.

It held, reinforced.

Back it came, the glowing arrow on its nose aimed for the doorknob. Again the huge ram lunged into the door. Splinters of wood flew through the air, but again the door held. Ustad cursed in Arabic. Sitting ducks—the worst of situations.

On the third attempt, the doorjamb dislodged. The next two collisions drove the door down the basement stairs in a cacophony of destruction. Ustad heard the all too familiar hand clap of small weapons fire, and saw a member of his team spin and fall to the floor. The man rolled over, wincing in agony, but not bleeding; the vest had saved his life; he had four broken ribs.

Ustad shouted, "Police!" stuck the barrel of the shotgun down the dark hole and fired off two rounds. Three to go.

Weapons firing. Voices shouting.

The sound of banging metal told Ustad the storm cellar had been breached as well. They had them from two perimeter positions. The Bad Guys were pinned.

"Drop the weapons!" echoed from below.

More gunfire, short and percussive.

Ustad heard a sliding sound directly overhead followed by the distinct snap of a marksman's rifle. He turned in time to see a body tumble off the roof into the backyard. The cookers had placed a lookout on the top floor. Watching the street instead of the backyard, he had missed the approach of the ERT unit and was hellbent on escape. Coming to his feet, he spun and let loose automatic weapons fire. Ustad was clipped in the shoulder by a bullet. Charged with adrenaline, he barely felt it. Instead, he hoisted his shotgun, got off a round and watched the fleeing man stagger with the hit. The escapee limped away following the same route Ustad and his squad had used.

Ustad depressed his radio-com button and shouted, "Devon, armed bird coming right at you!" Lightheaded, he sank to his knees, his full attention fixed on the shooter limping at a run toward the Allied moving van.

The back door of the trailer swung open and Devon Long jumped out, weapon in hand. Ustad saw him open his mouth to shout a warning but did not hear him over the surrounding chaos.

The escapee came to an abrupt stop and raised his weapon at Long.

Ustad mumbled, "No! No!"

Long elevated the barrel of his assault rifle but immediately identified that his weapon was trained in the direction of his own people. He could not fire at the escaping shooter without risk to his colleagues. Overeager, he had jumped from the trailer too soon.

Long dove to the dirt and rolled for a safer angle as the sniper unloaded his weapon wildly. A volley of muzzle flashes followed. The sniper spun and fell to the dirt. Long, favoring his right side and obviously hit, was over the man in an instant, kicking the weapon away and one good boot toe into the man's ribs.

Ustad smiled. He slumped forward, and passed out.

No deaths, Boldt reminded himself as he patiently waited for Lofgrin's SID technicians to finish with the downstairs so he could examine the second floor. No deaths. Four wounded—two on each side. But the bad guys were worse off, and the meth lab was the second largest lab bust in the city's history, netting huge quantities of meth and LSD.

The kitchen and basement were disaster areas of splintered wood, blood, discharged weapon shells, glass and debris. All was marked. All recorded. There would be more reports, more internal hearings than could possibly be justified to anyone outside the system. They would still be sorting things out on the Fourth of July. Labor Day if they weren't careful.

The kitchen was an evidentiary wasteland. Lofgrin wasn't going to find anything of interest to Boldt there. The grounds surrounding the house were no better, thanks to the army that had come and gone.

"When?" he shouted ahead at Lofgrin. It was three in the morning. He was going to need a cup of tea soon.

"You kept everyone out of there for a reason," Lofgrin reminded, meaning the upstairs. A pair of ERT officers had conducted a body hunt upstairs and then Boldt had sealed the area. He was anxious to get up there, but only behind Lofgrin's evidence technicians. With this extreme contamination, he wanted to maintain the best crime scene possible.

According to the evacuated neighbors, the house had been lived in by an elderly couple without children. The wife had recently died, sending the husband into a nursing home and leaving the place all but abandoned for the past few months. The neighbor to the east had removed the junk mail and tended to the flower beds. Newspapers found downstairs suggested the basement had been in use as a drug lab for the last six weeks, pointing Narcotics into a new area of investigation: meth cookers in decent neighborhoods.

Boldt walked a block and a half to air out his head, picked up a tea for himself and an armful of coffees and donuts and returned to the crime scene where press and the department's people of power shared microphones. Mulwright and Hill were there, as was Dunkin Hale from the FBI and a deputy prosecuting attorney. Boldt steered clear of all of them.

He passed out the coffees, winning points with the ID technicians, and then joined Lofgrin on the back porch. The man was smoking a cigarette.

"Since when do you smoke?" Boldt asked, astonished.

"Don't start, okay? I got enough with Diane."

"I've known you twenty-some years."

"I turn fifty next week, okay?"

Boldt knew about the birthday. He and Dixie had once planned to take Bernie to Victoria for a men-only jazz weekend, but Liz's illness and the task force had put the plan on hold. "Okay," Boldt said, making it sound as if he didn't know about this birthday in case they could still cook up a surprise.

"When I quit this shitty habit twenty-seven years ago, I promised myself that for the week leading up to my fiftieth birthday I could smoke. Then not again until I'm sixty-five, when I earn an entire month. At eighty, if I make it that far, all bets are off: no time limits. Smoke as much as I like, nonfilter or whatever. And to hell with anybody who has a problem with that, including Diane."

Boldt tried the tea. It was strong and to his liking despite the Styrofoam cup. "You're about as strange as they come. You know that?"

"Yeah, I know it. So what?"

"So nothing," Boldt replied. He returned to his tea. Lofgrin smoked the thing like it was his last on earth.

"You got lucky," the man said, exhaling a cloud. "If you could call it that."

"Extremely," Boldt replied. "A little bit this way or that and I'm responsible for a screwup."

"Learn anything?" Lofgrin asked him.

He couldn't tell if the man was serious or not. As a civilian, Lofgrin operated under a different set of rules than sworn officers. Boldt replied, "Only that I'm not looking forward to turning fifty." He finished the tea as Lofgrin laughed through his smoke and coughed until he had tears in his eyes. They returned inside together.

"Lou, you can come on up," Lofgrin told him forty minutes later. The sky was lighter in the east. A few birds made song in anticipation of dawn.

The second story contained old furniture, worn carpeting and tired wallpaper. There were two bedrooms, a bath and a linen closet. The rear-facing bedroom had been used as a sewing room and faced a slowly rising hill that offered a view of dozens of other homes. At four-thirty in the morning these homes were dark, streetlights etching their outlines in the fog.

Boldt heard heavy footsteps approaching and knew immediately that they belonged to LaMoia's ostrich boots. John stopped at the doorway and leaned against the jamb. Boldt was on his hands and knees engaged in carpet patrol.

"You know," LaMoia said, "if someone had bet me, I would have put big money on us tagging this asshole before he went for another one. Now we've lost Weinstein and I'm worried about a third."

"Don't think like that," Boldt warned. "Deadlines make you crazy, especially when the deadline passes."

Motioning for LaMoia to join him, he said, "Carpet patrol."

"What about ID?"

"Busy with the mess downstairs. Bernie asked us to take the carpet. What we've got is slightly confusing," Boldt explained. "We think the lookout for the cookers primarily used the front room. He's a smoker and that room reeks of it and there are butts and roaches everywhere. This room smells clean, and no butts. And yet that," he said, pointing out a cane seat chair by the window, "seems to indicate someone spent time at the back window."

"A different sentry. They took turns up here. One smoked, one didn't," LaMoia hypothesized.

Boldt had not shared Raymond's bit about the possibility of an exterminator on the premises with anyone. If he stumbled onto supporting evidence then it was admissible, but to do what he had done—use Narcotics to assist his own needs—was an outright manipulation of the system. To inform LaMoia would make him subject to the same risks that Boldt was taking. He said, "ID found some peat moss kicked up on the sill."

"In the rocker with his feet up," LaMoia suggested.

"Exactly. And peat moss?"

"Flower beds." LaMoia's jaw dropped. "Why do I get the feeling a bunch of meth rats would not be tending the primroses?" He sagged to his knees and joined Boldt in fingering through the carpet.

Boldt said, "P.S. No peat moss was found in the front room."

They worked methodically, using coins to mark the areas they searched.

"You know what I got to ask myself?" LaMoia said, busy with his fingers.

"What's that?"

"What the hell a lieutenant—Intelligence, no less—is doing on carpet patrol at four in the morning on a drug bust. Or are you just a Renaissance man?"

"The same could be asked of a Homicide sergeant running a task force investigation."

"Yeah? Except I'm here because you rudely woke me up and told me to get my butt down here."

"Two officers were wounded. I thought you were on rotation to investigate an officer-involved shooting."

"Sure you did," LaMoia said sarcastically. "I'm here because you needed someone assigned to the task force, and you weren't about to work with Mulwright even though his squad made the raid. Curiosity is what got me out of bed, Sarge. It wasn't loyalty this time. I'm too tired for loyalty."

"You know what Daphne says?" Boldt asked, avoiding a direct answer.

"I'm figuring you're about to tell me."

"That the Pied Piper is a planner."

Mention of the Pied Piper caused LaMoia to look up and lose his spot in the carpet.

Boldt said, "An advance man. He identifies them, we don't know how; watches them, we don't know from where; and only then strikes. Gets his advance work out of the way before the first kidnapping because he knows the public becomes more aware after the publicity hits. He either does the advance work himself or uses chumps like Anderson."

"Is that what I'm doing on my hands and knees?" LaMoia asked.

"It better be," Boldt said, "or we're going to have some rumors to live down."

LaMoia barked a laugh. "An attempt at humor at four in the morning. I ever tell you I love this job?"

It took several minutes for them to finish. Boldt's knees cracked loudly as he stood.

LaMoia wielded a small penlight, training its beam beneath the furniture. He ran the light up the wall and down into the window-sill.

"Sarge?" he asked expectantly.

Boldt moved to get a look at the object in the center of the light. A tiny chip of thick glass, caught against the screen's frame. With LaMoia training the light, Boldt opened the window saying, "He opens the window for some air . . . kicks his feet up on the window-sill."

Boldt placed the glass chip into a plastic evidence bag and marked it. Old times.

LaMoia said excitedly, "This guy is picking up automobile glass in shoes. Work boots. Waffle sole. That sort of thing."

"Yes he is," Boldt agreed, studying the chip.

Jumping to conclusions was both dangerous and foolish. The lab would have to check it against the other glass found at the Shotz and Weinstein homes. Nonetheless, Boldt was already won-

dering if the glass could be used to tie the Pied Piper to a location:
an auto glass shop, a car dealership.

They turned the evidence over to Bernie Lofgrin, who signed
for it. Twenty minutes later, the eastern horizon wore an azure
blue. Boldt drove away. Marina, who had spent the night, would
be awakening soon. His kids needed to be dressed and fed and
taken to day care. His worlds ran together, interdependent. Where
were the missing kids? Alive? Dead? Locked in a closet or a basement?

Try as he did to focus on his upcoming parental duties, he kept
returning to an image of the Pied Piper, dressed as an exterminator, sitting in the rocking chair, feet kicked up out the windowsill.

The question that begged to be asked was whether or not dead
Anderson had been after a possible thief stalking a neighborhood
as he had represented himself to his snitches, or was somehow
involved with the Pied Piper. Anyone could have killed Anderson—a client, a victim of Anderson's prying—one of the many
names on the caller-ID list. But the pollen on the knees of his
laundry matched the pollen found on the Shotz crib and in the
Taurus carpet fibers, evidence Boldt could not ignore. Anderson
was clearly involved—*up to his knees,* Boldt thought. Gaynes had
checked the entire block surrounding the Shotz residence and had
found no beds of knee-height yellow flowers.

Boldt slowed for a red light, but ran it. At five in the morning
he wasn't about to stop.

The caller-ID list! He suddenly understood the next logical step.

He dialed LaMoia's cellular. He had left him at the crime scene
with Lofgrin.

"Yo!" the man answered.

"Anderson's caller-ID," Boldt said.

"Right?"

"Anderson wasn't a guy working out of the kindness of his
heart. He worked for hire."

"I'm with you."

"I know Gaynes is checking his caller-ID list, John. That she
intends to speak with each of them. But cross-checking those calls

by *address* and comparing those addresses with the neighborhood that the Pied Piper may have had under surveillance—"

"Addresses?" LaMoia repeated softly, allowing a long silence as he attempted to follow Boldt's train of thought. "Gimme a second here," he vamped. "Oh shit!" LaMoia gasped. It had obviously connected for him the same way it had for Boldt. "Weinstein's house is in that direction. Anderson wasn't working for the Pied Piper, he was working for Weinstein!"

"Pleasant dreams," Boldt said, disconnecting, knowing damn well that LaMoia wouldn't sleep a wink.

17

Daphne selected the task force situation room for impact, its walls littered with photos both of the kidnapped children and of Anderson's corpse, an arm dangling half in, half out, of the bathtub. Suspects responded to environment, and she intended to treat Weinstein as a suspect.

Kay Kalidja held the door for Flemming, not the other way around. They entered ceremonially, Flemming instinctively reaching for the chair at the head of the large oval table and then reconsidering. "Where do you want me?" he asked Daphne.

"Wherever you're comfortable," she replied. "The head is fine. I want the suspect here," she pointed, "where he's forced to look at the shots of Anderson."

Kalidja shook hands with Daphne. "I wouldn't want to get on your bad side."

"No you wouldn't," Flemming contributed, letting Daphne know that he'd done his homework and knew about her. " 'Motivational Resources in the Criminally Disposed?' "

"I'm impressed," Daphne said as Flemming came up with the title of one of her papers. She searched her memory and fired back, " 'Human Extortion—Negotiating to Freedom.' "

"Gold star." Flemming faced Kalidja and demanded of her, "Background?"

"Father of victim number eleven: goes by Sidney. Graduated high school in Ohio. Antioch College. Earns sixty-eight thousand. Jewish. Wife is a gentile, Trish. Donations include Greenpeace and the Democratic National Party—small change—"

Flemming clucked his tongue at mention of Greenpeace.

Kalidja continued, "Has an eighty-thousand-dollar mortgage, twelve thousand left on his car loan. Credit cards pretty run up. No arrests. One moving violation, three years ago. Doesn't telephone out of state very often; when he does it's to a cousin and an aunt and uncle. Home phone number found on Anderson's caller-ID list. Seven calls total. Three in the week prior to the accident."

"Murder, don't you mean?" Daphne inquired of Flemming.

"Accident," Flemming insisted, leaning on the word. "You have two hundred and six hours of court time, Ms. Matthews—" she didn't even know this number herself "—as an expert witness. I would doubt seriously that even once that testimony involved evidentiary assets of any kind. Your realm is speculation—"

"It's science," she countered, feeling her face burn.

"—into motive, environment, a suspect's mental state. All helpful to the judicial process, but evidence is quite another matter. I have sixteen hundred hours in that same chair. At this point in time, Anderson was an accident. Something comes in to dispute this, we'll review it. Circumstantial evidence is just that. It may work for Columbo but it doesn't work in that chair. The Bureau doesn't arrest suspects, we convict them. Therein lies the difference between me and Ms. Hill."

She could feel resentment oozing from his every pore; he wanted control of the task force. He was a formidable presence. One didn't miss Gary Flemming, didn't pass him over with a casual glance. His black skin appeared iridescent in the room's artificial light. His voice warmed her chest like a preacher's.

Flemming held a degree in psychology from Georgetown, a master's in criminology from USC. He had been a federal marshal with the INS border patrol before joining the Bureau. With each two-year transfer he had received promotion. He served on the Girl Scouts national board and did the speaker circuit during vacation to promote a minor best seller he'd penned about his celebrity kidnapping cases. Single, Daphne recalled. Never married. This struck her as hard to believe. As a woman, she found the self-confidence, the penetrating brown eyes incredibly attractive. Perhaps, she thought, women came to him too easily. *Like La-Moia,* she thought.

Flemming drank a Diet Coke from the can, his strong black hand gripping the soda. Kalidja drank a Starbucks coffee. The psychologist in Daphne was glad for these few minutes of evaluation—it was important to know one's teammates. Flemming struck her as all business. His researcher, Kalidja, was all woman, sensual and fluid. She had expressive eyes and the lilting singsong voice of an islander. The ceramic beads ticked percussively behind her self-conscious toying with her hair. Daphne wondered if Flemming and Kalidja were more than colleagues.

Flemming's toy was a stainless steel pen. He made notations in his leather Day Timer, unable to sit still. When he allowed his face to settle, it carried exhaustion, tension and impatience. He worked to keep those from showing. He checked his watch and grunted disapproval. His life ran according to those two hands.

LaMoia appeared, looking unusually tired. He was followed in lockstep by Sidney Weinstein and a gray suit named Caldwell.

LaMoia made a half-baked gesture of greeting to Flemming, offered Kalidja an annoyingly fawning smile and acquiesced to Daphne's placement of the participants. Weinstein and his representative, Caldwell, sat across from the crime scene photos. Daphne focused on Weinstein, alert for changes in body language and expression.

Following introductions Caldwell spoke first, expounding his legal rhetoric. LaMoia reminded everyone that the interview was nothing more than an informal inquiry, a fact-finding mission. He said, "Mr. Weinstein, are you familiar with caller-ID, an electronic device that allows—"

"I know about it."

"Over a two-week period, you or your wife made four calls to one Bernard Chalmers Anderson, known locally as Ricky Anderson, Richey Anderson and most recently, Andy Anderson." Daphne logged the man's pained expression. Weinstein was no innocent.

Caldwell, the man's attorney, said, "Mr. Anderson was a private detective. As such—"

"Correction," LaMoia said, interrupting. "Anderson installed home security devices. He also provided everything from Polaroids of the wife caught doing the dirty to a dislocated limb or two when the situation called for it."

"Now wait just a minute!" the attorney protested.

"Easy," Flemming said in his low, resonant voice, the sound of which melted Daphne. "The sergeant just told you: There are no charges stemming from this. Settle down, Caldwell." The lawyer now focused on the SAC, knowing he was the one to watch.

LaMoia asked, "When did you last speak with Anderson, Mr. Weinstein?"

"Monday or Tuesday of this week," came the nervous answer.

"And have you tried since?" He advised, "Think carefully."

"Tuesday night."

LaMoia nodded. "At 9:52, to be precise. Lucky for you, that was two hours *after* Mr. Anderson's windpipe had been slightly rearranged, leaving him a little blue in the face, I'm afraid." Looking right at Weinstein he said, "Tongue as black as tire rubber and about the size of a rat. Dead. A nasty fall in the tub. Serves as a keen reminder of the importance of those rubber mats with the suction cups. Know the ones I mean?"

Weinstein went the color of toilet porcelain. Caldwell, off-guard, recovered in time to issue a line of objections as if in a trial.

LaMoia continued calmly, "So, what we're wondering about," motioning to the others, "is the nature of your professional arrangement with a.k.a. Andy Anderson. And I should caution you, Mr. Weinstein, that we take no prisoners here at SPD, if you know what I mean. If we all do the dance, it's a fun party. You sit in the corner like a wallflower with her finger up her nose and Agent Flemming, Lieutenant Matthews and I are gonna rain on your

parade until you're changing your shorts." He cut off Caldwell
with a raised hand. "And this Georgetown law professor can piss
all over us as much as he likes and we won't even feel it because
we got nothing to do with him. Our business is with you, just like
your business was with Andy Anderson. Know what I mean? So
my advice . . . personally . . . what I'm trying to say here . . . is
that you talk, you walk. You hold out on us and you're holding
out on little Hayes."

Flemming viewed LaMoia with an open mouth. Caldwell
coughed, got something stuck in his throat and gargled some
phlegm to clear it.

Flemming said cautiously, "Now is the time for the truth, Mr.
Weinstein. We don't need any fabrications, embellishments or
avoidances. Sergeant LaMoia is conducting a homicide investigation. That's all you need to know. You are not a suspect at this
time. We need a statement is all."

LaMoia added, "If you needed some knees broken, we're fine
with that. Dirty pictures? Hell, that's your business. A phone
tapped? A house watched? It's a free country." He flashed another of those disturbing smiles.

Caldwell whispered into the man's ear. Weinstein nodded. The
attorney asked, "Given that there is no recording taking place and
that this is an informal discussion—"

"Where have you been?" LaMoia asked, interrupting. "Why
don't we all just get out of Mr. Weinstein's way for a minute and
let him have some air."

For Weinstein, there was no one else in the room but LaMoia.
Daphne marveled at the detective's ability to win control in interrogations. Nothing he did was orthodox. He violated every rule
of questioning but one: He gained the subject's attention. "You
people wouldn't help," Weinstein complained. "I called. Told you
someone was watching us.

"So I asked this friend if he knew someone who could help me.
Not too expensive. He gives me Anderson's name, says he caught
this guy's wife with a neighbor. Said Anderson had gotten photos
for him. You guys didn't believe me, so I'd find out for myself."

He stabbed a finger toward LaMoia. "So I hire Anderson to check it out. Am I being watched or not?"

"Had you heard about the kidnapped child at this point?" Flemming asked.

"Shotz?" Weinstein asked. "This was *way* before that," he stated firmly. "LA, San Francisco and Portland. That was enough for me."

Daphne spoke up. "You sensed you were being watched by someone *before* the Shotz abduction." It supported her belief that the Pied Piper did his legwork in advance, reducing his profile once the kidnappings began.

"That's what I'm telling you."

Flemming said bluntly, "You hired Anderson in case it was the Pied Piper watching you."

Silence fell. Weinstein whined, "You put it like that . . . I guess that's right." He hung his head. "It wasn't exactly how I was thinking about it. No," he corrected. "Anderson said it was probably a thief. That made sense: Burglars stake out houses all the time. So we put some stuff in the safe deposit." His eyes clouded and Daphne knew he was thinking about his missing son. He cleared his eyes and said, "Hell, you know *anyone* in Seattle hasn't had their car stolen, or their house broken into? Anderson said catching these guys isn't so easy. They make you. They take off, stake out someplace else. I offered two hundred on the back side. That sealed the deal."

Too much television, Daphne thought. Every John Doe a cop.

Weinstein didn't strike Daphne as a target for a second-story man. Car theft maybe. She wondered if Anderson had simply strung the man along for the down payment.

"You called Anderson to check in. To see how he was doing," LaMoia stated.

Flemming glared at LaMoia, unhappy with the leading statements. Unorthodox.

"Protect my investment. Of course I did," Weinstein answered.

"And what did he tell you?"

"First time said he didn't have anything. So call back. Next time, a day or two later—"

"Two," LaMoia refreshed him.

"Said maybe some progress. He renegotiated. Said he could get pictures, but that expenses had gone up. Cleared it with me, I guess you could say. Expenses plus another fifty."

"And so you continued your arrangement," Daphne stated.

"Sure I did. He all but confirmed someone was watching the house. Actually all he said was that he was working on it. I didn't like him stretching me out for more money. That bothered me. Plus, a couple times he tried to sell me a home security system, an alarm system." He hesitated and asked, "Do you guys use them? At home, I mean?"

"Did you?" Flemming asked. "Buy one?"

"No. I'm not sure why. I just didn't feel like it, I guess. I will now. Hayes kidnapped. Anderson murdered."

"Anderson's death has been ruled an accident," Flemming corrected.

LaMoia and Daphne exchanged glances but neither challenged Flemming.

The attorney barked, "An accident or a homicide?"

Weinstein interrupted, "Listen, if you people had responded to my calls I wouldn't have hired him in the first place. Don't dump this on me. Is that what this is about?" He sounded a little hysterical. His attorney placed his hand on the man's arm to settle him, but Weinstein shook it off. "You guys got the pictures, didn't you." It was a statement. "You just don't know who's in them and you want me to tell you. But I didn't see them either."

There had been no mention of a camera in Anderson's property inventory.

"He had pictures for you?" Flemming asked.

LaMoia reminded, "You said he *renegotiated* to include photographs."

"That's right. I agreed to the fifty."

Flemming said heatedly, "Did he notify you about having these pictures?"

"No, he didn't," Weinstein answered. "Never. Listen! Screw the photos! What about my boy?"

Flemming ignored him, arguing to the group, "He would have

wanted payment for any such photographs. I think it's fairly safe to say he did *not* have any such photographs."

Daphne said, "Everything we're doing is in an attempt to get Hayes back as quickly as possible."

LaMoia made notes. "What do you think about the photos?" he asked Weinstein.

"I think he had shot some and was going back for more."

"And why is that?" Daphne inquired.

The attorney leaned over and whispered into his client's ear. Weinstein shook his head. "No," he answered audibly, and then to the others, "I never saw any photographs. I was never expressly told they existed."

Daphne pressed, "But you believed they did exist. Why?"

Weinstein turned slightly to face her. He wore a boyish, surprised expression. "He said he had something going for him. I don't remember the exact words." Weinstein anticipated her next question and said, "This came *after* the call about the extra fifty bucks. See?" Then a spark filled his eyes and he said matter-of-factly, "You know what it was? He said that he'd get his money when he delivered Mr. Stranger Danger. That's what it was."

Daphne felt a spike of heat from head to toe. To police, "Mr. Stranger Danger" referred to child abductors. The association with the Pied Piper seemed unmistakable. Pencils went to paper. Anderson had identified a suspect he believed a kidnapper of children.

If Weinstein had it right, it was the Pied Piper.

When Weinstein and his attorney had left, LaMoia offered for Flemming's agents to join in a second search of Anderson's duplex. In a surprise move, Flemming politely refused, implying he was happy to have SPD run his errands for him so long as any evidence discovered was shared. Flemming and Kalidja left together, leaving LaMoia and Daphne alone.

"So?" LaMoia inquired.

She said confidently, "Weinstein was nervous at first. Intimidated. But he loosened up. He's bankable. His respiration stayed regular. No noticeable perspiration, squinting, twitching. Not even much chair adjustment. He remained alert, focused—and we were throwing a lot at him."

"Had Caldwell prepped him?"

"It's a possibility. That would account for some of it."

"So we buy his statement?"

"Yes. Absolutely."

"What?" LaMoia asked, aware that something was bothering her.

She pursed her lips. "It's not Weinstein, it's Flemming. He remained pretty quiet until mention of the photography. At that point he became much more animated."

She asked, "Why did he pass on your offer to search Anderson's place for the camera?"

"That stunned me, I gotta admit."

"And what about his attempt to convince us that the photos didn't exist?"

LaMoia hung his head in thought. He said, "It makes sense if they've already worked the Anderson crime scene." He mumbled, "Fucking-A!"

Pouring ice into his veins, Daphne asked, "What if they already have Anderson's photos?"

CHAPTER

18

The Box, a small, rectangular interrogation room with gray walls, white vinyl floor tile and an acoustical ceiling, was hot. It held a single war-torn table, the metal legs of which were bolted to the floor, and, on that day, five gunmetal gray straight-backed chairs with padded seat cushions that *whooshed* when sat upon.

A woman officer by the name of Marsh accompanied Boldt and Daphne. Somehow McNee had identified the vacant house used for the drug lab; the Pied Piper had identified this same house, and that methodology was now critical to the investigation.

As a Narcotics detective, Marsh had the collar, but she granted Boldt this chance to work the suspect since the meth lab raid had been his idea. A previous interrogation already complete, Marsh was content merely to be present. She looked and dressed like an art student returned from Europe. She sat at the head of the table and remained silent. Boldt's plan was a simple one: Hit the man with everything they had.

On paper, Jeffry McNee was not someone Daphne had expected to find cooking at a meth lab: white, mid-twenties, with a degree in chemistry. Daphne had coached Boldt that McNee would likely test them to measure his opponents. He would sort them out, identify the weak player and work only with this person. She advised Boldt that if he wanted to lead, he should play dumb.

McNee being assigned a public defender surprised Boldt. It implied he hadn't the money or contacts to hire a lawyer specializing in drug defense. That fact suggested a rogue, freelance operation and offered Boldt some leverage. He might fear returning to the street more than going to jail. Drug turf was violently defended.

McNee had a boyish face with alert green eyes. With his black hair and ruddy complexion he belonged either in a Scottish kilt or selling junk bonds on Wall Street. The orange jumpsuit marked KING CO JAIL on the back did him an injustice. His attorney was a hundred and seventy pounds of Hawaiian mama, with enough mascara and lizard green eye shadow to qualify for stage work. She chewed gum vigorously and wore smudged eyeglasses. Her tent dress hung from her enormous breasts like a waterfall of lime green in a loud print. Her voice was a deep baritone, her teeth fake.

"My client wants to know what's in this for him," she said, from a chair all but swallowed by its gelatinous occupant.

"We're part of a homicide investigation," Daphne said, playing the role of the intelligent one. To the suspect she said, "A man who may have had your drug lab under surveillance was found murdered. Anyone in your position would take a dim view of such surveillance—"

"Give me a break!" the Muumuu sputtered like a big truck attempting to start.

"A conviction for which will earn you life," Daphne addressed McNee. "Not ten years. Not sixteen. Not with the current administration. Life without parole." McNee didn't seem the least bit ruffled. As she had expected. The stage was set for Boldt to do some damage.

"You sure about that?" Boldt asked Daphne, wearing a gumshoe expression of fatigue. "Can't we plea him down if we want to?"

"Trust me on this," Daphne said while simultaneously measuring the Muumuu for her take on Boldt. He had a reputation. If she knew of him, their ruse was unlikely to work. But she was unfamiliar to them both, most likely a newcomer to the public defender's rotation.

"You'll pardon me for interrupting," the suspect said calmly, "but do I detect a presumption of guilt or innocence?"

"Assumption of innocence," Daphne told him, "is a luxury afforded by those across the street." Her superior air helped McNee to quickly identify her as the enemy. Boldt was not yet so clearly defined.

The man addressed Boldt, "My pals and I were doing a little chemistry experiment. What's the big deal?"

"A man is dead," Daphne replied. "You have plenty of motive to want him that way. We can connect him to investigating a person or persons at the address of your lab. We will have documentation of that shortly. You would be well advised to play ball. Your attorney's shaking her head, telling you not to talk, but we can offer you a plea position on the dope charge."

"This is entirely inappropriate," Muumuu said. To her client she explained, "They can't offer this."

Daphne said, "No one can make any promises. But one thing is for sure, you go up for this, in the state of Washington, and you're gone for good. The key is tossed out. Ask her," she said, indicating the dress and the chewing gum.

"What do you want?" McNee asked Boldt. "What is it you want?"

"Don't do this," the attorney advised halfheartedly.

"What we want are a couple very simple answers," Boldt explained calmly. "What we have to offer is protection."

"Oh! This is bullshit!" the Muumuu complained. "Do *not* listen to them. They have no authority to plea you, and they cannot, will not, offer any reliable protection. Forget it," she told Boldt.

Ignoring her, Boldt informed McNee, "You take the dive and you end up in our big house. Everyone who's anyone in drugs has their people there. It isn't me that's been pinching Tommy Chen's turf. What do you suppose your life expectancy is?"

Daphne supplied the important piece of the puzzle. "A federal conviction would move you out of state."

"Safer," Boldt said. They had won McNee's interest.

"Don't threaten, people," Muumuu warned them. "And don't make promises you can't keep." But now even she seemed interested.

The suspect, who had acquired a sheen on his brow, looked silently between the two police officers.

Daphne said, "We'll put in a recommendation that the Feds take your case."

"How much do you know about Tommy Chen?" Boldt asked.

McNee did not answer.

"What about your parents?" Daphne inquired, thinking McNee too clean cut and too young. A degree in chemistry and nowhere to hide.

McNee went scarlet.

"Have you called them?" she drilled.

The suspect glared.

"The wire services have picked up the story," she explained. "Do your parents watch CNN?"

"My parents are not part of this."

"They could be, if you want them here," Boldt said naively.

Daphne asked, "Do I start the tape now? Or do we move this same offer down the hall?"

"Go," the suspect said.

"Under protest of counsel," the Muumuu growled.

Boldt started the cassette recording. He recited the particulars: date, time, location and the names of those in attendance.

Daphne went first. McNee had been recruited out of graduate school by Asians offering three times the starting salaries of other biochemical firms. Two months into his work McNee had faced the reality he was supplying elements to cook street drugs. Six months later, he asked for more money, and was threatened. McNee ran to Seattle, set up a roaming meth lab and sold wholesale to a street gang he refused to name.

Boldt asked, "Run it by me again how you picked your safe

houses? Did you know the owner or what? Someone next door? Down the street? I forget."

"I didn't say," the suspect answered.

The Muumuu fiddled with her watchband. It carried big lumps of turquoise fashioned as small turtles. "I don't see the relevancy," she complained, impatient now.

"Humor me," Boldt said to her. "I'm curious."

Muumuu glanced at her client and nodded.

Boldt appeared casually disinterested. In fact, the task force needed to know if the exterminator had a system for identifying his surveillance points.

McNee's face revealed a man wanting to guard a secret.

Boldt pretended to read some notes. "Okay. So tell me this: Did you use a point man? Was that exterminator yours?"

"What are you talking about?"

Daphne answered, "How you IDed the vacant house."

Boldt said, "A man was seen with a tank and a hose. An exterminator."

McNee looked confused. Daphne wondered if he was a good actor or ignorant.

The attorney said, "This exterminator wouldn't happen to be your vic, would he?" To her client she said, "Don't answer this." Her face flushed with anger and suspicion.

"Junk mail piling up by the door," Daphne guessed.

"No," McNee said.

"Don't answer this," the Muumuu repeated, sitting as tall as possible, a difficult task.

Boldt said, "You know about the exterminator," recalling his conversation with the snitch Raymond.

McNee looked nervously between Boldt and his attorney as Boldt said, "Tommy Chen's people would have killed some stranger creeping around his lab. Instead, we get a tip you guys have put the word out to ID the guy."

"We knew about him. It's true," McNee confirmed.

"The gang provided you protection. The shooters," Boldt guessed.

Daphne said, "You weren't going to kill a cop or—"

"We didn't kill *anyone*."

"You shot at us," Boldt said. "You wounded officers."

"*They* did."

"Their side was protection," Boldt repeated.

McNee nodded.

"That's enough!" the Muumuu protested.

"I don't see a street gang identifying vacant houses," Daphne said.

"A guy I know is a realtor," McNee allowed. "Is that what you wanted? Does that buy me the federal courts?"

Boldt glanced hotly at Daphne. He said to McNee, "A realtor."

"He's always looking to skim off the cream. He has a notebook filled with vacant, unlisted houses."

Daphne said, "We need a name."

"No way."

Muumuu said, "You've got too much already!"

"We need that name," Boldt confirmed.

"They must all do it," McNee said. "You show me the federal court and I'll give you a name."

Boldt signaled Daphne; he was in a hurry.

"All we can do is make the request," Daphne reminded.

"Make it," Muumuu said.

Boldt stood to leave.

McNee said, "What's going on?"

Chewing her gum like a dog eating its dinner, the Muumuu said, "Looks like you just became an expert witness."

CHAPTER

19

LaMoia looked forward to another meeting with Sherry Daech but could not escape the pressure of passing time. Rhonda Shotz and Hayes Weinstein were out there somewhere, counting on him. Hayes had been missing for four days; Rhonda, going on two weeks. The chances of finding them alive seemed slim. He had eaten only sporadically in the past few days. What time he found for sleep was bridled with insomnia.

Boldt had told him about McNee's realtor friend who kept current on abandoned houses.

"The guy probably watches the obits," Boldt had said.

"And who knows what else?"

"Find out."

LaMoia intended to do just that.

Sherry Daech did not answer any of her numbers, but LaMoia found her Hummer parked outside the agency offices, a small white clapboard house in Wallingford. The building was locked though some lights were on. He rang the doorbell and was greeted through the glass by a man in his youthful fifties, graying hair and blue eyes. LaMoia showed his shield through the glass and was admitted.

The building's interior felt more corporate than quaint. He entered her upstairs office with his usual swagger. However practiced and forced in junior high school, it had long since become part of his muscles and ligaments, and therefore a part of him. It telegraphed an overconfidence and conceit that his co-workers accepted and that strangers found outlandish. LaMoia was a modern-day carpetbagger; he took what he wanted. What he wanted from Sherry Daech was information. He needed a list from her; he would not leave until he had it.

Busy with paperwork, she did not look up immediately.

"Working late," he said, greeted then by an authentic smile.

She motioned to the stacks around her. "If you do this during the day, there's no time to sell."

"Your partner?" he asked motioning toward the hallway.

"Business partner," she clarified. "One of them." She drummed her painted nails on the desktop.

"A couple of questions," he said.

"Oh, darn." She flashed a smile and barked an eager laugh.

"I need some help."

"I thought you'd never ask." The eyelashes were dyed, but effective. They beat like little wings.

"We needed a realtor. I thought of you."

"I love making that kind of impression on people."

"I would imagine it's quite often."

"Complete with a silver tongue. You must need this help pretty badly."

"May I?" He motioned to the available chair. His legs were dog tired.

"I like you better when you're standing," she said, looking eye level at his rodeo belt buckle, "but okay."

He remained standing. "A realtor must track houses that are likely to come onto the market—try to get a jump on the competition and win the listing."

"Listings are the golden ring. Sales are great, but I get a piece of the listing even if someone else sells it."

"Ahead of time, I'm talking about."

"Of course. You stay ahead or you fall behind." She adjusted herself in the chair, enjoying his company, and said, "It's a rule that pertains to so many things in life."

"And how do you do this?" he asked. "Other than reading the obits?"

"You're not thinking of getting your license, are you?" She added, "I hate competition."

"Scout's honor."

"You were never a scout. Too many rules for a man like you."

"I wasn't a man then."

"I think you had better sit. You're distracting me. Good. There. All right. How do I do it?" she asked, chewing on a wry smile. "Okay. Obits, of course. Sure. Divorce filings can be a gold mine. I get a lot of play out of the divorce market—the separation filings are registered downtown. Early bird gets the worm. Construction permits are a good source: couples often fix up the house before trying to sell, or they start work on a future home before committing to listing the existing one. Tricks."

"Others?" LaMoia, for all his ability to think through crimes, had not come up with the divorce and construction angles.

"Oh, sure. I have lots of other tricks." The same smile, but a little more forced.

He appreciated her ability, her desire, to toy with him, to flirt. He knew the game and enjoyed playing it. He trusted her because of this. She demanded another's confidence in herself that only the best salespeople, attorneys and cops possessed. She was family. "Such as?"

"Don't tease, Detective."

"That is definitely the pot calling the kettle black."

"Smaller clues? Other sources?" she inquired, knowing what he sought. "Let's see . . . property taxes in arrears—that can point you toward a vacancy, and it's a matter of public record."

"Public records," LaMoia mumbled, writing fast.

"They are the easiest. City water being shut off is the biggie. Private records don't hurt, if you have access: phone, utilities. If you know someone in the insurance industry, multipolicy car insurance lapsing or a change in property coverage can signal a death. It's a long list. Maybe we should discuss it over a drink."

"Do you keep a list of these places? Some way to follow up?"

"A database on my machine. Sure I do. My secretary makes the cold calls for me. I do the follow-ups. It's one of those things always running in the background, you know? Low priority. Boiling away back there. A lot of it's wasted time, but every so often it pays off and I get a listing worth a trip to someplace warm and dry. The Biltmore in Phoenix. Ever been?"

"No."

"Friend and I own a two-bedroom suite in the hotel, a condo deal that works out great. We each get two weeks a year. It really *is* amazing weather down there. Rain is just another four-letter word. Not like here."

He asked, "Can I get a copy of the database?"

"Is this where I get to barter? Oh, goodie. How about you consider Arizona, and I consider giving you the database?"

"I'm a little busy right now." LaMoia thought about a weekend with this one at the Biltmore: white terry cloth robes, free shampoo. Where would he rather be? The decision came easy for him: with Sheila Hill.

She said, "What is all this about anyway? Still the kidnappings?" She curled a lock of yellow blonde hair. "What do vacant houses have to do with it anyway?"

LaMoia answered honestly, "That's what we're trying to find out."

He left with the promise of having the database by morning.

CHAPTER

20

Tuesday morning, day fourteen since the Shotz kidnapping, a fine cold mist sat across the city. Umbrellas were held against the weather, animating the sidewalks with color. It was a salt rain and tasted as such, tangy and tight in the nostrils, tart in the throat. A cloud-driven drenched darkness hung over the city.

Sherry Daech's list of confirmed vacant structures arrived by fax at quarter to ten. Thirty-two addresses. LaMoia checked with Sheila Hill, who agreed that by the start of the four o'clock task force meeting, the FBI would have to be provided the list and told of any progress for the remainder of the workday; however, SPD possessed this for themselves. It was LaMoia's job to work the evidence dry so that they surrendered nothing useful to the competition.

With the pressure of time and Hill's demand for success, he rounded up volunteers for the legwork: four members of his homicide squad, a Sex Crimes detective by the name of Cindy DuFur, a Narcotics cop called Runt who needed the overtime, Boldt and Gaynes. LaMoia assigned each cop several of the addresses to check. They were to door-to-door the neighbors for any activity at the houses, day or night, check the locks and look around the premises. If the owners could be contacted and admission legally gained and granted, then LaMoia wanted a look inside with attention paid to the upper stories. "Operation: Room with a View," he nicknamed it.

Excitement warmed him, countered by a chilling fear for the missing children.

The investigation still lacked key explanations to understanding and anticipating the Pied Piper, explanations required if the case were to be solved by anything other than blind luck. Chief among these was how the kidnapper identified his victims. The possibilities of their being random was infinitesimal—the Pied Piper was profiled as a careful planner. Whether the victims were identified through their parents or somehow through the infants themselves, no one knew. The parents seemed the more likely choice, all the children were of the same approximate age, all white. The kidnapper clearly knew about his victims. A variety of sources existed for such information, including the Internet, which posted national bulletin boards of births; its network carried full text copies of hundreds of small-town newspapers, all of which published news of new arrivals. The kidnapper might have used any of these.

The FBI, with its resources and nearly endless manpower, had been after this link between victims for nearly six months, and still seemed in the dark. How, LaMoia wondered, was SPD supposed to make such a discovery in the face of that?

Right behind selection of the victim was the physical and logistical execution of the crime—the *modus operandi*. For this reason, the discovery of a possible system of surveillance used by the kidnapper held a place of major importance.

For Lou Boldt, the fieldwork for which he had volunteered offered him a chance to air out his brain, clear his thoughts, refocus. Liz's proclamation of a spiritual awakening and an intention to abandon medical treatment struck him as nothing short of dementia. With his wife's survival so much in question, the notion of "leaving it up to God" was for him like deciding the easiest way to use the elevator was to cut the cable and allow gravity to deliver the car to the lobby. But there was no way he could think that would allow him to seize control and *force* her to take the treatments. To the contrary, he had to accept her decision, and his fear all but prevented that. This, in turn, caused him to face up to those fears, and he found it easier to run from them—to pursue fieldwork—than to look them in the eye.

So on a rainy Tuesday in March, Boldt found himself with his ear pinched to his cellular phone and his hand gripped on the wheel of the department-issue Chevy Cavalier he had driven for six years. The phone connected him to the owners, or the heirs, of the vacant structures. Boldt presented his need to enter the building, making no mention of writs or warrants. The more cautious of the group demanded to call back police headquarters and be transferred to Boldt, a situation made difficult due to his use of the cellular, but not an insurmountable hurdle. He slowly chipped away at suspicions, learning quickly to invoke a reference to the Pied Piper and approach the owners on an emotional level. One by one, he opened doors, making small checks on the list, suffering through congested traffic, struggling to put his personal issues behind him and to deliver some good police work.

He found the door-to-door interviews with neighbors the most satisfying, challenging him to carefully nurse from his potential witnesses facts that were often perceived as insignificant. For these two hours he left behind the world of chemical therapy and the smell of Betadine, the insatiate expressions of those marked to die. By hour three he was on to his last two addresses.

LaMoia favored him, like a teacher with a pet student, assigning Boldt four addresses closest to his own house, one of which bordered his neighborhood a half mile west of Green Lake. By doing so, LaMoia was offering Boldt the chance to head home early, ahead of the four o'clock duty rotation that would have sent him into rush hour traffic. Boldt understood this, but had no intention of going home early.

At the second to last house, he pulled to a stop and parked, checking the street for a white van or minivan. He waited, watching the house's windows for any movement, a shadow, a change of light, motion. After a few minutes of this he left the car in favor of a neighbor's house. He climbed the neighbor's steps, knocked, and was admitted into a small room with a faux leather recliner and needlepointed pillows depicting British bobbies, the London Bridge and Jesus at the Last Supper. A needlepoint in progress rested on the arm of the recliner along with a sweating glass of Coke. The chair faced a twenty-seven-inch color set tuned to the shopping channel. A cordless phone perched within reach.

Beyond the television, an open curtain revealed the adjacent vacant house.

The woman's figure implied cheeseburgers, fries and vanilla shakes. She wore blue rubber beach thongs on her pale swollen feet. She willfully closed the door behind him like a Floridian bracing for an unseen hurricane, and maintained her distance, crossing to the safety of her bowled chair in hurried little steps. Police shields bothered people.

"Can't stay long. Police or not." She picked up the phone like some cops handled their weapons.

"No need," Boldt said. She clearly had items to purchase. Some black-and-white fish occupied an aquarium with pink Bermuda sand that bubbled continuously. There was a ceramic sunken pirate's ship at the bottom that wore a green slimy film. "I need to ask you some questions about the vacant house next door. I wonder if you might turn the television down for a minute?" According to the uninterrupted narration, 170 peach cardigan sweaters had sold for $29.85; $6.50 tax, shipping and handling. Only two minutes left to go. She worked the remote and silenced the voice midsentence. "Thank you," he said. She watched the muted television, not him.

"Eleanor Pruitt breathed her last breath there not six months ago. Pancreas, it was."

He didn't want to be reminded of disease and death.

"No one living there, if that's what you wanted."

He wondered what she found so fascinating about the silent

colors flashing at her that she couldn't so much as glance at him. "Visitors?" His chest tightened.

"People wandering around, that sort of thing. At first I thought they might be church members. People used to bring Eleanor meals from time to time. But they weren't. Parasites is what they were—insurance men, real estate agents, tax assessors. Never knew all the fuss dying created. Been more activity over there since Eleanor died than when she was living."

"Recently?"

"I look right out that window, don't I? You can see that, can't you? It's distracting, people walking around like that. How do I know who they are?"

"Anyone been around recently?" Boldt repeated. "Quite recently?"

"I bought me a gun. It's legal," she informed him, making eye contact for the first time, but briefly. "Had it nearly two years now. They better not mess with me; I'll show them."

"Next door," Boldt said. "These people have been walking around recently? Ma'am?"

"You got earwigs where you live? Silverfish? I hate those damn things. Goddamn, they bother me."

He didn't look at the television. Perhaps it was selling a roach hotel. "Have you seen anyone recently, ma'am? Over next door, I mean."

"They hide in all the dark, damp places you know. Kitchen is the worst. Under the edges by the trash. Enough of 'em to make me sick. All I wanted was to know how much to get rid of them, you know? You'd think he could have told me that."

"Who's that?" Boldt asked, his thoughts finally connecting her words and his heart racing away.

Pointing to the television, she said, "That's Jerry. He sells all the electronic stuff. Could care less. It's Dorothy I like. The clothes. Haven't you ever watched this? Where you been?"

"Who was it you were asking about silverfish?" Boldt asked.

"The man spraying," she answered matter-of-factly.

"The house next door," Boldt supplied, violating a fundamental precept of interrogation. "Someone spraying the house next door?"

" 'I'd have to call the office for a quote,' he said. Screw him. Didn't even give me a card. I'll tell you something: If you're too busy for my trade, then someone else gets it. Plain and simple, far as I'm concerned."

"You spoke with him. You got a look at this exterminator," Boldt stated. He wanted this badly. The Pied Piper had used his exterminator disguise to scout the home, or as an excuse to be seen entering. This woman was an eyewitness.

"You kidding? Wouldn't give me the time a day. Never even so much as turned around." She added incredulously, "You've never actually watched this channel?"

"Was he spraying the vacant house?" Boldt asked. "Is that what you're telling me? When?"

"They had a housedress I really wanted. Kind of like this one, only red."

"Mrs.—" He searched for the name. Couldn't find it. A year earlier it would have been on the tip of his tongue.

"The housedress was up at the same time I saw him, and I thought about those earwigs in there and I thought, 'That's who I need.' So I get up and go out back and shout over to him. That's a big deal for me—going out like that. And could he care less? How's someone that rude stay in business anyway?"

"The housedress," Boldt said in earnest, returning to the language of her world. There were no minutes and hours, only items for sale. "What day was that?"

She looked up at him for only the second time. "He's been around a couple of times, but hell if I'm going to give him the time of day."

"You've seen him more than once?" It had been a long time since Boldt had conducted this kind of interrogation, and he felt out of sorts, his timing off. It was an art form when done right. Handled incorrectly, even the best witness could become confused and begin to believe he or she had it wrong. "When? How often?" He was rushing her, pushing her, supplying her with the

answers he wanted to hear. If he had seen one of his detectives
handling a questioning that same way, he would have been livid.

"Couple a times. At a distance. Sure I have. But to hell with
him."

"When?" He had trapped himself; he couldn't seem to break
out of what he knew to be poor practice, like bogging down in an
argument going nowhere.

"Yesterday maybe. The day before."

"Recently."

"I said 'yesterday,' didn't I? How recent do you want?"

"Have you seen him today?" Boldt asked.

"No."

Boldt handed her his card. "My number," he said, "in case you
remember anything else about him. We'll want to talk with you
some more."

"Not this time of day you won't. You wait until the gadget part
of the show. Who cares about computers and VCRs anyway?"
Eyeing Boldt's business card, she allowed a large grin to superimpose itself upon her features. "Say," she said, causing Boldt to
turn from the door to face her, "you know anyone sprays for
earwigs?"

Boldt tried LaMoia from the cellular, his intention to inform
him that he was going to enter the residence on a determination
of probable cause. He couldn't get through, but penned a note of
his attempt in his notebook. He walked around back of the vacant
house, not wanting to draw any attention, his senses on full alert.
It took him a total of three minutes to find the spare key—under
a potted plant. He paused at the back door and unsnapped his
service handgun.

The brief touch of the weapon brought with it dread and anxiety. Fieldwork was for the younger officers—he understood this
well.

He moved cautiously through the building, clearing rooms in
succession, allowing for no surprises. The house smelled dusty
and shuttered. Boldt climbed the stairs as silently as possible,
slowly and carefully. His imagination attempted to suggest the

Pied Piper was upstairs at that very moment. A confrontation. Violence. He pushed the images aside and measured every footfall, listening intently after each. Anxious cops made mistakes, he reminded himself. They shot small kids who surprised them, allowing adrenaline and imagination to distort reality, they shot the legal residents, they got addresses wrong, they believed witnesses without a second source.

The upstairs landing came into view. The clarity of such moments astounded him. He could make out the dust particles like beach sand on the upstairs floor planks. They swirled in the air like a curtain of mist in a silent and slow dance. The pounding blood in his ears was deafening—*ba-bump* . . . *ba-bump* . . . *ba-bump*. He understood that fear corrupted such moments, caused poor decisions and overreactions. He stood away from it as he stepped onto the upper landing and faced a hallway with four doors—all closed.

He threw open the first, shielding himself behind the jamb. He searched the room and its closet, but found no one and nothing of interest.

The second room was the same, no one, the smell of old age and medicines in the air.

He cleared the next two as well, one a bedroom, the other a guest bath. He returned his weapon to its holster. He examined the three bedrooms more carefully. The street-facing bedroom had a wooden rocker that faced a window, the curtains to which were pulled partially shut, unlike the other curtains in the room. The placement of this rocker reminded him of that of the chair in the sewing room at the makeshift drug lab—an unmistakable similarity.

He could visualize the Pied Piper sitting in the chair, rocking and watching, the gap in the curtains framing his target. Boldt sat down into the rocking chair, its frame creaking beneath his weight, his fingers held away from its frame.

He looked out across the geometric landscape of a hundred houses or more. Leaning back, he saw the curtains restricted this to thirty or so houses over six to ten blocks. Somewhere in this limited field of view was the Pied Piper's next target.

Boldt combed the landscape and the houses presented him. It was said one couldn't see the forest for the trees, and no one knew this better than a cop.

His eyes searched each roof, each tree, each street. Suddenly, among all the houses, driveways, porches, windows and roofs, Boldt's eye caught something indelibly familiar. He strained to see more clearly at such a distance. Could it be? And then, all at once: *yes!* He was looking directly at his own house.

Boldt left the place at a sprint, found himself inside the Chevy, foot to the floor.

Some cops attracted trouble, the way a good-looking girl incited catcalls. Paroled cons stalked them, threatened them, assaulted them; attorneys filed lawsuits against them. Boldt had only once been such a target. The thought that his children, not him, might be the true target hurried him blindly through intersections, through traffic and down quiet residential streets.

He skidded to a stop in his own driveway, the left door open, the engine running, and ran to the back door, charging inside and startling his housekeeper so that she dropped an armful of clean laundry onto the kitchen floor and ran screaming from the room.

"Marina!" he called out. "The kids?"

She returned sheepishly. "Day care," she answered in her thick Mexican accent, her face flushed.

"You took them yourself?"

"Who else?"

Marina had a temper. He had to watch himself. He settled down: The kids were not going to be kidnapped from day care. Nonetheless, he called Millie Wiggins and confirmed. Could coincidence explain his seeing his own house from that window? He hated the word. There was no case history to support his fears. Cops' children had not been targeted in any of the previous cities.

Nonetheless, coincidence was not in his detective's vocabulary. In police work, things happened for reasons.

The Pied Piper hunted white children under ten months old. Sarah was two, Miles, four.

"I take the children. I always take the children. What you mean coming in here like that? You scar-ed me half to death like that. Look at this laundry! On the floor. A mess. I have to wash it over."

"It's fine."

"It is not fine. You scar-ed me half to death like that . . . coming in that way like that. Shouting! Of *course* I take them to day care. What do you think? Mother of Jesus—you scar-ed me half to death!"

"Have you seen anyone around the house, Marina? Think! An extermina— . . . a man spraying for the bugs?"

"No such man."

"You're sure?"

Her nostrils flared. Trouble. He asked, "Am I picking them up, or you?" His heart rate settled back down. Without Liz around, Boldt deferred to the woman's decisions. Convinced that when it came to raising the children, any woman knew better than any man, Boldt kept his mouth shut. If he made Marina mad, Liz would have his head.

"*You* picking them up," she informed him. She shook her head in disgust, her rich brown eyes trained on him in disapproval. "After work. What are you doing here, anyway? It is too early."

"I was in the neighborhood," he confessed.

"Yes? Well, I am not through the cleaning. And you know how I am about people being in this house when I am to do the cleaning."

"I'm leaving."

"Yes, and you are picking up the children."

"I'm picking them up."

"Mother of Jesus, the t'ings I put up with around here!"

Boldt returned to the vacant house and relocked the door. Back at the office he avoided making a report to LaMoia ahead of the four o'clock, so that LaMoia would not have to share the information. SPD would keep the vacant houses under surveillance through the night, Boldt's discovery at the top of their list. To this end he chased down Gaynes, who was noisily eating biscotti in the coffee lounge.

"Any luck?" she asked, her mouth full.

"A home west of Green Lake. Neighbor saw an exterminator casing the place."

She stopped chewing and stared at him. Then, through the biscotti, she said, "Better than what I got." She formed her fingers into a zero. "You check it out?"

"Promising. Chair aimed at a window on the second floor. I want to get back over there."

"You mean you want me to get back over there," she corrected, understanding him. "You? You've got kids and a wife to worry about." She said quickly, "I didn't mean it like that."

He asked her, "What about Anderson's security tape?"

"I'm through about half of it. It's my late-night viewing—finger on the fast forward button. Not the best plot. I tend to fall asleep pretty quickly. And if you're sending me out tonight . . ."

"I'm not sending anybody anywhere. I work upstairs."

"I'm volunteering then," she said. "The point is, I won't be watching much tape. I'll take the first shift. Eight to two. That okay?"

"It's LaMoia's call," he reminded.

"You could always barge in on the four o'clock and see if Flemming's boys would like to help out."

He grinned. "What about—"

"Dixie did Anderson today," she said, interrupting, referring to the medical examiner. Gaynes had a way of anticipating Boldt's thoughts. It endeared her to him.

"All done?"

She nodded and said, "All but the pen and ink," and continued to chew. "Guy did the rubber ducky all right. Hit his throat on the tub. But the tub didn't do him. It was a twist to cervical vertebra number three. And that came *before* the rubber ducky by the Doc's account."

"Before."

"Doc says the twist and shout came *before* the fall. It won't get any better than theory. But he does have lividity and a hematoma to suggest blockage of the carotid artery—although the rubber ducky was a little too on target to be absolutely sure."

"The doer knows his anatomy?"

"That rubber ducky was either done by someone hoping to intentionally muddle an autopsy or simply in a hurry trying to cover his crime, and he got lucky."

"Carotid artery," Boldt repeated. "Strangled? From behind?"

"Cervical vertebra three is what iced him," she reminded. It was her turn to test him.

"From behind?" he guessed. The contact between the two might have explained the pollen being found on Anderson's clothing, although he doubted it: The knees of Anderson's pants had been covered with the yellow pollen.

"Snap, crackle, pop."

"Anderson turned his back on his visitor—and good night. So it's a person tall enough and strong enough to work Anderson from behind. A man as paranoid as Anderson. The two must have known each other. At the very least Anderson trusted him enough to invite him in."

She asked, "One of his snitches? Someone like that? You start talking about the guy's head and you sound more like Matthews than yourself, you know that?"

The comment stung him; he didn't want anyone connecting them too closely. The ghost of their one night together, years earlier, still lingered. He had put it behind him, as had she.

Gaynes consumed the rest of the biscotti greedily and wiped ashen crumbs from her pouty lips. She carried a tomboy look, much of it from her man-tailored clothing. She said, "Doc has some more tests to run before it's welded."

"When it's official, I want to know. Anderson's important to us . . . to LaMoia," he corrected.

She eyed him amusedly, but then her expression changed gravely. "A victim," she whispered knowingly.

"Yes," he conceded. If pieced together correctly, Andy Anderson could talk to him from the grave and lead him and the investigation to the Pied Piper. A victim. He prayed silently there would be no more.

CHAPTER

21

LaMoia entered the hotel lobby, anxious to see her. His pager had alerted him an hour earlier. The phone number belonged to The Inn at the Market, an upscale sixty-five-room hotel overlooking the Public Market and the churning marble green waters of Elliott Bay beyond.

He didn't know where she came up with the money for these rooms. The Inn was pricey and didn't rent by the hour. He supposed that she knew the right people—veteran captains often peddled their influence. Years of fighting the fight had its perks. Or perhaps the rumors that Sheila Hill's East Coast heritage came complete with a trust fund were accurate. He had never had the nerve to ask.

She answered the door using it as a screen in case of any stray eyes in the hallway. Sheila Hill was careful. She wore a hotel robe and her hair pulled back, her cheeks flushed as if coming off a workout. The bathroom mirror was fogged from the shower. His heart pounded at the sight of her. He missed her company while at work, bothered that their only contact was official.

She hung out the privacy tag and locked the door and pulled

on the robe's belt and it fell open, revealing her carefully waxed crotch and a smooth, tight stomach. "All work and no play," she said. "It's in the interest of the task force that you've come here."

She affected him both emotionally and physically. Something new for him. Like a thirsty animal to water, he needed to fill her, to hear her cry out for him. But he wanted her laugh as well, her ideas, her insight—she understood people so completely—her calm guidance, her company. He unbuttoned his shirt, unfastened his rodeo belt and opened his jeans. She fell to her knees.

"Let's wait a minute," he complained, stunned by his own words. He always pursued the physical women, the hungry women. Since when did he want to talk? He hardly knew himself.

She stood and turned to the wall.

Spreading her legs, she said, "Take me. Now. Right here."

She leaned against the louvered mirror that served as the closet door and watched.

LaMoia obeyed, driven frantically to please her. The smells and sounds overcame them both. "Faster, and harder," she ordered in a tone that he found demeaning. She was not his lover, but the captain ordering this.

"We have work to do," he said, briefly staying with a rhythm she suggested with her hips.

"You're doing yours right now," she returned. "I'll handle the investigation."

He withdrew from her. "Don't talk to me like that."

"You bastard." She spun around, a playful expression creasing her face as she decided he was simply toying with her.

LaMoia walked slowly backward into the room, Sheila Hill pursuing him in matched steps. "What now?" she asked. "All fours?"

"I'm not your play toy," he complained.

"Of course you are." She approached, both hands suddenly busy on her own body. She knew him and his pressure points. "That's exactly what you are. You love it. We both love it. Because it comes without baggage. But it comes, and it comes hard." She repeated, "What now? You want to watch?"

He did want to watch—she knew this about him—but he was too far along to stand back and do so. He stepped forward, turned her, and threw her to the bed. She laughed as she bounced. "You're so easy," she said. "It drives you crazy when I do that, doesn't it?"

"Shut up!"

"Make me."

In the minutes that passed, she gasped between surges of pleasure, her back arched, her smiles twisted and pained.

When it was over, she lay on the bed a glowing ruby, spent and exhausted. LaMoia showered. He returned to find her in the exact same position, but her eyes were open, deliriously taking in the whiteness of the ceiling and the flashing light of the smoke detector.

"Let's take room service," she suggested.

"Let's talk about the surveillance—"

"It can wait. You made the assignments. Everyone's in place. We have our pagers. We do room service, and another go."

"I just showered," he complained.

"And you will again."

She laughed and sat up on the bed. She looked older and more worn. He wasn't sure what he was doing there. He wasn't sure how to leave. It was going wrong for him.

"I'll call it in," she said. "What's your pleasure?"

But it wasn't about his pleasure; it was about hers. Nonetheless, he answered, "A burger."

"They don't do a burger, darling. This isn't White Tower." A disapproving, condescending voice of a disappointed mother. "New York Strip? Fillet?"

"Whatever."

"A salad?"

"What, you're a waitress now?" he asked, trying to lessen her. But it wasn't his game; it was hers.

"If you want me to be. Whatever you want me to be, baby. Have I ever refused you?"

He felt trapped, someplace he didn't want to be, but didn't want to leave. "I want to talk," he complained.

"Whatever you want, baby." But she didn't mean it.

And yet he stayed. Same as always.

CHAPTER

22

The following morning began simply for Boldt,
the scare of the evening before behind him. Marina's husband,
Felipe, was to accompany his wife and Boldt's children to Millie's
Day Care, where Boldt felt they would be safe. His eyes tired
from paperwork, he freed up time to pursue credit records of
earlier Pied Piper victims only to discover those records "locked"
by order of the FBI, an unexpected twist.

He placed a call to Kay Kalidja for an explanation but was unable to reach her.

Several times his computer beeped, signaling incoming E-mail.
Not every cop was on the system yet, but each unit was, from
accounting to Special Ops. Intelligence had been one of the first
on-line.

Boldt did not yet fully appreciate the network—the intranet—
although he understood how to operate it. E-mail was a nuisance.
It piled up worse than voice mail. He recognized its enormous
potential but reserved the right to use his E-mail at his own conve-
nience. Just because his computer beeped did not mean he responded.

His focus remained on the Pied Piper investigation, and on several crime scene reports that were still being stonewalled by Flemming. Under orders from Hill, Boldt was to get those files. "No tears." He was not to let her down.

Boldt had homicide contacts in most major cities and was on a first-name basis with many of Portland's finest. So he tried Portland first; if he could present Hill an early victory, she might ease up on him.

The computer beeped at him again. More E-mail. That made six since he had sat down. It irritated him: He didn't want to be counting beeps while he worked. (He knew the beeping could be switched off but had yet to learn how—another bothersome aspect of computers; the simplest thing required twenty minutes of figuring out how to do it.)

The overnight surveillance of vacant homes had failed to turn up any suspects or suspicious movements, a major disappointment. A few minutes past noon, LaMoia shared Daech's list of vacant houses with the Bureau, along with Boldt's discovery of the rocking chair facing a window. By early afternoon, in the first real show of a coordinated effort, the Bureau and SPD combined resources to identify any and all parental couples within visible range of the surveillance house discovered by Boldt. Ironically, it was through this effort that major progress was made in pinpointing how the Pied Piper selected his victims.

It was also through this effort that Boldt finally connected with Kay Kalidja.

"I received your voice mail. Sorry about the delay in getting back to you," she apologized in her creamy island singsong. "It has been a little crazy around here this morning."

"Here too."

She said, "Your people are pursuing recently issued birth certificates—a smart angle. We have gained access to state tax filings that we can sort by ZIP code, though with April fifteenth less than a month away and the targets under a year old, they will not show up as deductions. We also have access to applications for new social security numbers. We have asked for those as well."

Boldt offered the information he was anxious to share with her, believing that the Bureau had the authority to make the requests and receive the information days, perhaps weeks, ahead of SPD—something unmentionable around the hallways of Public Safety. "Baby catalogs, parenting magazines. I know from experience that once you have a baby, you're on every list there is. The offers they send you . . ."

The profound silence he encountered told him he had hit the mark. "This is good."

"We should have been on this a long time ago," he suggested.

"You mean *we* should have been. Point taken. This is very good, Lieutenant."

"You, the Bureau, would have quicker access to those mailing lists. The publishers will be out-of-state." He added, "You didn't hear that from me."

"Are you telling me this is ours?" the disbelief in her voice unmistakable.

"As far as I'm concerned, you thought of it, Ms. Kalidja, not me. It's all yours."

"I do not know what to say. This kind of cooperation . . . well, it has not been the norm."

Boldt asked, "Quid pro quo?"

"Ah . . . so that's it! You know, Lieutenant, I think you would get along well with my S-A-C. Perhaps you would like to bring this up with him."

"I didn't ask for Flemming, I asked for you."

"Exactly," she replied.

"That's because Flemming has locked down all credit information on past victims. I can't get access to any of it. I figure he put you up to that."

Another prolonged silence. Boldt didn't want a story from her; he hoped she wasn't dreaming one up for him.

She said, "A precaution is all. Keep the media from disseminating information ahead of time."

"Or to keep local investigators from looking at it?" he asked.

"Lieutenant . . ."

"I need the financial records—credit history, bank accounts, credit card activity—of every family the Pied Piper targeted. You

can understand that, I'm sure. It's where an investigation like this
starts. I put that request in to you personally, long *before* there
ever was a Shotz or a Weinstein. When it failed to arrive, after
numerous subsequent requests, I attempted to obtain those records myself and discovered they are stonewalled. Blocked. Now,
since you're Flemming's Intelligence officer, you must have done
this. I've got to tell you that I didn't even know such a thing could
be done. It must have been one hell of a Herculean effort to pull
this off. But now that you've done it—and so successfully—I respectfully request that all such information be delivered to me by
this afternoon."

"But—"

"Or," he added quickly, "Flemming's little end run will find its
way to both local and national media, and all the efforts in the
world won't keep at least some of it from going public. It's going
to come apart on you."

"You're threatening me?"

"I'm an information gatherer, Ms. Kalidja. I leave the threatening to others. But if I were to threaten anyone, it would be Flemming, not you. From what I know about him, Flemming is a man
who gets the job done. Nothing wrong with that. He's known to
like things his way. I've been there myself. But I wouldn't threaten
a man like Flemming; I'd just expose him and let him deal with it.
No, what I'm offering is a trade. I'm trading you a damn good
lead for information I should have had in my hands two weeks
ago. Who's getting the better end of this one?"

"I don't have the information you request, Lieutenant." Her
voice held a note of apology.

"You're the Intelligence officer. Any such information would
have gone through your office."

"It may have passed through," she conceded, "but it did . . .
not . . . stick."

She was giving him something, revealing something. Boldt
could hear the tentative reluctance in her silky voice.

At SPD such information would have been copied, filed and
disseminated to those with a Need to Know. The Bureau couldn't
be much different, and yet what she was telling him was that she

had either failed to make copies or had been ordered not to do so. Either explanation was insufficient and yet intriguing. What the hell was going on over there? Local FBI against the nationals? Perhaps the lockdown had little to do with keeping local police away from it and everything to do with preventing their own FBI field office investigators from running with it.

He asked, "What office received that information, Special Agent?"

"I cannot say."

"We're doing each other favors here."

"And I am afraid mine have run out. If you are dissatisfied and would like to take back—"

"No," he said, "it's yours. I don't go back on a trade, even when I get the short shrift."

"I will see what I can do. That is the best I can offer."

"That is as much as any of us can offer," he said gratefully, "and I thank you for that."

"Lieutenant, I am certain you did background checks on us coming into this, and of course we did the same—or rather, *I* did. Let me just say that from everything I have read, I have great respect for you, both as a person and your service record. Quite frankly, as Intelligence officer, it was my job to speculate on who would head SPD's task force, and I suggested to my superiors it would be you. I am aware of your wife's illness, and I offer my sympathies and those of this agency. I have to think that given other circumstances it would have been you running the show over there, and I think they could use you. I value greatly the information you have just given me, and I hope to earn your respect as well, as the investigation continues."

"I'd be happier," Boldt confided in her, "if it didn't continue, if it stopped today."

"Yes, of course."

Boldt thanked her, hung up and spun around in his chair with the sounding of the beep that signaled his E-mail. On his computer screen, a menu appeared with a full list of the waiting mail. This most recent arrival was a reminder—a second message—

from the mail room that Boldt had received a package marked "urgent."

As Intelligence officer, with snitches and informants spread around the city like traffic lights, Boldt could ill afford to leave any urgent package gathering dust. Some informants used the phones, others—politicians and white collars mostly—abhorred them, preferring the written word, always "anonymous."

By the time Boldt picked up his package, it had been X-rayed, electronically sniffed for explosives and run through a magnetometer for metal density—as safe as modern technology could make it for opening.

Ronnie Lyte ran mail room security. "It's a CD maybe."

Boldt realized he had hurried down to the basement mail room for nothing. The ME, Doc Dixon, and he exchanged favorite jazz works all the time. Along with SID's Bernie Lofgrin, they had something of a jazz enthusiasts' club. Boldt's love leaned to keyboards and tenor. Until Liz's illness, Boldt had occasionally held a happy hour piano gig at Bear Berenson's comedy club. Doc Dixon leaned toward trumpet players, though he also had a keen ear for tenor sax. Lofgrin was drummers and bass players: He considered the rhythm section of any group the most important. Boldt immediately mistook this CD as a gift from Dixon, whose offices were a mile away in the basement of Harbor View Medical Center.

The padded envelope had been stapled three times at the fold. The package bore no stamps, no postage meter label, no stamp or sticker from one of the city's many messenger services. This offered Boldt the first twinge of unease. His name and the address had been printed by computer on regular paper, and the paper taped to the package using two pieces of wide, clear packing tape. Boldt studied all this. "How'd we get it?"

"No clue," Ronnie Lyte said.

The mail room was run by three Asian civilians, administered by Sue Lu. Boldt shouted across to Lu, "Someone sign for this?"

"Don't remember it."

"Black kid delivered it," one of her assistants answered. "No signature required, except from you that is."

"A messenger?"

"Not someone I'm familiar with," the young man answered. "Not a regular."

"A cold drop? Is that what you're telling me?"

"A delivery, Lieutenant," the young man replied. "Guy said it was urgent."

"But what guy?" Boldt said, exasperated.

"We get a couple dozen couriers in here a day," Lu explained to Boldt, defending her assistant and herself.

"Was it logged?" Boldt asked.

"Every arrival is logged," the assistant confirmed, checking a computer terminal. "Arrived twenty minutes ago. We sent you an E-mail."

"I don't care about the E-mail! I care about how it arrived, who delivered it." He felt a growing sense of anxiety in his chest; a part of him did not want to open it, another part could not wait. But he wanted the details straight first. The label and the lack of postage had triggered a series of internal alarms. If the envelope contained cash, and not a CD, Boldt wanted witnesses to its being opened. Intelligence officers regularly faced attempts to compromise them; the smarter people behind such attempts left all details off the delivery of the bribe, waiting to make later contact. The CD might be a ruse, the true contents a roll of a couple hundred, a couple thousand, dollars in cash. Boldt needed witnesses.

"I'm opening it here," he announced. He marked the time aloud. This won the attention of Sue Lu, who joined him knowing he was requesting a witness. She checked her own watch and confirmed the time.

Boldt opened the padded envelope and disgorged its contents: a single gold-colored CD in a clear jeweler's box. The words OPTICAL MEDIA were printed on the disk along with some manufacturing information. No letter or note. No explanation. Everything about this bothered him. He handed the padded envelope to Lu, who looked it over.

"Empty," she said.

"Just the CD," he agreed.

"It's a CD-R," she informed him, pointing out the initials on the disk. "It's marked data, not music. For use with a computer CD-ROM."

"I need a computer with a CD-ROM player?" Boldt asked her, both testing that he had it right and asking her for advice where he might find one.

"Tech Services' media lab," she informed him. Adding, "They have everything in there."

Tech Services occupied two glorified basement closets that communicated by a doorway cut through a cement block wall. An array of electronic gear, predominantly audio/video and computer, occupied black rack mounts that in some instances ran floor to ceiling—linoleum to acoustic tile. Twice the rooms had experienced water damage due to errant plumbing, damaging gear and blowing circuit breakers. As a precaution against such accidents, a clear plastic canopy had been installed as a kind of shortstop. The sheets of plastic were taped together with silver duct tape, in places partially obscuring the overhead fluorescent tube. Boldt was shown to a computer terminal in the corner of the back room.

"We're working on some audio tapes in the other room," the technician explained, offering Boldt a set of headphones that were in bad condition. He plugged them into one of the rack-mounted devices.

"I don't think it's music," Boldt said, not understanding the offer of headphones. "I've got a CD player in my office."

"It's CD-R," the tech explained. "Recordable CD-ROM. Multimedia, probably, or why not just send a disk? These babies hold six hundred and forty megs of data, that's why. With compression? Shit, it's damn near bottomless."

"What do I do?"

The man set up the disk in the machine. "Double click this baby when you're ready," he said, pointing to the screen. "It should do the rest." He reminded, "Don't forget the disk when you're done. People are always forgetting their disks." He tapped his earlobe.

"You go through this a lot, do you?" Boldt asked sarcastically.

"Headphones," the man reminded.

Boldt slipped the headphones on as the tech left him. He double clicked the CD icon and sat back, watching the screen, his anxiety still with him. Someone had gone to a lot of trouble. The average snitch liked things simple: money for information. This felt more white collar, more upmarket, and that generally meant power and influence—entities that Intelligence ran up against from time to time.

The computer took a moment to access the CD-ROM. The word WAIT flashed in the message bar, as if he had a choice. The screen suddenly changed to a light gray background, and a credit card–sized box appeared in the center of the screen. Ambient room sound hissed in his ear, reminding Boldt of interrogation tapes. But there was something else in the sound: a radio or TV.

The small box in the center of the screen showed a small child—a girl—in a chair. He scrambled for his reading glasses. The girl appeared bound to the chair. Worse, she looked alarmingly like his own Sarah, although the room was unfamiliar to him: a pale yellow wall behind her, grandmother curtains on a window behind her and to her right. To the child's left, a television set played CNN, the voices of the news anchors distant and vague.

All at once the image animated. The girl looked left in a movement all too familiar to Boldt. The reading glasses found their way to Boldt's eyes, and he leaned in for a better look.

Not possible, a voice inside him warned. Terror stung him.

As she spoke, as he heard that voice, all doubt was removed. Sarah screamed, "Daddy!" She rocked violently, her arms taped to the chair. "Daddy!"

The video image went black, replaced by a typewritten message in the same small box. Boldt could not read it for the tears in his eyes.

He saw her all at once as a small fragile creature, cradled between his open palm and elbow, a tiny little newborn, a treasure of expressions and sounds. A promise of life; the enormous responsibility he felt to nurture and protect her.

He wiped away his tears, returned the glasses and read the message on the screen.

Sarah is safe and unharmed. She will remain so as long as the task force's investigation wanders. Do not allow it to focus. Do not allow any suspect to be pursued. If you are clever, your daughter lives and is returned to you happy and safe. This I promise. If you speak of this to another living soul, if the investigation should net a suspect, you will never see your sweet Sarah again. Think clearly. This is a choice you must make. Make it wisely.

Boldt reread the warning, stood from the chair and then sagged back down. He closed the file and took the CD out of the machine. *Think!* he demanded of himself, no thoughts able to land, his balance gone, the room spinning. He drew in a deep breath and exhaled slowly. The Pied Piper might have spies anywhere. Paranoia overtook him. Boldt stood up slowly, like an invalid testing his unsure legs. Chills rushed up and down his spine. His face burned. Someone spoke to him in the hall, and again on the elevator and in the garage—he saw their mouths move, he heard the shapes of sound, but not the words. He was someplace no one could reach him. He ran several red lights on his way to the yellow house where Sarah and Miles spent their middays with fifteen other children.

He bounded the stairs two at a time and attempted to turn the doorknob. Locked! He pounded hard—too hard, too loudly, too furiously.

If you speak of this to another living soul . . .

Hurried footsteps approached noisily. The fish-eye peephole momentarily darkened as someone inspected him from the other side. *Hurry up!* he wanted to shout, but collected himself as the door came open.

Millie Wiggins stood before him, surprised. "Mr. Boldt!"

"Sarah?" he asked, his voice cracking as he stepped past the woman and into the playroom. Sight of the children playing choked him and squeezed tears close to the surface. "Sarah?" he called loudly into the room, drawing blank expressions from the children. A pair of tiny arms clutched at his leg and he looked down to see his son beaming up at him. He reached down and hoisted Miles into his arms.

"Sarah?" he pleaded to Millie Wiggins.

"You called," she whispered, reminding him. "The police officers you sent picked her up." She glanced at the large Mickey Mouse clock on the wall. "That was nine-thirty."

He too glanced up at the clock. Five hours had passed. A lifetime.

He tried to speak, to contradict her, but the policeman inside him, the father, caught his tongue. He turned away and cleared his eyes as Miles tugged on his tie.

Millie Wiggins spoke in a gravel voice. An attractive woman in her mid-forties, she wore jeans and a white turtleneck. "I called you back, don't forget. To verify, I mean." Her hands wormed in concern. He could not afford the truth. He measured how far to push.

"Two officers, right?" he asked. She had used the plural.

She nodded. "A woman and a man. Exactly as you said. It's okay, isn't it?" She looked him over. "Is everything all right?" She added reluctantly, "With Mrs. Boldt?"

"Mommy?" Miles asked his father.

"Fine . . . fine . . . ," he said, avoiding sending the wrong signal. Sarah . . . He needed to collect himself, time to think. He needed answers. Sarah's chance depended on the next few minutes. *And for how long after that?* he wondered.

He wanted desperately to take Miles with him, but if the kidnappers had wanted Miles, then the boy wouldn't have been there. If the day care center was being watched—if Boldt was under surveillance . . . He mired down in uncertainty and paranoia, up to his axles in it. Poisoned with fear, faint and weak, he placed his son down and said to Millie Wiggins, "I didn't want Miles feeling left out. Thought I should stop by," hoping this might sound convincing. It fell short. His mind whirred. "It's one of those mornings where I can't tell up from down. I even forget where I was when we spoke this morning. Which line did you call?"

"I called nine-one-one, just as you told me," she reported. "I spoke to you, hung up, and dialed nine-one-one. They put me through."

The ECC lacked any means to relay a call to headquarters. It was technically impossible. Boldt knew this; Millie Wiggins clearly did not. Her explanation baffled him. "You sure it was nine-eleven—nine-one-one, and not—"

"You told me to call you back on nine-one-one!" she reminded him, viewing him suspiciously.

She had it wrong. It was the only explanation. Why should she remember? he wondered. It was important only to him. Memory played tricks on people.

He declined to push her any further. He felt aimless and lost.

She snapped her fingers. "I almost forgot." She hurried into the busy room and returned as quickly. She brought her hand up for him to see. "The lady police officer wanted me to give you this. Said it was a private joke, that you'd understand."

In her outstretched hands she held a dime-store pennywhistle.

CHAPTER

23

Unaccustomed to an invitation for coffee from Boldt, Daphne Matthews found herself caught by surprise. Neither of them drank coffee, and they didn't arrange secret meetings. Not any longer.

Du Jour, a small lunch cafe on First Avenue, offered yuppie chow and an expansive view of the bay. This choice also surprised her. Boldt leaned more toward tea and scones at the Four Seasons Olympic. He was known as a regular in the Garden Room.

He occupied a table pressed up against the huge glass window overlooking the bay and the lush green of the islands beyond. She bought herself a tea at the cafeteria-style counter, her eyes on Boldt, understanding immediately and with great certainty that something was terribly wrong. *Liz,* she thought.

As she approached, she noticed his slouched shoulders, the redness of his eyes and nose and his cup of tea, which was not steaming and had gone untouched. He hadn't added the milk yet. She recognized grief when she saw it.

"Hey," she said casually, pulling out her own chair. He didn't stand. Not the Lou Boldt she knew.

"Ah!" he said, looking up at her woodenly, taking no time to express any kind of welcome. She felt unimportant. She sat down.

"I need a favor, Daffy, and it's perfectly fine if you don't want to do it, but if you're willing to do it, to help me out, then all I ask is that you don't ask any questions. None. Not one. It's important for both of us, for everybody, that you not ask any questions."

"Does that include now?"

He looked up at her and then to the door of the cafe. "That's a question," he informed her. He seemed to have aged a dozen years. Liz, she thought again. She felt sad. He had broken—frankly, she had expected it sooner.

"No questions at all?"

"Better that way," he answered. "Safer." A furtive check toward the front of the restaurant. Grief could cause strange behavior in the strongest of people.

"You can't go back to the office looking like this," she warned. "And that is *not* a question."

He never quite got his clothes right, tending to carry a part of his last meal on them somewhere. The new breeds of permanent press were made with him in mind, but he stayed with natural fibers, all cottons and wools, and as a result looked like an unmade bed most of the time. He rarely shaved without missing a spot or two.

"I'll pull it together," he said.

"And keep it there?" she asked.

His eyes betrayed him. Her question brought threatening tears. He understood his own vulnerability. This was significant to her.

"Lou, one of the slogans I use is, 'Dare to Share.' It takes some nerve, but it's worth the risk." She waited a moment, hoping this might sink in, might trigger an effort. "Trust me. Please."

He leaned the weight of his head into the crutch of his open palm, covering his mouth and stretching his eyes open grotesquely. He spoke through his fingers, muddying his speech. "It's a favor is all. It'll take you most of the rest of the day."

"At the hospital? At home?"

"A drive."

"A drive," she repeated. "You and me? Me alone?"

"All questions," he answered, his eyes betraying his pain.

She hated herself. "Let me start all over. Please, please forgive me. Let me just say yes. Whatever it is, whatever it entails: Yes. The answer is yes."

"The thing is," he explained in a lifeless drone, "I'm preoccupied with something else and Marina is out. It's you, or Bear, or Dixie. I'm asking you first is all. It doesn't mean you have to do it."

"And I'm honored. I have already accepted," Daphne reminded him. "I could use a drive." She added, "Where to, what for?" Then she caught herself in another question and apologized softly. He needed soft at the moment.

"You remember the Lux-Wash up above Green Lake? The arson case?"

"Of course."

"Be there in an hour." He checked his watch. "One hour."

She tensed at the request. Intelligence involved itself in a variety of complex investigations, from political corruption conspiracies to eavesdropping on the Asian mob. Was this work-related or personal? Had she gotten it wrong? "One hour at the Lux-Wash," she repeated dryly.

"I can make it sooner if you want. But no later," he cautioned.

"An hour is fine. Plenty of time."

"An hour then. Park to the east out on Eightieth. I'll pull past. I won't honk or anything; you'll have to be watching. You'll come in behind me and we pull into the line that way: me directly ahead of you. Decline the interior cleaning. That means you can stay in your car and won't go into the waiting room. You'll need a full tank. Maybe a snack. Animal Crackers," he blurted out, as if picking her snack.

"Miles," she said, suddenly understanding. She had been around the boy enough to make that connection.

His eyes flashed angrily. "Maybe an apple. Granny Smiths."

"Got it." It *was* Miles. Sarah too? she wondered. She wanted to ask about car seats, but didn't.

Genuinely concerned, he asked her, "You're sure you don't

mind?" He glanced once again toward the cash register as if expecting someone else.

"One hour at the Lux-Wash," she repeated.

"Do exactly as I've told you," he stated harshly. Then he stood, the chair legs crying against the floor.

"Yes," she agreed.

"Don't follow out for several minutes."

"No."

"That's important. Several minutes."

"I understand." She didn't at all.

He walked out of the cafe, filling the light in the doorway, moving into silhouette, which removed all identity. It was raining again. Gray begetting gray. She wanted springtime. She wanted Boldt well again. She kept track of the time on her watch, knowing from experience that minutes took forever to pass when she was rattled. A ferry sounded, its call haunting and lonely. It reminded her of him, vacant and distant and casting no reflection.

She checked her watch again. Three minutes had passed. In fifty-seven more she was due at the car wash.

She waited for him, parked on 80th Street North, her attention trained on the outboard rearview mirror. He was five minutes late, which was not like him. She understood the car wash routine. They had used similar tricks before. Life as a cop was part deception. Of all the cops on the force, she was the most devoted to Boldt.

His Chevy pulled past. No acknowledgment. She couldn't see into his car through the light drizzle, but she suspected Miles was in there.

She remained attentive as she followed him into the car wash entrance.

The Chevy rounded the back corner, and an attendant, armed with a long vacuum hose, arrived at the driver's door carrying an umbrella. Boldt waved him off.

Daphne pushed the SEND button on the cell phone at the same time as she rolled down her driver's window and also de-

clined the interior work. Two in a row was too much for the attendant. He looked at her with a slack jaw and asked, "No?"

"No," she answered definitely, rolling up the window and hoping Boldt would answer his own cellular.

The Chevy pulled into the foaming shower of soap and spray
followed a moment later by her Honda, both cars swallowed by
the machinery. The rinse water followed, and immediately behind
that, powerful jets of air that drove rivulets of water out across the
hood and up the windshield like a silver fan. Within that blur,
Boldt emerged from his car carrying a large child seat with his son
strapped inside. In his other hand he carried a duffle bag. The
exchange happened quickly, and in the bending, distorted light of
the car wash, Boldt appeared to jump across the front of her car
and, suddenly, was wrenching open her side door and working
the car seat into the back and fixing a seat belt across it as he
moved to keep pace with the wash conveyor. He handed her a
crushed and wrinkled sheet of paper saying something about it
being "their address." He told her not to stop at the end of the
wash—he would pay for her. He added, "You're not to use your
cell phone for any reason." The car door thumped shut. Soaking
wet, Boldt hurried and reentered the Chevy just before it emerged
from the throat of the machinery.

At a red light she reached down and unfolded the piece of paper
he had handed her. Katherine Sawyer. Boldt's sister. A street address in Wenatchee, Washington. A phone number. A long drive
ahead of her.

Where was Sarah? she wondered. A moment later, another,
more terrifying thought occurred: Was this the question Boldt did
not want asked?

CHAPTER

24

Boldt sequestered himself in his office, phones off, to decide what to do, well aware that whatever his decision, it would determine not only his future but his daughter's as well.

The weather did not coincide with his mood, the heavy cloud cover having given way to warm sunlight the color of daffodils. He pulled down the office's slatted blinds to darken the room, but ended up with a striped floor, desk, walls and chair, surrounded appropriately enough in a cage of light. Jailed, just as he felt.

The kidnapper might have asked for money; for all of Boldt's worldly goods; he might have asked that Liz use her banking authority in some way, a false account, a fake loan; but instead he asked the impossible: that Boldt subvert an investigation.

In the balance hung his daughter's life. There was not, therefore, any decision to be made—the choice was obvious. And yet Boldt found himself engaged in debate, understanding how the Pied Piper had kept from being caught, had frustrated Flemming and his team, had moved city to city with a license to pluck infant children from their parents' arms. It was no wonder he hadn't been caught, that investigators had so few leads; the deck had been stacked in each city.

Once committed, there was no turning back. His powers far-reaching, the lieutenant of Intelligence had only to pick up the phone to initiate interdepartmental wiretapping. If he were to compromise the investigation, then he needed every piece of it, every whisper, every consideration. Information was everything. He had to know it all. He ran the names off to the civilian who ran Tech Services: "Hill, Mulwright, LaMoia, Gaynes, Lofgrin." He waited for some kind of acknowledgment. When the man on the other end failed to speak, Boldt said, "Do you have that?"

"I've got it. Record all of them," he stated. "Twenty-four hour loops or real time?"

"Real time." He added, "What happened to live monitoring?"

"This is too many lines, unless you can provide the personnel."

"No other choices?"

"AI," the man offered, "artificial intelligence. It's a new system, prone to bugs, but we've used it a couple times to good effect."

"You lost me."

"The software monitors the phone lines, listening for key words. You put in 'coke' or 'smack' and if the words come up, the conversation is flagged. When it works, it works beautifully, but the bugs aren't out. It crashes from time to time; I gotta be honest with you."

He ordered the phone lines monitored by AI.

To wiretap lines out of office required warrants, and therefore a visit to a judge. Boldt worked with only one judge, the most liberal in the state—this judge had been passed to him by the former lieutenant of the squad, like a mentor.

After hearing Boldt's arguments, viewing the numbers requested and understanding their significance, the judge asked only one question of him. "I take it you see no other way to monitor the situation, or you wouldn't ask."

"There's an insider," Boldt said blankly, knowing full well he was describing himself. "Has to be. Someone compromising the investigation. Steering it off course. We find that person, and the investigation just might have a fighting chance."

The gray head nodded. The pen came out of the drawer. The signature went down. Boldt had authority to wiretap the FBI.

"They have ways of protecting themselves from such things, don't they?" the judge asked.

"The warrant gives us access to the landlines themselves. I'm told by our tech people that it makes all the difference. We go through the US West switching station."

"I don't care who you go through, the shit's going to fly if they get onto this. You and I are going to be right in the middle of it, and that means you," he warned.

"He who complains the loudest is the first person we investigate," Boldt countered. *It's me*, he wanted to say. But who would listen? Lou Boldt compromise a task force investigation? Not likely.

He did it for Sarah, he reminded himself repeatedly. For Liz. For the family. But with each step he took toward his darker side, he questioned his decision. And he knew even then that before long, he would wish that he could take it all back.

CHAPTER

25

Boldt reached his wife's hospital room, but stopped at the door. For these last weeks of her treatment and the complications surrounding it, his single greatest responsibility had been their children. Time and again she had offered him options, from Marina moving in with him and the kids to parking the kids with various family members until Liz was home again. But Boldt had taken these as a test, both from her and from himself: Could he handle the kids alone? With a few hours from Marina—which he could afford on his lieutenant's salary—could he make the family work? The larger, unspoken question had to do with his abilities if he lost Liz, if the cancer claimed her as the doctors suggested it would. He needed to know, and so he had repeatedly declined her proposals, reassuring her he had everything under control.

But now at the hospital room door, tears were stealing his vision for the umpteenth time, because nothing was in control. In one moment his life had become a runaway train. Nurses passing by took him as a grieving husband. Here on the C ward beds emptied quickly and forever; images like the one of Boldt weeping at his wife's door were not at all uncommon.

Despite his rehearsal on the way over, what did he hope to say to her? How would he explain the loss of their child? What effect might it have on her health? Could he live with the responsibility of knocking her out of remission and back into the hell of her disease?

Racked by ill conscience, he allowed himself the lie that he might recover Sarah in a matter of a day or two. He had every key player in the task force under wire surveillance. He had Kay Kalidja working on the victims' financials. He had Millie Wiggins' statement from the day care center about calling 911 and being put through to Boldt: an impossibility that required further investigation. Leads, the cop in him convinced the father and husband. Somewhere, something would break. And when it did, Sarah would be home again, the incident in past tense, an acceptable scenario.

"Lou?" her voice called out from the other side of the door. "Honey?"

Had she recognized the sound of her husband's tears or had her uncanny prescience of late detected his presence there?

He stepped back and away and into the center of the hall, afraid.

"Honey?" he heard her voice again.

He turned and walked as fast as his feet would carry him, tempted toward an all-out run. He might have been paged; he might have been called or summoned back to the office. It happened all the time. What of it? A dozen excuses hung there in the offering, awaiting him, memorized from decades of use. But useless because he knew the truth.

"Lies," his own voice echoed in his head. A voice unfamiliar to him. A voice he was learning to live with.

Once begun, there was no turning back. The infection was rampant. Of the two of them, Liz was no longer the terminally ill, he was.

CHAPTER

26

Daphne approached the regular four o'clock ago-
nized over her assignment. Hill had requested a snapshot evaluation of every member of the task force—all of whom would be in
attendance. Hill had offered no explanation for the unusual request, leaving Daphne anxious.

Hill had her own grand entrance planned for a few minutes into
the meeting. She wanted Daphne's attention paid to this moment.
"Reactions and attitude changes," she had explained. Sheila Hill
remained a nut Daphne found hard to crack.

More photographs had been added to the situation room's
walls. Death and abduction. Children's faces everywhere.

In attendance were Mulwright, LaMoia, Hale, Flemming, Kalidja and herself. SID's Lofgrin had delivered a report and was
available as necessary. Boldt was two floors away.

Mulwright kicked things off by complaining to Flemming about
the FBI lab's failure to report back on the automotive glass found
at several of the crime scenes. The lab had been asked to help ID
the product number found on one of the pieces. SPD had heard
nothing. Flemming defended the delay, citing recent political and
media pressure that had adversely affected the FBI lab.

Daphne studied tone of voice, eye movement and body language of each and every participant. State of mind was more difficult.

The group worked well together when dealing with specifics. They anxiously awaited the analysis of the pollen, the lab work on the glass chips, and put great hope in the surveillance of the vacant houses. The proposed direction for the investigation segregated down departmental lines: SPD put faith in Anderson's killing and a possible connection to the abductions; Flemming wanted little to do with Anderson, insisting that Kay Kalidja's suggestion to pursue catalog and magazine subscriptions offered the greatest chance for a breakthrough.

Mulwright proposed concentrating all manpower on surveillance of families with infant children that lived within sight of the abandoned house Boldt had discovered. Flemming argued against this, citing manpower demands. He suggested they notify all parents in the area, reminding, "No child has been taken from a parent—only from baby sitters and relatives of the family."

In the two weeks since the Shotz abduction, this was the first mention of this, and for Daphne it went to the psychology of the Pied Piper. She blurted out, "He doesn't want the confrontation a parent would offer. He's afraid of violence." All heads turned to face her.

"My point is," Flemming said, "that if a parent stays with that child there will be no kidnapping."

Daphne said, "He's punishing the parent for leaving the child in someone else's care." Silence overtook the room. She said, "He's giving those children to parents desperate for their own; parents who care. Parents who won't leave that child for anything."

"Mumbo jumbo," Hale quipped.

Flemming reprimanded his agent with a stern look. To the others he said, "The point is, if we alert the public now, we may save some children."

Sheila Hill came through the door without knocking. She won the immediate attention of nearly every man in the room, drawn like moths to light. She wore a plain gray suit, white shirt and black flats. A simple silver necklace hung over her collarbone. Her lipstick was flesh-toned, her hair brushed smooth and held with a clip. Nothing showy. The SPD officers stood for her. The FBI followed reluctantly. In that instant, the mood changed. Authority walked through that door. Even Flemming seemed to understand this.

Daphne sat up and took notice.

At a few minutes before four that same afternoon, a rainstorm relenting to the east, Lou Boldt crossed an internal threshold and, like an ex-drunk sitting in front of a bottle of whiskey, reached out and took his first sip. He simply couldn't sit there staring at it. If the two who had abducted his daughter had believed him capable of passivity, they had guessed wrong. The cop in him won out. The only way he would ever see his daughter alive again was to beat his own people to the Pied Piper, locate his daughter and do whatever had to be done to take her back. He ruled out nothing. The plan was a simple one—eat or be eaten. His choice was made.

Tech Services was to provide him twice daily with cassettes of conversations that contained the key words he'd specified: "kidnap," "kidnapping," "abduction," "babies," "infants," "task force," and the names of every player, including the victims and Andy Anderson. The tapes were delivered in an interdepartmental envelope that had to be signed for by Boldt himself. Just another day in Intelligence, but this time Boldt was eavesdropping on his own people.

He listened to most of the conversations with the tape speed doubled. Voices like chipmunks, but the spoken words understandable. A two-minute phone call became one. Life in half time.

As he listened, he thought that he had failed as a father, husband and cop. A dozen should-have-dones presented themselves, but all in hindsight.

He recalled bottle-feeding Sarah in the living room as the morning sun warmed a darkened sky, the smell of the top of her head, the delicious sounds she made while eating. He recalled the softness of her feet and the strong grip of her toes. He ached beyond anything he had ever experienced. A knot of pain seized his chest, unrelenting. Adding to this anguish was the solitude of his secret. He could not face people. He shut and locked his office door and turned off his phone. But he locked himself in another room as well.

The father in him—the failure—wouldn't let him out of the dark room of his guilt and grief. A glimpse of a family photo, Sarah's crayon art, the tiny baby shoes on the bookshelf. These were the personal reminders he could not live with, and yet could not bear to remove.

From this point of utter desperation, he struggled back, reaching the most difficult decision of his life: The Pied Piper was not going to dictate his actions. He would turn on his own people if necessary, but Sarah would not be used to allow other children to be kidnapped.

As lead, LaMoia had both the Anderson file and the task force "book" on the Pied Piper in his possession.

Boldt could have submitted official requests for any such reports and files—he considered doing that—but then a more ominous question presented itself: Did the Pied Piper have a way of monitoring Boldt's activities? Was there a second insider? Had a second cop been compromised? Was someone monitoring his every move?

Boldt had to conduct his own investigation while hindering the efforts of the task force, to be seen obeying the ransom demands while secretly working to locate Sarah and get her back. Any sudden interest on his part in evidence records and case files might send the wrong signal.

If he couldn't request them, he had to steal them.

Flemming glanced over at his subordinate Dunkin Hale in what Daphne realized was a signal.

Addressing Mulwright, Hale said, "Lieutenant, if you agree, we would like to suggest SPD canvass pawnshops for Anderson's camera."

Mulwright countered in a sharply sarcastic tone, "It would help if we knew what kind of camera we're looking for, Special Agent."

Hill caught on and said, "Are you suggesting that Anderson was a heist gone bad, not a murder associated with the kidnappings?"

"It's possible," Hale replied. He then informed the group, "The camera is a Kodak DC-40, a digital camera that Anderson's credit card records show he purchased in November of last year."

Hill's face went scarlet. "We want the camera, yes. But for the record, Anderson connects via the pollen," she protested.

Flemming said calmly, "Anderson's computer may contain digitally stored photographs. It has been sent to Washington for analysis."

"You shipped it east without so much as telling us?" LaMoia complained. What he did not divulge was that the SID technicians had discovered a number of backup disks in Anderson's bookshelf that were currently being analyzed. If the disks contained digital photographs, SPD would have them ahead of Flemming.

"I'm telling you now," Flemming said. "We use the four o'clocks to share information."

Not all of us, LaMoia thought. He smiled and said, "Thanks for sharing."

The clock clicked into place: 4:20 P.M. LaMoia would still be at the four o'clock, his office cubicle unattended.

Boldt did not miss the irony of approaching an office cubicle and desk that had once been his own. At 4:00 P.M. the duty rotation had occurred and LaMoia's squad had technically gone off their day shift. Because of the caseload demands of the Pied Piper investigation, most of his team kept right on working, logging coveted overtime. Combining the two squads could have meant a

chaotic fifth floor, but it didn't work out that way because of the
surveillance duty. Adding to the floor's peace and quiet was that
the civilian employees—the secretaries, clerks, receptionists—had
gone home.

As Boldt entered Homicide, he glanced first toward the lieutenant's office, a large room with two desks shared by Shoswitz and
Davidson. The lights were on. Boldt kept his head down and
moved quickly. It was rare that both lieutenants occupied the
room at the same time—they handled separate rotations—but the
chaos of the task force had added hours to both men's watch. If
either lieutenant spotted him he would need to come up with an
excuse for roaming around Homicide. Head down, he slipped
past and headed directly to LaMoia's desk, where a deerskin
jacket hung on the back of the chair. The adjacent desk belonged
to Leon Kreuter, a detective on Davidson's squad, another of the
middle-aged Homicide detectives who felt that Boldt's prolonged
years as sergeant had hurt their promotions—an argument Boldt
didn't buy. Kreuter was a talker. He would make a point of nosing
into Boldt's affairs. LaMoia's desk would not be safe for long.

His heart pounding heavily, Boldt hurried to LaMoia's cubicle
and sat down. Twice the size of any other file, the task force book
was easy to spot. Anderson's was more elusive. He ran through
the paperwork in plain sight but struck out. He pulled on the
desk drawer and found it locked. At the same instant, two voices
boomed from down the hall, the louder of which belonged to
Leon Kreuter.

Sitting at his former desk, he suddenly realized that in the
course of transition, he had handed the desk key over to LaMoia
but not the duplicate key he had always kept in his wallet. He
didn't remember having ever disposed of the key. He dug into his
wallet's warm sticky leather and came up with it.

Kreuter's voice moved toward him all of a sudden; the topic
not cop talk but the performance of four-wheel-drive utility vehicles versus pickup trucks.

A detective's desk area was off-limits. Chain of custody rules
for active files required the signatures of both officers. Searching

the contents of another officer's desk—even a friend's—was simply not done.

Worse, an Intelligence officer caught snooping around Homicide would sound alarms. As much as Boldt felt a part of this floor, his new posting cast him as an outsider even to members of his former squad.

While considering all this, he unlocked the desk.

Kreuter's laughing voice drew closer.

Boldt slid the center drawer open: no files. Next drawer.

Anderson's file had been placed on top of a Kleenex box. Boldt grabbed it and slid the drawer shut. He tried to turn the small key but it slipped out of his fingers and fell to the carpet.

Kreuter said clearly, "And she handles turns like a dream. You can't believe the thing is four-wheel."

Forced to leave the desk unlocked, Boldt fled toward the copy room, both files clutched tightly under his arm, his heart painful in his chest, his face stinging hot.

Homicide's copy room looked like a paper warehouse, its walls adorned with dozens of Far Side cartoons, its shelves stacked with reams of paper products. The copier itself was the size of a freezer locker; it hummed loudly, green display lights lit up like a Christmas tree. The room was always a good fifteen degrees warmer than any other, making it a sweatshop. It smelled of paper, bleach and body odor. The door did not lock; nor was it *ever* seen closed, so Boldt left it open, feeling vulnerable. His back to the hall. He had never worked undercover. He didn't know how people did it. A greater offense than lifting the files was to be caught copying them—cause for immediate internal review. Knowledge remained the key to Sarah's chances.

He fed the copier groups of pages and it devoured them. The Anderson file took less than two minutes. He started in on the task force book, a formidable job.

A pair of voices approached from down the hallway. Boldt collected the paperwork in a rush of adrenaline, but then the voices faded past him, and again he returned to copying. He checked his watch as he fed another stack into the machine. Twenty minutes had lapsed since his entering Homicide. He bundled the photocopies into a stack and tucked it up under his shirt against his spine, held snug by the waist of his pants. His sport coat further hid it from view. He clamped the original folders under his arm and marched with purpose back down the hall.

All went well until he glanced over and spotted Doris Shotz keeping vigil in one of Homicide's formed fiberglass chairs. Boldt stopped and stared, understanding this woman's agony for the first time. Doris Shotz looked over at him, and Boldt felt her helplessness, her frustration and anger. They briefly met eyes.

"What is it?" she asked him from across the room, suddenly agitated, her hands worming in her lap. Her eyes dropped to the folders he was carrying, searching for answers.

Boldt shifted them to the opposing arm. As he did so, the strained voice of Lt. Peter Davidson said, "Inciting the natives?"

Davidson was an ex-football type with the chest and the attitude to prove it. His beer gut and spiderweb blood vessels spoke of his favorite pastime. "Don't get her fired up," he complained, "and don't get her hopes up either. Just leave her alone."

"She is alone," Boldt said, understanding perfectly well. "That's the problem."

"What are you doing on this floor anyway?" He looked Boldt over, looked right at the files in Boldt's hands. "Spying on us? Spying on your former squad?"

Boldt kept his arm to where it covered the tabs on the files. "Of course I am," Boldt said sarcastically, tapping the files. "Spying on all of you."

Davidson smiled. "Right. I thought so."

Boldt headed directly to LaMoia's desk, relieved to see Kreuter's cubicle empty once again—some cops spent all their time between the coffee lounge and the men's room. He returned both files to the drawer.

Finding his key proved more difficult. He looked where he expected it to be—beneath the desk—but didn't see it. If LaMoia found his desk unlocked . . . that was unacceptable.

Boldt intentionally dropped his pen, toed it under the desk, and then kneeled to retrieve it. He didn't see the key. He shoved aside the trash can, and there it was.

At the moment he retrieved the key, the door to Homicide buzzed and Boldt looked back to see a pair of ostrich cowboy boots approaching.

"While you're at it, fella', empty the trash," LaMoia teased. "If you're planting a bug, forget it. I'm onto you."

With mention of the bug, Boldt bumped his head on the underside of the desk.

Boldt's only chance to lock the desk was to put his body between LaMoia and the man's desk. He backed out from under, stood and feigned a sudden loss of balance. Leaning onto the desk for support, he blindly attempted to fit the key into the lock, but couldn't get it. He mumbled, "Stood a little too fast," his fingers working furiously. The key slipped in the lock. He pocketed it.

"You okay?" a concerned LaMoia asked.

"Fine," Boldt answered, wondering what kind of person deceived his closest friends. Wanting LaMoia's thoughts elsewhere, he asked, "How'd the four o'clock go?" He felt so cheap. *Desperate people take desperate measures,* he recalled Daphne once saying.

"Hill wants you in her office," LaMoia advised him.

"Me?"

LaMoia nodded and teased, "You're not in trouble, are you, Sarge? Your boys been putting cameras in the girls' locker room again?"

Had Hill found out about the wiretapping? Boldt felt the color drain from his face. Too much deceit to keep the lies straight. One day into it and he couldn't keep himself together!

"Maybe you ought'a sit down," LaMoia said.

"I'm fine," Boldt lied.

By design, task force books did not necessarily duplicate one another. The copy of LaMoia's was packed with evidence reports, SID workups, Daphne's psychology profiles and Boldt's Intelligence summaries. It contained the most recent SID forensics sweep of Anderson's apartment and a short write-up on the backup disks. With Anderson their only palpable victim, Boldt read carefully, his tired eyes working down each sheet. LaMoia's idea of organization differed from his; he found navigating the paperwork difficult.

Finally he reached the photocopies of the crime scene photographs, including two series from Anderson's apartment. He scrutinized these. On his third pass he grinned. He picked up the phone and dialed Gaynes.

A few minutes later, they met in the lobby, his paranoia forcing him to recognize that if he could so easily eavesdrop on others, the reverse was also true.

He walked her to a nearby restaurant caught up in happy hour. Dark wood, marble and polished brass, gleaming mirrors—suits, soft wools, spike heels, cigars. The noise level was deafening. Not a cop to be seen.

Bobbie did not turn heads, though if attitude had been looks, she would have silenced the place. He found a pair of stools in the corner looking out at an avenue crowded with buses. Her legs were a little too short to reach the stool's footrest.

"Since when do you buy me a drink, Sarge?" Gaynes was always out front with him. It was part of the reason for his enormous respect for her. "Especially at digs like this."

"Buying favors. Why else?"

"Why else indeed? Thing is, Sarge, you don't need to buy them. Know what I mean?"

"Depends on what they are."

"No, actually it doesn't," she said, waving the busy waitress over to them. She had an extraordinary presence, this one.

"Two things," Boldt said, keeping his voice to a level where it reached only her ears.

"Go," she said, studying him carefully. "You look like shit, by the way."

He hadn't changed clothes in forty-eight hours. "True story," he answered.

"Is it your wife?"

"You can sign off on Anderson's file," he said, not wanting any more of that.

"I had better be able to. I'm lead on Anderson," she reminded proudly.

"That's what I'm saying."

"Go."

"So you'll do that—you'll get the file back from LaMoia."

"Understood." A Scotch was delivered, neat. She sampled it and approved.

"You'll go through the SID crime scene photos. The more re-cent ones, not the March twenty group. Something is going to occur to you."

She placed down the Scotch, studied him and nodded grimly. "Go," she said, though less enthusiastically.

"You found Anderson's clothes on the bathroom floor, includ-ing shoes that were still tied. That was good work. In an abstract way we can match those clothes with those shoes. So, what are we missing when it comes to the clothes in the hamper?"

"Shoes."

"You're a peach, Bobbie, you know that?" He waited for her.

"I'm looking for shoes in the SID photos," she stated.

"Shoes or . . ."

"Boots," she answered.

"I want the lab report on those boots twenty-four hours before anyone else sees it."

Her eyes revealed her shock. Boldt did not make end runs.

"Sarge?"

He pulled out a five-dollar bill and placed it on the counter that fronted the window. Outside a homeless man was trolling for rush-hour philanthropy. He had a three-legged dog with mangy fur.

Gaynes took out her notebook and neatly wrote out several re-minders.

This time, she waited for him. "Sarge, whatever it is—and I don't to want to know, thank you very much—you're not alone, okay?"

His eyes stung with encroaching tears. If there was one thing he felt, it was alone. "Thanks," he said.

She drank the Scotch in two swigs and banged the glass down.

She cleared her throat, burned by the drink. Without looking at him, she added, "You need a shoulder, I'm here."

"What about Anderson's front door video? Any progress?"

"I'll be through it by tonight, promise."

"Didn't you say that last time?" He checked his own notes. "And the earwax?" he asked. "Anderson's earwax?"

"I put in the request with the Doc. He should a sent it over to SID."

"Follow it up," he instructed.

"Can I ask something?" she asked.

"No," he answered bluntly, surprising her. He tempered it by saying, "No, I'd rather you didn't."

He had hurt her. "Fine," she said, toying with the empty Scotch glass. She slipped off the stool. "I'll let you know what I find out."

"Bobbie!" he called out, wishing he'd handled her differently.

Some guy in red suspenders turned his head. He looked about twelve years old and was smoking an illegal cigar. "What?" he said. "I'm Bobby. What the hell you want?"

Boldt walked past him, too annoyed to think what to say.

Sheila Hill's office lacked any feminine touches. Cluttered with paperwork, newspapers and stacks of files, it nonetheless had an image of control. She motioned Boldt into one of the two straight-backed gunmetal gray chairs and clicked a shoe off unseen under her desk. "You mind?" she asked, lighting up a cigarette. It was illegal in a public building. "First things first," she said. "Anderson's computer. How we let the Feds get hold of it is beyond me. It's obvious we need to know whatever they know the minute they know it."

"I can try," Boldt said, thinking of Kalidja, "but it's not as if I have ears over there."

"Yeah? Well get some. Get a line on them—this is Need to Know, this is no bullshit."

"They sent it to Washington," Boldt reminded. "Bernie knows a couple civilians in the lab."

"Whatever it takes. Which brings me to my more important point."

He felt it coming: She knew about the wiretap and she was about to cut him off at the knees.

She stood and checked her door. She locked it. She took the smoke over to the window, sat down, turned toward Boldt and faced him with her stockinged feet up on the desk. She spoke unusually softly for her. "This goes no further than us." Boldt felt a chill up his spine. He was busted; he felt certain of it. "Okay. Are you with me?"

Boldt nodded tentatively. Hill had an imposing femininity about her. Sitting so close to her, Boldt felt drawn into her. Captivated.

"We're all thinking adoption ring at this point. Okay? So if we're right then there's some serious money in play. Market price for an illegal is anywhere from twenty to seventy thousand. White babies on the high side. That's a million bucks and counting."

Boldt wondered why Hill had waited to weigh in behind the adoption theory. Where was she leading?

"Plenty of spare change for a few favors." She met eyes with Boldt. "You see what I'm driving at?"

"Maybe I do," he said.

"You look at these reports, and you realize that in each and every city the Pied Piper blows town only days ahead of a major attempt to collar him. San Francisco. Portland. It's fairly obvious, isn't it?" she asked.

"Fairly," he answered.

"And *you*," she said strongly. "You're in the perfect position."

"Me?"

"Of course."

He had never understood the idea of a person's world collapsing in an instant—worlds took time to collapse—but all at once that was how he felt, as if the walls, furniture, the ceiling and floor began to suck in toward him, crushing air out of the room and him along with it. She knew! She had found out. Next came his confession about Sarah, and then what?

"Me?" he repeated, his voice breaking.

"Who else?" she asked, confirming she had thought long and hard about this. "It's your world, isn't it?"

"Yes," he let slip in a sad, quiet voice. She understood too much. His daughter was his world. He and Liz had taken a bath with Sarah not two months ago, her little feet frantic in the water—a different world now for everyone.

"You're positioned so perfectly. Who would think?"

He felt true hatred. "Who would think?" he repeated.

"Are you with me on this? Do you feel all right? You're looking awfully pale, Lou."

How should I feel? he wanted to say. "With you."

"Who else? Not Mulwright. Not John. They're too close to the center."

"You see, I differ there," Boldt objected. "The closer to the center the better, if it was me."

"Forest for the trees, in my opinion. I thought about Matthews, and maybe she becomes part of this—"

"She's *not* involved," Boldt interrupted strongly.

"But she *could* be. If you wanted her to be, she could be. In some ways she's perfect for this."

"I've barely spoken to her in the past few days," he protested. *But I tapped her phone! And yours . . . and LaMoia's!*

"But if you wanted her to, she could help you on something like this."

A high-voltage spike struck him; his fingers tingled. He had misconstrued everything she had said. "Captain . . . ," he began. "Sheila . . . what the hell are we talking about here? Me? Matthews?"

"I'm thinking it's a reporter. You know: exclusive rights for a little cooperation. Book deal. TV movie. It happens," she added with a strong twinge of regret.

"Are we talking the same thing?"

"A hundred grand? Two hundred?" she added quickly. "I'm thinking a reporter is buying inside stuff and supplying it back to the Pied Piper in exchange for exclusive rights. One of the tabloids."

Boldt took a long deep swallow. "Just to clarify," Boldt said dryly, "you're asking *me* to flush out an insider?"

She cautioned, "One of the Feds would make the most sense. Hell of a source. A little cash under the table. Happens all the time."

"You want *me* to flush the insider?" He felt giddy, he nearly laughed aloud at the irony: She was asking him to trap himself.

She said, "Yes. How else has this person gone undetected for so long? Inside information. Has to be."

"We sting the Feds with disinformation," Boldt proposed, "and see who surfaces."

"Whatever you can come up with." Unknowingly, Sheila Hill had just provided him the justification for the wiretaps he had ordered.

He would need to go through with something—no matter how poorly conceived—to placate her. Maybe use Daphne, maybe not.

"I think you're onto something, Captain. It makes sense."

"You're damn right it does. We get this insider out of play—we keep our efforts from being sabotaged—and we just might collar the Pied Piper."

"Right," Boldt agreed. It was all he could think of.

CHAPTER

27

Boldt parked outside the Shotz house shortly after 8:00 P.M. that same Thursday. The warm evening air carried the scent of a budding earth—rich, black, wet soil pushing up life after months of sponging up the sky's discharge. Boldt recalled an early winter evening when just he and Sarah had been home. He had put a Scott Hamilton CD on the stereo, a cup of hot tea on the table and little Sarah warmly into his lap. Flipping pages of *The Lovables*—he remembered the book so clearly—he had been pointing out the pictures to her when suddenly she had wheeled her head around and up and had met eyes with him, her father, so absolute a connection, so strong, this little person making contact, real contact with him, and then the long, sustained smile, gradually forming and then occupying her entire face, and an overwhelming sense of love choking his heart, filling his throat and unleashing from his eyes. Father crying, baby smiling, the book slipping to the floor, its pages slowly shutting.

Daphne's red Honda arrived a few minutes later, and she joined him in the front seat of the Chevy. She smelled of lilac and her face carried worry poorly. For a moment they sat in silence, and he knew she was mad at him for not explaining his moving Miles out of the city. But there wasn't any explaining to do; he wasn't going to start now. He had dug himself in too deeply.

"I've had time to go over the files, found some interesting coincidences." Everyone, including Daphne, knew he abhorred the word. "Take a look at these," he said, handing her a stack of lab prelims from the task force book. She would not question his being in possession of these. Boldt worked evidence—it was his lot.

"The parents' statements," she observed, reading.

"One is Shotz," he explained. "The other is taken from a report the Bureau provided. It's Portland . . . the Portland kidnapping."

"You want me to read these?" she said impatiently.

"Skim is okay."

"Portland is in interview form," she noted.

"All right. Here!" he said, pointing, ". . . swaddled in a receiving blanket at the time of the abduction. The mother calls it a 'custom' blanket."

"All mothers think that," Daphne said.

"No, no, no! She calls it a *custom* blanket. No one asks anything more. Here!" he said, rearranging the pages. "Doris Shotz says her baby was wearing 'an outfit with her picture on it.' Her words."

"Custom," Daphne said, following his logic.

"Custom," he agreed.

"Weinstein?"

"No mention I can find. No reference. But that's why we're here," he informed her. "Doris Shotz is organized. She'll know what we're after."

"And me? What's my role in this?"

"Downplay it. I don't want it going to the press. I need this to be a conversation, not an interrogation. She's a wreck."

"You don't look so swift yourself. You setting a record on that shirt or what?"

"He picks his victims somehow."

"Custom blanket?"

"Why not?"

"Just asking." She informed him, "The Bureau is pursuing magazine subscriptions and catalogs. It came up in the four o'clock."

"No kidding," Boldt said, hoping to sound surprised.

She knew him too well. "I won't ask," she said. "I promised not to ask. But I sure as hell hope you know what you're doing."

"Me too."

Doris Shotz answered the door with her three-year-old son clutched in her arms. Boldt had seen her only a few hours earlier outside Davidson's office and knew of her vigils over the past two weeks. In an environment that could and did cast humor onto any subject no matter how grim, Boldt did not know of a single joke that had been voiced about Doris Shotz. Each day she returned, unwilling to give up on her daughter. She was admired by captain and patrol officer alike.

A woman in her thirties, she had the look of an old lady on her deathbed, wan and thin. She admitted Boldt and Daphne, but they were not welcome. Doris Shotz had quickly developed a deep-seated hatred for the police.

The kitchen table held two empty place mats from an earlier dinner. Shotz never let go of her boy while preparing coffee and tea, even though she looked as if she might snap under the weight. Boldt and Daphne took tea. Paul Shotz poured himself a cup of coffee laced with rum, despite his wife's protests. He had the unfocused glass eyes of a taxidermied rat. He had shaved carelessly, a day or two gone by, lending him a worn and beleaguered look. His shirt had been slept in, on the living room couch if Boldt had it right. Sitting at the table with them, Paul Shotz stared beyond Boldt—right through him—so that the detective had the feeling that someone was standing right behind him.

"What is it you want?" Doris Shotz asked impolitely. Two weeks earlier she would have done anything to help; but now she had little room left for hope. The Pied Piper claimed far more lives than just the children he abducted.

Daphne said, "We're making headway—real headway—in the case, Mrs. Shotz. Police work is about fitting pieces together.

We're here in search of more of those. We need to seize chances when they arise. That's why we're here. Some of what we'd like to discuss has been brought up before, perhaps so many times that you're sick of it, that you think we already have the answers. If we did, we wouldn't be here. What we need to do, all of us," she said, including the dazed husband, "is do our best to imagine that none of this has been discussed before. Erase the slate. Allow things to rise to the surface through the grief and pain of your loss. We all want Rhonda back home. As much hostility and anger as you feel toward us, it's important you believe that, trust that, because it is the truth: We're in this together." She shot Boldt a look—this last statement aimed at him.

Losing her patience, Doris Shotz said, "We have been over all of it a dozen times. You take notes. Don't you read them?"

"What happens," Boldt informed her, "is that answers change."

"Shock affects memory," Daphne said. "You think you've told us something because it's so clear in your mind, but in fact it never made it into words. The mind can play tricks. It's the same with us: We can be so caught up in pursuing one line of evidence that we hear, but don't process, an important fact. When that resurfaces—if it ever does—the entire investigation may change." She added, "In just a little over three weeks, Mrs. Shotz, we've made significant progress. We came here to listen. Help us, please. Help us find Rhonda."

"Rhonda," the intoxicated husband mumbled. "You never even met her." He looked at all three of them as a silence fell between them.

The wife took in the husband as if tolerating an unwelcome stranger. She looked back at Daphne with despair in her eyes. "We'll try," she said.

Boldt explained, "The report filed with our department lists a missing receiving blanket. Her 'Rhonda blanket,' you called it."

"Her Rhonda blanket," the woman echoed. "Yes."

Daphne glanced to Boldt signaling that she wanted to lead. Boldt gave a slight nod.

"Can you describe the item for us?" Daphne asked. "Was it personalized in some way?"

"I did this already . . . I'm sure I told you," Doris Shotz complained.

"It's not the point, Doris," the husband admonished drunkenly. "You're so damn concerned about who's to blame here." He tapped the coffee cup against the table rhythmically. "It's not their fault. It's not mine. It's not yours. It just happened. They took her."

"Things like this don't just happen! If we hadn't taken that dinner train . . . "

"Oh, bullshit!" the husband roared. "What? We would have been back here an hour sooner. So what? She still would have been gone, Doro. They took her. They took our baby—" He sniffled. His rheumy eyes spilled tears. He stood and poured himself another rum, the coffee abandoned as unnecessary.

"We might have misplaced the description," Daphne allowed, hoping to avoid a domestic battle.

"It had her picture on it," Doris Shotz explained.

"Gail, wasn't it?" the husband asked, returning to the table with his mug full of rum.

"Paul's sister gave it to us."

"A gift?" Daphne nudged. She needed the woman to stay focused.

Boldt withdrew his notepad, trying not to attract attention to it. Most people were intimidated by their words being written down.

"It was cute," the woman explained. She scratched absentmindedly at the table.

"We sent out a photo with our announcements," the husband explained. "Gail found some place that silk-screened the photo onto the baby blanket. It was a really good job. Doro used it all the time."

"Silk-screened," Boldt repeated.

"Digitally enhanced," said the computer repairman. "Nice color, good resolution." He rocked the bottom edge of the mug in circles against the table.

The mother said mournfully, "It was adorable."

"She was wrapped in it that night?" Boldt asked cautiously.

The woman lifted her eyes to meet Boldt's, and he saw in there a building uncertainty. "It was missing. I assumed I had her in it."

Trying to keep the excitement out of her voice, Daphne asked, "But now?"

"It's definitely missing," the drunken man replied.

Doris Shotz shook her head slowly side to side. She glanced back to Boldt. "This is important, isn't it?"

"It's all important to us." He didn't want to fuel her hope unfairly, but they needed her attention focused on the blanket.

She said, "A drawer was found open." Adding, "It wasn't us. Julie maybe—the sitter."

Boldt nodded. He had read about the drawer in the report. It was what had focused him onto the possessions of the victims. He wrote into his notebook: *the sitter?*

Boldt said to the husband, "If you could provide a way for us to reach your sister?"

"Sure." He motioned for Boldt's pen and paper. His handwriting was more of a scrawl.

Boldt thanked him.

Doris Shotz said out of her silence, "It was a cute name. On the label. Mirror Image? I don't remember. Something cute. Does that help?"

Boldt took this down.

Daphne reached over and touched Doris Shotz's nervous hand. "Can you get a picture in your head of that label?"

She squinted. "No, not the label. The blanket, sure."

"But not the label?"

"No."

Boldt's sense of time had been destroyed by Sarah's abduction—everything took too long. His patience frayed. He spoke somewhat harshly to the husband. "Tell me about the dinner train again . . . who knew you'd be on that train?"

"It was supposed to be a surprise," he said, eyeing his wife. "We've been over this."

"You booked it yourself," Boldt stated.

"Yeah. There's a number you call. All there is to it. Pick up the tickets when you get there."

"You must have guaranteed them. What? A credit card?"

"Sure." The man repeated, "All there is to it."

"And you don't remember telling anyone at all—at work, a neighbor, a best friend? Maybe a friend recommended the train and you mentioned to him that you had booked an evening?"

The man ran his hand through his oily hair. "No, that isn't true. I didn't tell nobody—*anybody*," he corrected.

"Do you have the credit card statement?" Boldt asked.

The man looked a little fuzzy.

"Think, honey," Doris Shotz pleaded.

He screwed his face into a knot. "I probably got it, yeah, I suppose. I booked it ahead of time, you know." He reached out for his wife's hand, but she pulled hers away.

"Get it for them," the wife demanded.

"I can't."

"I'd appreciate the statements from the last three months for any credit cards you have," Boldt clarified. The husband looked crestfallen.

The wife remembered something then. She said, "We turned all that over to the other people—the FBI."

"All your finances," Boldt said, perfectly calmly. Inside, he boiled.

"The girl," her husband said, "the one with the accent. She took our bank statements, credit card stuff, everything."

Kay Kalidja, Boldt realized.

Before they left, Daphne and Boldt visited the child's nursery. He stepped into the room knowing full well what it was like to live with such emptiness. He had spent the night in Sarah's room, rocking in the rocking chair, staring into darkness, hating himself. He absorbed as much of the environment as he could, a new eye to the crime scene. The carpet was marked in three places where chips of automobile glass had been found. The glass connected the crimes to a single assailant, reminding Boldt of its importance. The dresser and the windowsills were clouded with fingerprint dust. Stuffed animals; children's books on a hand-painted bookshelf; a musical mobile of pandas with red and yellow feet; a changing table.

He visualized the Pied Piper entering the room and heading straight to the crib. Knowing what he was after. Boldt turned toward the dresser: The Pied Piper had taken time to search the dresser. Why? Did he need a change of outfits for the child? Or was he worried about leaving evidence behind? Had that silk-screened blanket been wrapped around the child, or had it been in the drawer that still remained open?

Blanket in hand, or not, he turns toward the crib. He needs to disguise or conceal the child before abducting her. He wraps her in a second blanket? He places her in a bag or toolbox?

The open drawer continued to tug at Boldt. The missing blanket had to be significant.

Daphne reminded, "He's an organized personality. If he took that particular blanket there's a reason."

"Mrs. Shotz!" he called out. The woman stopped at the door to the room, unable to enter. Her eyes welled with tears and she crossed her arms tightly as if to ward off the cold.

"You do the laundry?"

"Paul doesn't, I can tell you that."

"How many receiving blankets do you own?" he asked. Boldt did the laundry in his house. He grilled the meat, washed dishes and was much better with an iron than Liz. She paid for the housecleaner and they split Marina's check. Liz did their book-keeping, cooked most of the meals—all of the vegetables—and answered the mail and phone calls. He wanted his life back.

Liz had nine bras, two that she wore more often than the others. He knew the outfits that Miles wore by heart. They had eleven burp rags and seven receiving blankets—*enchiladas*, Boldt called them, because that was how they looked as infants, swaddled tightly before sleep.

"Four," she said, without the slightest hesitation. Boldt trusted the number.

"And how many are here?" he asked.

She looked at him, her face drained of expression. Fear stole into her eyes. "I never counted."

"No reason to," Daphne encouraged.

"Count them now, please," Boldt said.

Doris Shotz headed for the drawer that had been left partially open. Exactly what Boldt had hoped for: That drawer held the blankets. She corrected herself immediately, "Four, other than the new one, the one with the picture."

"I understand," Boldt said. "Five total then."

"I don't machine wash the one with Ronnie's picture. I hand wash it."

"Fine."

She rummaged through the drawer, glanced back sharply at Boldt and then started over, checking for a second time. "I don't know why I didn't think to count," she said, distracted by her own guilty feelings. She went through the drawer a third time.

"Only three?" Boldt asked.

The woman hurried from the room. A moment later she returned, several shades paler. "Not in the wash," she mumbled.

"How many?" Boldt asked her again.

"Three," she answered. "But how did you know two would be missing?"

Ten minutes later Daphne and Boldt stood by the Chevy. Her eyes sparkled with excitement.

"What about the credit cards? What was that about?" she asked.

"We all buy tickets, we book travel, we charge our meals, our shopping, all on credit cards. If there are any patterns to our lives, the two places they show up are our checkbooks and our credit cards."

"But Trish Weinstein was at the supermarket at the time of abduction," she protested.

"Frequent flyer miles. People charge groceries to credit cards now. Liz does it sometimes."

"Jesus," she muttered.

"The Bureau gave it away without meaning to. They've locked

us out of the credit histories on the earlier victims. We've been asking for them for weeks. Why hog them all to themselves unless they've spotted a pattern?"

"And the blanket?"

"We got lucky," he said modestly. "No one picked up the pattern."

"Next?"

"We contact Portland and see if the custom outfit mentioned in that interview had a silk-screened photo on it."

"We need the name of that company—the silk screens," she said.

Boldt nodded. "Might be the link we've been missing." He moved toward the driver's door.

"We're not done here," she stated.

"We have to move on this."

"Look over my shoulder," she instructed. "I'll bet you a month's salary she's watching us from the window."

Boldt did as he was told. "Are you showing off?"

"Of course I am. Did you notice the way she kept repositioning her little boy?"

"He's a heavy little boy." After a dismissive look from her, he said, "Okay. What'd I miss?"

"Only an eyewitness," she said.

Boldt opened the car door and retrieved the thick task force book. He sifted through the contents until reaching the Shotz file, mumbling, "Baby sitter . . . mother and father . . . neighbor . . . real estate agent . . . neighbor . . . neighbor—"

She interrupted. "John and I did the parents together. Spent a long time. We never spoke one word to little Henry."

"Little Henry was there."

"Little Henry is three, keep in mind."

"Miles is four. I know three very well, thank you," Boldt said.

"Too young for a witness?"

"Maybe for a courtroom, but not for me. I broke a lamp of Liz's last year—she'd had it since college. I swept it up and threw it out, and thought I would wait for a good time to tell her. You know," he explained sheepishly, "there are good times and bad times for that sort of thing. Well, Miles beat me to it. He reported the entire incident, point by point, the minute she got home. Three years old. He not only remembered everything I'd done but articulated it. Three years old? I'll take a three-year-old witness. Bring him on." He asked, "Can you deliver little Henry?"

"Not if Mama has anything to say about it. I'd bet anything that Doris knows Henry saw something. Ironically, no matter how much she wants Rhonda back, she can't bring herself to involve Henry. One child lost, one child left. She won't do anything to jeopardize that. The guilt we're seeing all over her face has more to do with her withholding Henry from us than with her being on that dinner train."

"Then why did you let me leave?"

"Because she needed to see us out here in a discussion. She needs to lose some of that protective confidence before we stand a chance with her. Henry can help Rhonda. The mother in Doris knows that. But she waited too long to tell us, she vented too much anger on us to come creeping back. But now that anger has turned inward. She has dug herself a hole.

"I can offer her a way out," she continued, "but it will only take if she accepts responsibility for her past actions. Oddly, the way I get her there is fear. Her imagination can make this worse than we will. We need to let that stew."

Boldt rocked his wrist as if checking his watch. "Yeah? Well, if she won't talk, I'll hold her in contempt for obstruction of justice and drag her downtown." He started walking toward the house, the task force book still in hand.

"Since when did you become cop, judge and juror?" Daphne asked, requiring a half run to keep up with him.

"Shit happens," he said on the fly.

She stopped abruptly as if slapped, and then hurried to catch back up to him. "Since when do you swear?"

"Same answer." He reached the front door and knocked more loudly than necessary.

"Lou," she said, grabbing his upper arm forcibly, "I'm serious. This isn't you."

"So am I. Yes it is. This is me, the new me. Take it or leave it."

"Leave it!" she said. "What's going on?" She still held him.

"I said no questions," he whispered dryly. "Remember?"

She released her hold on him. "Let me do the talking," she demanded. "This one has special handling written all over it. She needs force, but a special kind of force." They locked eyes. His were sunken and darkly colored. "Please," she begged.

Footsteps approached.

Her eyes held him, unrelenting. She, of all people, knew this man; and yet she didn't know him.

"If that kid, if that woman," he said angrily, "has kept something from us . . ." He didn't complete the statement. He said only, "Lives are at stake here!" The front door swung open.

Doris Shotz answered, a mask of concern and caution. Daphne's attention remained fixed on Boldt. The woman at the door said, "I've had about enough for one day—"

"We need to talk," Daphne interrupted her, still facing Boldt. "Now," she said strongly, snapping her head toward the woman and pushing her way past and inside. "We need to talk with Henry," Daphne completed.

"No! You cannot—"

"Yes, we can," Boldt corrected, cutting her off and silencing her. He and Doris Shotz met eyes, and she cowered under his haunted look.

"Where is he?" Daphne asked once the three of them were inside the living room and Doris Shotz realized they meant business.

"You can't do this."

Boldt responded, "You'd prefer attorneys and the press?"

"Your son was never interviewed as a witness," Daphne stated. The immediate tension in the mother's eyes confirmed Daphne had guessed correctly. "We understand your reluctance to involve him in—"

"He is three years old!" the mother objected. "How could he possibly help?"

"We also understand how important it is to you that we make every effort to locate Rhonda just as soon as we can."

If there had been any tears left for Doris Shotz, she might have spilled them, but her well was dry. She shook her head, holding on to what little protest remained in her.

"Let us talk to Henry. Help us find Rhonda, *please*," Daphne urged.

"He bit the man," the mother confessed, her chin wobbling. "I know I should have told you. Downtown . . . sitting there, just sitting there . . . I knew I should tell someone."

Boldt glanced over at Daphne; he wanted the interview *now*.

"Please," Daphne repeated.

"In our bedroom," the mother replied.

Down a narrow hall, she showed them into a cluttered bedroom. The boy had a set of blocks out on the floor, reminding Boldt of Miles, and in turn making him think of Sarah.

"Honey," the mother said, "these people are going to help us find Ronnie. They want to talk to you. I told them they could. Okay?"

The boy averted his eyes shyly, down at the toes of his Air Nikes.

Boldt said, "I understand Henry is quite the hero."

"A brave little boy," Daphne agreed. "We're just going to ask you some questions. Okay?"

The boy checked again with his mother, who sat down on the floor and took the boy in her arms from behind so the child faced Boldt and Daphne. Daphne signaled Boldt to lose some altitude. He joined her on the floor so he no longer towered over the boy. "Please, honey? We like these people. They want to help Ronnie." She prompted, "You bit the man, didn't you?" The boy nodded.

"On the leg?" Daphne asked.

The boy shook his head no. Henry had several of his teeth and a small scar on his chin. His s's whistled when he spoke.

The mother said, "Would you tell me again about what happened when the man came for Ronnie?" The child vigorously shook his head no. The mother encouraged, "You heard them in the kitchen."

"Me hearded Ronnie crying. Me shout for Julie."

"The baby sitter," Daphne said.

Henry nodded.

"And when she didn't answer, did that scare you?"

He nodded again. He was a cute boy with a round face and his mother's large blue eyes.

"And then what happened?" Daphne asked.

"Me go into kitchen."

"*Went* into the kitchen," the mother corrected. Boldt shot her a hot look. No time for home schooling.

"What did you see in the kitchen?" Daphne inquired.

The boy grew restless in his mother's arms. His voice was excited. "Julie asleep on the floor. The man with a bag. Ronnie crying."

"Did you see *him?*" Boldt asked. "The man carrying the bag?"

"Julie sleeping on the floor." He looked frightened all of a sudden.

Daphne signaled Boldt off with her eyes.

"What did you do then?" Daphne asked.

His voice sped up with his description. "Me pulled on his arm. He kicked me. Me screamed." He hung his head.

"You tried to help Ronnie, didn't you?"

"I bit him," Henry said, proudly.

"Yes," Daphne returned quickly. "On the leg . . . on the—"

"His arm," Henry interrupted.

Boldt restrained himself from interrupting, his heart racing painfully.

Without prompting, the boy continued, "Me bit him and I fell down and hit my head and it hurt." He rubbed the back of his head. "There was a bump, wasn't there, Mommy?"

"There sure was." Doris Shotz grimaced. She didn't want to relive any of this.

"It hurt!" the boy declared, still rubbing his head.

"I bet you hurt him more," Boldt said.

"He bleeded."

He smiled up at Boldt. All the innocence of the world was in that smile. What powers ultimately corrupted such innocence? he wondered. How was it so quickly lost? Because of the Pied Pipers of this world, he realized. Because detectives asked painful questions.

"I bit him on the birdie," the boy blurted. Doris Shotz was as surprised to hear this as Boldt and Matthews.

"A birdie?" Boldt asked. "On his arm?" The boy nodded. "A drawing?" Another nod.

A tattoo was as good as a fingerprint with a jury, and juries loved child witnesses.

"What kind of birdie? Do you remember?" Boldt asked.

Daphne let him go. Boldt had opened up the tattoo information.

"Like on TV."

Boldt was on pins and needles. He needed a detailed description of the tattoo, and the chances of that from a three-year-old were slim.

"Big Bird?" Boldt asked.

"No, the *real* bird," the boy replied, confirming he knew the difference.

"Is the bird on a show?" Daphne asked.

He shook his head no.

"A commercial?"

He half nodded, half shrugged his shoulders in puzzlement.

"Which commercial would that be?" she asked.

Henry offered Daphne a silly expression and said, "The one with the bird in it!" He giggled.

Daphne maintained her composure, but Boldt barked out spontaneous laughter.

Henry said, "Big bird flying over the river."

"An airplane?" Daphne asked.

"A bird!" the child repeated. "We deliver, we deliver!"

"The post office!" the mother said.

"An eagle," Boldt announced.

Henry turned toward him and nodded vigorously. "An eagle!" he repeated.

Daphne was not pleased with Boldt, and her eyes told him so. He had fed the witness an answer. In the process of answering questions a witness reached a heightened state of wanting to please. Especially children. That desire, combined with the frustration of a blocked or vacant memory, would often jump at the first offering, even if it meant answering erroneously. Boldt had planted a word in the boy's head to go along with whatever image lingered. No matter what the bird looked like, the word eagle would now be used.

"Where was this bird on his arm?" Daphne asked, avoiding mention of the species.

Henry Shotz pointed to the top of his forearm.

Boldt said, "If a friend of ours sketched the bird, drew the bird, do you think you might recognize it?"

The boy shrugged.

The mother said, "Henry loves picture books." The boy nodded agreement.

Boldt wanted a sketch artist with the child in a hurry.

"So what happened after you bit him?" Daphne asked, adding to her notes.

"The man ran out. I gone to Julie, but she was sleeping."

They repeated the line of questions a second time and got the same answers, a detective's dream. Boldt took more detailed notes the second pass. They left at 9:07 P.M. Boldt made note of this as well. Daphne was watching him, expecting this of him. Illusion was everything.

On their way back to their cars, Boldt stopped Daphne and told her he would take care of arranging a sketch artist. If they got a decent sketch, he'd pass it on to LaMoia to present to the task force. Daphne accepted this—as staff psychologist she had no part in evidence collection. But it was her role to assist in artist rendition sessions where the subject's state of mind was critical.

She mentioned her participation as if pro forma. "You'll let me know time and place," she said. "I have a ten o'clock tomorrow, so anytime after eleven will work. I'd suggest the sketch be done here, by the way. A three-year-old doesn't need any additional stimulus. Environment is everything."

"Good," Boldt said. "I got all that." He thanked her and they said good night and he walked to his car. He would arrange the interview for ten the following morning. He would use Tommy Thompson, whose studios were on Vashon Island. And if anything came of the session, no one would hear about it but him.

Thompson was perfect: retired and reclusive. No one would ever know.

Boldt approached the Weinsteins' front door alone, painfully aware that the Pied Piper had walked these same steps posing as a delivery man. The eerie sensation he experienced had to do with retracing the kidnapper's steps, with picturing his two victims: Phyllis Weinstein, and her grandson, Hayes.

"It's nine-thirty, Detective!" Sidney Weinstein objected. Dressed in a ratty cardigan, a wrinkled white button-down shirt and a pair of khakis that fit too loosely, Weinstein smelled of brandy.

"It's Lieutenant," Boldt corrected. "Crime waits for no man," he said.

"My hearing has been delayed while I undergo 'psychiatric treatment,' " he said, distastefully drawing the quotes. "Careful. I might shoot you. I suggest you leave."

"I need to talk to you and your wife."

"My attorney might have something to say about that. Are you part of my son's investigation or mine?" He smirked. "Wonderful world, isn't it?"

The question put Boldt in a difficult position that, if answered directly, required he misrepresent himself. His only association with the task force, other than as an adviser, was a covert assignment to flush out an informer. His visit to Weinstein was difficult if not impossible to justify if Weinstein made a production of it and brought in his attorney. Trish Weinstein appeared behind her husband. She looked dazed and exhausted.

Boldt spoke over Weinstein's shoulder to the man's wife as if absolutely certain of what he was saying. "Hayes had a blanket, a shirt, an outfit—I don't know which—that carried a photo silk-screened image of him." He spotted the hit of recognition in her eyes. "You know what I'm talking about."

The husband stepped back and regarded his wife and then

Boldt with suspicion and confusion. "Don't listen to him," he said. "They want to put me away, Trish."

"No one is even thinking of putting you away, and you know it. Your attorney has certainly told you that much. You stole an officer's sidearm. There is more paperwork involved in that one action, more internal reviews, than you can imagine. It will take us weeks, possibly months, to sort it all out. That is why your hearing has been delayed, that and because no one wants to see you face any charges, and that's not an easy thing to swing when a person has stolen an officer's sidearm and trained it onto half the fifth floor. You see a psychiatrist or a psychologist a couple times; we do our paperwork; a lenient judge gets assigned your case, and it's all over. In your position, any of us might have done the same thing." Smiling oddly, he emphasized, "*Any* of us!" knowing it was true.

Having silenced Weinstein, Boldt returned to the woman. "You know the item I'm talking about."

She allowed a faint nod.

"Is it here? Is it still here, or did it go missing the night of the kidnapping?"

She shook her head. She didn't know.

"You can't come barging in here!" the husband protested.

"No," Boldt agreed. Looking at the wife, he said, "Without a warrant, I have to be invited."

"Come in," the woman said, her voice trancelike.

"What?" Weinstein shouted in protest.

To her husband she said, "He knows what clothes Hayes owns. How could he know such a thing unless it's important? He's here to help us get our child back, Sidney. Are you going to prevent that?"

Sidney Weinstein stepped clear of the door. "Come in," he said to Boldt, motioning him inside.

"It might have been in the wash at the time," Trish Weinstein explained minutes later, rummaging through drawers. "I can't say for sure."

"But to your knowledge, the drawers, the closets weren't searched?"

"Your people were all over this place," Sidney Weinstein reminded. "They went through everything. Everything was searched," he emphasized. "How can we know who went through what? A drawer here, a closet there. What's to see?"

"Here!" the wife said, hoisting a small outfit from the third drawer. She looked at it, drew away and dropped it to the floor, her open hands raised to cover her face and hide her tears.

"See?" Weinstein barked. "See what you do to her?"

Boldt picked up the garment. It was a baby's onesie with three snaps at the crotch. On the chest was a square color photograph of the baby, slightly faded from washing; the mother had chosen this garment often for her child. The baby's face was adorable, reminding Boldt once again of an infant's profound innocence. Of Sarah.

Boldt checked for the label. There was none. It clearly had been cut out. He questioned Trish about this, and she nodded. "I snip all the labels. They're so big these days with all the washing instructions. They're horrible."

"You cut it out yourself," Boldt said, disappointed.

"I do it to everything. I hate those labels."

"And the company's name?" he asked, hoisting the garment.

She shook her head, reflecting. "Mirror Image . . . Double Image . . . something like that."

"A gift?" Boldt asked.

"Yes," Trish replied. "We sent out photos—that photo—to our close friends and all our family."

"One of them gave us the outfit," Weinstein said.

"Do you remember who?" Boldt asked.

"No chance," Weinstein replied.

Boldt focused on Trish.

The wife said, "No. Neither do I."

Boldt felt the failure weigh down his fatigue; he hadn't slept in two days. Investigations could drag out forever and never be cleared. Perhaps in this case it was a good thing, he thought. It was one case he didn't want solved. He just needed to make sure no one else could solve it either.

"But I don't have to," Trish Weinstein continued, coming more alive. "I kept a thank you book, a diary of all the gifts. It's got to be in there."

Moments later, she was busy flipping pages in a hand-bound diary with a Florentine cover. "Daniel!" she said, looking up at her husband.

"My cousin Danny," the husband told Boldt. "Wouldn't you know it! You get Danny on the phone, you never get off."

Daniel Weinstein lived in Cambridge, Massachusetts, where he managed a chain bookstore. He spoke to Boldt on the phone for over ten minutes, the upshot of which was a few bursts of hard information. He'd placed the order for the custom garment over the Internet. He remembered this distinctly, because he had scanned the baby's photo and sent it electronically. He did not remember the company's name, did not remember how he had found the company on the Internet, and promised to go back on-line and try to find it again. "It was over six months ago," he complained. "I surf every night, two or three hours a night. I bookmark about one out of every hundred sites I visit. I did not bookmark a baby clothes retailer, I promise you that."

"But you paid for the garment," Boldt suggested.

After a pause the man agreed, saying, "I guess that's why you're the detective." He laughed nervously.

"By credit card?"

"Of course. Would have to be. I buy all sorts of shit off the net. All by plastic."

"Then it would be on a statement," Boldt informed him. "And that statement would be a great deal of help to me and your nephew."

"I'm all over that."

Boldt gave him his direct fax number and reiterated the importance of the information. He added, "If you find it on the Internet, I'd appreciate that address."

"Hey, give me a good excuse and I'll spend all night on-line."

"You want motivation?" Boldt asked. "A dozen children like Hayes, Mr. Weinstein. There's your motivation."

"Hell," the concerned man replied, "I'm not really sleeping anyway. Not since the kidnapping. . . . You tell Sid and Trish I'm all over this. My VISA statement's in your hands by midnight. If that site still exists, I'll have it by tomorrow morning." He added, "Just tell me one thing."

"What's that?"

"Did I do something wrong here? Did I set up my own cousin?"

"We don't know. But you've done nothing wrong."

" 'Cause you'll forgive me, Lieutenant, but if some schmo used me to get at that child, my cousin's child . . . I know there're laws against this shit, and it may be your job to enforce them, but that guy's a dead man. That guy is dead."

Boldt stayed on the line, trying his best to bite his tongue, to keep from saying what a cop could not say, but what a father had to. He saw Sarah swing her face toward the camera in anguish, heard her shrill plea for help. The only help he could give her went against twenty-four years of experience and violated every friendship he had built over that time. "Yeah, I know what you mean," Boldt said. Before cradling the phone, he added, "I'm all over that."

He swayed with the rocking of the ferry, wind tossing his hair, his eyes unfocused and distant. He processed information as quickly as he could conceive it, working more vigorously than behind his desk.

The artist's rendition of an eagle, its wings wrapped like a robe around itself, traveled with Boldt back to Seattle.

There was no one better than Thompson: The eagle tattoo looked alive on the page. That a three-year-old had guided Thompson's hand was something that would go unsaid as long as Boldt could manage. The tattoo itself would go undiscussed and unpublished. Boldt was studying it when Daphne entered his office uninvited. He covered it quickly, not wanting her or anyone to see.

"You're avoiding me," she complained. She looked flushed and awake, from another world than his.

"Nonsense." Boldt adjusted himself in his chair, prepared for the deceit of a lifetime. Daphne Matthews knew him intimately; she was not someone to whom he could easily lie. "We're both very busy," he said. As a cop he had learned when and how to stretch the truth, but outright lying came from a different, more central place inside oneself, and he found it repugnant.

He did not offer her a cup of tea as was their custom, knowing that would send its own signal. He wanted her out of here. He was, at that moment, expecting Gaynes, who had called to tell him that the SID lab had completed several tests including the analysis of the mud from Anderson's boots. The results were being sent upstairs to the fifth floor for her signature. She, in turn, planned to run the results up to Boldt before showing them to anyone else. He did not know if Daphne would pick up on this or not, but Gaynes had no business reporting to him, and it seemed quite possible to him that Daphne might make that connection. He needed her gone.

"You took him to Tommy Thompson without telling me," she said irritably.

"Tommy only had the morning open," Boldt explained. "You were busy."

CHAPTER

28

The session with sketch artist Tommy Thompson occupied all of Boldt's Friday morning and the early hours of his afternoon. He, Doris and little Henry Shotz rode the ferry across the undulating olive skin of the sound, pursued by the white flights and cries of seagulls as the city's skyline receded until it nearly joined the horizon. The sea air was alive with pine and cedar. A few pleasure craft split the green marble along the shores, etching a gray wake. Sight of the boats reminded him of Hill's theory about the Pied Piper moving between coastal cities by vessel, that this might explain the kidnapper's ability to avoid roadblocks and dragnets in San Francisco and Portland. Within fifteen minutes of their departure, Boldt's mind was too preoccupied to remember he had missed placing a phone call to Liz and another to Miles, had forgotten to leave Marina her check, had failed to give Hill an update, and had not shaved.

But he was not too preoccupied to remember bathing his daughter in the bathtub and the small rubber sailboat that would cause her to giggle and splash. He looked out on the water, and it was this red rubber boat he saw, not the ketch running downwind, its spinnaker full.

"The man paints seagull art for curio shops and you're telling me he was too busy?"

"I can't dictate the schedule to him," Boldt complained. "It's a freebie for him."

"Which begs the question: Why didn't you use one of the in-house artists? Why go all the way over to Vashon?"

"He's the best there is. Tommy's the best."

She had yet to sit down, in part because he had not asked her to, and so she stood, arms crossed indignantly, her high breasts cradled tightly. She wasn't buying this. Boldt had a problem. She drew in a long, deep breath and exhaled slowly in an effort to settle down. "Do you want to talk?"

"I want to find Rhonda Shotz and the Weinstein boy. I want to stop another kidnapping from happening."

"How did the sketch come out? Thompson's sketch?"

"Worthless," Boldt answered, consumed in the lie. She was his closest female friend outside of his wife. Lying to her was the worst and yet it came so easily.

"Tommy said a five- or six-year-old might have worked out. Henry lacked both the patience and the vocabulary."

"And we got to him too late," she said, taken in. "Three-year-olds are not long on visual memory."

In point of fact, Henry Shotz had done a brilliant job.

"I'd just as soon the tattoo not be mentioned at the four o'clock."

She tensed. "But why not?"

"Doris Shotz. I promised her—"

"I remember."

"The press will crush her."

"They might not be told."

"Then Mulwright will crush her," he said. "The point is that the tattoo is weak or even useless until and unless we get a second witness."

"But who will look for collaborative evidence if no one hears about it?" she asked. "Chicken and the egg."

"Leave it," Boldt said sharply, stinging her. "I made her a promise."

"You made me promise not to ask questions. When is that quarantine lifted?"

"Don't," he said.

"When do we talk about whatever it is you don't want to talk about?"

His throat constricted and he felt his jaw muscles lock.

She said, "Did I tell you I called Marina and asked about Liz and she said she's coming home this weekend? Because she's better, Lou, or because she's worse? Talk to me."

He coughed and turned his head away. He searched for a way to change the subject. He said, "I wanted the kids out of the house for the first few days. That's all." He knew what she was thinking.

"Why doesn't that make any sense to me? I'm getting conflicting signals. Mommy's coming home and you send the children away? You think she's coming home to see you?" She stepped closer and repeated, "Talk to me."

"Daffy!"

"Have you told Liz? Did you involve her in this decision? Is she coming home to live or to die, Lou? That's important." She moved around the desk toward him. "I know you. You take matters into your own hands. You make decisions, no matter how boneheaded. I'm a woman, Lou. Liz wants the kids home regardless of the added pressures it puts on you, regardless of what the doctors have to say about it. The kids will heal her, Lou, emotionally, sometimes even physically." She reached out and took a firm grip on his shoulder. "You're reacting as a controller. You want to control her environment, make it peaceful for her. Make her better. Heal her. Good intentions, wrong action. Get the kids back home."

It was these last words that pushed Boldt to tears, and his friendship with this woman that made him look up into her eyes and reveal himself, expose his vulnerability.

She clearly took the tears to mean Liz was coming home to die. She moved even closer and cradled his head. It was this contact that triggered his pulling away. He wasn't going to tell her, wasn't going to give her the opportunity to coax the truth out of him—she could milk the truth from anyone; it was her expertise.

He judged the situation quickly and said, "I'm not much of a father, am I? Who would abandon their kids because his workload makes home life too difficult? This isn't about Liz. I moved the kids before I heard Liz was coming home." He forced out a small bark of laughter. The lies came too easily all of a sudden. With truth his only tie to sanity, he felt himself slipping away, like trying to run on ice. "Worse, I haven't told Liz. I know you are right."

Her eyes darted back and forth between his. Her expression changed from relief to concern. "I almost believe you. You're good. You're very good."

"What's not to believe?" he said, knowing not to break eye contact. This strength served to confuse her. She studied him.

"What the hell is going on, Lou? You're selling me a bill of goods here." She waited and said, "How do I account for these changes in your behavior? Professional stress? Home life?" She added, "Sheila Hill is playing politics. At yesterday's four o'clock I was told to take measure of all those present. Today she's dropping hints that I may want to pay you a visit, and I'm taking that to mean she wants the book on you as well. My guess?" she asked rhetorically. "A little task force housecleaning is in order. She's not getting results and the axe is about to fall."

"It isn't that," Boldt said.

"I'm on orders here, *Lieutenant*. If I'm by the book I tell her that you're a physical and emotional wreck, that you appear exhausted, short-tempered and that you have gone steadily downhill over the past three days. I tell her that you don't appear fit for duty."

Boldt said calmly, "Hill thinks there's a conduit inside the task force, possibly supplying information to the Pied Piper. As Intelligence, I'm to turn him or her. She suggested I work in concert with you. Thinks we should try an inside-out: Sting him with disinformation and watch for the bubbles on the surface. It's big and it's complicated, and it comes at a time when I have a few other things on my mind."

She stepped back as if he had pushed her.

"Me?" Boldt asked. "I'd like an afternoon tea at the Olympic, a lamb dinner with roasted potatoes and a video of Bogie and

Bacall. The phone off; the kids asleep and Liz complaining into my ear that there isn't enough time in the day. But I'm stuck with this, and now you are, too. I wasn't going to drag you into it. I resisted. But she pushed and you fell for it. It's Need to Know. It's you and me and no one else except Hill."

"Disinformation," she said, still dazed. New territory for her, but with nearly as much ambition as Hill, she would jump at the chance.

"She's thinking a tabloid reporter has compromised someone at the Bureau, that the reporter is in cahoots with the Pied Piper. Or maybe the kidnapper has compromised one of us. If it's illegal adoption, then there's a lot of money at play. If spread around correctly—"

"One of *us*?" she gasped.

"What the hell? It could be you or me," Boldt said. "Never know."

"Yeah, right: Lou Boldt, the Pied Piper's insider," she said sarcastically.

"Preposterous, isn't it?" he said. But a thought remained: The Pied Piper had identified Boldt both as a father and as someone close enough to the investigation to influence it. He recalled Kay Kalidja explaining to him that the FBI had believed he, Boldt, would lead the task force. Who else might have guessed that?

Her eyes shined. "So what's really going on?"

A pinprick of light stabbed through the darkness of his existence. Someone had identified him, had passed his name on to the Pied Piper. Perhaps Sheila Hill was closer to the truth than Boldt had credited her.

A knock at the door was followed by Bobbie Gaynes.

Daphne moved toward the door automatically. "Call me," she said. "We'll play with some ideas."

"Draw something up," he suggested.

"Will do." Daphne passed Gaynes at the door and offered a friendly exchange. But Boldt could feel her mind working already, sizing up Gaynes and wondering what she was doing there.

How much did she know? he wondered. Daphne could be like an iceberg: far more lurking underneath than showed on the surface. He appreciated her as an ally, and yet feared the clarity of her insight.

Gaynes radiated an energy he envied. She stepped up to his desk and placed the lab results in front of him with authority—she liked whatever was in that file. She did not take a seat. She appeared slightly uncomfortable as she said, "You wanted to see this before anyone else."

"Yes I did." Boldt read from the file.

"It's important that I get it to LaMoia right away," she said. Answering Boldt's look of disappointment, she added, "If I don't tell him, the lab will."

Without reading a line, Boldt told her, "The soil on Anderson's boot contained a pesticide, a fertilizer, something like that. His earwax contained traces of the same pollen found at the Shotzes' and on Anderson's khakis."

Astonishment opened her features, her eyes wide, her teeth showing. "Fertilizer, not a pesticide. The thing about you . . . sometimes I wonder why we bother with lab tests at all. Third line," she told him. The report confirmed much of what he had just guessed. As a former student of his, she had quoted him quickly, "I know . . . I know . . . . A good detective uses the lab to confirm his suspicions, not bring him surprises."

He said, "If pollen was discovered in his earwax, then it suggests Anderson did more than rub up against someone. It means he was standing in a garden, a greenhouse or a field, and that evidence being found at the Shotzes' connects to the Pied Piper." He told her, "Run it by the university's ag-school. See if the pollen and this pesticide suggest a particular flower. Have them contact you directly, and when you hear back —"

"Tell you first," she interrupted. She said carefully, "What's going on, Sarge?"

A few minutes earlier he had felt despair. Suddenly he felt awash with hope. Evidence, when interpreted correctly, painted a particular, unique story. The mud on Anderson's boots, when combined with the pollen in his earwax and on his clothing, was certain to tell a story.

"It's good work," he told her. "I appreciate it."

Still facing him, she said, "Let me know if I can help."

He thanked her.

She said, "I liked it better when you were on the fifth floor."

"Me too," Boldt confessed.

His phone rang, and Gaynes understood that she should go. Boldt handed her the report and thanked her.

She turned and walked out.

He sat alone, a snitch complaining into his ear, an undigested bubble of guilt consuming him. The truth was nowhere left to be seen. Gone, and Boldt along with it. The truth, which Boldt had held as an absolute, was suddenly a product of context. One could distort it, bastardize it, destroy it as one saw fit.

The Pied Piper had not only stolen his daughter, he had stolen his life.

CHAPTER

29

Theresa Russo worked freelance out of a sprawling ranch home that overlooked Puget Sound and the white-capped Olympics. Boldt had met her through Liz, whose bank had arranged a nine-million-dollar loan for the woman to expand a multimedia software start-up. Russo had paid back the loan in eleven months, took the company public a year later and retired to entrepreneurial work, reportedly twenty million dollars richer. With Russo well outside of law enforcement, Boldt had sworn her to secrecy, making no mention of Sarah's name or her relationship. She was a missing child. Russo probed no further.

An African American with boot-polish black skin and straightened hair she kept pulled back tightly, she wore blue jeans, a green cotton sweater, and green Converse All-Star high-tops. She was twenty-seven years old and single. Russo worked from a padded leather throne on a forty-inch monitor mounted in the wall using a wireless keyboard and pointing device. For all the stunning views, her office shades were drawn to restrict sunlight.

Boldt was anxious to be shown whatever it was this woman deemed worthy. He had not told her the child on the CD-ROM he had received was his and Liz's daughter, only that the analysis could not be done in-house for reasons of security. Russo had a strong handshake and bright green eyes. For Boldt, the challenge was to keep all mention of Sarah out of their conversation.

Russo spoke in a matter-of-fact tone, her attention on the huge monitor. She worked the keyboard and trackball with a dexterity reserved for those who spent eighteen hours a day behind their machines.

She said, "First of all, let me answer a couple of questions you raised when you asked me to take a look at this. The CD-ROM is not unique. Many thousands of home users have CD-Rs and can burn their own disks. The disk itself is encoded with a manufacturer's batch number, but it won't get you anywhere in terms of tracking down its sale. Unfortunately, the disk is unremarkable, but it's a clever way to deliver such a message. E-mail would have left a far better trail. She's done a good job, for what it's worth—"

"She?"

"We'll get to that."

Boldt's mind raced: the Pied Piper a woman! He was hooked. He tried to keep from interrupting.

"We know she has a working knowledge of home computers and can read a computer manual. No big deal. I'm sorry it isn't better news."

Boldt put his pen to work. The contrast of pen and paper to the media in front of him was inescapable.

She said, "I called you because I came across some interesting stuff early on."

The image of Sarah moved on the screen. Her voice, amplified by surround-sound, screamed, "Daddy," and Boldt felt his bowels loosen. "A couple of details that may be relevant. It's true that video imaging on PCs has made leaps and bounds in the last few years. The home market software is good, but not up to the capabilities of the commercial players. What we have here is strictly home market—an off-the-shelf package. The result is a fairly low-resolution image. In order to give it a palatable look, you need to box the video in a pretty small screen."

Boldt felt a spring of tension in his neck. He couldn't lose her earlier reference to a woman. Millie Wiggins, who ran Sarah's day care, had mentioned a pair of uniformed cops, a man and a *woman*. This was a possible confirmation. He kept his mouth shut, Russo had her own way of doing things.

"The point being that I can size the screen however I like. Larger is typically less resolution, though as it happens," she grinned, "my equipment is a little better than average." She dragged the corner of the viewing box that contained Sarah's image so that it enlarged on her screen. "I use a res-enhancement program that we created ourselves."

The images enlarged. Russo replayed the video several times. "Do you see it?"

Boldt saw only his little girl. Try as he might to pull his eyes away from her, it was impossible. "Tell me."

"Here," she indicated with the computer's small white arrow. As the image replayed, Boldt forced himself to focus away from Sarah and onto the room's window, where Russo pointed. "In the smaller format, at regular speed, all we picked up was a slight change of color. But res-enhanced and enlarged it's actually a blurred image. If we slow down the playback," she said, working her magic, "we get an altogether different look at it."

The video advanced slowly like a replay in a sporting event. During the first playback, Boldt, once again, could not take his eyes off his daughter: Her head swiveled in tight jerky motions; the whites of her eyes showed. For the second playback he focused on the window behind and to his daughter's right. A stream of purple bled from right to left. She glanced at him, testing him, then replayed the image for a third time. She advised, "Try squinting your eyes." Boldt still could not make it out.

"Traffic of some sort," Boldt guessed.

"Let me slow it some more."

The images advanced in a series of a freeze-frames. Tiny moments of time strung together like beads on a necklace. "Orange and blue."

"Warmer," she said. "Let me isolate it." She dramatically enlarged just the window, creating an abstract maze of colorful dots.

"This takes some creative vision, mind you," she warned. "This is a different kind of detective work."

Boldt watched it several times. "If I let my imagination go, I'm not sure what that is. But logic says it's a window, and movement behind a window implies a road, and color on a road suggests a truck."

"Exactly."

"But I'm not actually *seeing* the truck. Not per se."

"I understand. You're doing great. Now watch the blue and the orange you pointed out. It's coming up." She inched the video forward frame by frame. The colors froze and then blurred together. The blue formed the letter F. The orange framed an E.

Boldt saw it. "FedEx. It's a FedEx truck!"

She beamed at him and then fixed her attention on the computer and returned the image to its original contents, though still enlarged. "Yes. A FedEx truck. Good. That is part one. Watch closely please." She enlarged an area behind and to Sarah's left that contained the room's television. "You were given a date stamp, as I'm sure you're aware of. To confirm her condition. Intentionally or not, she gave us a time stamp as well, by nature of the program. That anchor team goes on at 10:00 A.M. our time. I'm a CNN junkie," she said. "CNN Atlanta will be able to tell you the precise time—down to the fraction of a second."

Boldt's tired brain began to assimilate the information. He found the excitement in her voice contagious. "The FedEx system is computerized," he mumbled, knowing where she was headed. "The routes and the scheduling of every truck are a matter of record." He cautioned her, and himself as well, "There are a couple of hundred trucks on the road on any given day. Granted, we may be able to approximate the location of those hundreds of trucks at the time of the video—and it's great stuff, don't get me wrong—but it's too much for us. We don't have that kind of manpower." He was a department of one.

"That's true, if we're talking Seattle," she said, baiting him. She advanced the image of the television to the last few frames before the video went dark. Reducing the size, the resolution tightened, and although tiny, the result was clear: A small blue band crept across the television screen from right to left. "Did you see it?" she tested. Boldt said yes.

"Bear with me." She enlarged the area around the television set, behind and to Sarah's left. Then she enlarged the television itself. When the blue weather warning appeared on the bottom of the screen, she told him, "Local cable carriers have the authority to superimpose weather warnings, news bulletins or natural disasters. They shrink the satellite feed and insert their own moving band of text. I haven't had the time to do the legwork, but I guarantee you each and every cable system can tell you if they posted a weather bulletin on this particular date at this particular time. Given the limited number of cable companies left anymore, it's a matter of a half dozen phone calls or so." Sensing his impatience, Russo said, "We're not finished. I've saved the best for last."

"The woman," Boldt guessed.

She smiled. "If you think you needed your imagination for the FedEx truck, you ain't seen nothing yet. I haven't had any time to work with this image, and I do have a few tricks still up my sleeve—some really nice high-speed res-enhancement engines and pixel predictors, some work we did for NASA—it's graphics software that uses AI, to make best-guess image correction on degraded data. I need more time to complete that work. But I want to show you what I've got, so far. Watch the little girl's legs," she said, directing his attention to the lower section of the small video image. She replayed the video. Sarah's knees appeared, then her feet. Boldt knew those shoes. He had helped her into them that day. His throat tightened. Russo explained, "For whatever reason, the person running the camera zooms back on the image. Presumably, to show the girl's entire body, that she wasn't harmed in any way. The zoom continues to the end of segment. In the process, it gives us a look over here," she said, pointing with a pink painted fingernail to the very edge of the frame. She played the video again, and light winked from where she had pointed. "Did you see that?"

"Yes."

"If I enlarge it," she said, quickly doing it, "and I separate it out, I get only this." From top to bottom, it was nothing but a band of light, followed by a band of dark. It appeared slightly curved. "Now I warned you this requires imagination, and I do want to run some enhancement and see if we can clean it up, but . . ." She drew her short fingernail the length of the fuzzy image. "You see this tiny square of light right here? I think we're looking at something hanging on the wall, a painting maybe. A photograph."

Boldt saw the square of light. "A mirror?" he asked.

"You *do* see." She nodded. "Why not? Yes, the edge of a mirror, I think, and it's reflecting back at us. Okay? I know it's hard to see. But if it is a mirror, then what image is likely to be caught in it?" she asked rhetorically. "The camera person," she answered. She indicated a bump, a curving shape that ran top to bottom. Boldt had focused on that same image but couldn't identify it. She hinted, "That shape moves in the mirror, winking light at us." She waited for him to see it, but her impatience won out and she sat up straight, heaving out her chest, and saying simultaneously, "It's a silhouette of her chest." Running her hand down her shirt and over her breast, she announced proudly, "This video was shot by a woman."

CHAPTER

30

There was no view from the hotel room window, only the gray concrete of an adjacent building separated by a narrow alley, home to a row of Dumpsters. Sheila Hill admitted him, using the door as a screen, so that when she shut it behind him, he turned to see her dressed in only a white lace bra and matching high-cut underwear, smooth and tight against her crotch. She maintained an indoor tan throughout winter.

He carried a plastic shopping bag about which she was immediately curious, but he held it high and away from her, not letting her have at it and forcing her to press herself against him to reach for it. As she did, he took her by the back of the head and planted a long hungry kiss across lips that held a little more red lipstick than usual. The lipstick smeared on their faces.

Physically hot to the touch, she had an appetite that penetrated through his clothes and aroused him; she enjoyed rubbing up against him—it was for her pleasure, not his—and used the excuse of the package to make contact.

"Let me see it," she whined.

"All in due time, my pretty," LaMoia replied. He kissed her

again, drawing the breath out of her so that she cooed darkly. He loved the tease that existed between them. She thrilled him. Her fuse, once lit, was difficult to extinguish. She walked a fine line, once free of her clothing.

LaMoia dropped the bag and cupped her between the legs with his strong right hand, squeezing and lifting her off the floor to where she squealed with excitement. His tongue slipped wetly into her bra. Her breathing slow and heavy, she squinted at him playfully.

He carried her across the room this way, like a puppet held awkwardly, his teeth nibbling at her breast. He threw her onto the bed.

"Hurry," she ordered him, slapping her knees together.

"Touch yourself," he told her.

She viewed him curiously, actually blushing. "What?"

"Did I tell you that someone got inside my desk?" he asked her.

"We're *not* talking business. Not now, anyway."

"Then touch yourself." He paused and informed her, "I can't say for sure, but I'm pretty sure that whoever it was got a look at my files—my copy of the task force book."

She slipped her hand down her underwear and blushed again. Seeing Sheila Hill blush was worth the price of admission. She giggled nervously and slipped out of her underwear.

He said, "Show me what you do when you're alone and the shades are pulled."

A fine sheen of perspiration shined on her skin, so that she glowed golden as if dipped in wet paint. A moment later she lay naked on the bedspread.

"I like to watch you undress," she said.

"How do you feel?" he asked.

"Mmmm," she hummed, her eyes fluctuating between tightly closed and straining for a glimpse of him pulling down his pants.

"Good?" he asked.

"Come over here," she said, her voice breaking again.

He tore open the bag and the box that was in it. "Don't stop," he said, banging around the end table to the side of the bed. He found the electrical outlet, plugged in the cord and turned the device to high. "For you," he said, switching it on.

She accepted the device and put it to use. Her face knotted in pleasure. She held her breath for a long time and then cried loudly into the room.

With LaMoia inside her, she bit his shoulder to bleeding.

She smoked two cigarettes by the open window, stark naked, her feet kicked up onto the round table that bore tented cardboard advertisers heralding pizza delivered to the room. She hadn't spoken a word. Either mad at him, he thought, or out of gas.

He said, "Have you heard the rumor that Liz Boldt is coming home?"

"Coming home to die, I hear."

"Don't say that."

"You asked," she said, entwined with a large cloud of cigarette smoke. She stared through the gauze curtains at the cement wall across the alley. "Leave Boldt to me. Don't you worry about Boldt. You worry about the evidence. About how long I'll put up with a task force that isn't delivering."

"Meaning?"

"Read between the lines," she said, flipping him her three middle fingers held together like a scouting hand sign. "You're not exempt, John. Fucking me a couple times a week does not buy you exemption. It's nice, don't get me wrong. You are very good. But you have to prove you're a good cop as well, one capable of running other men. I want something useful out of those glass chips, and don't tell me about FBI delays—you sort that out. I want financials. I want some progress I can take to Mr. and Mrs. Shotz and the Weinsteins. Having their children back would do just fine, thank you very much. You've got a wonderful sense of timing, but that won't cut it at the four o'clock. Don't think you're the teacher's pet just because you've got your hand up her skirt. To the contrary—" now she chose to look back at him, "if anything that makes you more of a liability. We get caught like this and the shit is going to fly. They'll say it could compromise the task force. Thing is, they don't know me. It compromises nothing."

"That's all this is to you?" LaMoia blurted out. "Some fluids? Some sweating? What, I'm your gigolo?"

LaMoia dressed without showering and was out the door, but not before Sheila Hill called out, "You can go away mad, but you'll be back. You enjoy screwing the teacher. Nothing wrong with that, John. Teacher likes it too."

He slammed the door and was still tucking in his shirt by the time he reached the elevators where a mother and small child stood waiting. Sight of the child stung LaMoia. They boarded, but he declined to join them. He couldn't stand that close to a child. He took the stairs. Running hard. Running fast. Running away.

CHAPTER

31

David and Carlie Kittridge, both setters on the Mick's Grill volleyball team that had taken third in the inter-city competition a year earlier, had their eye on the big prize this year, thanks to a Boeing recruit who had played for USC's junior varsity. The guy could spike and block right up there with the best of them. The Kittridges were such fanatics that they had timed Carlie's pregnancy so that she delivered between the summer outdoor and the winter indoor seasons. Trudy was a week shy of five months old. Reddish blonde hair, green eyes—the cutest, most precious baby since Evelyn, her older sister.

The Wednesday night games took place in the gym of Rainier Junior High, just four blocks from the cheapest gasoline in Seattle. Carlie teased her husband for always managing to leave his tank empty until Wednesday night. After the game they would stop and he would fill up, proud of his savings. Summer months he brought his lawnmower tank along as well. If there was a deal to be had, David was first in line.

The winner of Wednesday's game would go on to represent Wallingford in the indoor championships. Carlie Kittridge pre-

pared to serve against the brick wall thirty feet away where a line
was painted eight feet high. Hers wasn't the most powerful serve
on the team, but it was arguably the most difficult to return because of a wicked reverse spin she had perfected.

As she stood in the backcourt preparing to serve, Carlie Kittridge glanced down at Trudy's car seat to make sure her daughter
was content, and saw the little angel's eyes closed. Evelyn was at
day care. All was well. She smacked the ball and watched its beautiful rotation, the seams running back toward her. Wednesday was
only a few short days away. She looked forward to it with an antsy
hunger. Mick's Grill was currently ranked number-one inter-city.
David and Carlie had every intention of keeping it that way.

CHAPTER

Boldt had put off telling Liz for two days. He had a decision to make regarding the most recent evidence—the FedEx truck in Sarah's ransom—and he needed Liz's involvement, illness or not. He elected the hospital stairs over the elevator, to buy him time to compose his thoughts.

He found her in bed reading a small pamphlet. Her roommate's bed was lived in but empty. Her face had its natural color back, not makeup. Her eyes had lost their dullness. She looked tired and older than the woman he knew, but far better than the Liz Boldt who had been admitted some weeks earlier.

"You look great," he said, kissing her on the lips.

"Wish I could say the same. Not that it isn't good to see you. We've been playing phone tag. I've missed you." She waited for him to say something. When he failed to do so, she asked carefully, "Is it her?" The face behind the question twisted as she sized him up. She drew in a sharp breath. "It is, isn't it?" She gasped, drained of color.

Boldt choked on his attempts to speak, implying acknowledgment. She meant Daphne; she had it all wrong.

"We can work through anything," she said bravely.

Boldt teared up, confused and sorry and angry.

Her eyes held a softness, seen for the first time in months. Her pain was gone, he realized.

"Where is she?" he asked, indicating the roommate's empty bed.

Liz pointed to the bathroom door.

"Feel like a walk?" he asked, offering his hand.

She swung her legs out of the raised bed. "I'll need my robe," she said. "Home tomorrow. I need the practice." Believing her husband in the midst of an affair, she nonetheless held her composure. He stood there in awe of her, feeling small and pitiful. There was a girl involved, but he couldn't bring himself to explain it. He handed her the robe and fished her slippers out from under the bed. Her bottom showed as he helped her into the robe. It was different than the one he remembered. She needed twenty pounds. He ached, praying for her health.

He walked alongside of her down a corridor void of character to an empty waiting room called the Solarium. He turned down the TV and they sat in a far corner. "It's not *that*, Liz. Not even close. My love for you . . . it's stronger, more clear to me than it's ever been. My admiration for what you've been through . . . for the strength . . . the courage—"

"It's not me, love. It's much bigger than me. But thank you." Studying him she said, "We can get through anything, you know."

Did she mean money? The banker in her had a way of neatly tracing most problems back to money, of seeing most solutions in financial management.

"I'm not so sure," he said, thinking aloud.

She smiled warmly. "Whatever it is, we're in it together."

He burst out crying, so suddenly, unexpectedly, that he buried his face first in his arm, and then on her shoulder. She held him and rubbed him. "We're almost out of this, love."

He wasn't going to tell her with his eyes buried. He leaned back, frozen by her expression. There was no good time. All his rehearsal failed him—paralyzed by her soft eyes.

"It's Sarah," he blurted out.

Her face went blank, her words caught in her throat. Tears spurted from her eyes, raining onto him. Her face collapsed and she struggled to swallow.

"An accident?" she mumbled.

He shook his head, no. "They took her . . . kidnapped her out of day care."

Her face pale, her chin trembling, she offered only a blank stare. He had lost her to anger, as palpable as the bones in her back.

"Alive?" she whispered.

"Yes."

"Kidnapped?"

"Yes."

"You were looking after them. You said . . . You said you could handle it!" Her eyes pleaded him to tell her it wasn't so. He couldn't think what to say.

"They need her alive," he said stupidly.

She pushed away and crossed her arms. She glanced around as if looking for a place to hide. "You did this? You let them take my baby?" She fired at him quickly, "Miles?"

"With Kathy."

"You bastard! That's why you vanished. You coward."

"We had some leads," he exaggerated. He caught himself worming his hands, just like Doris Shotz. He understood suicide then. A place for everything.

"Get out," she ordered through blurred eyes. She repeated herself until it became a mantra.

"Liz," he pleaded.

She curled up on herself like a crab retreating into its shell. Speaking wetly into her knees, she said, "You get out, and you bring me back my daughter."

"I need you, Liz. I need you to help me with this."

"This is your world, not mine," she fired back. "I wanted none of this."

She had asked him to quit the department too many times to count. He had nothing to say. It was a point she could hold to and that he could not argue.

He said, "She needs us both, Elizabeth."

"You bastard!" She pulled in on herself even more tightly. "You bring me my baby!"

"I'm going to find her," he said, his decision made, but his policeman's logic countering everything he said. "I'm going to get her back." He felt small and cowardly.

She pointed, her bone-thin ashen arm aimed stridently toward the door.

Boldt reached out to touch her, but she jerked away, revolted. "Liz, I . . ." He could not think what to say. Her arm trembled, still holding point. Wiping back tears, he moved reluctantly toward the door. A sense of nothingness overwhelmed him, a feeling of being horribly alone. He left without another word. He knew what had to be done.

CHAPTER

33

Boldt drove into his driveway and then, before
killing the engine, threw it into reverse, backed up and sped away.
The same for the last several days: The house was Sarah. He
couldn't go in there.

He returned to the office, too sick to eat, and spent all of Friday
night into the wee hours reviewing the computer printouts from
Tech Services that detailed conversations caught by the electronic
trickery of their AI eavesdropping software. For one who hated
coincidences, Boldt was forced to live with the fact that had Seattle not been a port city used to smuggle everything from chopped
autos to crack cocaine to illegals, and a reputed hub of organized
Asian crime, his department's Tech Services unit would never
have had such sophisticated software. But with the current administration's emphasis on returning law enforcement power to
the state level, they did have it, and by a fluke of good salesman-
ship combined with Sheila Hill's unquenched ambitions, it was
Boldt's to misuse legally.

Nonetheless, the software proved mediocre at best. Boldt spent
hours listening to outtakes of conversations of little value, and

additional hours to sections of tape the printout did not list at all. Of interest to him was that within SPD there was a good deal of dialogue. Between the FBI and SPD, nothing.

Several excerpts from the phone of Kay Kalidja intrigued Boldt, as she clearly attempted to gather in the victims' financial statements as he had asked. She had left repeated voice mail for Dunkin Hale, and it was from these tapes, not his own phone system, that Boldt heard a message she left for him. The irony of picking up his voice mail by wiretapping did not escape him.

> Lieutenant Boldt, Kay Kalidja. I wanted you to know that I have not forgotten your request, and although slower than I would like, I am making some progress. You will find some of the financial information you requested posted to your E-mail, which I thought more confidential than a pool fax, and I did not know if the fax number I have for you is direct or not. Sorry it has taken so long. I will try to speed things up. Call me if I can be of further assistance.

Ironically, it was Kalidja's apparent willingness to help that insinuated Boldt's first suspicions of her. He had encountered so much resistance from Flemming and Hale, both overt and otherwise, that an agent's sudden readiness to give him information refused by others left him a little cold in the heart. Had someone gotten to her? He wondered if the information being forwarded was tainted and meant to throw SPD's investigation, if Kalidja had been compromised by the Pied Piper, just as he had. Could that be it? Had she seen fear in his eyes? Did she know his child was missing? Suspicion bred suspicion the same way that lies begot lies.

He downloaded and printed Kalidja's E-mail. She had sent him the full financial records—over thirty pages—for two of the former victims: one from Portland, the last city targeted; the other from Rancho Santa Fe, just outside San Diego, the first city struck by the Pied Piper. The gap in between was profound and impossible to miss. The stonewalling continued.

He reviewed the statements while he continued to listen in on dozens of phone calls, many of which overlapped in content and spread before him the complex tapestry of the ongoing investigation. By the sound of it, LaMoia had himself not a runaway train but a rudderless ship, meandering in a half-dozen different directions, some evidence driven, some driven by what could be described only as wild hunches. Many of the threads made sense to Boldt: the attempt to ID the pollen; the desire for lab reports on the automobile glass; the pursuit of Anderson's missing photographs; the massive ongoing surveillance of transportation hubs and vacant structures around the city believed to be part of the Pied Piper's MO. But woven together, these threads presented more an abstract image than a clear picture. The investigation appeared to be stumbling along well enough by itself, needing little hindrance from Boldt to fail.

He was going to find Sarah and rescue her, and he was going to do so without anyone's knowing.

The FedEx manifests needed pursuing, as did the chemical analysis from Anderson's boots that Gaynes had brought him. Even more promising was the possibility of the involvement— intentional or not—of an unidentified photo silk-screening company, and it was this lead he pursued arduously with the arrival, first of Kalidja's E-mail and then, at six Saturday morning, of a fax received from Daniel Weinstein, cousin of Sidney and the giver of the silk-screened outfit.

March 27, Seattle, Washington

Dear Lieutenant Boldt:

I am pleased to include the following Internet address for the silk-screen company: HTTP//:retail.fashion.childrens.SpitIm@EMall.com

Also "enclosed" are my credit card statements. I drew an arrow by the charge for Spitting Image, which is what I think you wanted. It jumped right out at me, and helped me find them on the Web.

Assuming you are not only busy but somewhat hamstrung by your constitutional requirements, I am taking the liberty of pursuing this

myself, and should have something for you by the time you read this.
(This fax was intentionally delayed.) You can thank me later.

Sincerely,

Daniel Weinstein

Boldt immediately dialed the man's number, reaching only an answering machine that said, "I'm unavailable until Wednesday, the first. Leave a message after the beep, and I'll get back to you."

Boldt frantically phoned the Weinstein home and reached a groggy voice that belonged to Trish. Initially she said that both Sidney and his cousin were in town. Once Boldt explained the fax he'd received and convinced her that her out-of-state husband was in violation of his bail, she confessed that they had left for northern California early Friday afternoon. He asked if Daniel was the kind of man to follow through with such threats.

"Threats?" she returned. "They think they're doing you people a favor. They think it'll take you two weeks to get all the warrants and get down there and do something. Threats? They're trying to find our baby."

"Can you reach them?"

"Only if Sid calls tonight. If they get drinking, he won't. He knows I don't like the drinking. And my guess is, this is more an excuse for the two to go on a tear than to save our child. Sid, and Daniel too, they're people who have to do something. You know? There are doers and there are people who sit around, Lieutenant. Sid and his side of the family—they are definite doers."

Around the cop shop a "doer" was a criminal. Boldt did not miss the irony. "Did they give you an address, a town, anything?"

"No. Just that name, Spitting Image. But you already know that, don't you?"

"I want you to listen to this next question carefully, and understand that the only way I can help them is to know everything. I have no jurisdiction out of this city, much less out of this state, Mrs. Weinstein. If I help, it's as a private citizen. As a friend. Do you understand?"

"Yes."

"Okay. Listen carefully: To your knowledge, does either of them own a gun?"

She gasped over the phone line, settled herself and replied, "Yes."

"A handgun, or a rifle, or both?"

"Both," she answered. "Daniel does some hunting."

"Let's hope not," Boldt said. "If your husband calls—"

"I tell him to get his butt home," she interrupted.

"First you find a way to get the name of the town and the place he's calling from. That first! A motel, a bar, it doesn't matter. Then, and only then, you try to get him home." He read her his cell phone number and made sure she took it down correctly. "It's on twenty-four hours a day. You call the minute you hear."

"I'll call," she promised, "but he won't."

With the help of Theresa Russo's computer expertise, Boldt avoided including anyone in his search for Spitting Image's home page. Within minutes of reading her the Internet address supplied by Daniel Weinstein she was reading back to him the company's physical address, E-mail address, and phone and fax numbers. Russo kept him on the line while she used an Internet mapping service to pinpoint the location of the company, and faxed him the resulting map. Within five minutes of phoning her, he had an address and map and was headed for the residential community of Felton, California, north of Santa Cruz.

A flight from Sea-Tac left for San Jose less than an hour later.

CHAPTER

34

Boldt had seen Sidney Weinstein in action with a weapon once before. He had no desire to face the two men alone. He called LaMoia from his car phone, awakening him. Weekend mornings were the detective's only opportunity to sleep in; Boldt destroyed this chance. "I'm about to break your investigation wide open," Boldt told him, assuming the Romeo was with a woman and probably sporting a Scotch-induced headache. "Southwest flight 192 leaves in fifty minutes." He hung up, knowing that if he stayed on to argue his point LaMoia would worm his way out. As it was, LaMoia arrived at the gate with seven minutes to spare. He wore dark glasses, wet hair, a fresh pair of pressed jeans and his signature black leather jacket and ostrich boots. He drank buckets of coffee and ate pretzels for breakfast.

"You're not going to tell me anything?" the detective complained from the front seat of the rental car.

"Of primary importance—" Boldt began to repeat himself.

"Yeah, I know. I heard you. It's yours over in Intelligence for the first forty-eight hours. I keep my mouth shut for two days."

He added, "Two days is an eternity for those babies, you don't mind me saying so."

"Don't push, John. You're going to come out smelling like a rose."

LaMoia burped on cue. "Better than I smell now," he said.

Boldt stepped him through the evidence reports, the interviews with the Shotzes and Weinsteins, Daniel Weinstein's credit card statements, the Internet site.

"Damn Internet," LaMoia said. From homosexual abductions to fraud, the World Wide Web had brought police added case-loads. Only the white-collar crime boys sang its praises. "So this Daniel Weinstein, along with our pal Sid, are down here boozing it up with heat in the trunk. Does that about recap it?"

The drive was made longer by a thousand cars all trying to get to different places ahead of anyone else. The same in Seattle. A predictable impatience. Any lane, any highway, always the same race. LaMoia felt it too. "They don't drive for pleasure. Not like the Italians. They drive to *get somewhere*. To beat the clock, save gas, bring home the bacon. I hate California." He slouched down in the seat, napping behind his dark glasses. They ran past card-board houses cut out and pasted onto hills dotted with live oaks that looked too beautiful to be real. The crush of humanity de-pressed him. LaMoia, who couldn't nap if he'd been awake a week, reached out and dialed in a talk radio station.

"You're depressing me," Boldt said.

"What? You got no interest in prostate cancer? This is good Saturday morning stuff." He kept searching until he found sports talk. "There we go," he said. "I love this country!"

"I like to travel alone," Boldt said.

"Should have thought of that."

The housing developments streamed past. Pieces on a Monop-oly board. Boldt said, "Aren't the basketball play-offs still a cou-ple months off?"

"Na, not the start of them. Besides, with the talk stations you just gotta go with it. Know what I mean?"

"I don't think so."

"No, you probably don't." LaMoia passed some wind and cracked open the window.

"Wider," Boldt said.

LaMoia turned off the radio. As much as Boldt disliked talk radio, he didn't want to talk, and he knew LaMoia too well. The detective said suddenly, "The thing about Matthews I can't figure out is what she wants, you know? What she's up to. You know? First the engagement to Adler is on, then it's off. Now, maybe on again, I hear.

"I collar a few bad guys along the way," he continued. "You know? But Matthews—all she wants is to get inside their heads, take the gears out of their clocks. Wouldn't you think that would get a little old? You ask me, we're talking about a screwed-up childhood or something."

"Who's trying to get inside whose head?" Boldt asked. "She's complicated. That's what you don't like about her. She's more than perfume and lace and you can't get close."

LaMoia clutched his chest. "Oh! You're killing me here!" He glanced over. "You don't want to talk sports, you don't want to talk legs." He shook his head. "You know, we don't talk all that much, Sarge, I mean aside from business."

It wasn't true and both men knew it. LaMoia was close to Boldt's family, especially the kids. A long silence overcame them as Boldt negotiated several severe turns. LaMoia, one of the best drivers on the force, said, "I should have been wheel man."

The road climbed out of the developments and into thick woods, winding through sharp turns. Cabins had been tucked up into the hill; many went unseen, marked only by numbered mailboxes. The air smelled thickly of pine sap. The bows of the towering firs hung heavy with age, like a ballerina's upturned arms, her fingers drooping.

Boldt slowed and negotiated the turns carefully. The street numbers indicated they were close.

"We work these people as a team. Who knows if they're connected or not."

LaMoia sat up. "Providing the Weinsteins haven't killed them."

"Maybe no one's here. Maybe they are the Pied Piper. Maybe they know nothing about it."

"I'm hip," LaMoia said.

"If we need to role-play," Boldt said, "I'm sweet, you're sour."

"How else could we play it?"

Boldt passed the mailbox, backed up and pulled the car into the driveway.

The sign out front read Tiny Tots—Home Schooling. Hanging from this shingle was another smaller one: Spitting Image Designs. A cottage industry, literally. It was a small log house tucked up into and surrounded by tall evergreens. No lawn to speak of, just forest floor. A walkway of chainsawed slices of tree trunks led from the drive to the front door, past a six-year-old Chevy four-wheel-drive with body rust behind the rear wheels. Everything in these woods—living and inanimate—was in a constant state of rot.

A woman answered the door with a welcoming smile. Nearly six feet tall and sporting an imposing nose, she reminded Boldt of a high school phys. ed. teacher. She wore a faded blue sweatshirt and gray sweatpants, suede Birkenstocks with yellow socks. Her hair was pulled back into a black fuzzy band. "Hi," she said, studying them as a pair. "If you've come about enrollment, we're all filled up. But I can put you on the waiting—"

"Us?" LaMoia gasped, believing she was mistaking them as a married gay couple.

Displaying the badge, he said, "Sergeant John LaMoia, Lieutenant Lou Boldt." He put the badge away quickly before she identified them as Seattle. "We'd like to talk to you, if you don't mind?"

She nodded limply, displaying none of the defensiveness Boldt would have expected of the Pied Piper or an associate. He said, "And you are?"

"Donna Stonebeck," she answered him.

The woman showed them in to a small pine table. The house smelled vaguely of paint, although there was no silk-screen equipment in sight. The small living room had been converted into a preschool classroom.

Boldt opened his briefcase and handed her a stack of photos. "Look carefully," he said. "Do you know any of these children?"

Studying them, she looked a little frightened, understanding this was no social call. She shook her head at each photo, looked through them a second time more quickly and passed them back to Boldt. "They weren't students here. We have never had a single complaint."

"It's not that," LaMoia surprised her by saying. "It's a kidnapping case. A serial kidnapper."

The horror on her face appeared genuine. Disappointment stung Boldt.

"Kidnapping?" she whispered. If an act, it was a damn good one.

Boldt heard small footsteps racing downstairs followed by three children who appeared around the corner and stopped abruptly. One was Asian, one Caucasian, and one a beautiful cream skin. They all seemed the same age, around five or six. Stonebeck, still stunned, told them, "I'll be up in a minute."

The kids ran back upstairs at the same frantic speed.

Stonebeck apparently felt compelled to explain. "I take up to five boarders. I have those three at the moment. Children of violent divorces, orphans whose extended family can't take them in yet but who can afford private care—we offer a better environment than the public institutions."

"A regular Florence Nightingale," LaMoia quipped.

"It's not entirely benevolent. I'm paid quite well for my boarders." Without flinching, the woman offered, "Tea or coffee for either of you?"

Boldt asked for tea with milk and sugar. LaMoia took coffee.

Donna Stonebeck asked from the kitchen, "Are you interested in the preschool or Spitting Image?"

"Spitting Image is located here?" LaMoia asked.

"I've got a basement full of it," she told him, setting the water on to boil.

"You do much business?" LaMoia asked.

"I have two people downstairs full time while I'm up here with the kids," the woman said proudly. "It keeps growing like this,

and I'm going to need more space. We created a Web page—oh,
about a year ago now—and our orders have doubled in the last
three months. We're shipping all over the world now. Japan is big
for some reason. Korea. Germany. Finland. We've got five orders
for Japan right now."

"The T-shirts mostly?" Boldt inquired.

The woman stood waiting for the pot to boil. She didn't appear
nervous in the least. Boldt wanted her nervous, he wanted her a
part of it. "We don't do T-shirts, per se. Too crowded a field. We
do infant clothing, but it's our crib products that are zooming: the
blankets, quilts, duvet covers and pillows. We're doing twenty,
thirty baby blankets a week. At fifty bucks a blanket," she added.
"We've got a new velvet product. Comes out like velvet art, you
know? Elvis? Only it's your kid's face. Hundred bucks per unit.
Can't keep up with orders."

"Business is booming," LaMoia said.

"I won't give up the preschool," she directed to Boldt. "I mean,
one's for love, one's for money, right?"

"What kind of records do you keep?" LaMoia asked coldly.

"Are you two IRS?" She laughed as if caught. "Oh my God, I
should have looked closer at that badge!"

"Police," Boldt answered, attempting to reassure her. "Kidnapping," he reminded.

"All of those kids, or was I supposed to recognize one of
them?" Then a wave of realization crashed over her and she cried,
"You don't think I have something to do with this?"

Boldt's cell phone rang. He rose and took the call in the corner.

LaMoia asked her, "How do you keep track of each order?"

"The artwork? The paperwork? What?" she asked, distracted
by Boldt mumbling in the far corner.

"Artwork. Paperwork."

"Artwork, goes back with the product. Our paperwork—"

"Invoices," he clarified, interrupting. "Customer names. Addresses. That sort of thing. I give you a name, you pull the order."

"Specific customers? We file by month," Stonebeck said.

"If I give you a name?"

"A date *and* name would be better, but yeah, we could do it.

We're alphabetized by month. But can I promise we'd have it? This is not Land's End," she said. "A year ago we were doing five pieces a week. Now it's maybe twenty-five. Last year we invoiced by quarter. This year by month. Used to pay our bills by hand. Now we use Quicken." She said sarcastically, "We're real cutting edge around here."

"Could I check out your invoices?" LaMoia asked. "The last six months?"

"Do you have a warrant?" she said. "That's what I'm supposed to ask, isn't it?"

"No warrant," Boldt answered, returning to the conversation. "We had hoped to keep this as informal as possible."

"But you want to rifle my invoices? That's cute."

LaMoia glanced at Boldt, who nodded his consent. He said, "In your estimation how secure is your Web page?"

"Meaning?"

"What precautions have you taken to secure your Web page?"

"This is a cottage industry, fellows. I keep telling you—it's not Land's End. We post the same warning everyone else does—you play at your own risk. We encourage customers to call us direct and place the order that way. You know what it costs me to file with one of these security providers? Forget it. Arm and a leg. Maybe down the road."

"To call you is a toll call or an 800 number?"

"Do I look like I'd have an 800 number? I'm out of my basement. I do a couple dozen pieces a week."

"So they place the orders through the Internet to save the toll charges."

"The orders come to me as E-mail. E-mail is pretty secure, right?"

"We're interested in attempting to identify some of your customers," LaMoia explained.

"No kidding?" she asked sarcastically. The water boiled. She poured the beverages and delivered them. "What I want to know is why?"

"We just want to check a couple of names," Boldt said as respectfully as possible.

"Yeah, but how's it connect to these kidnappers?"

"That's police business," LaMoia said harshly.

"I kinda figured that," the woman fired back, "or you wouldn't be here."

"If you wouldn't mind?" Boldt asked. "Time is our biggest enemy."

She put down her tea and stood. "You can see whatever you like." She asked cautiously, "Am *I* in any kind of trouble here?"

LaMoia grinned that LaMoia grin that showed his teeth and bent his mustache into a pair of wings. "Not yet," he said, joining her.

"You single?"

To Boldt, LaMoia said, "Wait here, Lieutenant."

As their voices descended the stairs, Boldt heard her say, "Maybe I like you after all, Mr. Smooth. Which one are you?"

"LaMoia."

"Italian?"

"Every inch."

"Don't go getting personal on me."

Boldt listened in, thinking only LaMoia got away with such things. One of these days his libido would get him in trouble. Sooner than later. After twenty minutes he emerged, that same irritating self-confident smile pasted under his mustache. In his right hand he carried a number of invoices. "Bingo!" he said, waving the paperwork.

"So the doer, soon to become the Pied Piper, decides he wants to establish a little under-the-table adoption business." LaMoia drove the curves effortlessly and at twice the speed, like water running through a pipe. "He needs product: white babies, good solid stock."

"You have a real poetry about you," Boldt sniped. He studied the man's use of gas and brake, marveling the car could ride so smoothly. LaMoia was the same with women: It came naturally to him. Boldt studied the Spitting Image invoices. The backseat contained a cardboard filing box going back two years. Stonebeck had cooperated. Boldt thumbed his way through December a year earlier, starting at the beginning as a cop always did, looking for San Diego, Los Angeles, San Francisco, Portland—looking for a paper trail. Shotz and Weinstein had both been found.

"He needs clients too. Maybe word of mouth. Maybe he simply runs credit checks on names he finds on adoption waiting lists, IDs the high rollers and makes a phone solicitation: You pay, you play. Must be plenty of those types waiting out there. Some of those lists run five, six, seven years deep, and then your name comes up and you get offered a five-month-old with learning disabilities. Fuckin' A, I'd buy from this guy."

"You probably would," Boldt said, but it stung his former detective.

"I'm just talking hypothetically," LaMoia complained. "I'm brainstorming here."

Boldt said, "He gets the bright idea to hack an Internet site devoted to children's clothing—"

"He stumbles onto Spitting Image. It's perfect for him. Some of the orders, like Daniel Weinstein's, include digitized photos, and suddenly he knows that he's getting a white kid with the right looks. What a sicko."

"He's got a shipping name and address, almost always the residence. If he's a good hacker, or if he has access to credit histories, he can lift credit card records—"

"Which is how he knew the Shotzes would be on that train, that Trish Weinstein would be at the supermarket—"

The pieces clicked into place for Boldt: isolating his targets; establishing a schedule or routine to time his hits. His fatigue lifted like a fog burning off. "So he has computer skills," he said.

"They teach computers in the Big House, Sarge. Could be one of the family."

"If we had all the invoices, I'd feel a little better," Boldt said. "The fact that she remembered a couple of shipments to Seattle doesn't leave me with the best feeling."

LaMoia said, "It's her E-mail orders we want."

"We'll get them," Boldt reminded. "She's forwarding them."

"Thank God they were backed up."

Boldt checked the map. "Next exit. Then east."

"You're sure they're there?"

"Trish Weinstein said he called. She got the name of the motel out of him and then told him to get his butt home before he ended up in jail. She said he sounded pretty convinced."

LaMoia said, "So now we help convince the cousins Weinstein to turn the show around."

"And maybe some day we thank them," Boldt replied.

"How's that?"

"If Weinstein and cousin Daniel hadn't headed down here to pay a call on Ms. Stonebeck, would we have jumped on that plane?"

"Point taken."

"We tough them up," Boldt advised. "We put the fear of God into them if they get within ten miles of Ms. Stonebeck."

"I love this job," LaMoia said, slouching down behind the wheel and letting out a long sigh, "but this rental is a piece of shit."

CHAPTER

35

Boldt pored over the Spitting Images documents, the time pressures nearly too much to bear. Rhonda Shotz, Hayes Weinstein, his own Sarah . . . Stonebeck had underestimated her sales volume by a factor of two or three, but even so, five or ten detectives working in concert could have completed the work in a matter of hours. For Sarah, Boldt handled it alone, cross-checking names and dates against the Pied Piper victims. Slowly he built convincing, and finally irrefutable, evidence that the custom silk-screener linked at least four of the Pied Piper's victims. Such information could set a task force on fire and provide the good, solid leads that led to real suspects.

Boldt kept it all to himself.

The stakes were high enough. Added to them was the possibility that within these documents or Stonebeck's E-mailed orders—which she had promised to deliver to Boldt—existed the name and address of the Pied Piper's next Seattle victim. For Boldt to hoard such information not only was a crime but went against everything in his nature. To share this would be to advance the investigation, prohibited in the ransom. But his commitment to

proceed with his own investigation forbade expansion. He didn't
know how long he could keep LaMoia at bay, but he believed
he could stall longer than the forty-eight-hour grace period using
Intelligence's Need to Know exclusion as his excuse. As a last
resort he could share the secret of Sarah's abduction and pray that
LaMoia's loyalty would hold.

Boldt's trying to balance these two forces, Sarah's well-being
versus the abduction of another innocent child, failed with each
internal argument. "You picked the wrong man," he mumbled
nearly incoherently at his desk. "You picked the wrong cop."

On some of the Spitting Image invoices the handwriting barely
rose above a scrawl, making Boldt's task even more difficult. In-
terestingly, the numbers read fine.

Name by name, date by date, month by month, Boldt slogged
through the paperwork. If he could find another Seattle customer,
he might have a way to locate and follow the Pied Piper back to
his daughter. Twice he fell asleep and had to start farther back in
the pile, finding an invoice he clearly recognized. In between
pages, he glanced furtively at the wall clock, feeling the minute
hand like blows to his chest. *You're risking another child,* the voice
inside him reminded. He thumbed faster and fell asleep a third
time.

John LaMoia wondered what kind of importance Intelligence
could assume over the needs of the task force. How could Boldt
care about busting someone or protecting sources when the lives
of children were at stake? Or was Intelligence, a unit that thrived
on secrecy, directly involved in the Pied Piper investigation without the knowledge of the task force? The only reason LaMoia
kept his promise to Boldt was that he trusted the man in ways he
trusted no other.

His decision came more easily due to the fact that he was overwhelmed with paperwork of his own. On Saturday night, he
worked at his cubicle reviewing property damage reports he had
sought for the better part of a week. He hoped Hill might show

up and offer a night together; he caught himself glancing toward the door each time it was opened. But Sheila Hill never showed. He worked alone.

Even in the greatest of emergencies, the incompetence of SPD's bureaucracy lived up to its stereotype. People could move quickly, meeting to meeting, floor to floor; paperwork never did. It lumbered under the control of a civilian labor force, many of whom worked for minimum wage and to whom the word urgent was seen so often that it blended into any request form. The joke around SPD was that if you needed a vacation, if you wanted to slow an investigation down to a crawl, place a request for an archived file.

Ironically, LaMoia was working off of a suggestion made by Boldt, the theory being that the chips of automobile glass might be the product of vandalism or theft—car windows shattered for kicks by teens, or for profit by petty thieves looking for car stereos—that the Pied Piper may have repeatedly walked through a field of such glass and, by the rule of mutual exchange, carried the evidence into his crime scenes. It was vintage Boldt.

Frustrated by the failure of the FBI to deliver a lab report on the glass, LaMoia turned to the time-honored process of reading each and every property damage report filed in the prior six weeks, trusting that for insurance the owners of the vehicles would report any damage to the police—a requirement for insurance reimbursements. He read reports on every kind of damage conceivable, from the bizarre to the mundane—from thousand-dollar leather jackets torn by bar bouncers to a home stereo thrown across an apartment and out a patio window by a jealous lover; random vandalism, including spray painting, rock throwing and minor arson. Any such report involving a vehicle, LaMoia read carefully. If a shattered windshield, or any vehicular glass was listed anywhere in the report, or if it seemed to LaMoia that the only way a dashboard might have been torn apart was to break into the vehicle and therefore smash a car window, he set aside the report.

One by one these separated reports stacked up. He had been reviewing documents for over three hours when the first hint emerged. Establishing a pattern—any pattern—was reason for excitement.

Human behavior could be broken down into a series of learned patterns. In the shower, a person soaped his or her body parts in the same order, day after day. A man shaved in the same sequence. The cop's job was to identify as many of these patterns as possible in his suspect's behavior or his crimes. Patterns proved predictable. Predictability meant arrests.

At first there was nothing to tie one broken car window to another—a truck, a car, a minivan; the parking lot of a mall, a Sonics game, a supermarket. But when the fourth property damage report indicating window damage cited a northbound I-5 Park and Ride, the similarity jumped out at LaMoia. Two of the four dates were the same, but two others were not, meaning the Park and Ride had been hit a minimum of three times on different dates, which in turn meant that an individual or gang had targeted the Park and Ride as a good place to pick up car stereos. The Pied Piper might have picked up the broken glass anywhere—from his own garage, to an auto shop, to any of the locations listed on the reports he was collecting into a stack—but police work meant playing percentages, and the area of highest percentage was this Park and Ride. LaMoia saw one clear way to narrow the field. He picked up the phone and called Bernie Lofgrin at home despite the late hour.

LaMoia spent five minutes describing his discoveries to Lofgrin, the head of SPD's Scientific Identification Division. Lofgrin, a civilian, did not work weekends unless on call and attending a crime scene, neither of which was the case, but he took to LaMoia's discoveries like a bloodhound on a scent. The detective pointed out the increasing importance of determining the make and model of the vehicle or vehicles from which the chips had come. Whatever pressure Lofgrin could apply to the FBI's Washington, D.C., forensics lab would be appreciated.

At the same time, LaMoia elected to place the Park and Ride under twenty-four-hour surveillance, hoping to use a combination of detectives under the direction of Bobbie Gaynes. In a political nod to Sheila Hill and the politics of the task force, he took his recommendations to Patrick Mulwright, whose Special Operations unit was the department's premiere surveillance squad. Mulwright, who had undergone a suspension ten months earlier for boozing on the job, was caught drunk as a sailor by LaMoia's midnight call. After a rambling attempt to sound coherent, the lieutenant assigned the surveillance back to LaMoia, mistakenly assuming LaMoia was currently on call. LaMoia awakened Gaynes and told her to organize a rotation. Reminding him that with over a dozen vacant houses under surveillance and Hill squawking about overtime pay, the manpower was not there, she suggested he rethink the assignment. "So work the uni's," LaMoia told her. Uniformed patrol officers would, on occasion, work plainclothes detail *gratis* for the chance to be noticed and recommended for advancement.

"Do it yourself if you have to, just get that Park and Ride covered."

CHAPTER

36

Boldt sensed someone behind him, spun in his chair in time to see a woman at his office door, emaciated and pale. His wife.

Her release had been postponed twenty-four hours because of a scheduling conflict. He did not expect her, and so for a moment simply stared.

"Forgive me," she said calmly. She stepped inside and closed the door.

Forgive *you?* he thought, a bubble of painful guilt overwhelming him. No words came out. He stood and approached her.

"I've acted foolishly," she said, "unchristian in every way, and I—"

Boldt hugged her unfamiliar body, once soft but now sharp with bone. "No. You have every right—"

"Nonsense. I was horrible to you. I apologize. Please forgive me."

They spoke, simultaneously, their apologies blurred.

"We'll get her back," the wife said.

"We'll get her back," the husband echoed.

"The two of us."

"I never thought—"

"Tell me," she said, gently breaking the embrace and holding him at a distance. "Tell me everything. Time is against us, isn't it? I know it is. And yet I also know that God will not allow this. God will see her safely returned. But not without you, love. You're the best cop there is."

Words he had lived to hear spoken; words she had never said, instead voicing resentment, anger and frustration at the demands and risks of his job. Words he would have gladly given back in a heartbeat for Sarah's safe return.

Sensing his every emotion, she said, "We aren't alone in this."

His enormous emptiness waned. A state of mind, he realized, not reality, for what else could explain it passing so quickly and completely? With Liz in the picture, everything changed.

"Together," he said, his lips gracing her ear, her cheek hot against his neck.

His wife gave in to her tears like a tree uprooted by the wind, begrudgingly and with much protest. "Together," she agreed. "Bring her home." She wept openly.

For a moment Boldt thought she meant him, but then she whispered so closely that he felt it clear through to his soul, "Please God, bring her home."

"Together," Boldt repeated, a single word as healing as any he had known.

CHAPTER

37

Boldt awakened Liz at four in the morning from a deep sleep. She came awake, arms flailing, from either the clutches of a nightmare or reaching out for a husband who had not slept by her side for far too long.

There had been no lovemaking between them—Liz needed more strength—but the loving had been intense and more intimate than many other nights shared physically. Boldt had found a brief piece of the sleep that for days had eluded him.

"Something you said," he told her.

"Love? What is it," she said, using her private name for him.

"You said we aren't alone—"

"I meant that God—"

"Yes, I know. But it's more than that, you see? I think I know now why we have never received the Portland file. The same for San Francisco. What if it wasn't the Bureau dragging its feet, but the police departments themselves, someone in our exact situation?"

"Wouldn't you know that by now?"

"Would I? Does anyone know about us? About Sarah?" He

switched on the room light and she flinched. He said, "I let myself believe that. But why should anyone know? Hill's wrong about a reporter working an insider. It's not one, but a string of insiders, a string of cops, city to city, in the same situation as we are."

"And what if it is?" she questioned, confused and even frightened by his excitement.

"Then there's evidence that has been withheld. Victims we don't know about, some of whom may have information they've never disclosed."

"Like you with this clothes company," she said.

"Exactly. I don't know anyone on the San Francisco force, but in Portland a CAP sergeant named Tom Bowler—a guy I know pretty well—was lead on the kidnapping, and the Serious Crimes committee, their version of a task force. Bowler has two kids."

"It's four in the morning, love."

"I'm going down there, to Portland."

He spun his legs out of bed and sat up.

"Now?"

"Be there by morning." He asked, "Okay with you? It's a Sunday. It's the only day I could get away with this, without somebody questioning it."

"You need sleep. Rest. You need to be thinking clearly."

"I'm going down there."

"Love, has it occurred to you that you can't do this alone? If we're going to obey the ransom, it's one thing. But we aren't, are we?"

"No."

"So you need help."

"No. We can't." Standing, he told her to get some sleep. "I'll be back afternoonish. Cell phone is on if you need me."

"I need you," she assured him.

She was back asleep before he was into street clothes.

At 7:30 A.M., the Columbia River was caught in the dusk of sunrise, its swirling dark waters reflecting back a rose-hued sky

with patches of white cotton clouds. Shorebirds and gulls flew low while a barge and tug cut white-feathered wakes into its surface. The noise of traffic obscured any sounds, so that if one stared long enough, he might believe it was the river making that noise.

Boldt ate scrambled eggs with his four cups of tea at a trucker's diner. The waitress was too old for the hairstyle and too friendly for the hour.

At 9:00 A.M. Connie Bowler claimed her husband was running errands. At ten, when Boldt called back, he heard the twinges of panic in her voice as she fired off an excuse. Boldt had met Connie only once. He reintroduced himself, asked after their kids, and said he was passing through town and would love to see Tom. She said the kids were fine, but there was relief in her voice. Boldt pressed her about Tom. She carefully volunteered the name and address of The Shanty Lantern.

The watering hole was six blocks from the Portland Police Department, in a basement area beneath a Chinese restaurant named Wang Hong's. Entering from sunlight, it was several minutes before he could see clearly. The bar smelled strongly of egg rolls, but it had an Irish decor. It was not a happy bar, but a drinker's bar; Boldt had played piano in both kinds. It was not a cop bar either. Police were a strange breed. After spending eight-hour shifts together, cops tended to spend another two hours together getting pasted before heading home. They shared war stories. They bragged. They exaggerated. They talked sports and cars and, in the right company, women. Daphne would have all sorts of explanations for cop bars, some of which might make sense to scholars, but at the heart of such a place was that police work was teamwork. After the bruising, the team enjoyed a moment or two on the lighter side.

The Shanty Lantern was no such haunt. On a Sunday morning it played host to ten determined souls, all of whom struggled to either continue their drunk, or find one. Tom Bowler owned a table, a pack of cigarettes and a disconnected look. He paid no attention to the sports discussion on the overhead Sony. He had a Scotch in front of him—half empty. By the way the man stared into space, Boldt knew it wasn't his first.

Bowler looked all wrong for a man in his late thirties. Boldt might not have spotted him had he not been looking for him. He wore a wrinkled white shirt that was stained with either ketchup or blood. When he saw Boldt, he shook his head, refusing the visit.

Boldt took a chair at the man's table, sat down and stared at him.

The bartender interrupted, attempting to rescue her regular customer. She was the owner of a great deal of dyed hair, a pair of artificially large breasts and a vivid shade of blue eye shadow that could be seen even in the cavelike atmosphere of The Shanty Lantern.

Boldt ordered an orange juice for himself and a cup of coffee for Bowler.

"Who put you in charge?" the man asked, correcting the coffee to another Scotch.

"We've never received your file, Tom," Boldt said, deciding to play it straight. "You were lead," Boldt reminded.

"Queen for a Day, you mean. Flemming shows up, my brass bends over and greases up the old red eye and says, 'Park it here please, Mr. Federal Officer.' We form a serious Crimes Unit, but all we end up with is bottle washers for Flemming's suits. He's a monster, you know—Flemming, I'm talking about. A dictator. Eyes in the back of his head, an ear to every wall. Knows what you're thinking before you do. On edge. I had the feeling that at any moment . . . he used us. Manipulated us, worked us—and the brass seemed to never catch on. We processed the evidence, but they analyzed it. I gotta admit, he played it brilliantly, like a quarterback working a cheerleader to get her panties down. We get the public exposure, the blame, if it goes south; Flemming gets the real control. Knows which wheels to grease, which buttons to push. Has our chief bragging at cocktail parties that he's taking phone calls and sharing beverages with our U.S. Senator. It's all politics, Boldt. Blame management: Who's to blame if the investigation goes south? Who takes the front page if the guy walks into the seventh precinct and gives himself up? Let me tell you this: Talk radio has done in law enforcement. The public is like a child, you know? You give them too much information too soon and they're dangerous with it." He killed the Scotch. "To hell with it."

"How're the kids?" Boldt asked.

Tom Bowler's jaw set and his eyes grew large as they met and held Boldt's. He shouted a little too loudly. "Ginger?" Barroom shorthand. She delivered the two drinks. "What about my kids?"

Boldt said, "Let me run a hypothetical situation past you, Tom, and maybe you can help me see clear of it."

"What about the kids?" the man asked, mean in a way only a drunk can get.

Boldt had won the man's attention. The room suddenly felt warmer.

"What the—?"

"Sarah's going to be two. Can you believe it?" Boldt sipped his juice. It was from a can. He set it aside. He locked into Bowler, saying no more. The man's expression slowly hardened. He knew why Boldt had made the trip. "So let's just say, hypothetically," Boldt continued, "that a cop is working a case, a big case, like a string of kidnappings or something."

Bowler shifted uncomfortably.

Boldt continued, "And let's say the doer is no dummy. He knows he either has to have an enormous string of luck or someone pulling strings for him. He knows the Feds will be players. Tens of thousands of kids vanish every year. Few, if any, of these disappearances are ever connected. Fewer prosecuted. But this guy is making a statement. He leaves a calling card."

"A penny flute."

"Exactly." Boldt hesitated. Other than Liz he had not told a soul. He couldn't bring himself to. Instead he said, "The doer understands it's the local cops who will work the crime scenes for evidence, the locals who will most likely process the lab work on that evidence. In that way it's the locals' case to give away, not the other way around. The Bureau may be running things, maybe not, but the local cops control the evidence and therefore the success or failure of the investigation."

A bead of sweat ran from Bowler's sideburn into his collar. He looked jaundiced. Malarial.

"One other thing: The doer is much more frightened of the Feds than he is of local law." He paused briefly. "Did I ask you about your kids?"

Bowler coaxed the shiny surface of the Scotch into a swirling disk of light suspended in the glass. "You wasted a trip," he said.

"I'm just talking hypothetically," Boldt reminded.

"How's Liz?"

"Cancer," Boldt fired back harshly. Mentioning it didn't sting him the way it used to. If he expected Bowler to talk to him, then he had to reciprocate. "They cut her open. They ran her full of drugs and radiation. Now she's found religion."

"Connie's joined the God squad. Me?" He lifted the Scotch.

"Is it working?" Boldt asked. Maybe it was the fear loosening him up. Maybe it was the look in Bowler's eye that confirmed Boldt was right. His voice faltered as he said, "I'm begging you here, Tom."

"The Sonics are murdering us this year. Once we lost Clive the Glide it was all over. They should have thrown it in back then."

"Let's say this guy—the doer—has something that's mine," Boldt said angrily, "and I don't know whether or not I can trust it'll be returned in one piece." He stared at the man, hoping he might win eye contact, but it was a bust. "Let's say that made my interest in the Portland file all the stronger."

"I took the file—the master file—home one night. Stopped for a drink right here. Car was busted into. My car! Briefcase was stolen. The file was gone. Hey, we got triplicates, but it takes a while to pull it all together."

"I need it to pull together, Tom. I need any leads I can get."

"No, that's wrong. You know your best bet? Play by the rules. You'll be glad you did." He waited for this to sink in, and met eyes with Boldt. He held him in a prolonged stare and said, "Penny is *fine*. Did I mention that? Thanks for asking."

Tom Bowler stood, sliding his chair back with the effort. The legs cried out on the tile floor sending chills down Boldt's spine. Bowler was unsteady on his legs. And he was dead inside. He had apparently played by the rules and had a daughter to show for it. But Boldt's daughter was gone. The Shotzes'. The Weinsteins'. Bowler had to live with that, or try to. The man walked past Boldt and said something to Ginger about his tab. He left without looking back.

CHAPTER

38

Daphne hurriedly changed her outfit for the third time, studying herself in the full-length mirror that attached to the back of her houseboat's bathroom door, and decided she looked too contrived: Annie Hall on a Sunday stroll. She hadn't been this clothes-conscious since her dinner a month earlier with Owen Adler, her former fiancé, perhaps her future fiancé as well.

She undressed to her bikini underwear, shedding the underwire bra in the process and leaving it in a pile with the rest of her failures. Her body was winter pale, but her stomach flat and firm, her hips wide and her thighs lean. Her breasts were high on her chest, her nipples angling up and out to the sides. Men found her breasts attractive because of that; why, she wasn't sure. She worked hard at preservation, chased her youth like a dog after a moving car—four miles a day, weight training—these weren't God-given assets, she earned them through a daily regime. She ran through the houseboat all but naked hoping to death no one was happening down the dock, for one of the front blinds was open. She scrambled up the narrow ladder to the tiny loft bedroom where she kept her underwear, socks and bras separate from her other clothing—for reasons she had never fully understood. The rest of her wardrobe was divided between two closets, a trunk and a chest of drawers, all located down by the bathroom. She stuffed herself into a constricting jog bra, feeling much better. Hide the chest. Baggy is best.

Bailing out of any attempt to invent herself otherwise, she returned to a pair of gardening blue jeans that were a little too big in the back and a pink cotton sweater that revealed nothing of what it contained.

She brushed her dark hair back and shook her head, reconsidered and tried a hair band and settled finally with it pulled back sharply into a "squishy," as she called the elastic fabric bands. She liked the results: plain, confident, but boyish and even a bit severe.

She drove the Honda at warp speeds, picking out a route that allowed a lot of turns on red.

Liz Boldt had never invited her to anything.

She approached the front door aware of her stride. She had a sexy, athletic gait that came naturally, and she dismantled it as best she could in the event Liz Boldt might be watching her. She walked stiffly.

The closer she drew to the house, the closer to an internal honesty. There had been several years of her life when she would have willingly exchanged places with this woman, when her need of Lou Boldt had built to an obsession that had driven her to prove herself not only professionally but as a woman. When her moment with Boldt finally occurred—a passionate and tumultuous tumble under a dining room table—it only drove her further over the edge. For months she had thought of nothing but possessing him, consuming him so that he would abandon his wife for her. She loved his kids and the way he was with them—she wanted her own with him; Liz be damned.

And now Liz was damned, and Daphne lived with the guilt of her former hopes and ambitions. She had broken off an engagement because of her inability to settle for less than Boldt, and now she felt ready to renew that commitment to Owen Adler, with none of her former passion for Boldt, but strangely with a form of love for him still intact. How this transition had occurred would puzzle the psychologist part of her for the rest of her days, but she no longer had to own Boldt, did not want to. Knowing him, working with him, was enjoyable, but her heart no longer fluttered when he entered the room. Her greatest fear was that this ability in her to let go might have coincided with the discovery of Liz's illness—that only by facing the possibility of getting what she wanted did she discover she did not want it. She didn't know if this were true or not, but even the possibility terrified her. If Liz died, if Boldt made advances, would she reject him? She caught herself standing at the door unable to lift her arm to knock. She wanted to turn around and run.

The door came open.

"You look great," Daphne said, nervous and lacking the composure that was her trademark.

"I look awful." Liz smiled and tugged on the wig, making a point of it. "Bald as an eagle under this thing." Another smile.

The poor woman was all bones and cosmetics—there wasn't a hair on her body.

"It takes a generous person to say otherwise. Thank you." Showing her into the living room, Liz offered Daphne a cup of tea, the pot steaming on the coffee table.

Passing her a cup, Liz said, "You're puzzled by the invitation."

"I'm honored, actually. Your first day home, isn't it? I didn't think—"

"It's probably not what the doctors would call for, but neither is attending church, and I did that this morning, so why not break all the rules?" She placed her own tea back on the table. "I'll tell you something about cancer: It changes you. It changes everything about you." She paused and Daphne could see the woman searching for the right words, the way an athlete concentrates just before competition. "You and I share a mutual interest. For the last couple of years, I've allowed that to threaten me. You're quite beautiful, extremely smart—if Lou's opinion is to be trusted—and you have clearly captivated a part of Lou's heart. He cares for you deeply—"

"Liz—"

She cut her off with a raised hand. "He does. What of it? Why shouldn't he? You've got a hell of a lot going for you."

Was she intending to tell her that her husband was fair game after she died? Was she going to get morbid and coach her competition on the raising of the children? Daphne wondered why she'd come. She should have seen clear of the trap. Liz Boldt intended to punish Daphne for her brief love affair. She wanted out of there.

"My point is, he trusts you. He believes in you." Her eyes teared up. "That's extremely important right now."

"He believes in your recovery, too," Daphne said. "We all do."

"Oh no, is that what you think? That this is about *me*? That I called you because— Oh, no. I'm sorry. I'm so sorry! A dying woman's maudlin attempts to—" She laughed and looked around the room as if suddenly seeing it for the first time. "I'm not dying. I'm healed." She said freshly, "Miles is coming home tomorrow."

"I'm glad."

"You drove him to Kathy's. Lou told me. Drove him without ever asking why. You see the kind of person you are? You know what that means to us, that kind of trust?"

She couldn't stand the tension. She blurted out, "Why exactly *did* you ask me over?"

"It's Lou," she said, tears flooding her eyes. But she would not give in to them. This woman who looked so frail had the strength of ten. She reached down and took Daphne's warm hands in hers, as cold as tile. "I'm trusting in you as I've never trusted in anyone. In part because of Lou's high opinion of you—we don't really know each other, do we? In part because your profession requires a great deal of confidentiality, and I trust, I assume, that that is a skill one acquires, that that is something once learned can be applied to so many relationships."

Relationships? Confidentiality? Was she going to bring up the affair? Had Lou told her? She looked down at their hands entwined together. Guilt and fear rose in her chest to a knot of pain—she couldn't breathe. The damn bra was too tight!

Would she lie outright to this woman if asked?

Liz Boldt squeezed her hands tightly and said, "Something terrible has happened. We desperately need your help."

CHAPTER

39

The treasure revealed itself like the gold of the pharaohs. On Monday morning, March 30, the lab delivered sixty-seven full-color computer printouts to LaMoia—all photographs made with Anderson's digital camera, all from a backup disk found hidden in Anderson's bookshelves. As an added bonus, each was dated and time-stamped. He leafed through a series of a businessman climbing out of his car in a motel parking lot, entering a room, and leaving forty minutes later, followed shortly thereafter by a worn-looking creature bearing the heavy posture of someone defeated. Two of the many subjects depicted were shown engaged, in partial nudity or unmistakable poses, with adolescent members of the same sex. How Anderson had gone about his work was likely to have puzzled some of his clients, but it showed little imagination or creativity to LaMoia. In some cases Anderson had taken the adjacent motel room and bribed a housecleaner into unlocking the communicating door. In one daring effort, the sleuth appeared to have been hiding inside a closet with shuttered doors, implying that he had paid off the prostitute.

There had been a time early in his career that LaMoia would have found one or more of such photos suggestive enough to arouse him, but those days were long gone. More than anything, he felt numb to it all, frightened for the missing children, guilt-ridden over his failure to rescue them. So many of humankind elected to lead sordid, twisted, perverted lives that any detective came to expect it rather than be fascinated by it. After a time one forgot that these people were only a fraction of society. Because of their staggering numbers, they seemed more the norm.

There were photos of storefronts, school buses, city parks, top-less dancers, a bank teller, an interior of a Starbucks. Seven shots of a woman shopping various department stores. Three of a teen-age girl—a daughter? a baby sitter?—giving her boyfriend head in the family hot tub, her face partially underwater, the smooth flawless skin of her bare back cresting the surface of the bubbling water like a breaching whale.

Thrown into the mix near the end of the stack, he finally reached the series that he'd been waiting for: five images from a computer file Anderson had named weinstn.pix.

The first of these, one that easily caught his attention, depicted the now familiar clapboard house that had contained Jeffry Mc-Nee's meth lab. Closer study revealed that one of the vehicles parked in front was a white minivan, its back windows made opaque by either paint or butcher paper. On the driver's door was an unreadable sign. LaMoia was guessing it advertised an exterminator service. Hard evidence was, on occasion, as good as sex.

The second of the five photos showed a figure walking along the building's perimeter carrying a spray tank and hose, his head down and hidden by a gray baseball cap and a pair of goggles. He wore coveralls and looked to be about six feet tall. There was no face to pull from the shot. LaMoia silently and reluctantly con-gratulated him on his choice of disguises. It was no wonder they had never gotten a decent eyewitness description: nothing of him to identify but a pair of bland-colored coveralls and matching cap.

LaMoia placed the third of the images in front of himself like a poker player rolling his cards. This was of a boating marina on a gray day. The depth of field was bad, the image blurred. He wasn't sure they would ever identify the marina from such a poor picture. The same could be said for the two figures at its center— *two,* LaMoia noticed. Shot at such a great distance they were little more than stick figures. Anderson had been careful not to get too close. The man wore a colorful sweatshirt, baseball cap pulled low and blue jeans. The woman wore jeans, shades and a hat. Unidentifiable. LaMoia's initial enthusiasm was tempered by these discoveries. Anderson knew how to follow people—a photographer, he wasn't. He cursed the man for managing a shot with no identifiable landmarks or signage. Anderson confirmed his standing as a nickel hustler, nothing more.

LaMoia dwelled on this photo for a long time, first working the magnifying glass, then the loupe. The resolution was too poor, the focus too blurred, to give up any secrets.

The penultimate image related to the final of the five shots and contributed to the story that formed the mystery of Anderson's homicide. The scene was a greenway—a running path. It showed a man, perhaps six feet tall, in running clothes. Again, this man wore a cap on his head and sunglasses, again the shot was taken at too great a distance. The final photo, and the telling one, was nearly identical—shot in the same minute—except that the jogger's head was turned toward the camera. But Anderson had panicked, this shot was the most blurred of all. The story of Anderson's death unfolded for LaMoia as clearly as if Anderson had still been alive to tell it.

"So?" LaMoia asked Boldt, standing slightly behind him and looking over his shoulder.

"So?" Boldt fired back. He understood perfectly the significance of Anderson's photographs: If handled correctly, if traced to the right marina, every possibility existed that SPD might identify a suspect. Boldt had to prevent that, but at the same time he wanted every scrap of information the photos provided. He felt incredibly tempted to share his secret with LaMoia to double his manpower, but he didn't dare. The ransom note haunted him.

Boldt prided himself on his organization and neatness, but the clutter of his desk and office told a different story, and he wondered how much of this LaMoia picked up on. The room smelled of his fear. Two dozen or more white and blue telephone memo slips littered his desktop in various piles. They represented unreturned calls, or calls in which Boldt had no interest. He was intentionally allowing his Intelligence work to lapse; the unit was in shambles.

These memos were interspersed with hand-scrawled scraps of notes that, if viewed as a complete work, revealed a mind in turmoil, a man, a husband, a father, an investigator saddled with internal conflict. There was an empty bottle of aspirin open by the phone, the lid missing. A mug containing a moldy scum that had once been tea. Several stacks of paperwork carried office dandruff—the visible dust of neglect. If he had caught one of his detectives with a work area in similar disarray he would have chastised the guilty party.

"So the pictures tell a story," LaMoia said. "The Pied Piper clearly made Anderson—in that last shot it's so obvious. The thing is dated March 15, 4:22 P.M., which fits with the angle of light. Two days later Anderson does the swan dive in the tub."

Playing devil's advocate, Boldt said, "The photographs show no crime being committed. They are of an unknown subject in an unknown location. They are from a computer disk that, according to you, has never been mentioned at a four o'clock, never presented to the task force. Is there proper paperwork on the removal of the disk from Anderson's residence?"

"I wrote it up. Hill knows all about it."

Boldt warned, "Okay. So let's say the evidence holds in court. It still shows no crime."

"The file has Weinstein's name on it."

"It has a piece of Weinstein's name," the more veteran cop corrected.

"In computers, that's the same thing."

"Maybe, maybe not." He couldn't afford LaMoia running to the task force with these photos. He needed first crack at them if he were to have any chance of finding Sarah. He looked for La-Moia's angle in bringing them to him first. It wasn't the good student wanting to show off to his former teacher—LaMoia wanted something more than praise or evaluation. But what? And could Boldt turn whatever it was to his own advantage?

"So?" LaMoia asked, forcing Boldt to make a hasty assessment.

His basic problem was that he couldn't think clearly, certainly not quickly. He felt drugged, not himself. Fatigue swam in his head as if his ears were filled with water. Aspirin dulled it briefly, but did not remove this pain. It was his to live with. Why? he asked himself again. He voiced the only thought that entered his weary mind. "You're reluctant to turn this over to Flemming."

LaMoia took this as an accusation. "Their lab has had Anderson's computer forever. If they had come across these same pix when would we have heard about it? I'll tell you when: Once they had located that marina and made inquiries—and only then, and don't you believe otherwise."

"I don't," Boldt said, rubbing his neck with as strong a grip as he could muster. That was the other thing: He had lost his strength. He walked at half his former pace. His arms felt heavy, as if someone else's. "You're right, I'm sure of it." He said, "And if you so much as breathe a word of this—"

"They'll run with it. They're pigs in shit with this kind of evidence. Fly a few more suits in to canvass marinas, and once they find the place we'll read about the Piper's arrest on the front page."

"Probably right," Boldt said, not believing a word of it. He had no great love for the Bureau—he'd been bitten as many times as he'd been fed, but Flemming struck him differently than most. The man wanted this over, wanted the Pied Piper in custody as badly as anyone. Boldt wasn't certain how he had managed to

remain on the case as long as he had; the Bureau had a way of
exorcising inefficiency. Typically, Flemming would have been off
the case by the San Francisco kidnappings, having failed in the
previous two cities. He either had friends in the right places, or
his reputation as their top kidnap cop was well founded.

"You're damn right I'm right." LaMoia could get worked up.

Boldt played on that. "Unless you beat them to it. This is our
city, John. Those are our marinas."

"Exactly! Don't I know it? Damn right. *Our* city, god damn it!
But the shot! Look at those two pictures. There's nothing in them
but a bunch of masts. Nothing to identify them. It's like Anderson
worked on screwing it up. You know how many boatyards and
marinas there are? Lake Union. Lake Washington. The shore.
Mercer Island. Kirkland. Medina. Jesus! Vashon. The islands, for
Chrissakes. It's endless."

"And you want me to find it for you," Boldt said, knowing and
exploiting LaMoia's needs. Intentionally misusing their friendship. He wanted to crawl into a hole and die.

The comment sobered LaMoia's hysteria. He looked his former sergeant in the eye and nodded grimly. "You mean I'm using
you?" he asked, getting it all wrong. "Yeah, that's about right. If I
have anything to do with this, the existence of Anderson's photos
gets out and I'm butting heads with Flemming, which means I'm
butting heads with Hill, which means I'm screwed. Anyone I ask
to look into this is going to know it's task force related. But Intelligence? No one knows what the hell you do up here all day. Everyone's worried you're looking up *their* skirt. And with manpower
being what it is—"

"I use the snitches to do the legwork."

LaMoia acted slightly embarrassed. "That's what I was thinking. Yeah. A color Xerox. Pass 'em around and see if we can't
kick a location."

"My snitches don't exactly work the yachting circuit. They
aren't the deck-shoe set, John." He couldn't jump at the offer
without raising suspicions. No cop glorified himself with extra
work; he or she spent too much time and effort defending turf

and protecting positions. Boldt had to dismiss the offer. "You could use a few uniforms."

"It would leak."

"It might." Both knew damn well it would.

"I gave you forty-eight hours with the Spitting Image evidence," he reminded, playing the trump card Boldt hoped he might use.

"I was doing the legwork. This is a little different," Boldt countered. It took all his strength not to agree too quickly.

"Seventy-two hours," LaMoia requested. "Work the photos for three days. After that, I take it to the task force."

"Forty-eight." Boldt wanted the evidence for a week or two, and there he was suggesting a shorter period than he was being offered.

"It'll take you one day just to get the pix out on the street. Right? Once they're out there, you're giving me forty-eight, same as I'm giving you." And then the word LaMoia rarely, if ever, spoke. "Please, Sarge."

"You've changed," Boldt said, knowing correctly that LaMoia would take it as a backhanded compliment.

" 'You don't work cases, you work deals,' " LaMoia quoted the man sitting in front of him. "A wise old soldier once told me that."

"Get out of here," Boldt said, his fingers sweating on the photographs he held.

As had LaMoia before him, Boldt worked the photocopies with a magnifying glass and a jeweler's loupe. He pored over the images for the better part of an hour and then, just ready to give it up, he noticed what he had missed in all the other passes. It came under the heading "forest for the trees."

Of late, he realized, a detective mined his crime scene for evidence that he then turned over to SID for lab tests. Too often, that reliance translated into a dependence on the lab—a belief that the lab had all the answers. In the process, old-fashioned police work suffered.

For an hour, Boldt searched the photos for a readable license plate, a landmark, any unique piece of evidence that might help. He sought out patterns, anything unique.

What he discovered was easily missed. It was not a sign, nor a number or a name. It was much more simple. It was right there in the center of the photo. Right there staring back.

CHAPTER

40

Dr. Ronald Dixon's home was an impressive three-story Victorian, on the west side of 16th East, near Volunteer Park. Appointed with marble and antiques, Heriz rugs and a Steinway Concert grand, the living room had at its center two couches that faced each other across a low walnut coffee table and were perpendicular to the fireplace, its mantel painted an eggshell enamel white and holding a glass-encased clock whose pendulum issued a steady click, click, click.

Boldt knew the living room well, having spent many hours there exchanging jazz favorites with Dixie, who opened the front door admitting Boldt. Dixie thanked him for coming over.

"You made it sound so urgent," Boldt said of the request for a lunchtime meeting. Their friendship went back decades, not years. Dixie rarely, if ever, asked favors.

His host motioned Boldt toward the living room. The lieutenant rounded the corner and stopped cold, glancing back at his trusted friend and then into the room again and the people assembled there. A trap! Boldt realized, his first instinct to run. Run and never trust anyone again.

Daphne Matthews stood admiring one of the antiques, a hammered brass lamp and mica lamp shade.

LaMoia also stood, though with his back pressed firmly against the mantel, his bloodshot eyes trained on his mentor. SID's Bernie Lofgrin was on the couch working a beer. Bobbie Gaynes occupied the end of the piano bench. She straddled it, legs spread, leaning on her hands planted together in front of her. A group that knew each other well, a working family. Boldt did not like the looks, nor the silence. He had been found out! By whom? LaMoia? Daphne?

But one other person appeared to his right, stepping out of the sunroom. Liz said, "This is an intervention."

It was not Boldt's life that passed before his eyes, but the image of Sarah on the video clip: the pleading eyes, the frightened voice, "Daddy!" It wasn't these people to whom she was calling out, but to him, her father. He wanted no part of an intervention, whatever the hell that meant; he wasn't an alcoholic, he was a cop who wanted his daughter back.

Liz said, "You can't do this alone, love. No matter how badly you want to, and God knows I love you for it—" She was crying now, "You can't. *We* can't. We made the decision to save her. These are our closest friends. They can help."

"Liz!" he protested.

"If we're careful—" Daphne began, immediately interrupted.

"No one asked you!" Boldt shouted, his skin numb and tingling. Liz had killed their child . . . , "or you, or you," he said to the others.

"Your wife asked me," Daphne contradicted in the voice of a friend, not a psychologist.

"You could have told us," an angry LaMoia delivered. "What'd you think I'd do, rat on you?"

Daphne said, "This isn't about you, it's about Sarah—"

"Don't lecture me on what this is about." To his wife he complained bitterly, "We talked about this. *No one was to know.*"

"And no one does," Dixie pointed out in his resonant baritone. "Only we know, Lou. Only those of us in this room. It isn't a conspiracy with only one person. You *need* us."

LaMoia jumped in. "You want to find her, we'll find her. You want to screw up the task force, brother we'll fuck it up but good!" He smiled a patented LaMoia smile. Overconfident to the point of cocky.

Lofgrin said, "We can misplace some evidence if necessary."

Bobbie Gaynes stood from the piano bench. "Sarge, I got to get back to the Park and Ride surveillance. What you got to know—we're with you on this. We all love little Sarah. We all love you. So stop being so ungrateful and figure out a way to put us all to work. John, you'll catch me up?"

"Got you covered."

Gaynes walked to Boldt, leaned forward on her tiptoes and kissed him on the cheek. She had never done this before and it brought a frog to his throat. "You got your own secret little task force now, Sarge. Take advantage of it." She left, the large front door thumping shut behind her.

LaMoia checked his watch. "We got about two hours to debrief you and get a game plan before we raise suspicion by being away from the office."

Dixie said, "There's tea water on. And sandwiches."

"Have a seat, Sarge," LaMoia said, patting the couch.

Boldt sat down, not by his detective but by his wife. The meeting began in earnest a few minutes later.

CHAPTER

The Intelligence offices were a quiet place to work. Boldt had learned to appreciate the quiet. Phones purred softly, answered in hushed voices that didn't carry. Secrets. A two-way street of constantly shifting information. Computers hummed. Outside, the sun appeared for the first time in several days, painting brushstrokes of silver in the windows of neighboring buildings.

Surrendering his secret added to Boldt's exhaustion, driven by an overwhelming sense of relief. The burden of withholding the truth of his daughter's situation released, he found himself able to concentrate, focus and redirect his energies. He spent his time reviewing the Spitting Image invoices, including the E-mail orders he had received from Stonebeck earlier that same morning.

He attempted to contact the various cable television companies that served northwest Washington, hoping to determine which of them had run a weather alert at 12:02 P.M., March 25, the moment of Sarah's video ransom, and he was in the middle of just such a call when he was interrupted by a patrol officer. "You have a visitor, Lieutenant. A woman."

"No visitors," he said, believing it a snitch. "Pass her off to someone else."

"She's from out of town. Says it's urgent. It's not a squirrel, Lieutenant. This one is Talbots and Eddie Bauer. You know? What should I tell her?" the uniform asked.

"Out of town?"

"She didn't say where."

"An attorney. You've got to at least get a name. I'm busy here."

The uniformed woman stood up artificially erect. "She wouldn't give me a name. But she did say that you spoke to her yesterday."

"Yesterday?" He couldn't remember back twenty-four hours. He glanced at the call sheet he kept by the phone. Sunday. Nothing. It didn't make sense to him. It was someone trying to weasel an unscheduled appointment out of him. He had spent most of the day before, in, or en route to, Portland.

He dragged himself out of the chair. The patrol officer stepped out of his way. Boldt peered around the jamb.

In her mid-thirties, she dressed well, wore her hair extremely short and wire glasses that added a thoughtful intelligence. The face seemed familiar to him, but he couldn't come up with a name. He stared at her searching for a name. She sensed it and turned and met eyes with him.

"Connie," he called out. "Connie *Bowler*." He had in fact spoken to her the day before. She had helped him to locate her drunken husband. It felt as if a week had gone by.

Boldt showed her to a seat and shut the office door for privacy.

She clutched her purse tightly. Sarah had a favorite blanket she held to this same way. Beneath the purse lay a bulging oversized mailer. Boldt found it difficult to take his eyes off that envelope. Connie Bowler spoke in a high, rushed voice. "If Tom asks, I'll say I drove up here to do some shopping. But he won't ask, so it doesn't matter." She rattled on, "It's a bit of a stretch, because the shopping in Portland is just as good, but we do have a few friends up here," she said, thinking aloud, "you and Elizabeth among them, but I wouldn't dare use that because he might follow up on it."

"How long has Tom been drinking like that?" Boldt asked, getting directly to the point.

"How is Elizabeth?" she asked, avoiding an answer. "I was so sorry to hear—"

"Better, I think." He didn't want a twenty-minute heaping of sympathy. He had grown to resent such offers. "I wanted to work with Tom on this kidnapping case—"

"The Pied Piper."

"Yes," he answered.

She toyed with the chain to her purse, eyes cast down in avoidance. She pulled out the manila folder and Boldt stepped up to accept it. He did not open it despite himself. He set it aside. "That's why I'm here. Why I came. Tom—" She caught herself and glanced over at his office door as if to make sure it was closed, their conversation private. "We don't know each other very well, do we?"

He knew Bowler from the constant traffic of information between departments, and because Bowler had once chaired a conference of Northwest Law Enforcement at which Boldt had been one of the speakers. "Well enough," he attempted to reassure her.

"Tom was lead detective on the Pied Piper. Did you know that?"

"Yes. That's why I came down yesterday." He added, "To ask about Penny."

She blushed—an involuntary act that spoke volumes. Boldt felt flooded with anxiety. Connie Bowler glanced quickly at the door again, drawn perhaps by a uniform passing close to the office.

Once the uniform was well out of earshot, she whispered, "Penny was taken from us in the middle of the second week of the investigation."

For Boldt, this meant the Pied Piper had routinely blackmailed local police officers, that in all likelihood, the evidence from each city was tainted, that Flemming and the FBI had been following bad information all along. Sheila Hill had suspected as much. Connie Bowler now confirmed it.

"Tom won't talk about it, but I know he concealed evidence. He said the case file was stolen, and he kept it from the FBI that way. That's not right. I can't let it happen again. I mean . . . it already has, hasn't it? Sarah. He told me. And these other children up here. I'm *so* sorry. I know that if Tom . . . but you have to understand . . . we got her back safely. Penny . . . It was all we dreamed for." The woman's eyes brimmed with tears, her lips quivered and her face collapsed like a balloon losing air. She shrank down into herself, suddenly half her size. Her tears spilled onto her blouse, leaving constellations on her chest. "And Tom? He's convinced that if it came out how he intentionally threw the case—for whatever reason—that they'd pull his badge and his benefits and kick him out into the street. And the way it is, we're just not prepared to start over like that. You know? The kids and all."

As he waited for her to continue, he understood that he had already violated the ransom demands, and a sinking terror filled him that he had done the wrong thing in giving in to the intervention. But in the same thought he realized that Bowler could not live with what he'd done.

Connie Bowler's tear-streaked face confronted Boldt, who caught movement out of the corner of his eye. He lifted his hand to stop Daphne from entering his office. Connie looked in Daphne's direction, but by the time she did, she saw only her back as Daphne walked away, no questions asked.

Connie said softly, "Penny's fine. Not a scratch on her. No sign of . . . you know . . . nothing. He'd done nothing bad to her."

"He?"

The question puzzled her. "The kidnapper. A woman couldn't possibly put a child through this."

Playing his cards closely, Boldt said nothing to contradict her. "Did Tom make contact with him?"

She shook her head. "No. He would have told me." She teared up again. "We heard nothing for over three weeks."

Sarah had been missing six days; he could not fathom the concept of three weeks.

"She was found in the Clackamas Town Center. It's a mall. Her name, our address and phone number were found on a card in her pocket. Left there like a lost package." She sprouted more tears and mumbled, repeating, "Nothing was wrong with her. She was fine. Just a little scared was all."

"The card. Handwritten or typed?"

"On a computer, Tom said." She forced a smile. "It's funny that that would matter to both of you, isn't it? I remember he mentioned it was a computer. It struck me as so strange that he would care about that."

Boldt's speech came out hoarse and dry. "I will need to talk with Tom about his case."

"I told him he had to talk to you, that we couldn't allow it to continue, but he said that Penny came first, that he had gone to the devil to save Penny and keep her safe and that he wasn't going to throw that all away now."

Boldt wasn't sure he had the courage to do what Connie Bowler had done—to get Sarah back safely and then risk it all over again.

"What we went through . . . what we've gone through . . . well, you know, don't you." She made it a statement. "You of all people would understand. That's what I tried to tell Tom. If we can tell anyone . . ." She teared up again and spoke to Boldt the father, the parent, her voice earnest and strong. "No one should ever have to go through what we went through. It has to stop." Holding his gaze, she silently pleaded with him. Then she stood, wiping away her tears, and indicated the thick manila envelope. "I put our address on top. Mail it back to me, please. He still looks at it occasionally."

Boldt offered to copy the file while she waited. This appealed to her, and Boldt left her in his office while he copied it, the action reminding him of copying LaMoia's task force book only days earlier.

If he did not act, if he allowed the Pied Piper to continue the abductions, in all likelihood Sarah would be returned unharmed. This possibility tugged at him but was quickly replaced by an image of Bowler cradling the glass of Scotch. The child had been saved but the father lost—the family broken.

CHAPTER

The FBI's Washington State Field Office, located in Seattle's new Federal Building, smelled of perfumed disinfectant that Daphne Matthews associated with a doctor's waiting room. She was repulsed by the smell because it reminded her of a particular car deodorizer that came in the shape of a small green pine tree and hung from the rearview mirror or inside the trunk, the smell of which was seared into her memory where it would remain forever. Just the smell of it made her want to run. She was supposed to trick an FBI agent into supplying information the Bureau had yet to release to SPD. No small task. The intervention had gone well. Boldt—and Sarah with him—was now supported by a team of competent and fiercely loyal individuals bent on the girl's rescue.

As Flemming's Intelligence officer, Kay Kalidja had unrestricted access to Bureau resources, making her an invaluable ally. By not making an appointment, Daphne denied Kalidja any preparation for her visit. She was kept waiting for ten minutes in a small reception area. Behind the receptionist hung a photo of the president, another of the FBI chief and a third of WSFO's special agent in charge. Kalidja appeared at the secured door and greeted Daphne, apologizing for keeping her waiting. Daphne followed her inside. "The digs here aren't much for those of us from out-of-town. I'm sharing an office with two others."

She showed Daphne into the cramped and cluttered office and closed the door. "They resent us, of course—the local agents. They don't want Washington coming in and dictating procedure. On the surface, it's business as usual, but the resentment is there. Have a seat, if you can find one." The office walls held book-shelves crowded with loose-leaf binders bearing the FBI logo.

They faced each other from opposite sides of the desk.

Daphne lied for the sake of her efforts. "They assign me all the no-brainers, assignments they wouldn't dare ask a male officer to do."

"Same thing here, I promise," Kalidja said, sympathetically.

"They assume we're incapable of using our brains," Daphne said, hoping to strike a common chord.

"And it's not our brains they're thinking about," Kalidja said. She laughed. Her neck was long and elegant. She might have made it as a model had she tried.

Daphne met eyes with the woman and said, "Have you ever noticed how quickly your ideas become someone else's? Suddenly all the credit is going down the table?"

Special Agent Kay Kalidja did not break the eye contact, under-standing perfectly well that Daphne had come for a favor. Daphne placed Thompson's rendition of the tattoo in front of Kalidja and let it sit there. She said, "VICAP and your other data-bases keep track of body markings, don't they?"

Kalidja fingered the photocopy.

"Left forearm," Daphne said.

"*His?*" Kalidja nearly shouted. "The Pied Piper's?"

Daphne nodded. "If it pans out, we unveil it at a four o'clock, the two of us. With two of us, one SPD, one FBI, they can't take it away from us. Everyone's talking up joint cooperation, but doing little if anything to make it happen." She paused. "What do you think?"

"You mean keep it from our own people?" Kalidja was clearly

afraid of the idea. Flemming ran a tight ship. "Where did you get this?"

"We keep it between us until we know if we're going to look like fools or geniuses." Daphne broke into a sweat.

A smile slowly crept onto Kalidja's face, illuminating her features and lending her an attractive innocence, younger and less formal. "I could have something this afternoon. Tomorrow at the latest," Kalidja said, eyes sparkling with excitement.

Daphne settled back in the chair and relaxed. She had her right where she wanted her.

CHAPTER

43

Wednesday morning greeted Carlie Kittridge with excitement beating in her chest, her focus on the volleyball game later that evening. She climbed out of bed the moment she heard Trudy's little coughs over the baby monitor. The coughs signaled a gagging sound followed by outright crying—hunger—and she attempted to fend off that stage whenever possible.

The house was small but the master bath oversized, and so she kept the cradle in the bathroom alongside the tub and in front of the windows, with the beige cafe curtains, that faced the Wallingford Bridge. She unwrapped and pulled away the receiving blanket, talking silly at little Trudy and planting a gentle kiss on the five-month-old's forehead, amazed at the softness of the skin and its sweet cream smell.

Just before Trudy's impatience built to a peal, her mother scooped her up gently and pulled her tightly against the warmth of her chest. Carlie, wearing a terry cloth robe, immediately planted her daughter onto her left breast, who suckled hungrily. She held her effortlessly there, remembering briefly how unnatural it had all felt in Evelyn's first week on earth, how far mother, father and family had come since then. With Trudy, everything seemed second nature for Carlie, as simple as could be.

Carlie quickly glanced over her shoulder, experiencing the disquieting sensation that she was being watched. She wrote it off to the exposure of her bare breast—she still felt self-conscious about the nursing.

With Trudy gumming and nibbling at her, Carlie walked a little faster downstairs through the morning darkness and changed her girl's diaper in the nursery. She entered the kitchen and brought a bottle of formula from the refrigerator, the automatic light spreading white over her and again instilling a sense of vulnerability.

Carlie ran some hot water to warm the bottle and switched Trudy to her right breast without a thought. Weaning was the worst, she enjoyed the breast-feeding so much, but her milk had not come in as strongly for Trudy as it had for Evelyn, and so she had been supplementing with the bottle. She was on a schedule to have Trudy completely off the breast by the time the summer sand leagues started. No sense in having engorged and painful breasts all summer long.

She tuned the stereo to a light rock station and burped Trudy to cuts from the Beatles' *White Album*. With Trudy in the mechanical swing, Carlie slipped into a pair of fresh underwear, shorts, socks and a jog bra. Her sweatshirt was from the university bookstore. As the sun broke over the eastern horizon, she carried Trudy upstairs and awakened David. She held the child while David freshened up, and then, with Trudy safely in her father's arms, Carlie broke out into the crisp moist morning air, alive and vital, but harboring that same unsettling feeling that someone was indeed watching. The evening game would be upon them before she knew it.

Lou Boldt dismissed the first call from sketch artist Tommy Thompson as a cry for payment. Thompson, a freelancer and former employee of the police department, understood he faced a four- to six-week wait for his check. Boldt believed Thompson was merely attempting to hasten the process by applying some pressure.

He reluctantly heeded the second call, however, because the word "urgent" was conveniently tacked onto the message. If Thompson was misusing their relationship, Boldt would give him a piece of his mind, but as it was he owed him the professional courtesy of a return call.

"You're either getting sloppy, lazy or both," Thompson began their telephone conversation.

"I put in for payment the minute I got back, Tommy. You did great work with that tattoo. If I had my way I would have paid you on the spot."

"I'm not talking about my check, I'm talking about your lack of hindsight, that is, covering your tail end."

Boldt understood the implication immediately—that he had been followed to Vashon Island and the session with Thompson— and felt sick to his stomach. The Pied Piper had warned him in the ransom note to derail the investigation, not work to improve their evidence. He experienced a flutter in his chest and a light-headedness that bordered on nausea. If the Pied Piper knew about Thompson, then Boldt had just sabotaged his own daughter.

"You were contacted?" Boldt nearly screamed into the receiver, furious at himself for having let down his guard. He had not thought to look for a tail the day of that ferry ride.

"You might call it more of an interrogation," Thompson said. "I got a little door-to-door from a blue suit named Hale, Dunkin Hale. You know him?"

"I know him," Boldt confirmed.

"Was interested in a little bird-watching."

"As in eagles?"

"You got it."

"You showed him the sketch?" Boldt complained into the phone.

Thompson snapped sarcastically, "No. I told him to go screw himself. I do that with all the FBI agents who come knocking."

"If I had wanted the thing broadcast," Boldt reminded, "I would have done it in-house."

"Yeah? I trained every one of them kids. We both know why you made the ferry trip." He added, "Listen, he told me not to say a word about his visit. Told me the IRS loves to audit artists working out of their houses. A real peach, this one. Meaning, you put it back onto him and I'm a screwed pooch. You got that?"

"I got it."

"Intelligence," Thompson mused. "What exactly does that mean, anyway?"

Boldt wondered how Hale had found out about Henry Shotz. Would Doris Shotz, reluctant to involve her son in the first place, volunteer to the FBI that she'd withheld information from them? Doubtful. Had Hale placed a tail on Boldt? Had he wiretapped Boldt, the same way Boldt had wiretapped him? Perhaps Boldt had just found him.

CHAPTER

The idea of running one investigation inside another appealed to LaMoia in the same way as did the secrecy of having an affair.

At 11:30 that Wednesday morning he was paged to the Four Seasons Olympic, arguably the best hotel in the city. He drew attention as he passed through the elegantly appointed lobby, in part because of his cocky body language. He rode up to the fifth floor along with a Chinese woman laden with Nordstrom shopping bags. A few minutes past twelve noon, he knocked sharply on the door to room 512.

The routine nearly always the same, the room door came open for him and LaMoia stepped inside. Sheila Hill had pulled the window's gauzy inner curtain so that the noonday light bled across her skin in an induced twilight. She wore a black underwire bra that forced her breasts up invitingly and black high-cut underwear revealing her tanned flank.

She stepped toward him with her practiced hungry look in her polished eyes and LaMoia suddenly wondered what he was doing there. She allowed him a modicum of control by eagerly submit-

ting to various fantasies, but her reason for being there was a form
of addiction, whereas his was a desire for companionship: He had
dated twenty-year-olds for too long.

He turned away from her, taking in the room with its glimpse
of the sound's gray-green waters and shipping traffic. He wanted
a conversation, something more than G-strings and the Kama
Sutra. He told her, "Boldt was able to get some of the credit
records from the Bureau—you don't want to ask."

"I don't want to *talk*," she corrected, swaying toward him, but
stopping short of making contact. "Let's see what can make you
stop talking."

She slipped off a shoulder strap and sucked on her fingertip.

"We've got to talk," he dared. "This isn't working for me."

"How 'bout this?" she inquired, slipping off the other strap. "It
certainly worked last time." She placed her hand between her legs.

"Can't we just *talk* for a change?"

"Damn you!" she said, her act over, though her chest and
cheeks flushed with anticipation. She stormed over to her pack of
cigarettes, all femininity gone, and lit a smoke. Until that moment
he hadn't fully allowed himself to realize how much of her was an
act. "So talk."

LaMoia said, "Not like that. I mean *talk*."

"About?"

"Something other than work and sex," he said.

"And the leading candidates are?"

"What if we just had dinner tonight? A bottle of wine, some
pasta."

"I hate pasta. I bloat up. What has gotten into you?"

"We shouldn't be doing this at lunch hour," he complained,
regretting his earlier line of argument. Born of guilt and concern
over Sarah's abduction, he said, "Those kids need us on this
'round the clock."

"What the hell have you been smoking?"

She sucked on the cigarette though didn't seem to notice it. She
appraised him like a tailor, paying no mind whatsoever to her own
partial nudity. Reaching for the table, she tossed him a key ring
and said, "Make me a gin and tonic." She indicated the minibar.

"It's lunchtime, *Captain.*"

"Yeah. Okay. Make it a double. And make one for you too."

"I don't think so."

"*Make one for you too.* I'm not drinking alone, cowboy."

LaMoia obeyed her, observing himself as if watching another. He poured the drinks, a stranger to himself. From where did she extract such power over him? He even went down the hall for ice. The drinks were poured strong. The cigarette smoke annoyed him.

She circled him as she drank. "More important question," she said. "Why would you give a shit about conversation? Hmm?" She dipped her finger into her drink and offered it to his lips, and he sucked on it. "Tongue," she said, and he obeyed. "Are you going soft on me, so to speak?" She plopped herself down onto the bed, the drink spilling onto her hand. She licked off the excess lasciviously, making a great show of her abnormally long tongue.

"I want more than nooners," he blurted out.

"Not from me you don't." She leaned back and poured a stream from her drink so that a silver line of liquid jumped through the delicate white hairs on her belly and vanished into the underwear's black elastic. "Ready or not," she said again, rocking her legs open and closed. She giggled girlishly. He knew that was part of it as well—she was someone else in these hotel rooms.

LaMoia upended the drink. She liked his long neck and its angular Adam's apple. He did this for her, again not understanding why.

Her thighs slapped softly.

She poured another stream down her belly to where it disappeared. "Come and get it!" She waved the cigarette at him.

LaMoia slipped it from her fingers and extinguished it, suddenly boiling mad. With the reactions of a snake, he knocked the drink from her hand, snagged her wrist, and pulled her so hard and so quickly toward the head of the bed that he pulled her out of her underwear. It rolled into a lump between her knees.

"Whee!" she squealed, possibly appreciating that he had mixed her drink as a triple and his own as a single.

"Take a few minutes to think about us," he said, cuffing her left wrist to the headboard. She made an exaggerated expression of concern and said, "Oh, you're scaring me!"

The liquor glass rolled to a stop.

LaMoia hurried to the closet and returned with two terry cloth bathrobe belts. A moment later the underwear was on the floor and her ankles bound to the bed.

"Something new!" she said excitedly. "Have we done handcuffs?"

"You've been rude to me, Sheila. Demeaning."

"Rank has its privileges," she fired back at him, waiting for him to undress. "Once you're captain, I'll make the drinks. But you'll still come when I call. And you know why? The twenty-year-olds gratify the ego all right, but not the loin."

LaMoia tugged the comforter off the bed, then the blanket out from under her and the flat sheet. Hill, naked and writhing, legs bound, one hand in the cuffs, didn't know what to make of this. She forced a smile, beginning to question his actions. He reached beneath her, and she cooperated, arching her back. He freed the corner of the fitted sheet and also stripped this from the bed, pulling a mattress pad with it. Nothing left with which to cover herself.

"What the hell?" she said.

He showed her the handcuff key as he carefully set it down in plain sight next to the television.

She looked around searchingly, suddenly understanding the game. "No way," she said, believing it a joke.

"Phone's in reach," he said, pointing.

"You will not do this," she shouted. "I am stark naked!"

He nodded. "And you know something? You'll call me again—"

"You're *dead* you do this!" She squirmed but wasn't getting loose. Her free arm could not reach her ankle.

He moved toward the door. "And you know why? Because you've never had it like this. Those fifty-year-olds just don't do it for you." LaMoia pulled the door shut, her insults filling the hall. He wondered how long until she made the phone call to room service.

CHAPTER

45

With the volleyball tossed and hanging in the air, awaiting her open palm, Carlie Kittridge suddenly worried over having left Trudy with a sitter. She knew this stemmed from the pregame discussion about the kidnapper called the Pied Piper that had focused on news stories warning parents not to leave their children in the care of others until the kidnapper was captured.

Carlie caught the ball rather than serve it. Her husband shouted back at her, "Let's go! Serve 'em up a beauty."

Instead, Carlie bounced the ball toward Jenny, their weakest player but the only woman on the bench. Conference rules required gender-balanced teams.

Her husband chastised, "What the hell?"

She felt no need to have to explain herself. A mother's prerogative. She searched for the car keys in the pocket of David's warm-ups. Possession of those keys lent her a great sense of freedom and relief. "Have Danny drop you off," she told him.

Her husband's expression conveyed a sense of treason. "Danny?" he croaked incredulously.

Jenny stepped up to the service line, having little sense of her own inability to play the game. A member of the opposing team complained loudly about the substitution taking too long and demanded a serve.

"At least serve out the game," David pleaded.

Jenny called out the score and served a lofting floater to the opponent's backcourt. The resulting bump was a perfect set for the front line. The spike came right at David, who failed to block it. Side out.

Carlie hurried out of the gym.

A stunned and defeated David Kittridge shouted after his wife, far too late to be heard, "Don't forget it's damn near out of gas."

Carlie Kittridge had forgotten. She ran out of gas eleven blocks from home, at the corner of 42nd and Stoneway. Blinded by her fear for her baby, she failed to pull the truck entirely off the roadway, leaving it dead, angled toward the curb and blocking traffic, the lights still on.

She came out of the truck's cab at a full sprint, already warmed up from her volleyball, came out running like a thoroughbred from the gate. Seattle traffic being what it was, she left most of it behind as if it were standing still, blowing through intersections without looking, without slowing her pace in the slightest, her hysteria feeding off her charged system. The harder she ran, the more convinced she was of the trouble that lay ahead.

Ironically, it was the disabled pickup truck abandoned midlane that brought the police into it, not the abduction of Trudy Kittridge. Fearing a car-jacking, an abduction or simply a vehicle stolen for a joyride, the reporting motor patrol officer requested a black-and-white do a drive-by inquiry at the Kittridge residence—the name and address lifted from his wireless computer terminal that accessed DMV's mainframe.

As Carlie Kittridge rounded the corner of 35th and Stoneway she was in abject horror and running faster than she had ever run in her life.

She approached the kitchen door already calling out for Gena, a neighbor's fourteen-year-old daughter in whom Carlie had placed an enormous amount of deserved trust. Gena was fourteen going on thirty. She loved Trudy like a member of the family, and her own mother—a fantastic friend—lived just four houses down the block.

"Gena, it's me," she called out loudly, swinging open the kitchen door. Gena lay there on the floor, her clothes torn, her fourteen-year-old body exposed.

Carlie Kittridge's scream was heard for several blocks.

CHAPTER

46

LaMoia awakened from a comatose sleep, summoned by the irritating beeping of his pager. His first response was anger, his second was a feeling of fear and dread. 8:00 P.M. He had fallen asleep at his kitchen table. He could conceive of very few reasons for the summons, not one of which he wanted to face.

He read the phone number from the device and heaved a sigh of relief. Sheila Hill's home telephone, an unpublished number. She had decided to talk. He complimented himself for understanding her. She was not an easy keeper.

"It's me," he announced over the phone.

"Their name is Kittridge." Her blank tone of voice and the announcement drained all color from his face. She read off an address. "Handle it."

She hung up, leaving him with a hollow, panicked feeling.

Another kidnapping.

Within an hour, photocopies of Trudy Kittridge's face were faxed to airports, train stations, ferry companies, the image being shown to cab drivers, limo drivers, bus drivers. Within the next hour every local television station would cut away to the same photo. Hundreds of thousands of people would see that face, and yet if the Pied Piper lived up to his reputation, no one would see the child.

Daphne awaited him as he pulled up, her face grim, her fists clenched tightly. Her job, to define the Pied Piper in terms of behavior, was taking its toll. She looked exhausted.

LaMoia said, "You take the parents, I'll take the scene. We gotta work fast. This place'll be jumping in a couple minutes. We need the head start. We pow-wow in the kitchen in ten minutes. You believe in miracles?"

"No," she answered.

"Me neither."

LaMoia had never smoked. He drank beer, but only socially. He had been blind drunk twice in his life, and had hated the lack of control. But at that moment he envied the habitual, whatever the vice, because it gave the person a preoccupation, an object of distraction. He had only the first officer's description of the four-teen-year-old unconscious on the kitchen floor to occupy his thoughts. He would have given anything to erase it from his mind. He could visualize her lying there where now there was some litter from the EMT's medical work and AFIDs from the air TASER. Sight of the AFIDs reminded him of the stonewalling of evidence. Sarah and the others deserved better than this.

Daphne joined him in the kitchen as planned.

She told him, "The mother is real clear on the Spitting Image outfit. It was a tiny little sweatshirt. A gift. Knew the name and everything."

"Did you tell her not to share said same with our distinguished colleagues?"

"That's suppressing evidence, John."

"Well shame on us."

A pair of Lincoln Town Cars pulled up in front.

LaMoia said to her, "Stall them. Give me as much time as you can." He took two steps, turned and asked, "Where are they?"

"Upstairs. To the left."

LaMoia threw open the bedroom door, stepped inside, and closed it quickly behind himself. "Mr. and Mrs. Kittridge?" The couple was trashed, the man worse than the wife, who looked as if she had run a marathon. He knew about the volleyball game, though he wasn't sure how the Pied Piper had made the connection.

He displayed his badge and introduced himself. He edged over to the window and peered out. Flemming, Hale and Kalidja. The full team. They walked as a group with strict determination. Flemming held an intensity that LaMoia did not want to experience firsthand—the guy's career was in flames, and SPD was pouring on the gasoline.

"You've just spoken with Ms. Matthews about a certain garment that your child . . . that Trudy . . . received as a gift." He glanced out the window nervously for a second time. Daphne wouldn't be able to hold them for long. If the Bureau made the Spitting Image connection, then they were likely to close in on a suspect, perhaps ahead of Boldt, and Sarah's chances went down the drain. He owed this effort to Boldt, who had made the Spitting Image connection in the first place.

"The sweatshirt," the wife muttered.

Nervous perspiration breaking out all over, he spoke quickly to the parents, knowing he had one, and only one, shot at an explanation. "Okay. Here's the thing. What I'm about to tell you is opinion. My opinion. But keep in mind, I'm lead detective for Seattle Police on this case. Okay? Just keep that in mind. This information, this Spitting Image connection, is what we call a good lead. You understand? It's *important* information to us. Very important. To the investigation, I'm talking about. To getting Trudy back. But there are other people investigating these kidnappings, okay? The FBI I'm talking about. And they aren't exactly our bosom buddies, if you know what I mean. They've had this investigation for nearly *six months,* and parents, just like you, are still waiting for news of their children. Okay? Six months. Gimme a break! These guys can't even remember the kids' names! You know what a leak is? Good. That's great. Well," he lied, "we think there is a leak inside the FBI. We think information like this—the Spitting Image information—is better kept close to home." He heard footsteps growing closer. Flemming and his team. LaMoia felt a bead of sweat run down his chin. He wiped it off. "Better kept right here in Seattle. You want to deal with three-piece suits and black shoes, you go right ahead. It's a free country. I can't stop you. But me, I'm right down the street. You pick up the phone, I'm there. Okay? Public Safety building. Right downtown. These guys? Go ahead and try to reach them on the phone. *I* can't even reach them. What chance do you have?" The footsteps were only a few yards away. "What chance does *Trudy* have? That's what you've got to ask yourself. Six months they've had this. Think about that. They're trying to handle a *dozen* cases. What's to show for it? Why? Because somebody's not clean, that's why."

A strong hand knocked on the door—Flemming—LaMoia knew this before the door opened.

LaMoia repeated, "It's a free country. I can't tell you what to do. *They* can't tell you what to do. No one can make you say anything you don't want to." He shouted toward the door. "Yeah?"

Flemming threw the door open. In his strong, rich baritone, he addressed the parents, "Mr. and Mrs. Kittridge, I'm terribly sorry for your loss." He glanced over at LaMoia venomously, for not waiting, and then back to the parents. He introduced himself and his two special agents. "I'm sure Detective LaMoia—"

"Sergeant," LaMoia corrected, interrupting. He said, "You still don't know my rank?"

"—has asked you a few questions. We'd like to start all over if you don't mind. The sooner we get this information, the better our chances of getting your daughter back."

"Trudy," Kay Kalidja supplied.

"Trudy," Flemming repeated.

David Kittridge glanced over at LaMoia and then complained to Flemming, "Just like you've gotten all the other children back?"

LaMoia felt the warm rush of success as Flemming flashed him another angry look.

David Kittridge lifted his right hand, holding it out for everyone to see. Gripped tightly between white, bloodless fingers was a tin penny flute.

CHAPTER

"Do you know the aquarium well, the big viewing room that is under all the fish?" the creamy female voice inquired.

"Yes," Daphne answered.

"Can you be there in fifteen minutes?"

"See you there."

The walk to the aquarium felt good, in part because it was nearly entirely downhill. Daphne worked herself up to a good heart rate, past cranes and Caterpillars and jackhammers all busy making the population deaf. The city refused to stop growing. Unable to spread out, it grew up now, the new buildings pushing higher and higher into the sky, winning views of the bay and blocking the view of others. The streets closed in around the pedestrians. The town of Seattle was gone, a city having replaced it.

Elliott Bay's restless, wind-scuffed green waters caught the sunshine in highlights, like Italian marble with flecks of mica angled to the sun. Freighters and ferries, their white wakes flowing behind them like wedding veils, called out in deep-throated cries. A jet rocked its wings on final approach, its wheels like tiny talons reaching for the ground.

On its best day, no city was as beautiful, no city held her heart as this one. She knew she would never leave, although she had considered doing so—distance would force a fresh start. She also knew that if she stayed she would likely marry Owen Adler. Fear had led to her breaking off the engagement the first time. Fear of being filthy rich, of attending fund-raising dinners and ribbon-cutting ceremonies instead of working psych profiles and would-be suicides. Fear of losing her identity, *not* a fear of her love for this man. She trusted her love. She appreciated his humor, the attention he paid her, his intelligence, confidence and determination, the way he put others first, especially Corky, his adopted daughter. She loved Corky nearly as much as he did.

She walked right past the aquarium before she realized what she had done. Owen was like that—he could occupy her in ways no other man ever had.

The aquarium was crowded with tourists and a busload of students on a field trip. Most of the display areas were kept dark, the visitor's attention focused on the fish tanks in the walls. She navigated her way through the throng and made her way to the descending ramp that led down into the center of an enormous tank, where the humans became the observed, surrounded on all sides and overhead by coral, water and fish of a dozen varieties.

Special Agent Kay Kalidja occupied one of the two viewing benches, her purse and sweater set beside her holding a spot for Daphne, who sat down. The glass arched above them, fish swimming directly overhead, passing from one side of the tank to the other. Kalidja did not look at Daphne but at the fish. She pointed out a sand shark with a suckerfish attached. "I feel like that sometimes," she said in her pleasing island lilt, "the one attached."

"Yes."

"Made to follow, to stay close."

Kalidja's choosing a neutral site forewarned of the significance of the meeting. Excitement filled Daphne, as she nudged, "You ran the tattoo."

"The contents of many of the Bureau's databases are classified. As you must know, we track everything from violent offenders to suspected double agents in the State Department. For this reason there are levels of access imposed, levels of security, pass codes, log-in records. It is extremely well-protected data. Hackers have fooled with our Web site before, but no one—to my knowledge—has ever come close to compromising these databases." Kalidja found it difficult to share the information. She struggled to admit, "Yes. The tattoos." She then said, pointing out a pair of blue and yellow fish, "Spectacular."

"The system tracks access," Kalidja continued. "It maintains a computerized log. Not only can internal investigators see who has been working what information, but it also allows agents to see who else has worked the information, to *share* that information. An agent in Chicago can call an agent in Dallas who has been requesting the same information. Perhaps they are pursuing the same suspect and were unaware of the connection. The database actually alerts them. Those alerts are automatic now, offering a kind of investigative bibliography."

"Impressive," Daphne said, suppressing her anxiety over where Kalidja was headed.

The agent faced Daphne for the first time and spoke quickly but extremely softly, "Special Agent Dunkin Hale requested any and all information on eagle tattoos—photographs of those on file, tattoo artists known for wrapping the wings around the bird like a cape. Everything he could think of."

Daphne had expected nothing like this. She had a dozen questions to ask, but held her tongue. Kalidja was not finished.

"Special Agent Hale has never mentioned any such tattoo in any of our meetings. Never. Not once."

"And you had said nothing to him about it?"

"Absolutely not."

"Perhaps he saw it on your desk—"

"Never! I accepted this information from you in the strictest of confidence. I've told no one! Shown no one!"

Daphne tried to make sense of it. The schools of fish swimming over, above and around her added to her sense of confusion.

"VI-CIM, our Violent Criminal Identification and Markings database, has produced two hits, two similar tattoos," she said, producing photocopies and showing them to Daphne. "One of

the tattoos was shown on the biceps, the other on a pectoral."
They were, in fact, both unmistakably similar to the rendition
drawn by Tommy Thompson: a bald eagle looking straight ahead,
the wings wrapped around like a cape. "One is dead. The other is
two years into serving a life sentence. Mind you, we only show
federal offenders in the database, and only a limited number of
them. It is by no means complete."

"It's not our boy. His was on the forearm."

"No, but the same artist perhaps. Special Agent Hale pursued
the name of the artist. I can tell that from the database requests."

Daphne sniped, "Imagine calling this artwork." Studying the
photos, she asked, "Wait a second! Are you saying these two cons
are from the same region?"

"The same *city*," Kalidja answered. "Both arrested and convicted in New Orleans, Louisiana."

"The tattoo shop is in New Orleans."

"Exactly."

Because of Boldt, Daphne knew a great deal about the investigation that Kay Kalidja and the FBI did not, including that the
Pied Piper had used a 911 telephone scam to convince the day
care center into handing over Sarah to the two uniformed cops.
Con artists were continually arrested and even occasionally convicted. Using this new information, she wondered if she couldn't
work the New Orleans police or prosecuting attorney's office to
ID any con artists using 911 telephone scams. The location was a
huge find. It would shift the entire investigation. Boldt often spoke
of an investigation gaining momentum, that there came a time
when the evidence outweighed the mystery, when the huge rock
of knowledge assembled by a squad in an uphill manner suddenly
crested that hill and began the journey down. She believed that
combined with Kalidja's information, the Pied Piper investigation
had just crested. It would pick up steam now, and eventually that
rock would crush the Pied Piper in its path.

Daphne said, "What do you intend to do with this?"

Kalidja looked a little frightened. "Honestly, Ms. Matthews, if
I had not discovered that Special Agent Hale already has this same
information, I was intending that we—you and I—should present

the information to the task force, as we discussed. But now? I have to wonder why Special Agent Hale would withhold such information. Yes? I am, unfortunately, not in a position to take this directly to S-A-C Flemming."

"We call that an end run."

"Yes. I deal with the S-A-C all the time, but by design, any information, especially information such as this, must go through Special Agent Hale. S-A-C Flemming is careful to insulate himself in this manner. He has managed to keep control of this investigation far longer than others might have, in no small part because he is so carefully insulated. Special Agent Hale and I were not brought on until Portland.

"This assignment has been a graveyard. Three of the S-A-C's former deputies and two of his former intelligence officers were removed prior to Portland. He shoots the messenger, you see. It allows him to preserve his position." She looked Daphne up and down, head to toe, and then met eyes with her. "There is something else, something far more disturbing," she said softly. "I overheard Special Agent Hale inform the S-A-C that the task force was his whenever he wanted it."

"Meaning?"

"Those were his words exactly: 'yours whenever you want it.' S-A-C Flemming does not like Captain Hill having control over the task force—we all know that, but he is an astute politician. He will not take control of a sinking ship. Nonetheless, I believe Special Agent Hale has discovered a way to push Captain Hill out of her chair when and if the time comes. If the time comes. Your Captain would do well to watch her back." Looking at the fish, she said, "I do not care to see men ganging up on a woman just because she holds the position of power."

Daphne recalled Hill's request that she study and report on each member of the task force. "Captain Hill is quite the politician herself. I wouldn't count her out."

"Do not underestimate S-A-C Flemming. He is a brilliant man and a brilliant investigator. If the Pied Piper is caught, it will not be Sheila Hill's collar. This I promise you. There will be only one person giving the press conference, and that person will be S-A-C Flemming."

"And these?" Daphne asked, indicating the photocopies of the database information. "Why don't I follow up on this for you?"

Kalidja had clearly been hoping for such an offer. "It is not for me to act upon information."

"Your name will now appear as having accessed the same database."

"Yes."

"Hale may notice that."

"Only if he seeks the same information a second time. I see no reason he would do that."

"I accept," Daphne took the envelope, to her a treasure.

"Watch out for Special Agent Hale," Kalidja said in a hushed voice. She stood and straightened her knee-length skirt.

"Message received."

Boldt, LaMoia and Daphne took a walk around Pioneer Square in order to avoid ears within Public Safety. Dodging tourists, panhandlers and ticket scalpers, they passed a sax player and Boldt left a dollar bill in his case, much to LaMoia's disapproval.

"You just encourage them," LaMoia complained.

"It's how he makes his living."

"You can't call that music. You of all people—you know music. So why give up your hard-earned money?"

"They are con artists," Daphne said. "The nine-one-one scam tells us that much. Their world is illusion. He could have been arrested and charged by the state, not the Feds. They wouldn't have him in their database."

"Hale is ahead of us?" LaMoia complained. "You know what that means for Sarah?"

Daphne answered, "We don't know that for sure. We know only that he searched the same information that Kalidja supplied us. He probably got the names of the two cons with the same eagle tattoo."

"It had to be Indiana, Michigan, Denver or New Orleans," Boldt informed them. "New Orleans fits," he confirmed.

"And just how the hell do you know that?" LaMoia protested.

"Anderson's photos," he answered. "The ones *you* gave me."

"I went over those things a dozen times. Two dozen. There was no license plate, no markers or identifiers of any kind to indicate—"

"The sweatshirt," Boldt supplied. "Coming down the dock he's facing the camera. You can't see his face because of the hat, but the sweatshirt has two colors on it: purple and gold. School colors. Those same colors are used by colleges in—"

"Indiana, Michigan, Denver and New Orleans," LaMoia completed, understanding the logic.

"There was the off-chance it might have been high school colors, but I was betting university or college."

"So it *is* New Orleans," LaMoia said.

"Our suspect spent time there," Daphne said, picking up on the reasoning. "Maybe went to school there. More than likely got a tattoo there. Could have spent time locked up. Kalidja stressed that only some of the inmates end up on the database."

"May still have contacts there," LaMoia added, "or a sheet."

Boldt warned, "If we involve the law down there it will have to be done carefully. The ransom demand. . . ," he reminded.

LaMoia asked, "Why would Hale stonewall this from his own people?"

"Flemming's attitude fosters independents," Daphne said. "Kalidja warned me of that."

Boldt suggested, "We need that tattoo shop."

"Agreed," LaMoia echoed.

"I have the address," Daphne announced proudly, drawing looks of astonishment from both men. "You think I wanted fresh air?" she asked sarcastically.

Boldt asked, "Hale?"

"Probably has it too," she admitted. "It was in their database."

Boldt warned, "We can't have him IDing a suspect."

"No," Daphne agreed.

"We going to Cajun Country?" LaMoia asked. "We gotta find this tattoo shop ahead of Hale."

"I'll book the flights," Boldt said.

Boldt's phone was ringing as he reentered his office. He caught it before voice mail picked up. He answered tersely, having no interest in Intelligence work, the pressure of Hale's advance work threatening Sarah.

"What it is, my man," the deep voice uttered into the phone.

He recognized the drawl immediately. "Not now, Raymond."

"What has one tail but two assholes?" the snitch asked.

"Am I paying for this bit of entertainment?"

"What has a nice set of tits, a dick and two wings?"

Boldt didn't want to be playing games. He told the man so.

"I thought you cops were good at solving shit like this."

Boldt answered, "Two people on a plane: a man and a woman."

"Damn!"

"So why do I care?"

"Because one of the assholes is this visiting heat, this FBI brother who's been all over the TV. The other is one fine piece of trim."

Boldt's chest tightened: Flemming and Kalidja. "Where did you get this, Raymond?"

"A brother just came by the Air Strip. The G-man and the G-string jumped a private jet fifteen minutes ago."

Flemming had a government Lear at his disposal. The information held together.

Boldt informed his informer, "There's a fifty in it if you can give me their destination. And I need it quickly."

"Right back to you." The phone went dead. For Flemming and Kalidja to leave the city together without letting the task force know meant something big was in the works. Bigger than big: huge. Boldt suspected their destination was New Orleans, that Flemming had the jump on the tattoo shop, that Sarah's chances were diminishing with every hour. Boldt called a travel agent and booked himself and LaMoia nonrefundable tickets to New Orleans on the earliest flight available. If need be, he would appeal to Flemming in person, revealing Sarah's abduction.

In the midst of booking the flights, Boldt's other line rang, and he answered it.

"Boise, Idaho," Raymond announced. "The G-man jet filed for Boise."

"Idaho?"

"As in potatoes."

"It's going down in the book," Boldt acknowledged, confirming the payment.

"And the rich get richer." Raymond hung up.

Boldt steadied his hand as he dialed Boise's police department. He knew several cops there. If Flemming had a suspect already in custody. . .

Minutes later, Boldt connected with Detective Hank Langford.

Boldt reintroduced himself to Langford as an Intelligence officer investigating the Pied Piper kidnappings, electing a strategy of us-against-them. He made assumptions and took chances that a week earlier he would have been unwilling to take. "Hank, as I'm sure you are aware, you have a situation over there that may involve our investigation. Our friends in the FBI are on their way there as we speak. We at SPD were hoping you might enlighten us a little so we don't end up with mud on our faces."

"Mud or shit, Lieutenant?"

"I see we understand each other."

"I don't have a clue what you're talking 'bout. Closest thing we've got to 'a situation' is a five-car fender bender out on the interstate. A diesel jockey fell asleep at the wheel, rolled his eighteen-wheeler, and dumped about a hundred microwave ovens out on the highway like some kind of garage sale. Right there in front of the airport. The trucker was decapitated. Around here we let the state police boys clean up those messes. A lot of blood in a decapitation. You ever seen one?"

"Would you know anybody with state police who might know about extending an invitation to the Bureau?"

"This is Idaho. From God's lips to your ears, we aren't real fond of the federal government. They tend to grab our land, try for our water and steal our checkbooks."

"Could you make a call for me?"

"Could and will. Sit tight. Won't be a minute."

It was seven minutes. Boldt counted each one along with his elevated heart rate.

Langford sounded a little more excited on the second call. "Seems you're onto something. The FBI was in fact contacted."

"Do we know why?"

"I told you about the pileup. One of those cars was found abandoned. No driver. No passenger. What *was* found was baby bottles, dirty diapers and such. The car came back an Econo-Drive rental out of Seattle. That's when the Feds were notified." He added, "Whoever was driving abandoned the scene of an accident and took an infant child with them. Leaving the scene is a crime in and of itself."

Boldt asked desperately, "Any sign of a second child being in that car? An older child?"

"Didn't hear nothing about it."

"If you hear anything more . . . ," Boldt said.

"Got you covered."

Flemming was pulling an end run. It was information he should have shared.

Any evidence trail would begin in that wrecked car. Boldt wanted that crime scene, but he needed it ahead of the Bureau and that wasn't going to happen. He couldn't allow any of this to distract him: The pull remained New Orleans and identifying a suspect—preventing Hale from doing so.

The decision was a simple one. Let Hill aim the task force at Boise, convincing her that LaMoia was best left behind in Seattle. Then jump the plane for New Orleans stealing LaMoia and staying ahead of the race.

Screaming into the phone, Sheila Hill ordered Boldt to keep trying for details and to stay by his phone. Boldt, in turn, pleaded with her to assign Mulwright to Boise.

"Don't tell me my job, Lieutenant." She hung up.

Boldt spent the next fifteen minutes finding Daphne and La-Moia and keeping them current. LaMoia was asked to pursue Econo-Drive and run the charge history on the credit card used to rent the abandoned car. Daphne, with her people skills, was asked to work NOPD by phone for any con artists who used a 911 telephone scam. She wasn't to mention her association with the task force.

As he was debating buying Daphne a ticket to New Orleans as well, his wife called him to announce a visitor: Sergeant Tom Bowler, Portland Police Department, was sitting in Boldt's living room.

CHAPTER

49

Bowler was sober, making him a different man than the last time Boldt had seen him. He had clear eyes that wore concern at their edges, though he possessed the soft, bloated look of a man lost to the bottle. Boldt noticed the liver spots on the back of the man's hand and felt its coldness as they shook hands in greeting.

"Tom." Boldt felt jumpy and edgy. There was too much going on inside his head to stay focused, too many lies to keep straight. He had seen suspects this way—frayed and scattered. He worried he was becoming the very person he sought.

Liz, her wig perfectly in place, her clothes hanging loosely, explained patiently, "Tom drove all the way from Portland to talk to you. I've been boring him with the details of my recovery."

"Not at all," Bowler said, generously.

She called it her recovery—her decision to walk out of treatment, to turn to "God's healing powers." As supportive as Boldt had felt about it only days earlier, he feared that any setback might rob her of her ability to mentally fight the battle. She preached, to those who would listen, the healing powers of her faith. Ironically,

Boldt could only pray that she wouldn't lose that same faith if the beast grabbed hold of her again.

Boldt sat down alongside his wife but could hardly stay still. Bowler had gone to a great deal of trouble to come here. Pushed by Connie, or of his own accord; therein lay the important difference.

Liz offered to leave the room. Boldt, and Bowler immediately after him, told her she was welcome to remain. "It involves us both," Boldt told his wife, his eyes on their visitor.

"Yes, both of you," Bowler began. "I know what you're going through. I also accept that in no small way I'm responsible." Liz sat up straight and her lips quivered; the facade she had offered Bowler was crumbling. Boldt took her hand.

He said to Boldt, "When you came down to see me, I was an asshole. I was drinking. We were threatened—Connie and me. I just could not, would not, put us into that same position again." He sat in the chair, leaning forward, elbows on his knees, hands steepled at his chin. He looked as if he might be praying too. "And then this Kittridge girl."

Liz knew only the rough details of the Kittridge case, what Boldt had told her from the bathtub. Like her husband, she was a practiced listener.

Bowler said, "That changed things. I don't know if it was Connie or Sarah and this Kittridge girl, but something convinced me it has to stop. Maybe it was your visit," he told Boldt. "Seeing that you were willing to take him on, that I wish I had. I was pissed—pissed that you had the strength I lacked. I wasn't about to help you." He said to Liz, "You got a good man here." Liz sobbed and squeezed Boldt's hand.

Boldt corrected him. Returning her affection, he told Bowler, "We made that decision together."

Bowler said, "We were working the vic's possessions. Anything that might link the kidnappings. I informed the Bureau that I had a good, solid lead—"

Boldt interrupted, "Spitting Image."

He nodded. "You do your homework, don't you?"

"We stumbled onto it."

"So I ask for a meeting, to get this out on the table." He blinked furiously, his eyes glossy. "Penny's gone the next day. Needless to say, because of the demands I cancel the meeting and keep my trap shut."

"The next day?"

"The Pied Piper knew I had requested that meeting—has to be."

"Your contact over there?"

"The island girl—legs to the ceiling."

Kalidja, Boldt realized. Had Hill been right about an insider? Had Daphne played right into that?

Bowler said, "I'm making lame excuses for skipping the dance; she's breathing fire down my throat. I'd been after them to run rental car *reservations*, not the actual agreements, using a list of valid cards I had."

"Which were?" Boldt asked.

"The Spitting Image customers. If you know about Spitting Image, then you know she has a Web page; I got to the Web page first, never did interview her. But one of our pocket protectors hacked into her site without any hassle. Said a sixth grader coulda done it. Lifts a couple dozen valid credit cards. The woman was using E-mail for her orders! Jesus! And I'm thinking—"

"This guy's had experience counterfeiting credit cards," Boldt supplied.

"Got to be. Right? Credit cards, documentation. It's all available to him. He needs fake cards to get things done. But first he needs valid numbers, and Spitting Image all but hands them to him."

"Not the victims' cards."

"No way. Have to be punch drunk to use those; but the other card numbers? Why not?"

"Did you ever connect it?" Boldt asked.

"Did I ever! The AFIDs."

"We've never seen a report."

"Yeah, well, Hale has one. The cartridges for the air TASER were bought all at one time. Las Vegas, a year ago. One time charge to a valid credit card—"

"Which later turned out to be—"

"Much later, yeah," Bowler answered.

"What?" Liz asked irritably.

The two men answered nearly simultaneously, "A Spitting Image customer."

"And that's when you thought to follow the cards," Boldt said.

"The guy is lifting his vics off the Internet. Why make things harder on himself? He does up a valid credit card, maybe a driver's license all from the same hack. He gets into those files once, he never needs to go back again. Clean and simple."

"Is someone going to explain this to me?" Liz asked indignantly. "How does his using some silk-screen customer's credit card connect to rental cars?"

Bowler answered shamefully, "I never followed it up, never chased it. Maybe it does, maybe it doesn't."

Boldt told her, "The Pied Piper needs valid credit cards and a valid ID to rent cars, take plane flights, whatever. If he's using Spitting Image customers—and I agree it makes sense that he might—then we may be able to track him." Boldt told Bowler, "The problem with it that I see is that we know he accessed the victims' credit card records—it's how he knew their movements, how he predicted when to strike."

This was clearly news to Bowler, who attempted to digest it. Boldt continued, "If he had that kind of access to credit records, he doesn't need the Spitting Image list."

Bowler contradicted, "Sure he does. He needs expiration dates. Those aren't available from a TRW or some credit service. He's got some ex-con who can pull that kind of information for him," Bowler speculated. "It doesn't mean he's got valid cards."

Liz, the banker, said, "He's right, love. He would need the expiration dates for a successful counterfeit."

"What you've got here is someone who knows computers. With a color scanner you can forge hundred dollar bills. How difficult can a driver's license be?"

Boldt thought back to the CD-R of Sarah—video embedded on a CD-ROM. He said, "They teach computer skills in prison."

Bowler looked up and said, "Our tax dollars hard at work."

CHAPTER

Boldt returned to the office as fast as the Chevy would safely take him, a dozen ideas competing inside his head for his attention. Kalidja. Hale. Sarah's situation. Time running out. He couldn't hold all the loose ends together.

LaMoia pushed shut both doors to the fifth-floor corner coffee lounge, windows overlooking the secretary pool to one side and the bullpen to the other. The situation room, which offered far more privacy, had become task force headquarters and churned with activity. Daphne warmed her hands on a tea cup. There were no smiles, only anxiety-ridden expressions.

"I'm toast," LaMoia said. "I'm out of here." He had called the others to the impromptu meeting.

"Boise?" Boldt asked.

"Sheila—Hill," he corrected himself, a little late, "wants me on the six o'clock flight, wants me running down every stinking piece of evidence there is—some of which I've already done, incidentally, though I didn't tell her."

"Econo-Drive," Boldt supplied. He had asked LaMoia to look into the car rental records.

"Yeah. I had no trouble getting that: The abandoned car in the pileup," LaMoia said, "was rented to one Lena Robertson."

"A woman," Daphne said. "Then it *is* a team." Boldt could feel her processing the information. She had been among the first to insist that the kidnapped children were intended for illegal adoption, and that if true, the Pied Piper more than likely needed an accomplice to help care for and transport the infants. Boldt's revelation of two uniformed cops, a man and a woman, abducting Sarah from day care had supported her theory and led her to investigate previously arrested or convicted con artist couples on a national level. Con games were often played out in pairs.

"Hold that thought right there," Boldt said, hurrying from the coffee lounge. Once through Homicide's secure door he started for the elevator but changed his mind and ran the stairs. The climb up was arduous and reinforced his utter exhaustion, reminding him of how little sleep he had gotten over the past ten days and how poorly he had eaten. He reached for some of those dangling strings, knowing that the SPD task force—and their FBI counterpart—was, at the very least, close to identifying and arresting the kidnapper's accomplice. If he could only count on a few pieces of good luck, he might yet beat Hale or Flemming to his daughter's abductor. But luck rarely ran when one needed it. It ran when least expected.

Boldt ran the hallway to his office, unlocked his file cabinet and secured the Spitting Image customer list. He was halfway back downstairs when he located the name on the run: Robertson, a baby quilt shipped in care of Durrel Robertson of Oakland, California.

"You look like you're about to come out of your skin," Daphne observed of Boldt on his return.

"Robertson was a Spitting Image customer. A baby blanket was shipped to that name in care of Durrel Robertson at what looks like a home address. It was charged to a VISA in the name of Lena Robertson." Daphne and LaMoia looked back at him blankly. He explained Bowler's visit and the possible connection—never proved and never brought to anyone's attention because of Pen-

RIDLEY PEARSON

ny's kidnapping—between the Pied Piper's possible identities and the Spitting Image customer list.

"You're telling me Bowler suddenly got a conscience?" LaMoia said skeptically, finding it impossible to conceal his dislike of a cop who would intentionally throw an investigation. "Or did he drive up here to sell you a bill of goods and stay with his original game plan?"

"You are the all-time cynic," Daphne said.

"Bowler put together Spitting Image just as we did. But he made a leap in logic that we did not: With a bunch of valid credit card numbers at your fingertips, why not put them to good use? It works for me," Boldt impressed upon LaMoia, referring to the customer list. "Robertson's card was used to rent a car here in Seattle that's later abandoned on the way to God knows where. Do we need it any clearer?"

"It's your call," LaMoia said irritably.

"You're just pissed that Hill can call the shots," Daphne, the psychologist, explained to him. LaMoia was no fan of her psychological evaluations. "You don't like a woman bossing you around. I know you, John. I know where this is coming from."

"You don't know shit about it."

"Hey!" Boldt chided. He told LaMoia, "The Bureau blocked the financial records of the victims, we assume so they could have it all to themselves. But we can pull credit card statements for the Spitting Image customers and look for charges that coincide with the Pied Piper's calendar. You see what they've done?" he asked, tapping the Spitting Image records. "The Pied Piper uses fresh, valid credit cards—Robertson ordered that blanket just last week. If he has the access we think he does, then he knows her statement dates; he knows she won't actually see any of his charges for a month or more. He's protected from discovery. What we want to do is get to those statements electronically ahead of time—we can do that—then we focus on car rentals in and around the abduction dates; gas charges, airfare, lodging, restaurants."

"They won't use the cards for small-ticket items," LaMoia countered. "The car rentals, sure—you have to show a card."

Daphne said, "And that card has to match your driver's license."

"Fake ID?" LaMoia asked. "So they could use a card and license to board a plane as well. I'd buy that." He added for Boldt's sake, "But I'm off to Boise to measure skid marks and work a traffic accident. That's what this is, you know?" he complained. "Hill is knocking me down to metro."

"I need both of you with me in New Orleans, if any of this pans out," Boldt announced. "Hill will have to settle for Mulwright."

LaMoia snapped, "Forget it. She's talking a minimum of two or three days over there."

"She's going too, isn't she?" Daphne speculated.

"It's where the press will be," LaMoia said, though he blushed and squirmed in his chair. "What do you think?"

"The press, are you sure?" Boldt questioned, the ramifications for Sarah echoing in his thoughts.

"I'm sure. They're all over it."

"Already?"

"Already."

"That couldn't have been what Flemming wanted," Boldt pointed out.

"Ten to one, the Captain did it, Sarge—Hill. She wanted Flemming slowed down; she wanted to punish him for trying the end run. What better way than to dump the press in his lap?"

"Games," Matthews said, disgusted.

"You gotta get me off the Boise assignment, Sarge. You've got tattoos to run, con artists, adoption records. A foreign town."

"How badly do you want off?"

"Whatever it takes," LaMoia answered.

"I'll go," Daphne confirmed. "I won't be missed."

Boldt asked LaMoia, "Straight answer. Is there any reason Hill would be mad at you?"

"Moi?"

"I need it straight, John, because from here, from what we know about what you face in Boise —"

LaMoia interrupted, "You mean failure? Trying to track down this driver and child *after* the Bureau has a substantial lead on us."

"It looks more like a setup. This may be the investigation's biggest lead, and if it goes nowhere—"

"Hill needs a scapegoat," Daphne said, following Boldt's reasoning.

"Or else there's a personal agenda at play," Boldt said, challenging LaMoia directly, "and she's either intentionally sending you off to Siberia, or getting you out of the way so you can't screw things up for her at home." He added, "How 'bout it?"

LaMoia didn't answer. He looked searchingly back and forth between Boldt and Matthews.

Boldt said, "Sarah's out of time. If the press picks up on the abandoned car . . ." His throat caught. To Daphne, he said, "Better go pack. We have seats on the red-eye."

CHAPTER

LaMoia boiled at the thought of pursuing dead leads in Boise, Idaho, while Boldt attempted to track the tattoo and criminal records to the actual suspect in a place like the Big Easy. The central question that needed answering—was Sarah better off with him in Boise—seemed obvious enough: Bobbie Gaynes or Patrick Mulwright could easily handle Boise. How Sheila Hill could have made such a call without discussion was beyond him. Once again she was using him, this time in a political move that left too many unanswered questions. Was she afraid of someone within the department? Was LaMoia a threat? Or did she simply want three days with him in a hotel out of town to mend their fences? He feared this latter thought the most: playing gigolo in Boise for an oversexed, overly ambitious woman who had the power to trash his own career. Exactly what had he gotten himself into? Perhaps his handcuffing incident had awakened her, had made her realize how strong his feelings were for her.

He had no choice but to obey orders. A police department was not a democracy. The Boise investigation could have been handled over the phone, and Sheila Hill knew it. But the cameras—along with the fresh sheets and room service—were in Boise.

LaMoia's calls to his credit services contacts produced immediate results. Cross-referencing the Spitting Image customer names with the dates that the Pied Piper was known to have been in specific cities produced billing records that suggested the kidnappers had counterfeited at least six credit cards. LaMoia was sorting through the information when his pager buzzed, interrupting his work. Tempted to ignore it, he obediently angled it to the light and read the overly long string of numbers on the display, immediately guessing these numbers would lead him to a hotel room, same as always. Sheila Hill wanted to talk; she had wisely reconsidered her decision. That, or she wanted to lay down ground rules for their Boise bed jumping. He cringed. A combination of resentment, anger and hope overcame him. Perhaps she wanted to apologize. Perhaps she knew in advance he had no intention of sharing showers with her in Boise. The New Orleans red-eye was only hours away. His own flight to Boise was much sooner.

One phone call, and LaMoia had the name of the hotel: a Days Inn south on I-5. Its close proximity to the airport annoyed him— she still expected him to board that plane to Boise.

He passed the credit card information along to Boldt, went home and quickly packed a bag, his anger continually resurfacing like a fire assumed out. He left an extra dish of dry food for his cat, Granite, and slipped a note under his neighbor's door that said he'd be gone for a few days. He stopped at an ATM and withdrew two hundred dollars cash, which he would then expense over the next few days.

On the drive south he promised himself that he would not, under any conditions, have sex with her.

He found himself passing the Days Inn registration desk and heading to the elevators. He found himself on the second floor, walking the long corridor in search of the number 214. He found himself practicing his first few lines so that she could not, would not, steer him off course, no matter what her intentions and appetites. He knocked sharply on the door and braced himself for whatever she threw at him.

The door came open to empty space and he knew immediately she was hiding behind the door, and he feared what she had in mind. Feeling like a trained German shepherd, he stepped into the room prepared to counter whatever awaited him. He walked straight ahead, intentionally not looking back, not playing to her game. If her clothes were laid out on a chair or on the bed, then he knew what to expect: reckless abandon. He couldn't wait to deny her that.

The TV was going loudly. Sheila Hill was a screamer. LaMoia knew at that moment that she intended to try to make up to him. Knew what she had in mind—something adventuresome, something daring, perhaps even dangerous. He cautioned himself against succumbing.

There was a big rat of a man in a padded chair pulled up to a faux-grain breakfast table, and LaMoia's first thought was that she had fantasies about a trio, but for him, the gender was all wrong. The rat was hairy and in his middle thirties. On the table in front of him, a cheap briefcase waited. LaMoia had never seen the man before, but sight of him set off a string of mental alarms. This was no sex partner of Sheila Hill's. Not only was someone in the wrong place at the wrong time, but the rat was the exact kind of man one saw in a lineup. He was a man made for numbers across the chest.

A squeaky male voice behind LaMoia wheezed, "Hands stay visible. Nothing fast. You move slow or you go."

LaMoia turned his head ever so slowly and took in a smaller man dressed in blue jeans and a black leather jacket. He had Asian blood in him, and maybe some speed. He hadn't seen the sun in a long time. He held a Glock in his left hand, as casually and comfortably as some people held cigarettes.

"I'm a cop," LaMoia announced, not a single muscle tensing. He found his center; he found his calm.

"Guy's a fucking genius," Ratman said in an East Coast baritone.

"You can count if you want, or you can take my word for it: The money's all there," the little one said, more irritated than only a moment earlier. "We're not about to short a cop."

The rat opened the briefcase. Inside were several dozen vials of what looked like crack cocaine and two stacks of cash. The top bills of each were hundreds. If the rest matched those, it amounted to some serious change.

A neon light lit up in LaMoia's mind. He looked at the little man with the gun curiously. "We got a small problem here," he said.

At that moment, the hotel room door swung open, blindingly fast. "Police!" a voice thundered. A pair of black blurs occupied a space by the door and suddenly the little guy and LaMoia were both pinned against the wall, faces pressed to the cheap wallpaper, arms wrenched up behind so painfully that LaMoia couldn't get his voice out. He hadn't so much as twitched when he saw the ERT coming in; he knew the drill. At first, he couldn't believe his good luck: that his own people had somehow come to his rescue, and so fast. But with his face kissing the cheap wallpaper and his shoulder about to dislocate, he reassessed. He heard a commotion behind him, which turned out to be the Ratman going down onto the floor.

"I'm a cop!" LaMoia finally gasped, his cheekbone welded with the wall, his ribs flattened by the pressure on his back.

"You *were* a cop," the ERT man hissed into his ear. LaMoia knew the voice. He searched for a name to go along with it. Lowering his voice even further, the ERT man added, "You're lucky you got witnesses, Floorshow, or I'd do you myself right here."

LaMoia had never experienced such feelings of disgrace, humiliation and frustration as he did over the next few hours. His badge and gun were taken from him. He was escorted in handcuffs to a police van amid a flurry of activity and jeering from his peers and driven downtown. The sting had involved a minimum of eight cops, possibly twice that—all of which added up to something big. He knew the players: Narcotics. Drugs, as they were called within the ranks. They traveled in a clique within the department, the same way Homicide did. He had been to Seahawks games with a couple of them. Decent guys who took their jobs a little too seriously. Drugs was rough duty, and it made the players that way too.

He professed his innocence, demanded representation, and otherwise kept his mouth shut. He was booked, printed and humiliated by a full body search. LaMoia's internal representative rescued him from an interrogation. No one seemed clear on the exact crime for which he was being accused. It involved the briefcase and crack cocaine. Sheila Hill had led him by his dick into a heap of trouble. For what? he wondered. Revenge?

Why get him arrested and suspended only a half hour before sending him to Siberia? Had she found out about Boldt's Gang of Five and the work being done behind her back? Was this retribution? Or was it repayment for leaving her handcuffed and naked?

LaMoia left Public Safety without his badge or gun—suspended without pay pending review. "It won't be review," his representative warned. "They intend to prosecute."

Boldt showed up as he was being released and offered a ride. LaMoia didn't know their destination until under way. Daphne's houseboat was a twenty-minute drive in good traffic. There was never good traffic.

LaMoia said, "Let me tell you something—you never want to be on the receiving end of our business. Never."

Boldt said. "What happened?"

LaMoia's hesitation caused Boldt to say, "The truth will work until you can think of something else."

"I've been snaking the captain."

Boldt released a pent-up sigh.

"I know . . . I know . . . okay?"

"Stupid, John. Very stupid."

LaMoia chewed at his mustache out of nervous habit. "It's usually lunch with us, but this time—today—it was afternoon. Next thing I know I'm in cuffs. What the hell?"

"Drugs made a good bust last night. This morning I'm t
there's an unidentified cop who plans to swap out ev
street-grade crack for what's currently in the evidence

"What's in there?" LaMoia asked.

"Bad formula. Freelance lab, just like McNee's. Six deaths in the last three weeks. Prosecutor was going for the death penalty, and she would have gotten it. The switch knocks it down to dealing. It's a first offense, a nonevent. Lab test will come back clean. No aggravated assault, no prosecutable deaths."

"I walked into that? Oh, shit."

"The bad cop is Kevin McCalister," Boldt informed him. The car bounced through construction.

"We know this?" LaMoia asked.

"Some of us do," Boldt answered. "It'll sort itself out. Faster, if you explain why you were there in the first place. It doesn't look so good, you know?"

"I can't do that. Not now. She'll deny it, of course. Besides, if I give up the captain, Flemming will take over the task force. You know that's true. And where does that leave Sarah?"

"Hale was overheard saying Flemming could win control of the task force. I guess we now know how."

"Where'd you get that?"

"Daphne, via Kalidja."

LaMoia said, "Something else, Sarge. I think my desk was broken into."

Boldt sidestepped the comment. "So you ride it out," he told him. "A trip to New Orleans will keep your mind off it."

LaMoia glanced over at Boldt.

Boldt explained, "Daphne got an emergency call from Kalidja, who is herself in Boise with Flemming. Dunkin Hale is AWOL. Flemming is furious."

"New Orleans?"

"Has to be," Boldt agreed. "The tattoos," he reminded. He turned off Fairmont and pulled to a stop where Daphne stood at the end of the dock by a box of mailboxes. A moment later they were headed south on I-5 toward the airport.

LaMoia told his story to Daphne, who offered no sympathy.

From the backseat, Daphne suggested to Boldt, "You aren't taking three of us to New Orleans based on an FBI agent's curiosity."

"No," Boldt confirmed.

LaMoia said to Boldt, "You worked the credit cards." He then told Daphne, "Six of the Spitting Image customers have contested charges on their cards in and around the dates of the earlier abductions."

Boldt explained, "The rental car abandoned in Boise was paid for using a credit card belonging to Lena Robertson, a Spitting Image customer. The rental agreement called for a drop-off in San Francisco. With the car turning up in Boise, it's fairly obvious San Francisco was never in the picture; she, or her accomplice, is smart enough to book the car for one destination and then drive it and deliver it to another. The rental company accepts the car and simply charges more. By using the rental car to get clear of the kidnap city—in this case Seattle—they avoid the law enforcement watching the airports.

"This morning," Boldt continued, "less than half an hour after the Boise pileup, another Spitting Image customer's card was used to book an Avis rental from Boise to Reno. She knew we would quickly have the Lena Robertson ID. The name on this second card is Julie DeChamps. The same card—DeChamps—was then used to book a plane flight from Salt Lake City to Cancún."

Daphne complained, "Cancún doesn't fit the profile. They are not taking these kids into Mexico. They know the FBI is involved. Immigration officers are alerted. They're not going to risk that."

Boldt nodded agreement and said, "The flight makes one stop." He caught Daphne's eyes in the rearview mirror, acknowledging her.

"In New Orleans," LaMoia guessed. "She rented the car in Boise with no intention of heading to Reno. She's headed for Salt Lake, for that flight."

"For New Orleans," Boldt confirmed. "That flight will be short passengers on the leg to Cancún."

Daphne said, "She's going down there to sell Trudy Kittridge into adoption."

"She thinks she is," Boldt corrected, driving well above the speed limit in the HOV lane, his dashboard flasher pulsing blue against the glass. He pushed the Chevy a little harder.

LaMoia said, "We can't stop her without putting Sarah at risk."

Daphne suggested, "Maybe we don't stop her. You can't beat 'em, join 'em."

An uncomfortable silence—the silence of frustration—filled the car. "The thing about blackened catfish," LaMoia told them, breaking that silence, "you either love it or you don't. But if you don't, you got no business being in the Big Easy."

CHAPTER

52

Boldt failed to see the romance of the French Quarter. For years he had heard stories about the mix of French and black cultures, of voodoo, umbrella drinks, of Creole bar girls with bodies like centerfolds, of blues and jazz drifting onto cobblestone streets at three in the morning and fresh oysters the size of golf balls. Instead, he saw only a giant tourist attraction, a Disneyland for alcoholics and unfaithful husbands masquerading as conventioneering businessmen. The locals provided color in street music, juggling and costuming, but to Boldt it felt contrived. The Quarter had been great once—it reeked of history—but the Chamber of Commerce and tourist board had cleaned it up for the McDonald's crowd in a way that left it too slick, too polished, too Kodak, too little of the soul that had once fueled its engines.

The tattoo shop was called Samantha's Body Art. Its wooden sign hanging out front depicted a large-breasted woman vampire clad in black lingerie and straddling a Harley holding a delicate paintbrush trained onto the naked form of a pale female ghost. Located outside the Quarter in an area of hairdressers, Tarot card readers and personal injury attorneys, the shop made the most of neon. The smell of pot and incense tainted the air.

Samantha did not exist. In a city of pretense, the tough behind the needle went by the name Maurice. He wore a silver stud in his left ear, had biceps the color and density of ebony and a shaved head that looked like an eight ball. He wore a T-shirt that showed two women fornicating in the palm of an outstretched hand. No explanation. The place was for bikers and sailors. Its walls bore hundreds of designs. It took Boldt a minute to locate the eagle, wedged as it was between the space shuttle and the butt end of a pig, but when he finally did identify it, the likeness to Tommy Thompson's rendition was unmistakable.

"Help you?" Maurice asked. A voice dipped in roofing tar saturated by nonfilters.

"I'm interested in this design," Boldt said, pointing out the eagle.

"You heat?"

"Who's asking? And why?"

"You ain't drunk enough and you ain't young enough to be wanting something like that. As for what you is, you got the look, you know? I can spot that look."

"Apparently you can," Boldt agreed. "But you missed with me. I'm private heat."

"Not from around here, you ain't."

"Not from around here, no."

Boldt pulled a fifty dollar bill from his pocket that he had waiting. "A client of mine is interested in a man who's wearing one of these birds on his forearm."

"It ain't a bird, it's an eagle."

"Do a lot of them, do you?" Boldt toyed with the fifty, a man who wasn't certain if he would spend it or keep it.

"Not many."

"I tell my client I paid fifty for information, and I get reimbursed whether I paid it out or not." He slipped it into his pocket and then pulled it back out.

"That's a good gig." The guy liked the sight of the fifty. The public wasn't exactly banging down his doors.

"I'd be pleased if you remembered a name or a face."

"Bet you would."

"A date, a time of year. Anything like that and the fifty's yours."

The man's fingers reminded Boldt of chocolate candy rolls, thumbs like cigar butts. One of those fingers pointed out a half dozen black vinyl photo albums chained to the wall and sitting atop a small counter. The counter was pockmarked with an army of cigarette burns, lined up like a regiment. The man explained, "They sell better in person. Look better than hanging on the wall. Besides, guys get off looking at all the tits and ass—you wouldn't believe some of the shit girls want, and where they put it. And we take pictures of all of it, man. 'Cause the way it works out—you think nobody never done something like that, but shit, then you see it there in the book and it don't look half bad and you think, maybe you want one too. Least that's the way it works out. Anything you can think of, it been done. And I personally have laid some art down on inner thighs, ass, pussy, tits, cocks—you name it. I seen it all, done it all."

"These are *photo* albums?"

"Damn straight."

Boldt opened one of the books. For shock value, he supposed, female genitalia and breasts occupied the first page. He blushed at what he saw exposed there, and what the owner of the tattoo had chosen to do to her body. One woman's shaved crotch had been painted into a face with an obvious mouth. It stood out from the snake winding up to an enlarged nipple, the daisy around the navel, the hummingbirds in cleavage, and the inner thigh with Cupid's arrow aiming at labia. "These are disgusting," he said, "you don't mind me saying so."

" 'Course I mind. It's art, man. You're looking all wrong. That there is quality work. Fine pitch, good solid color. A person wants to 'xpress hisself, that's a good thing. It's a free fucking country."

Boldt leafed through the plastic pages of Polaroids. "They let you take pictures like this?" he gasped. Page upon page of buttocks and breasts, penises, ankles, necks, eyelids, fingers. *Gray's Anatomy* courtesy of the Cartoon Network.

"It's not like you know who they are."

No, it's not, Boldt thought, wondering why he would bother to look on. Driven by a voyeuristic curiosity, he did just that, landing on a page of motorcycles and nudes on forearms, male chests and biceps. The detail and color were in fact extraordinary for flesh art. "It's good stuff," he said conversationally.

"A couple my pieces been in a gallery down in the Quarter," the man bragged. "A swan I done using a guy's dick, and another of Van Gogh's irises right up the bikini line, you know? This girl could'a walked the beach and you wouldn'ta even known she was bare ass."

"Impressive," Boldt muttered cynically. "You have repeats in here," he said.

"Same artwork, different body location. The images look different, depending where you put them. We try to show it all."

"You have eagles in here?"

"Third or fourth book, I think. One of 'em's nothing but animals: frogs, lizards, snakes. I do a lot of reptiles, for whatever reason."

"And you do all of this work?"

"I didn't do all of it, no. 'Course not. But I could. Sure. What my eye sees, my hands can paint."

"That includes the women?"

"Some guys get their girls to pose. I'm not shitting you. Imagination plays into it," said the artiste. He had a wide boyish smile, not at all what Boldt might have expected from such a brute.

Boldt worked through the lions, pussy cats, tigers, an aardvark, pandas, teddy bears and landed on a series of bald eagles. A profile of just the beak and head. An eagle in flight. A number of eagles with various messages or items clutched in the talons. An eagle with its wings wrapped around its body like a cape.

Boldt pointed it out.

"My own design. Maybe half what you see is original design. The rest I rip off from magazines, film or whatever, or I do custom from a photo or something. I charge extra for the custom work."

"Any others?" Boldt asked, flipping the page of Polaroids, his eye immediately answering his own question as it landed on an eagle drawn onto a knotty biceps. "You did this?"

"I told you: It's original. It's mine."

"There's one missing," Boldt stated.

"I don't think so."

"It's missing. Maurice," Boldt encouraged, making a point of the fifty, "it showed an eagle on a forearm, not a biceps."

"I don't think so."

"Someone else was here ahead of me," Boldt suggested to the man.

Boldt handed him the fifty. It had come out of his and Liz's joint account using the ATM card. The account was seventeen hundred dollars in the red, thanks to the hospital. More now with the airfare. "Guy looks like a surfer but has an attitude. He tell you who he was?"

Maurice considered the money. "Like I gotta ask? A suit like that?"

"He took a photo with him," Boldt stated. "He paid you how much?" Boldt asked.

Maurice pocketed Boldt's cash. "Not enough. Fucking prick Fed."

"Threatened to bust you."

"The half of it," the man said. Boldt produced another fifty. Maurice said, "I gave him the picture and I kept my door open for business."

"He told you how to reach him in case your memory came back." Boldt knew the routine. He pulled a third fifty out of his pocket.

"He might have mentioned the Hyatt." The fifty disappeared into the jeans.

"Anything you left out? Anything you forgot to tell him?" Boldt's time at the Intelligence desk had not been for naught.

The big stump of an index finger pointed out several other photos on the page. He flipped forward a page, then back two, and pointed out another row of photos. "You see that gray wall? The background? You know what that cement wall means?"

Many of the photos were shot against the same gray background. "Tell me, Maurice. What is the significance of that wall?"

"Couple times of year they bring one or another of us inside. Ends up like a fucking arts and crafts fair, know what I mean?"

Boldt felt his system charge with adrenaline. "We're talking about the penitentiary, Maurice. The guy with the eagle on the forearm—he was doing time."

"You got it."

"When?"

Maurice slipped out a photo and flipped it over. "Nineteen ninety-five."

"The suit . . . does he know this?"

"He didn't ask," Maurice said, his face spreading into a smile.

CHAPTER

"**J**esus, su-gar, what da hell dey got going up in Seattle we ain't got down here? You ever consider yourself a transfer, how 'bout looking down our way?"

NOPD's detectives division was a mismatch of gray metal government furniture, paddle fans and noisy, window-mounted air conditioners. Half the building had been remodeled, but they were working from the top down—from the chief to the garage—and the detectives division was low in the building and low on the list.

Daphne bristled at the man's sexist attitude but played to him rather than make trouble. Priorities.

Detective Broole was white, thirty-five, modestly good looking, with acne scars and sleepy brown eyes. He wore his hair like a Las Vegas showman and talked with a Dixie drawl that she had to mentally replay to understand.

"He was in your medium lockup in '95. He's white, with an eagle tattoo on his left forearm. Six foot, maybe six-one. In for fraud or bunco—"

"A confidence artist?" Broole said, planting his swagger down in front of an outdated computer terminal. "Well, hell, if that don't describe half the population, sugar." He hooked another chair with his toe and pulled it close to him on its casters. He lit up a nonfilter and blew the smoke away from her. "Shitty habit," he said, "but somebody's got to die young." He motioned for her to sit in the chair, but she remained standing.

"Maybe kiddie pornography. Stalking." She couldn't mention the abduction of children without risking connecting herself to the Pied Piper. "He may work with a female accomplice," she said.

"We'd all like one of those," he conceded, turning his sweaty face toward her.

"Maybe ran a telephone scam using nine-one-one," she suggested.

"That dial-back scam?"

"Which one is that?" she asked, hanging on his every word.

"That one didn't reach Seattle?" he asked. "Fella puts himself up as a cop. Was an embezzlement scam involving the elderly. To insure he really is a cop, he tells the mark to hang up and quickly call him back at the station using the nine-one-one line. Never mind that ain't possible. The mark hangs up. The line stays open—it won't go to dial tone on the receiving end. Did you know that? So the confidence man plays a recording of a dial tone into the phone; mark picks up the phone, hears the dial tone, dials nine-one-one. Trickster turns off the recording of the dial tone. Some of 'em use another voice, some an accomplice, but the line is answered something like, 'Emergency Services,' " he said, feigning a woman's voice. "The mark asks to speak to the cop; the con man comes on the line, and the mark is absolutely convinced from that moment on that she's talking to a cop. And that's all it takes. A person'll do just about anything for a man carrying a badge." He looked her body over a little too closely. "A woman carrying a badge too, I imagine."

"Do we know who went down for that one?"

"Su-gar, we got so many damn scams crawling out of the swamp, we don't hardly keep track. Holding down a job is the most common one we see. You know somebody's crooked if they got a nine-to-five job."

"Including cops?"

He smiled. He enjoyed his own company. "Last name? First name? You got anything more than nine-one-one for me?" He looked at her chest again and then lowered his eyes to her waist. "Anything at all?"

"I'll take everyone serving time in '95 for fraud and bunco. That's a good place to start."

"A better place to start is dinner at Commander's Palace. Then maybe a ride up the river on a jazz barge and a nice long, lazy look at the stars from around the pool at a little bungalow I know just outside the parish. In too close to the city the sky is all lit up and glowing and you don't see no stars at all. And let me tell you, there ain't nothing as pleasing to the eye as the Louisiana night sky." Having properly loaded his own statement, he added, "Excepting, that is, maybe you, su-gar. Seattle gotta be damn proud have you carrying their shield."

"Alphabetized. Fraud and bunco. If there's a way to isolate it to telephone scams—"

"There isn't," he fired back, the smoke peeling up his face and over his eyes. "This system is the Model T of networks. New system going on-line in another year or two. They're calling it an intranet. Now ain't *that* clever! We're calling it late." He confirmed that he was also the single greatest fan of his own jokes. "Give me overnight. You really ought to think about that dinner."

"I can call you?" she asked.

"Anytime, su-gar. Though I'd prefer to call *you*." He faked a smile for her. His teeth belonged to a heavy smoker.

She wasn't giving this guy any way to find her.

"I have a feeling we work together on this, and it might speed things up," he said. "Two heads are better than one."

She suggested, "What about I drop by later and we see what, if any, progress you've made."

"I just love incentive programs."

CHAPTER

54

Consumed by an unrelenting, twisting knot of worry, Boldt understood the criminal mind-set as never before. Lies started small and out of sheer necessity; they then mushroomed into gross untruths driven by selfishness and greed. Boldt's greed was centered around his daughter; the hunger a criminal felt for money or control, Boldt felt for an intact family. He held her in his arms and made up stories for her; he sat her on his lap and played jazz to her. He missed her in a way he had never missed another.

Daphne made contact with the most well-known, most active home for children, believing them experts on every aspect of adoption, legal and otherwise. For Boldt, this visit lit the candle at both ends: pursuing the Pied Piper from the evidence surrounding the kidnappings and from the result of the kidnappings— adoption. Sarah and Trudy Kittridge and ten other children remained in the candle's middle, flames licking toward them.

The Louis Charlemagne Home for Boys, an imposing stone edifice set back from the road by a semicircular gravel driveway, dominated the city block. It looked more like a country club than a halfway house. The towering door occupied a space between two tall Corinthian columns. A cheap electronic doorbell had been fitted alongside—a wart on an otherwise pretty face.

A black man with skin that shone with sweat answered the doorbell. He had thick forearms, a large head and a jutting brow that partially hid pinprick dark eyes. He ushered Boldt and Daphne into a cavernous stone foyer that carried the sour smell of a dull Skil saw burning its way through a two-by-four. A cloud of gray smoke hung heavy in the air.

"Dr. Montevette," Daphne said.

"Right down here," the man said, abandoning his small construction project. "He expecting ya?"

"Yes, we have an appointment."

"Whoa, Cardinal!" he shouted to a spotted puppy that appeared out of nowhere and peed onto the floor as the handyman snagged him. "What-cho doing loose?" He called out for "Evelyn," but received no answer. "Just down on your left," he advised his guests, raising his voice. "I best handle the Cardinal and his little mistake."

A professorial man wearing a checked shirt, brown corduroy pants and brown bucks greeted them from a distance, drawn by the handyman's voice. "Bernard Montevette," he introduced himself.

They shook hands all around. Montevette was a short man with kind eyes, half the hair he wanted and a delicious New Orleans slur to his words. A chandelier fan paddled the air languidly, gently cooling the rich, wood-paneled walls, the fading green carpet and the few antiques. The slow, lazy propeller strobed soft shadows down onto the room's walnut table that sat away from Montevette's enormous partners' desk. "Don't get out-of-town police as a rule. Can't think of the last time, and I've been involved with Charlemagne—well, I am, in fact, only the home's fourth director in its one-hundred-and-seventeen-year history; the first and only director to have been a former resident here."

"One of the boys?" Daphne inquired.

"Exactly. And the Charlemagne has the proud distinction of being the only boys' home in the country not to accept public funds. We operate privately from an endowment established just after the Second World War." The way he regarded them, Daphne had the uneasy feeling he was considering them as a couple intent on adopting a son. This was the first time the idea came to her of how to save Trudy Kittridge. It struck her all at once—a whole and complete plan—as only the best ideas hit her. She wanted to steal Boldt away immediately and run it by him.

"We're involved in an active investigation, Dr. Montevette," Boldt said, "that requires some discretion."

"Yes, so Ms. Matthews informed me earlier." He met eyes with each of them; his were an icy gray blue. "I am at your service, sir."

"Illegal adoption," Daphne reminded.

"Yes, so you said."

Daphne explained, "How one might go about it here in New Orleans. Successfully, that is. The way the law works—"

"Or doesn't," Boldt added.

"Private adoption," Montevette supplied, nodding. "I believe I have someone on my staff who might be able to help us. If you don't mind?"

"Not at all," Daphne answered.

He summoned a "Miss Lucy" over the phone. Announcing that she would join them shortly, he added, "The fact of the matter is that private adoption is something we all must contend with—that is, adoptions not arranged through a state organization. Private adoption is less regulated than state-arranged, although it still requires court appearances and proper paperwork. It is far more susceptible to human greed and abuse. What I think you will find here in New Orleans,"—*Naarlans*—"and I say this only because I've heard the stories myself, is that what you might call the lower end of the economic strata is far more *familiar* with this kind of practice than others."

"Paperwork?" Daphne asked.

"More than just paperwork," Montevette explained. "In the surrender of a child, the biological mother is required to make a court appearance in front of a sitting judge. She is advised by the judge that she is surrendering the child in perpetuity, and in a court of law, and that she is also surrendering her right to any legal recourse in the future. This is a fairly recent law, and one that has proved to simplify and qualify the process—a great improvement, I might add. At the time of adoption, a birth certificate is required, along with the document attesting to this court appearance and the surrender of the child. If the mother's medical costs are to be reimbursed, a copy of the medical bills are submitted. Ah! Miss Lucy! Come in, please. Won't you join us?" Montevette jumped to his feet and pulled back a chair for the young black woman. Miss Lucy Penneford wore a soft yellow dress and too much violet eye shadow. Her skin wrinkled when she smiled widely.

"Pleased to meet you," she said to them.

Montevette caught her up to date. ". . . how an illegal adoption might be carried out . . . And I was recalling that shake-up we had down to City Hall last year and how you—"

"Oh, yes. I think I can explain that," she said. She had an even thicker accent than Montevette. Her voice played musically in the room. The fan worked dark shadows across her face. The air smelled faintly of lavender. She had brought it with her.

She said, "It had evidently been going on for years. They worked down to the city office . . . what is that called?"

"The Bureau of Vital Statistics," Montevette supplied.

Daphne had the feeling Montevette knew more of the story, more of the answers, than he was willing to admit. She wondered why.

Miss Lucy continued, "And you know all those girls work for minimum wage down there, and it's just plain tough on minimum wage. Some man comes along and offers you a hundred dollars to process a birth certificate, and there's not a lot of thought that needs to be done on the subject."

"Which is just what was happening," Montevette contributed.

"Been going on for years, come to find out. Decades maybe. You need a birth certificate for a child, you simply come up with the hundred dollars."

"No adoption at all," Daphne said, amazed at the simplicity of the scam.

"No need," replied Montevette. "You obtain a fraudulent birth certificate for the child in your name, and he or she is legally a member of your family. Who's to question it?"

"It allows the mother to be paid for more than just hospital costs," Miss Lucy explained.

Boldt said, "It creates a viable black market."

Montevette agreed. "But it was closed down."

"I knew some of them girls," Miss Lucy told them. "Some of them is still doing time for that. And believe you me, that was the last of it. Don't even ask, Miss Matthews, because I can see you're about to, aren't you? That was the last of it. Honestly. They cracked down hard on those girls."

"But there are other ways," Boldt said, fishing for a back door through which he might locate the Pied Piper or his accomplice.

"Oh there are!" Miss Lucy said cheerily. "Another one I've heard about is this missing father thing." She explained to blank looks, "A single mother has a child and does not list a father on the birth certificate. Happens all the time. Either she wants no part of the man that put her in that condition, or she don't know who done it to her anyway. Maybe she's a drug addict, or in some other way where she don't exactly want the child no more. The way they do it, she sells a man—a complete stranger—the chance to put his name onto the birth certificate as the lawful father. Now this is the legal birth certificate we're talking about. This stranger is now the legal father of that child and has custody rights to that child, custody rights that she is willing to surrender for a price. It's a common means of adoption in the minority communities, believe me. Middle-class Cajun or blacks buy a blood right to a child. Cheap and easy."

"But not only with blacks," Daphne said.

"No, you're right. White trash, too. Maybe some suburban

teenage kids. Thing is, it's legal of course," she smiled, "as long as you ain't found out by no DNA test."

"Do the attorneys need special training, licenses, anything like that?" Boldt asked.

Montevette answered. "As far as I know, in Louisiana there are court fees to be paid, paperwork that must be filed. It's a specialty field, but by choice, not requirement."

"And if an attorney desired to bypass certain elements in the process?" Boldt asked.

"I see what you're driving at. Sure do. But he couldn't arrange a legal adoption without a judge on his side because of the requirement of a court appearance. Flat out, could not do it."

"But with a judge in his pocket?" Daphne asked.

Montevette and Miss Lucy exchanged looks. Miss Lucy said, "Miss Matthews, Louisiana ain't exactly like other places. An expression like that—it's offensive."

Montevette explained, "Let me tell you how we operate in New Orleans, Ms. Matthews. I have a little family farm not far from here. Not even an hour's drive. I own a farm vehicle, an old 1960 Ford half-ton. Use it on the farm to haul fallen limbs, move fence, that sort of thing. Run it into town on the odd day for groceries. The law requires I get that truck inspected once a year. Everything on it must function correctly in order for me to obtain my permit to operate the vehicle. It has been a long, long time indeed since everything on that truck has functioned properly, Ms. Matthews.

"Now there's a man named George," he continued, "whose job it is, for the price of a twenty-dollar permit fee, to inspect vehicles in our parish. I have known George for many, many years. Nearly as many as I have been driving that old Ford. I see him exactly once a year. For an extra twenty dollars George issues me my permit. Always has, always will. And that's just the way it's done around here. Guys like George, like me, we're everywhere. No one is hurting nobody. It is just the way business,"— *bidness*—"is done."

"Which might include business between attorneys and judges," Boldt suggested.

"Which on some level *definitely* includes attorneys and judges. *On some level.* Most definitely. And police, no doubt. And doctors and window washers and tree trimmers. Part of the culture, you might say. I am not condoning such behavior, but it is as inescapable as are so many elements of our fine culture. Southern culture."

Miss Lucy said, "If you are willing to pay for it, if you are willing to wait long enough to find the right person to help you, there is little you cannot do. Which is not to say it's a criminal place. I'm not implying that. It is not! We have crime and we have cops and we have courts, same as any other city."

"But as a people, we emphasize relationships over the letter of the law," Montevette said. "Black or white or Cajun, doesn't matter. We make relationships. The man who mows your lawn eats his breakfast alongside your children. Relationships," he repeated.

"An attorney could buy off a judge," Boldt said. "Forge documents of a mother surrendering a child, and the rest would all be perfectly legal. Even the adopting parents might never know the adoption was—"

"Improper," Montevette supplied. "It would not be *illegal*, you see. Not per se. Not with the proper paperwork in place. Only improper."

"Improper," Daphne echoed, getting a take on the man's attitude, and cringing internally.

"Mind you," he said, appealing to their curiosity, "there would be a paper trail to follow," he glanced at Miss Lucy, "if one was ambitious enough to pursue it."

Boldt understood the man was making an offer. "The names of the attorney and the judge would appear on the paperwork."

Montevette said, "The paperwork is filed in the parish where the judge sits. In a large parish, it might seem a little coincidental for the same judge and attorney to process too many adoptions."

"But not in a small parish," Miss Lucy informed the two visitors. "There may be only one judge in the entire parish."

"Certainly possible," Montevette agreed. The shadow of the fan pulsed across his face, like a curtain being pulled back. A thought had come to him. He said, "No, Miss Lucy, I believe we are wrong. The *originals* would remain with the parish. But in the case of a private adoption, copies would be filed either here in New Orleans, or in Lafayette, depending on the parish of record." He met eyes with Boldt and smiled coyly. He glanced at Miss Lucy and said to Daphne and Boldt, "It would be our pleasure to help you in this endeavor. I think you may find Louisiana a bit of a foreign country."

Miss Lucy said, "Perhaps we can translate for you."

Montevette, his eyes charged with excitement, slapped the table. "It's that paperwork we want to follow."

CHAPTER

55

Smiling John's Pleasure and Social Club, a corner establishment in an ethnically mixed neighborhood of Cajun, Caribbean and Afro-American, caught between the opulence of the Garden District and the commerce of downtown, smelled of a rude combination of perfume, stale beer and vanilla air freshener. The soles of LaMoia's ostrich boots stuck to the wooden plank flooring. Obnoxiously loud Cajun accordion music roared from distorted ceiling speakers as six women—girls really—played pinball.

He sidled up to a set of recently waxed legs that disappeared into a tiny piece of red leather. The look she offered LaMoia was sad and distant—a junkie. He passed. The second machine received its hip bumps from a Creole girl still in her teens who filled out the denim overall shorts and white camisole so that any man would want to take up farming.

"Hey," LaMoia said.

"Not now, sweetie. I got two thousand to go for the bonus."

"Got all the time in the world," he lied.

Alarms sounded, announcing she had crossed into bonus territory and sending her into a blinding frenzy of bumps and flipper thrusts. She kept the ball alive for three full minutes, having cleared the next bonus as well. He had never thought of pinball as sexy. The ball died on a bad left flipper.

"You could be here all day," he said.

"Unless I had a better offer." Her voice gave away her age, perhaps still a minor, although her equipment suggested otherwise.

"There's a guy works here name of Jimmy."

"So? Am I going to play this next ball or not?"

Before he could explain the twenty dollars he proffered onto the machine's glass surface, she advised him, "That won't even buy you a hummer, sweetie." She drew back the springed metal ram preparing to launch another ball, but LaMoia grabbed her hand, stopping her.

"Need a little face to face with Jim-bo, *sweetie*. The twenty's just to keep the meter running."

The twenty disappeared into the bib of the overalls. There wasn't a lot of room left up there.

"A location where I might find him would be nice."

She pointed to the ceiling. "He goes on in an hour. His is the first room on this side," she said. Eyeing LaMoia actively, she added, "Another twenty you go home with a smile on your face."

He offered her a big, toothy smile. "I'm smiling just thinking about it."

"You got a car with a backseat? Pull it around back. Lemme know."

"We'll talk," he said.

"No we won't," she corrected. She released the plunger and launched the steel ball into the flashing lights, bells and buzzers.

LaMoia found the stairs and climbed them to the second story. From the far side of the first door *Oprah* played loudly. He thought she had given him the wrong room—one of Smiling John's active employees, he thought. He knocked carefully.

"Yeah?" came a male smoker's voice.

LaMoia fished two twenties under the crack in the door. Probably a night's wage in a dump like this. The twenties disappeared.

LaMoia stood there for a full minute expecting an inquiry or the door to open. "Hey!" LaMoia spoke to the door.

Oprah went louder.

LaMoia knocked for a second time. He teased a hundred under the door, but brought it back to his side. He teased it through again. The information he sought could not be valued—nothing less than the Pied Piper's identity.

"I think you got the wrong room."

"Jimmy?"

"Heat?"

"Was once. Not anymore. Repo now. Don't want you. My thing is with an individual from your last known address."

"I don't think so." The forty came back through the door.

"The guy wears the same eagle as you do, only on his forearm. Yours is on your right biceps. That bird is the only connection to you. I'm not carrying any trouble for you. The artwork was done at your last address." LaMoia fished the hundred half through. "Take it." It sat there, and he suddenly saw it not as currency but as Sarah caught in a deadly tug of war.

The door came open a crack. Jimmy wore a goatee and glasses in dime-store frames. His dark hair was pulled into a ponytail. He looked dumb, like so many of them did.

"Three of you got the same tattoo. I checked with the prison. Of the three, they remembered you. You stayed a little longer than was on the original invitation."

"You gotta be heat."

"Was once," he repeated. "The guy—the one with the eagle on the forearm—is laying bad plastic from San Diego to Seattle. He's late on payments for a Taurus. I'm representing the car dealer."

"Never knew him."

"A name would help. That tattoo was seen laying down the plastic, but we got nothing but aliases. Medium security. You had to run into him."

The man glanced down at the hundred on the floor.

"Plus the forty," LaMoia said. "Name of a friend. Anything I can use?"

"Never knew him. Not personally. Not so as I knew a name or nothing."

"Listen, if you're milking me. . . . I'm light as it is—"

"It's not that. *I didn't know him.* You listening?" Disgusted, he said, "He was smooth, that's all I know about him. Talk his way into anything, out of anything. Was a stunt man—"

"Con artist."

"Right, a stunt man. In for some kind of something. Sucked up to the screws and the chief. Got his way: butts, weed, booze. Didn't want to know him. You know? Fuck the little kiss ass."

LaMoia ate up every detail. "But he got the same tattoo as you," he reminded, hoping to spur some rivalry. Inmates were little more than boys in this regard.

"Got mine first, Goddamn it. Everyone admiring it, like. Himself included." He eased the door open wider, more relaxed. *Oprah* was on a small color set that favored yellow. Jimmy saw LaMoia checking out the TV and he said, "Got hooked on that bitch in the joint. Can't give her up."

"Know what you mean."

"You watch?"

LaMoia shrugged. "You're saying all the sucking up won him special treatment. That's why you didn't hang with him."

"He got privileges," the man complained. " 'Jungle visits,' we called them."

"Conjugal visits."

"Only the butt suckers—the brownnosers—pulled off that kinda shit, I'll tell you what. Doing time and getting cheese a couple times a month. Gimme a fucking break!"

LaMoia knew it went against the rules, meaning the visits had been arranged by the guards as a form of payment. "He's married?"

"Two, three times a month he's sucking and banging the bitch who put them both in the joint the first place, way I heard it."

"She was *also* incarcerated?"

"A stunt team, they were. She gets driven over here from the slammer in Lamont, drops the lace and spreads 'em. They do the Dippity-Do and she's back in the van for Lamont."

Conjugal visits between two inmates was unheard of in Washington State. "Lamont?"

"It's the big house for chicks."

"The wife is doing hard time?" LaMoia sensed his chance to
identify the two. The conjugal visits were certainly not official,
which meant they would not carry any kind of paperwork. They
reeked instead of payoffs, or—knowing this team's record—a con
job. A few screws and a transport were involved at a minimum.
"He have money, this guy?"

"How you think he rubs up against the screws so good? 'Course
he had money, somewhere. And it must have been quite a few
yards. But I heard that about him—no one ran a stunt like this
guy. He was in for ripping off old hags, I think. Something like
that." He glanced back at the TV where Oprah paced in front of
the stage. "I don't know shit about him. Stayed clear of that shit."

LaMoia handed him the remaining forty to add to the hundred
on the floor. "You sure you don't remember a name?"

"No way."

"Looks?"

"Average. Your height. You gonna run stunts on people, you
gotta look average, know what I mean? They gotta trust you."

"Not me," LaMoia said. "I don't trust him an inch."

Boldt and Daphne's admission to the Bureau of Vital Statistics did not come from Montevette, the director of the boys' home, nor did it come through the front door. Miss Lucy made the contact—at the back door—and in a matter of an hour instead of what might have taken days or even weeks through proper channels. They had no warrant; they were well out of their jurisdictional authority. They possessed only Boldt's compelling urgency in his eyes and Daphne's internal calm. With both barrels loaded, no one could refuse them, least of all Walter, a black man in his early fifties who wore polyester trousers and a starched houndstooth shirt. Walter, whose hair was graying at the temples, walked like a man sacrificed at fullback on an overly competitive high school team. His nose had been flattened several times and left to wilt on his face like the curled thumb of an old leather glove. He wore half glasses that magnified a string of dark moles under his left eye.

Boldt and Daphne were led down a long narrow aisle between gunmetal gray shelves that stretched fourteen feet into the air toward bare-bulb funnel lights and the exposed steel trusses that supported the building's flat roof. The volume of paperwork overwhelmed Boldt, for this was but one of dozens and dozens of such rows. "I hope this isn't all adoptions," he said.

"This here is birth certificates," Walter replied, his strained voice absorbed like the spoken word in a snow-covered forest. "To your left, death and marriages—same thing, far as I'm concerned. That area toward that far wall is divorces. We got maybe twelve, fifteen stacks filled to the top with 'em." He turned right, left and right again. A maze of paperwork, marked only by tiny white labels on the shelves and typed stickers on the boxes, the place seemed artificial to Boldt, created simply to overwhelm him. The prospect of dust and gum and paper cuts loomed. His impatience mounted; perhaps he could leave Daphne here to sort through it. But no, he answered himself, two sets of eyes were critical to such an undertaking.

Another right, left and right—they were working their way to this, the top floor's far corner where a massive chain-link fence isolated the small reception area with its wood bench, wooden counter and black pens on chains. A woman named Amy glanced once when she heard Walter's approach and a second time as a double take when she saw him in company.

"I need Ole Blue a minute, Amy," Walter said, indicating the computer.

A computer! Boldt felt a rush of hope. "You're computerized?"

"I'm not," Walter replied, "but these stacks are all indexed on Ole Blue, and anything filed after nineteen hundred and eighty-eight is in his memory instead of on the shelves. Thank the lord." He said, "Although it did cost four jobs up here on the seventh." He smiled warmly at Daphne. "Seniority do have its privileges."

Amy came to Walter's rescue several times over the course of the next ninety minutes. He had trouble keeping the search targeted to all parishes, the system defaulting to citywide searches. The result was that adoption records were sorted parish by parish; neither of them could seem to convince the machine to do a districtwide search. The process was painstakingly slow.

Daphne requested printouts—the number of parishes stunned Boldt. Realizing he had the search dates wrong, Daphne explained patiently to Walter, "We're particularly interested in adoptions registered from sometime in the last five to six months, right up to the present."

"Nineteen hundred and eighty-eight to nineteen hundred and ninety-two, I wouldn't been able to help you." *Hep you.* "Ninety-two on they gone directly to the screen. Afore that we still done all the paperwork, but they filed it on computer and archived it on fiche. Now it's straight to the computer and they run two of 'em—two different locations—one watching the other, backing it up, you know. Only paperwork is the signatures and the court documents. They can't seem to figure this thing out completely. Always some kind of paperwork involved."

Boldt's patience, on the other hand, had run out. He kept his mouth shut and tried to stay out of things. Trudy Kittridge was going to be sold into adoption within a day or two—Boldt felt convinced of this.

With each search, Daphne requested another printout and then studied the results while Walter again isolated a particular parish and conducted the search. Boldt had the feeling that Amy might have accomplished this all much faster, but Walter and Miss Lucy shared an aunt or grandparent—some blood relative—and Walter was their man.

"Lou," Daphne whispered, gaining his attention.

He joined her at a metal desk, taking a rolling chair that squeaked when he leaned forward.

She contained her excitement, using only her index finger to direct him, so as not to be overheard. No telling who else Walter might know or be related to. Her nails held a clear finish and were cut short. She had filed them recently.

Boldt's eye followed the line she indicated. The filing was for January. The judge of record was Judge Terence Adams; the attorney, one Vincent Chevalier, whose mailing address placed him in the city. The very next adoption, recorded three weeks later, was again the work of Judge Adams and Vincent Chevalier. Her finger danced down the page. She glanced up and looked at him with wet, excited eyes.

Boldt withdrew his notebook and flipped pages hurriedly. The dates fit into the Pied Piper's schedule remarkably well—the adoptions coming four to eight working days after each of the abductions. He counted back and realized that if these entries indeed belonged to the Pied Piper, as he now believed, then he still had between two and six days in which to find Kittridge. The adoption process took slightly longer to arrange than he had foreseen. It was the first ray of hope he had felt.

The printout for Tanipahoa Parish showed eleven adoptions performed over the most recent six-month period, all with the same pair: Adams and Chevalier. All but two of the children had been placed with couples living out of state. Prior to November there had been no adoptions in the parish for five months.

"We've got them," Boldt whispered, disbelief permeating his words.

Daphne folded the printout, carefully aligning the corners and using her nail to make the fold. She said, "Now let's hope we're not too late."

CHAPTER

Central air-conditioning provided the New Orleans downtown public library with a large population of homeless, some of whom were effective at passing themselves off as readers, others who abandoned the ruse altogether, sitting at tables while fighting off the exhaustion of walking the streets at night. Technically, the library could not ask them to leave unless they fell asleep. Eyelids fluttered. An occasional page of a newspaper turned in keeping with the act.

The homeless seemed to collect in the periodicals section, perhaps because of its abundance of chairs and tables. Perhaps because of the sports section. Boldt and Daphne split up. Most of the news they sought they believed too recent to have reached microfiche.

Boldt refused Daphne's suggestion to approach NOPD's Detective Broole about the attorney Chevalier's dealings, this based on the assumption that a cop's curiosity could put the word out on the street, which in turn could jeopardize their efforts.

LaMoia, who wanted to work the husband and wife conviction, also wanted to consult Broole. "Cops know more than newspa-

pers," he repeated one too many times, bringing Boldt's wrath
down upon him. Assigned surveillance of the attorney, Chevalier,
LaMoia was halfway across town. He intended not only "to sit on
the man" but to install a caller-ID box on Chevalier's phone lines
in order to monitor the attorney's incoming calls. Legality was no
longer an issue; they had no way to trace Chevalier's outgoing
calls without the involvement of Broole. A warrant would have to
be justified. LaMoia had to justify that warrant, as well as keep an
eye out for Hale.

Boldt denied both suggestions, electing instead to gather intelligence. The more fact, the more hard information they brought
Broole, the better.

Boldt searched newspaper indexes for Vincent Chevalier.
Daphne took Judge Adams of Tanipahoa Parish. Thankfully, the
Times-Picayune ran a good crime beat.

The *Times-Picayune* was indexed monthly, available on the fifteenth of every month. The most recent index was for articles
published in February. Boldt searched the months of January and
February and found no reference on any Chevalier, including
Vincent. He then waited his turn to access a reference computer
terminal that at peak hours allowed each user only three consecutive searches, and maintained a line a half-dozen deep. Boldt was
not used to waiting in lines, except for the office copier. His shield
generally moved him to the front of any line.

Boldt restricted the search to the *Times-Picayune* database and
then typed in the name:

V_I_N_C_E_N_T _ C_H_E_V_A_L_I_E_R

The computer considered the request. Boldt caught himself
holding his breath. A moment later seven listings scrolled down
the screen, including publication date, partial headlines, page and
column numbers. Five of the seven articles had been published in
the paper nearly five years earlier. The first two listings had been
page 3 stories, implying a relative importance to them. The last
two were barely twelve months out of date. The partial headline
on the opening hit read: "POLICE DISCONNECT 911 SCAM . . ."

The last article listed had a title that began: "APPEALS COURT SHOOTS . . ." That first listing swimming in his head, Boldt signaled Daphne—and half those in the reference section—with a frantic wave of the hand. He asked the person in line behind him how to print out a copy of his search results. A few minutes later, he and Daphne took seats in adjacent microfiche viewing stations, the appropriately boxed issues in hand.

"A nine-one-one scam," he reminded urgently, clumsily threading the cumbersome roll of film into the antiquated machine. He threaded it upside down on his first effort; reversed, his second try.

"Yes, I caught that," Daphne said calmly, trying to contain him. She threaded her machine correctly the first time and was reading text before Boldt.

"As in Millie Wiggins' day care center," Boldt said, still fumbling.

"Yes."

"It's *them*," Boldt emphasized.

"It suggests a strong possibility, doesn't it?"

He glanced at her incredulously, as he failed with the machine for the third time. "Goddamn it!" he hollered too loudly, his fingers refusing to cooperate.

"Here." She leaned across him, corrected his mistake and restored the machine.

Boldt sped ahead to the article written five years earlier as Daphne returned to her station. "It was page three," he said, prior to actually locating the article. "You've got to think that means it was pretty big news at the time."

"Shh," Daphne chided. "I'm on to something here." But a moment later, as Boldt went silent, she couldn't resist. She slid her fiberglass chair up against Boldt's and looked on.

"Two hundred and eighty thousand," she read. "It was run on the elderly."

Boldt heard her but did not acknowledge. He read slowly and intently. He wanted every last detail committed to memory.

CITY BEAT—POLICE MADE TWO ARRESTS ON TUESDAY IN THE SO-CALLED 911 SCAM THAT HAD BEEN PUZZLING IN-

VESTIGATORS FOR WEEKS AND HAS COST AREA VICTIMS, MOSTLY THE ELDERLY, NEARLY $280,000. FOLLOWING A TELECOMMUNICATIONS STING INVOLVING COORDINATED TECHNOLOGIES LINKING AIR TOUCH CELLULAR, SOUTH-WESTERN BELL AND SPRINT COMMUNICATIONS, THE CON-FIDENCE GAME, WHICH PITTED THE FICTIONAL CALLER AS A LAW ENFORCEMENT OFFICER ATTEMPTING TO UNRAVEL A BANK EMBEZZLEMENT SCANDAL, WAS FINALLY PUT ON HOLD. ARRESTED WERE ROGER CROWLEY, 28, OF NEW ORLEANS, AND HIS WIFE, LISA. THE PAIR, WHO HAVE OPER-ATED UNDER AS MANY AS TWENTY-TWO ALIASES, ARE WANTED ON RELATED CHARGES IN FIVE OTHER STATES IN-CLUDING NEVADA, ARIZONA AND FLORIDA. IF CONVICTED, THE COUPLE INDIVIDUALLY FACE UP TO FIFTEEN YEARS JAIL TIME AND FINES EXCEEDING $200,000. THE CROW-LEYS' ATTORNEY, VINCENT CHEVALIER, SAID HE WOULD FILE FOR DISMISSAL BASED ON ENTRAPMENT. INSISTING HIS CLIENTS WERE VICTIMS THEMSELVES—OF A LAW EN-FORCEMENT WITCH-HUNT—CHEVALIER INSISTED ON HIS CLIENTS' INNOCENCE AND SUGGESTED TO REPORTERS THAT THE CASE WOULD NEVER REACH TRIAL.

Three subsequent articles proved Chevalier wrong. The case did go to trial, a jury trial, resulting in what to Boldt's eye was a ninth-inning plea bargain down to intent to defraud that cut short the trial and lessened the sentences to seven years each, restoration of the victims' assets and fines of ten thousand dollars each. Trans-lated, it meant release in two to three years, restoration at thirty cents on the dollar, and two, twenty-five-hundred-dollar fines. It was the Crowleys' first conviction after eleven years and twenty-seven separate arrests in five states. There was nothing in the arti-cles to connect the couple to any kidnapping, child abduction, child abuse or extortion.

Daphne made the connection ten minutes later. "Middle of last year, the Crowleys sued the state of Louisiana for blocking an *adoption* they had planned."

Boldt shot her a look of astonishment. He said, "Convicted fel-ons aren't allowed to adopt," well aware of the federal law.

Daphne continued, "The Crowleys took possession of an infant girl born in Arkansas. They might have pulled it off, except the biological mother was an unwed fourteen-year-old, a minor, and her parents contested the adoption. Vincent Chevalier both arranged the adoption and represented the Crowleys in their lawsuit and their appeal."

"Lost both," Boldt guessed.

"Yes."

"Motive enough for this spree," Boldt suggested.

"A couple denied parenthood?" she said. "Worse than the wrath of a woman scorned."

"Confirm with Broole that Roger Crowley has an eagle tattooed on his left forearm. Then convince him that Crowley's at large. We need a warrant to trap-and-trace telephone calls inside Chevalier's office, from his cellular, and from pay phones in and around the surrounding neighborhood. Whatever you do, don't mention the Pied Piper investigation."

Keeping up with Boldt's hurried strides, Daphne said, "Is there some water you want me to walk on in the meantime?"

"Just try."

"I will."

"What happens to them after the adoption is blocked?" he asked.

"Denied the adoption, they decided to pursue other means of obtaining a child. But not for themselves anymore. For others."

"Forget about it," he said.

"The penny flutes. They wanted the abductions connected. They're making a statement. It's the Robin Hood Syndrome. They see themselves as saviors. In their minds, their actions are perfectly justified. They know what it's like to be denied parenthood."

"Stop," he said harshly. "I don't want to hear this."

"You need to," she protested. "These are the people who have your daughter."

CHAPTER

Detective Broole returned to his desk carrying a swagger reminiscent of LaMoia and a thick manila folder that Daphne assumed belonged to Roger or Lisa Crowley. The detectives division suffered under the noisy strain of wall-mounted air conditioners unable to condition and the languid efforts of paddle fans that recycled the same stale air.

"You really know how to pick 'em, su-gar." Broole slapped the file down in front of her and then lit up a cigarette within yards of the sign forbidding the activity. His clichéd coif was gelled into a ducktail. "We've had this loser in cuffs more times than his tailor. How'd you find him?"

"Library."

"Ah yes, that font of public knowledge," he said sarcastically.

"But it didn't say anything about tattoos," she said, reminding him of her earlier criteria.

"Yeah? Well this does. Have a look," he said, leaning over from behind and opening the folder in front of her, using the effort to be physically close to her. Attached to the folder's inside flap was a series of a half dozen mug shots. Below these were two other photographs, both of tattoos: an eagle on the man's left forearm; a snake running down his leg to the right of his genitals that had been blacked out with marker. Her heart skipped a beat—they had a physical marking that could be offered as hard evidence— Roger Crowley was the Pied Piper.

Crowley's various mug shots revealed a man skilled at cosmetics. Light hair, dark hair. Short hair, long. Acned skin, baby face. Warts, scars and wounds. Bright eyes, dull eyes; round eyes, almond. Crowley was all of these people and yet none of them, she realized. The real man behind the crimes lay buried somewhere back on Crowley's personal time line. Daphne Matthews wanted a shot at that person—the one who remained hidden. She wanted into his mind, inside where others had not been.

As she sought an invention to convince Broole to wiretap Chavalier's phone lines, Broole revealed his own agenda. "Is this the Pied Piper?" he asked, still leaning over her, his sour cigarette breath warm on her neck. "And before you hand me some discontinued merchandise and try to sell me on the life of its warranty, I beg you to consider the truth carefully because maybe, just maybe, su-gar, I possess something of even greater value to you." He placed his left hand onto her shoulder and his long fingers dangled down her chest as he sucked on the cigarette from his right. A cold shiver pulsed through her. He quizzed her. "Now, I don't want to speak it, su-gar, not aloud that is, but thunderstorms produce not only rain and lightning but another meteorological element."

"Wind? Tornadoes?"

"Not aloud. Aloud is not allowed," he said, amusing himself. He touched a finger to her lips. She was suddenly very much afraid of him. "But no, not wind, not tornadoes." He took his finger away. "It is a hybrid of snow and rain, su-gar, this particular meteorological element—kind of rain and ice rolled into one. It is also something you might associate with a particular federal agency involved in law enforcement. It will benefit us both greatly if you do not speak his *name* aloud, for that will alter my own position greatly and put me in a difficult position where I am forced to take sides. And I don't believe it would be revealing any secrets to tell you I would much prefer to be on your side."

"Frozen rain," she said, repeating what he had said.

"*Precisement!*"

Hail, she thought. Hale. Special Agent. "I'm with you," she said.

"Which is more than any man could ever ask," he said, maintaining the intimacy and stroking her collarbone. "Let me repeat," he said, sparing no contact. "Is this the one you all are calling the Pied Piper?"

"He's a suspect," she conceded, wondering how much to give, how much to keep.

"And the connection to New Orleans, other than his past?"

"His past is what brought us here," she told him. It was not an outright lie; the use of the 911 con had in part led them to Crowley.

"The connection, su-gar? Don't play with me." He sucked on the cigarette. Some ash brushed her arm as it tumbled to the floor.

"An attorney named Chevalier. We need a wiretap. We need to stay a step ahead of our federal friends."

"Is the collar so all-important?"

"You like the Feds, you work with them," she offered. "We need his office, his cell phone, and any pay phones for several blocks. My job is to win your cooperation."

His fingers danced lower on her chest. "And what is it exactly that I get in return? Hmm? From you, I mean? What would such a favor be worth? I'll need a warrant, su-gar. I'll need a real good lie to convince a judge to give me one. What would all that be worth, do you think?"

"The lives of two little girls," she answered bluntly. "If the Feds beat us to the suspect, we lose at least one of the girls."

"And I'm all tears, you understand," Broole said, "but it's that night sky I'm thinking about. Some good company."

"We could try for the attorney's phone records without you," she said, "but we're a little out of our jurisdiction."

"Maybe you aren't listening."

"Dinner tonight?" she said, weighing Sarah in the balance.

Broole picked up the phone and made two calls, Daphne listening in. He found his way to a woman named Emily who was either a past girlfriend or a blood relation. There was a brief discussion. When he hung up from the second call he said, "Phone records for office phone, home phone, fax line and cellular. They'll be through on the fax in a matter of minutes."

"I shouldn't have told you what I did," she admitted, having had time to reconsider.

"Look at it this way, su-gar. If you hadn't, our meteorological friend would have been a step aheada you."

"He has already IDed Crowley?" she gasped.

"He looked through our photo albums. He had a list of the state's former guests with him. What he made of it all, he didn't say, but he did not leave here in a jovial mood. Even so, I wouldn't count a man like that out, if I was you. He seems bound and determined to make the most of his resources."

"We're not counting him out, no," she said. The fax of Chevalier's phone records arrived only minutes later.

CHAPTER

The phone records provided by Broole produced immediate results and instantly clarified Vincent Chevalier's role. They also necessitated Daphne requesting a rain check for her dinner with Broole: She was heading out of town.

Awaiting his flight's boarding call, Boldt told her for the third time, "I'll call your cellular at eight o'clock Eastern, your batteries okay?"

She nodded. "You know the drill? Go easy with them, Lou. It's doubtful they know the extent of what they're involved in. If they go crying foul to Chevalier—"

"Got it," he said brusquely, checking the overhead clock. It was her plan, not his. A part of Boldt resented that. But true to form, she had come up with something brilliant.

"There are moments in one's life that are never forgotten," she warned. "Weddings, deaths, traffic accidents. The space shuttle blowing up. Kennedy. Lady Di. Your visit to the Brehmers is one of those moments. Mine too, with the Hudsons. This evening their lives change forever. Remember that."

"All our lives have changed forever," Boldt reminded stoically.

"Every moment—every decision—is one of those moments you're talking about."

"They'll never forget our visits. We are walking into their living rooms and detonating a bomb. Go easy on them."

"Message received."

His flight was called. He glanced toward the developing line at the gate, back to the clock and finally to Daphne. They shared an awkward moment, not knowing how to part. They shook hands. Boldt felt right about that.

"Eight o'clock," he repeated. He walked to the gate carrying only a briefcase.

Amelia and Morgan Hudson owned a sprawling horse farm on the outskirts of Lexington, Kentucky. Surrounded by a white-washed board fence, acres of manicured bluegrass corrals interconnected like a patchwork quilt. With it too dark to see, Daphne imagined the ill-tempered stallions kicking and bucking, the complacent mare and foal pairs meandering the fence lines. She had been raised on a farm not unlike this one. Her parents lived not two hours away.

Having headed straight to the Hudson residence from the airport, she turned the rental down the long drive, recalling a dozen memories from her childhood.

The enormous brick house ran off in a variety of directions. A white-faced Negro riding a black horse in an English saddle welcomed visitors with an electric lantern held out to the side.

Chevalier's office and cellular phones carried a series of long distance calls to the Hudson household leading up to the date of the Shotz kidnapping. The day of the kidnapping, three separate calls had been placed. A week later, the calls suddenly stopped. Chevalier never called the couple again. Daphne knew what she would find inside—*who* she would find, though it did nothing to instill confidence in her. Her assignment was simple confirmation. Boldt had the more difficult task.

She dragged her briefcase heavily toward her. She had lied to the Hudsons three hours earlier in a call from the New Orleans airport. Now she had to reveal that lie and undo others. She double-checked that her weapon, concealed inside her purse, was loaded and working properly. She had no idea what kind of people she faced.

CHAPTER

Boldt toyed with LaMoia's pick gun from the backseat of the rental. The Brehmers' Houston, Texas, home showed no activity, as it had not for the last hour. Boldt had made a single call to it before leaving New Orleans. A woman's southern drawl had answered, "This is Cindy."

"Mrs. Evaston?" Boldt asked.

"This is Mrs. *Brehmer* speaking," she corrected.

"Sorry, wrong number." Boldt hung up. That was all he had needed to justify the trip, but now, from the backseat, he found himself having second thoughts. He was playing a solid hunch based on an attorney's phone records, but the impatience of the desperate father in him, in constant conflict with the meticulous detective, refused to waste more than another fifteen minutes. He climbed out of the car and headed around the house to find the back door. He had the perfect excuse available to him if someone turned out to be home—the police shield in his coat pocket.

The house was deceptive. It reached back into the lot, framing a lap pool, and with a substantial cottage pressed up against the back fence. A great deal of care had been taken with the landscaping, hiding corners and breaking the structure's more common lines.

Boldt walked up to the kitchen door and pounded sharply. He didn't care if neighbors saw him; he had Sarah, Trudy and the others on his mind. He knocked again. No answer.

The security system, visible through the kitchen door, was manufactured by Brinks and was currently armed, a single red LED flashing. Boldt flipped open his cellular and called the house number again to make certain he had called the right home. The phone rang inside a moment later and also went unanswered.

The next call went to LaMoia.

"Yo!"

"It's me."

"Nothing here. Chevalier is a workaholic. Ordered a sandwich delivered."

"I need every four-digit number that could possibly belong to the Brehmers, of 342 Magnolia. Cindy and Brad. Dates of birth. Cell phones. Social Security. Car registrations. Start there. Add anything else you can think of."

"Hang on, I'm writing this down," LaMoia said. "Cindy and Brad Brehmer."

"How long?" Boldt asked.

"Six o'clock in Seattle? I can do this. Fifteen or twenty for the easy stuff: birthdays, cell phones, Social Security. I don't know about the car registrations. I'll try the local law. They might help if I press them."

"Hurry," Boldt said.

"You on your cellular?"

"Right here," Boldt said. He disconnected. Boldt never questioned LaMoia's contacts, his ability to obtain information. Some said it was all the women he had been with. Others claimed he had once held a position in Army Intelligence, something Boldt knew to be untrue. Whatever the case, he would have made a better Intelligence officer than Boldt; he had contacts everywhere and at all levels.

Twenty minutes later Boldt's cellular vibrated at his side. La-

Moia provided him with two Social Security numbers, one cellular phone number, and the vanity plates from two cars: FNDRAZN and BRADH. He also had two other phone numbers for the same address, both unpublished. Boldt took these down as well, believing them to be the office phone and data line—both decent candidates for the home code.

Boldt asked, "How many retries on a Brinks home security system?"

"We're talking password entry?"

"Right."

"The system times out is all. User programmed. Ten-second intervals. Default is thirty seconds on most systems."

"That's true for Brinks? Do you know that for a fact?"

"Doesn't matter the make, only the commercial models limit the number of retries as far as I know. Home models use timers." He asked, "You going inside, Sarge?"

"The last plane out is at ten. I can't wait around if I'm wrong."

"And if you're right?"

"Then Matthews has a flight to book."

Boldt wrote out the numbers he'd been given as a list on a piece of notepaper. He timed himself, and using his cellular phone's numeric pad, practiced entering the various combinations of numbers. Within minutes, he determined he could not key in all the numbers provided him. He had to make selections. He reduced both Social Security numbers to their last four digits and he did the same to all the phone numbers. The birthdays were more troublesome, both containing six digits. He divided each into two sets of four digits: 12/24/59 became both 1224 and 2459. Boldt's edited list amounted to ten sets of four digits. After six practice runs it became clear to Boldt he would be physically unable to enter more than eight sets of numbers in the thirty-second window. He removed the home phone number—too obvious— and the first half of the wife's birthday, 1224; husbands were not the best at remembering their wife's birthday.

He started the rental's engine and left it running so that if he failed inputting the code, he would be in the car and out of there in a matter of seconds: no running lights, no stopping for the stop sign at the end of the short street, just a dark blur. He knew that the alarm signal first passed to the private security firm; then, if and when the security firm failed to reach the residents by phone, it would be handed off to the local police, who could not possibly dispatch a cruiser any sooner than five, and more likely forty, minutes from the time of notice. As long as he didn't panic, Boldt had little to worry about in the way of being caught. As an added precaution, he donned a pair of disposable crime scene gloves, his transformation to criminal complete.

He stood at the home's back door for several seconds mentally rehearsing his every movement, well aware that from the moment he keyed the door with LaMoia's pick gun, the thirty-second timer would be running. He donned his reading glasses, placed the pick gun in the lock, squeezed the trigger and turned. The door unlocked, but he did not open it. His heart sounded in small explosions radiating jolts of anxiety throughout his system.

By opening the door, he would sever his ties with law enforcement, would cross boundaries that separated cop from criminal— the legendary Blue Line. He knew absolutely that such actions inevitably and irrevocably brought one down, and yet he turned the doorknob, pushed open the door and stepped inside. Once committed, forever committed. Sarah was coming home.

The security device immediately sounded a high-pitched warning tone alerting the resident to disarm it. Using his list, Boldt keyed in the first four-digit numeral. The device's keypad light went dark and the beeping stopped, though only briefly. Then the light came back on and the beeping began anew. INVALID CODE flashed across the small display. Boldt keyed in the next number: INVALID CODE. *Ten seconds.* Another attempt, *thirteen seconds.* INVALID CODE. *Fifteen seconds.* Another: INVALID CODE. *Eighteen seconds.* The display flashed, the beeping stopped, and the red LED was replaced by one green. Boldt hesitated there, his finger outstretched. The device remained silent. He was inside.

He closed and locked the back door, briefly studying the security device in order to rearm it quickly, if necessary. Below the

number 9 was printed ARM ALL; below the 0, ARM PART. He circled the fifth number on his list. Preparations complete, he began
what he intended to be a thorough search in order to determine
the Brehmers' relationship to the New Orleans attorney. It took
him all of five minutes to locate the empty nursery down the hall.

CHAPTER

Boldt picked up Daphne at the door to baggage claim at 11:15 P.M., Central Time. She carried a hanging bag, a purse and a leather briefcase.

Boldt drove.

"I never want to go through that again," she said. "I'm not a very good liar."

"It worked?" he asked.

"They believed me. They bought into it. They trusted me." She glanced over at him, the oncoming headlights pulsing across her face. "Has it occurred to you that we've stooped to being exactly like them, like the Crowleys? You and me. We're con artists. We lie to people. We cheat them. I threw up during the flight. It wasn't air sickness."

Cars cried past in a whine of rubber and engine.

"But they bought it?" he asked, repeating himself. He wanted every detail.

"I walked into their home, flashed my badge too quickly for them to get a look and reintroduced myself as being with Health and Welfare. I visited their child asleep in the nursery. It was Rhonda Shotz."

Boldt glanced over at her, and back to the highway.

"I inspected the house, including their bedroom, the kitchen, the garage—even the child seat. I played my role."

"Paperwork?" he asked.

"Chevalier brokers the adoptions. My guess is that the Hudsons have no idea what they're into. They think they bought off an attorney to move them up a list. I worked the money issue. They were well rehearsed. I was shown a single check made out to one Gloria Afferton in the amount of her medical expenses: nine thousand and change. A second to Chevalier for services rendered: five thousand, the maximum allowed for a private adoption in Kentucky. I suppose the rest was cash or stocks or bonds. Who knows?"

"Their impression of Chevalier?"

"He's a little slick for their tastes. The wife believes their child is an unwanted baby from a prominent family, just as Chevalier represented it. They don't care. They would have bought any explanation. The rest of the process fit with Kentucky law for interstate adoptions: a Louisiana social worker, a woman, phoned several times with questions for them."

"Lisa Crowley," Boldt supplied.

"Probably." She spoke quietly, clearly rattled from the interview. "They sent the social worker videos of their home and their neighborhood; they notarized documents; they mailed their checks; they waited."

"Were they asked for photos of themselves? Videos?" Boldt asked. The issue was crucial to Daphne's plan.

"They claimed not. It makes sense. An adoption can't be refused based on how an adoptive parent looks. If anything, such a request could appear discriminatory."

Since it was critical to their success, Boldt hoped no photos had been sent. "Delivery?"

"The baby was brought to Chevalier's office by the social worker. They were in and out in less than an hour."

"Judge Adams?"

"They never met him, no. But his name is on the documents." She hesitated. "I saw the documents. As far as I could tell, they're in order, Lou. I think the Hudsons have what would pass as a legitimate adoption."

"Chevalier kept it all in order," he said. "He let them be the ones to transfer the child across interstate borders. Someone delivers the child to the city, the adoptive parents take the child away. He's careful."

"And Rhonda Shotz?" he asked.

"Peaceful. Asleep in her nursery. I gave them a clean bill of health and went my way. And you'll love this: They asked me to pass along their best wishes to Miss Chambers, the social worker. Lisa Crowley evidently makes a good impression."

"It's a living," Boldt said sarcastically.

"And the Brehmers?" she asked.

"They have a nursery all set up. Nothing's been used. Diaper Genie is empty. Most of the outfits still have their tags on them—haven't been washed yet. It's a nursery in waiting."

"That's it? That's all we have?"

"Calendar by the phone in the kitchen has a line through the weekend, the word NO underneath. Caps. New Orleans. It's them. Couldn't find the March phone bill, might not be there yet, but February they were calling Chevalier's office about once a week. It's them," he repeated. "Trudy Kittridge," he muttered.

"Damn," she said, turning away and rolling down the window to allow the air inside. "Awful business." Her shoulders tightened and he thought she was crying.

His cell phone vibrated and he answered it, met by a woman's distinctive voice that spoke the words, "Skagit County." Theresa Russo, the computer expert he had consulted on Sarah's ransom video.

"Come again?"

"The cable company that boxed in the severe weather notice around CNN. It provides service to Skagit. The notice concerned a flood warning."

"You're working late."

"Message was buried on my E-mail. Thirty-five new messages. It's been there two days, I'm afraid. Sorry about that. Thought you'd like to know."

"Skagit?" he asked. "We're certain about that?"

"Positive," she said. "It's good for your investigation, isn't it? I mean, how many FedEx trucks can be assigned to Skagit? A hell of a lot fewer than in downtown Seattle, I'll tell you that."

"Any contacts at FedEx?"

"I may know someone who knows someone in data processing," she said. "It's a pretty small community. We may even supply them—I'd have to check."

"Check," he said. "Data processing should have all the logs and manifests. That's what we're after."

"You want me to try, or do you want to do it?" she asked.

"You mind?"

"No problem. Routes and times for all Skagit deliveries?"

"March twenty-fifth."

"I've got that already." He could feel her hesitation before she asked, "How is Liz? I heard she's out, isn't she?"

The way she said it, it sounded to him more like a jail sentence. Maybe that was right. "She's home," he confirmed. "Doing fine." He glanced at the car's clock. He had promised to call but couldn't remember when they had arranged. He had no idea if she was doing fine or not. He said, "At the risk of sounding like a jerk, the sooner—"

"Understood. What do I do if I get something? E-mail it to you?"

"How about dropping it off with Liz?"

"Done. I'd love to see her anyway."

He thanked her and disconnected.

"Anything important?" Daphne asked, working a tissue at her nose.

She knew his voice too well, knew him too well. She had discerned his excitement, his anticipation. He had not told his team about the FedEx truck; he had kept that one to himself, though he wasn't certain why. More lies. They didn't bother him anymore. He knew he was in trouble.

He was saved from any discussion. The Brehmers' house appeared on their left.

CHAPTER

Boldt parked the rental on the street, certain that the next twenty to thirty minutes were crucial to the rescue of Trudy Kittridge and, thereby, Sarah. Together, he and Daphne climbed the slate steps toward the front door in silence, each reflecting on the importance of their performances. "You understand—"

"Yes," she interrupted. "I do. Perfectly well."

Boldt pushed the doorbell, which to him felt more like pulling a trigger. Brad Brehmer peered through the crack in the door—baby-faced but handsome. *Honest looking.* Boldt thought. A *churchgoer*, thought Daphne. He had dark hair, a sharp jaw, a sardonic smile. He wore khakis and a button-down blue Oxford shirt. It was past eleven. The news played in the background. "Help you?" he asked, with only a hint of a southern accent.

"This is Lt. Lou Boldt," she introduced. "I'm Daphne Matthews. We're police, Mr. Brehmer." They produced their identification, but quickly, hoping the man might miss their jurisdiction.

"SPD?" Brehmer inquired, his throat dry like the air. He hadn't missed a thing. "Where's that?"

"Seattle," she answered.

"You're a long way from home."

Boldt said, "It's late. Sorry about that."

Brehmer hesitated. The moment was awkward. "You mind if I see those again? You mind passing them through?"

They did as he asked. Brehmer shut and locked the front door. A long sixty seconds later, he reopened it and invited them inside.

"Is your wife at home, Mr. Brehmer?" Daphne asked. "We'd like to speak to both of you if we might."

"We were out tonight," he clarified as if asked. Appropriately nervous and anxious. Daphne approved. "A celebration dinner." The room looked bigger to Boldt with the lights on.

"Celebrating the adoption," Daphne said, stinging the man. Above all things, she needed to maintain the upper hand.

"Cindy!" the husband called out somewhat desperately, "put something on and get out here."

"Nice house," Boldt said.

"You want to show us the nursery?"

"Cindy."

Cindy Brehmer, a woman who would look twenty-five for the next ten years, entered the living room wearing a terry cloth robe that hung to mid-thigh. The moment she saw Boldt and Matthews, she reversed course abruptly. "My God, Brad!" she complained.

"Stay. They're police."

"I don't care who they are. You will please excuse me," she apologized, and beat a hasty retreat. Five minutes later, she returned with her face on, wearing jeans and a pajama top.

Introductions followed. Small, with a petite waist and frail hands, her large, expressive eyes and her dark coloring conveyed a demanding presence. With a thicker accent than her husband, she practiced her southern hospitality, enjoying the sound of her own voice as she prattled on about a visit she and a sorority sister had made to Seattle a decade earlier. She said, "I'm sure I've never had better crab cakes in my life."

Boldt missed the crab cakes, the smell of the water, the vivid sunsets over the Olympics. More than anything, he missed little Sarah.

The resulting silence hung heavily in the room.

The husband said, "They mentioned the adoption, Hon."

Daphne offered Boldt a side glance, drew in a deep breath and began cautiously. "It's a delicate matter. Confidential. We ask you to respect that."

"We'll respect it a lot better when you tell us what it is you want," Brad Brehmer said, impatiently. He knew how much they had paid Chevalier for the child. He sensed the trouble well ahead of his wife, who couldn't sit still.

Boldt explained, "We're investigating a series of kidnappings."

Clearly confusing them both, Daphne added, "Our purpose here is to inform you, to warn you, to attempt to keep you out of criminal proceedings, which are almost certain to happen if you adopt this child."

"Oh, God." Cindy Brehmer understood then what her husband already knew. "You *cannot* do this to us! Do you know what we've been through? This is our baby—our first baby."

Addressing the husband, Boldt said, "You have business relations with an attorney named Chevalier in New Orleans." Their faces drained of color, and the wife's theatrical smile faltered. "Before you go forward with this adoption, you need to be aware of the facts."

"There is still time to avoid criminal charges," Daphne reminded.

"This is *our* baby," the woman complained.

"No," Boldt countered. "If she is who we believe she is, she was kidnapped, transported across state lines and delivered in New Orleans within the last twenty-four hours."

"You're to take possession of the child in New Orleans," Daphne informed them with a threatening certainty.

"This is not happening," the husband said. "We've prayed about this. Chevalier was the answer to those prayers."

Boldt said, "There are parents in Seattle who are praying as well."

"It's all legal," the husband insisted, jumping ahead. "We haven't done anything illegal."

"Not yet," Boldt corrected. "But the moment you take possession of that child you will have. Knowingly or not, you are accessories to kidnapping."

"Oh dear God, no!" Cindy Brehmer's eyes clouded and she sprang up to save her face.

Daphne told Brehmer, "You'll be asked by the court to explain what you thought you were paying all that money for, why so much money."

Boldt contributed, "It's a felony to overpay for an adoption. There are federal statutes as well as state. How carefully did you hide the money trail, sir? Were you creative enough to fool forensic accountants?"

He might as well have slapped the man across the face. Dazed, Brehmer sputtered, unable to complete a thought. A siren wailed in the distance; perfect timing, Boldt thought.

Daphne explained, "If you cooperate, we may be able to keep you from being charged."

Boldt cautioned, "There are no guarantees."

"When are you scheduled to pick up the child?" Daphne asked.

"You are *not* taking this baby from me!" the wife said, leaning against the hallway wall.

"Cindy," the husband admonished. "They're offering us a choice. A chance. We need to listen to this."

The woman's face collapsed into tears. She staggered to her husband, embraced him and sobbed.

Daphne asked, "How much did you pay?"

"Expenses plus fifty," the husband answered matter-of-factly. "Three separate payments. About seventy in all." He checked with both his visitors. "He told us it was a prominent family, that it would be done very quietly. We were paying extra to get a white baby. That was never spoken, but it was understood."

"Have you ever met Chevalier?" Boldt asked.

"Never."

"Did you videotape yourselves or send photographs?"

"The house," the wife answered. "The neighborhood. Not us."

"Spoken with him?"

"He has called a few times. Spoken with Cindy mostly. About the timing, the schedule."

"The money?"

"That was with me," he answered. "Early on."

"How long ago?"

"Two, three months."

"He wouldn't necessarily know *your* voice then?" Boldt inquired.

"What is it you're getting at?" Brehmer asked curiously, beginning to understand.

Boldt told them, "Chevalier called your home yesterday."

Teary-eyed, the wife answered, "We're booked on a flight in the morning." She began to cry again. "We're booked into a hotel. We honeymooned there. We're to wait for his call."

Boldt met eyes with Brad Brehmer and waited for the man to feel his intensity. Then he shifted the same attention to the woman and told them both, "If we bust Chevalier ahead of time, we might never recover the child. The child is our priority. Right? For all of us," he said, including even Daphne. "The child comes first."

The woman nodded.

"Good," Boldt said.

"It's important we understand one another," Daphne added. "If this is to work, we need to communicate. We need to know you down to your core. Unfortunately, we need it now. Tonight. Before tomorrow morning."

"You're going to take our place," the husband said, correctly guessing Daphne's plan. "Is that what's going on here?"

Boldt answered, "You might want to make some coffee. It's going to be a long night."

CHAPTER

The following morning at 11:22, Boldt and Daphne checked into the Soniat House under the name Brehmer. Deep in the French Quarter on a quiet side street away from the T-shirts and the smell of stale beer, away from the movie crews and tourists swollen with crawfish and hot sauce, the hotel's office and courtyard were accessed through a single door painted kelly green. They stepped into another, older world, a New Orleans Boldt had not yet experienced, but one he quickly realized lingered beneath the surface glitz and souvenirs. Its cobblestone courtyard resplendent in a lush jungle of deep greens and sharp vivid colors, the Soniat House delivered the New Orleans of the nineteenth century.

The male receptionist wore a dark suit, looked Boldt in the eye and bowed his head slightly to Daphne. "We have a lovely room for you, Mr. and Mrs. Brehmer. Charles will show you the way. I note that your stay is open-ended. We will need notice day after tomorrow if you're intending to spend the weekend with us."

"That shouldn't be a problem." Boldt paused a beat too long as he signed the guest slip, in part because he had to remember to sign Brehmer's name—it was Brehmer's credit card he was using—in part because the daily room rate was twice his rental car's weekly rate.

As a couple they were shown through the courtyard and up a century-old set of winding wooden stairs, past a seven-foot-tall oil portrait of a southern general, and a smaller oil of a harlequin in full regalia. Boldt had no way of knowing how far Chevalier's influence reached, or what kind of underground existed in this city, but it didn't take an Intelligence officer to understand it was a place of influence peddling, of favors. For this reason, they had changed nothing about the Brehmers' hotel reservation or the couple's itinerary.

Charles keyed open the extremely narrow nine-foot wooden door and motioned for Daphne to lead the way. He heard her gasp as he followed into the long hardwood hallway, its walls covered with oil paintings, light sparkling from a cut glass chandelier. The hallway ended at a large bathroom all marble and brass. Through another pair of towering doors to the left was a sitting room with a crushed velvet love seat, two French chairs and three seven-foot windows that started at floor height and led out onto a balcony with flowering baskets issuing green waterfalls of tendrils and runners and overlooking the narrow street and a nunnery beyond.

Charles, the bellman, explained in his warm affected voice that a century earlier city property taxes had been assessed according to the number of a building's exterior doors, and so huge, double-hung windows had taken their place. He lifted one, admitting the sounds of the Quarter as a horse-drawn buggy passed and the driver's voice was heard lecturing his passengers on the Soniat House's place in the city's history. Breakfast—biscuits, juice and coffee—would be served on the balcony.

The bedroom held a four-poster with a red satin duvet, flanked by antique end tables hosting leaded glass lamps. A telephone was the only fixture that brought the suite into the current century. Boldt tipped the man, whose footsteps faded down the impossibly long hallway. The door to room 22 bumped shut.

Any of the hotel staff could be on Chevalier's payroll—

bellhops, chambermaids—their every move might be monitored. They would maintain the impression of being a married couple. The Brehmers had a dinner reservation arranged in advance by Chevalier that Boldt and Daphne would honor. There was no saying to what extent Chevalier screened his prospective buyers. Certainly he conducted credit reports. Perhaps he placed the adoptive parents under surveillance for a day or two preceding the adoption; this would help explain his having made various arrangements for both the Hudsons and the Brehmers. Any such possibility required Boldt and Daphne to play along, at least on a superficial level—a married couple excited by the prospect of an adoption.

"We had better practice our signatures," she said in a business-like manner.

She ordered a mint julep from room service; Boldt, a ginger ale. When the waiter had come and gone, they sat out on the balcony in green wicker chairs with chintz padded cushions, the sonorous clip-clop of horse and buggy carrying up the cobblestone street. They worked on their forged signatures. Intricate shadows from the wrought-iron artistry played onto the decking, black and white and gray, like Chinese shadow puppets. After attempting a page of signatures, Boldt glanced over at her, his face flushed from the heat. He said, "Want some irony?"

"The laundry service provides the irony," she said, clearly feeling the bourbon.

Boldt smirked, finished the ginger ale and said, "The irony is that the tables have turned. Now who are the con artists trying to steal a baby?"

CHAPTER

Commander's Palace roared with the music of gracious dining—cocktail patter, the chime of fine tableware, corks drawn from the necks of wine bottles. Boldt and Daphne, as the Brehmers, were shown to a table in the restaurant's lavishly painted second-story lunchroom. An army of waiters descended upon them, the men clearly taken in by Daphne's beauty.

She owned the place from the moment they arrived, the maître d' charmed by her fluent French and the plunging neckline of her afternoon purchase.

Boldt lowered his head and toyed with the butter on his bread plate.

"Don't sulk," she said.

"I'm not. I'm thinking about John's call."

LaMoia had tailed Chevalier the night before, following him north to the small town of Méchant. He had not been alone. A second car had also been following Chevalier. LaMoia had kept his distance, but he was guessing Dunkin Hale.

"So where's the Russian army?" Boldt asked Daphne. "The Bureau," he clarified. "They have an active field office here in the city, probably a fairly large one. An out-of-town agent working a case of national importance. Where's the backup?"

"I see what you mean." She lightly buttered a piece of bread and recommended he try it.

Boldt said, "The only explanation I can come up with is that he's running this advance work solely for Flemming, which means Flemming does not want the rest of the agency to know about New Orleans. Why?"

"There's a cornbread, and a rosemary. If you go with the pork tenderloin, the cornbread's the ticket."

"Is Flemming so political that he would bury this kind of connection until he has hard evidence?"

She said, "Kay Kalidja painted him exactly that way. Have you decided? It's a toss-up between the pork and the catfish."

"He must have traced the rental car to Salt Lake by now, which means he has the DeChamps identity—the credit card. How much more does he need?"

"I'm going with the catfish," she replied. She sampled a celery stick. In an exceptionally private voice, she said, "Do you know the real story of the Pied Piper?"

"The flute and the children," he said.

She waved the celery stick like a conductor's baton. "No. No. In the thirteenth century, the Pied Piper was hired by the German city of Hamelin to rid the town of its rat infestation. He did just that—got rid of the rats—and legend had it that he charmed them away with his flute; in fact he probably poisoned them. Once the rats were gone, the city refused him payment. He responded by killing over a hundred of the city's children."

"This is folklore, right?"

"No, some version of the man existed. One of our earliest documented serial killers. The folklore came from Goethe and Robert Browning, who retold the story with a little sugar on it." She placed down the celery. "The Crowleys served their time and then were denied an adoption. They are denying others children. You think his decision to play an exterminator is random? It fits his role as the Pied Piper. They could have kidnapped one of these children and kept it for themselves, but they did not. They elected to take from the fertile and give to the barren, combining Robin Hood with the Pied Piper. They hold a grudge. This is not about profit, this is about payback. I'd like to think they're predictable, but they are not. They feel justified in what they're doing. They understand the joy of adoption. It's been denied them. They're angry."

"We're all angry," Boldt replied.

Two hours later, a hazy moon rising in the sky, its light spilling into the Soniat House courtyard despite the illumination of the city, Daphne and Boldt slowly climbed the wooden staircase toward their suite in silence. She stopped at the top of the stairs and, gazing down into the courtyard, said, "No matter what, this is a beautiful hotel."

As Daphne prepared for bed in the bathroom, Boldt sat on the crushed velvet couch feeling both fatigue and anticipation: Chevalier was going to contact them about the adoption; his best opportunity for rescuing Sarah lay ahead.

He placed his gun and ID wallet in the bed's end table, emptied his pockets, hung up his sport coat and tie, removed his shoes—all the little rituals he had come to accept as preparation for bedtime.

Daphne appeared, wrapped snugly inside a hotel robe. "Which side?" she asked.

He pointed, as uncomfortable as she.

A few minutes later he entered the bedroom in boxer shorts and a T-shirt; thinner than he had been since his twenties, the terror and tension of the last few months starved off him.

Propped up against a number of pillows, her face caught in the bedside light like a half-moon in a summer sky, Daphne shone equally as brightly. She looked up from a tourist magazine, her brown eyes tracking him as he crossed the room and climbed into his side of the bed.

"This is weird," she said.

"Yes," he agreed.

"I think I snore," she said.

"That makes two of us."

He ate the chocolate that had been left and read the "tomorrow's forecast" card. Stormy. When she switched off the bedside lamp a knife blade of light sliced through a crack in the drapes, bathing the bedroom in an artificial dusk.

He rolled onto his stomach, thinking that Liz occupied a bed far from here, alone, frightened, concerned about their baby girl.

It was for her sake he said his prayer.

"Good night," Daphne sighed, exhausted.

"Good night," Boldt replied, knowing sleep would elude him once again.

At 8:00 A.M. exactly, the telephone rang in room 22 of the Soniat House. Daphne Matthews, wrapped in her hotel robe and drinking a cup of hot chocolate, secure beneath the porch overhang in one of the green wicker chairs, sat with her legs tucked up under her as a light rain stained the stone facade of the convent across the street. She placed down the hot chocolate cradled in her hands and hurried into the suite's antebellum sitting room hoping to give Boldt the needed rest, but he snagged the telephone.

"Hello? . . . Speaking . . . yes, Mr. Chevalier . . . ten o'clock? No, no. That's why we're here. We can't wait. Ten o'clock then." He hung up. "I guess we passed the test."

"I'll order up some tea." She felt as hungry as she'd ever been. Room service offered biscuits, and only biscuits. She ordered for two.

LaMoia heard from Boldt five separate times between 8:15 and 9:45 that Friday morning. They discussed photography, the importance of field notes, surveillance position, retrieving numbers from the caller-ID box LaMoia had fixed to Chevalier's line in the basement of his office. Boldt sounded as nervous as an actor on opening night.

LaMoia felt more like a ball player before the game—filled with the excitement of anticipation, his muscles restless in a welcome ache of need, his mind singular and focused. He had slept in only fits and starts since his return from Méchant late Wednesday night, early Thursday morning. Despite this, he felt refreshed. Ready.

He felt bound and determined to avenge himself and his professional dignity. His suspension would be removed from his record if the charges proved false, which they would. But to apprehend the Pied Piper—to receive a commendation in the middle of a suspension—would be the ultimate rat's tail up the ass of Internal Investigations. He licked his chops with expectation.

He had long since established his surveillance position when Boldt phoned him the first time. Chevalier's apartment communicated with his second-floor law office. His Cadillac had remained parked behind the building all night. Room lights had come on at 7:00 A.M. Chevalier had not left his rooms since that time. For Boldt and LaMoia, this presented one of three possibilities in terms of the Kittridge girl: Chevalier had phoned the girl's kidnapper; the kidnapper had called Chevalier; or arrangements had been made well in advance of the exchange and would go off as scheduled, unless otherwise notified. This last option made the most sense given the Pied Piper's penchant for preparedness, for it limited the number of phone calls between the two players and thus limited any chance of identifying the guardian's whereabouts; furthermore, it helped explain Chevalier's tight control of the actions of the adoptive parents—the kidnapped child was already scheduled for delivery, the purchasing parents had better show up.

But if either of the other two options proved true—a last-minute exchange of phone calls between the players—it presented investigators with the opportunity to locate the guardian's safe house ahead of the adoption meeting, meaning LaMoia might be able to establish surveillance on the safe house while Boldt or

Matthews followed whoever dropped the child, increasing their chances of identifying an individual to follow back to Sarah.

Matthews was, at that very moment, attempting to contact Broole in hopes of obtaining Chevalier's outgoing calls.

For his part, LaMoia needed access to the caller-ID well ahead of the 10:00 A.M. meeting to monitor what calls had been received by Chevalier.

He left the surveillance post he had established on the third floor of an arsoned building a half block down and across the street from Chevalier's office, and clawed his way into a pair of faded green coveralls purchased at the local Salvation Army outlet, pulled on an ill-fitting baseball cap and negotiated the back fire escape, leery of the building's central stairs, which were about as trustworthy as crisp toast. The ostrich cowboy boots stuck out from this ensemble, certainly capable of giving away his disguise, but some things a guy just couldn't compromise.

LaMoia believed a disguise, any disguise, was built primarily on one's presence. It was not the worker's coveralls, nor the banker's three-piece suit, nor the telephone lineman's rigging that convinced the unsuspecting; it was the way in which those clothes, that gear, was filled out. If a man dressed down as a street person but walked with the posture of a Marine, forget about it. If that same man exuded a primal menace, then the sidewalks would part to accommodate him. A building's maintenance man understood himself, believed others could not live without him, felt the control given him in the master key he carried, the wrench in his toolbox.

LaMoia approached the building's service entrance with his cocky attitude intact, as he had five times before. The pick gun admitted him effortlessly. He switched on the interior light, in no hurry to be seen ducking inside—he had every right to be in that place. He belonged. Fuck 'em all.

He reached the back room where he uncovered the caller-ID box he had placed on the attorney's two voice lines—so accommodating of the phone company to mark each line for him in advance; sometimes the juju went with you. To his regret, Chevalier had received not a single call since LaMoia's inspection of the system the night before. Popular guy.

Maybe Broole had something for them; Chevalier's outgoing calls were equally important. Or maybe they weren't going to be handed any bones. Maybe Sarah's chances came down to this one meeting in a sleazeball attorney's office in the middle of the hottest city on earth. Maybe it was all up to his own abilities to follow whoever delivered the Kittridge kid, follow him or her for as long as it took, follow this person right back to the elusive Pied Piper and little Sarah Boldt.

He liked the sound of that. Maybe destiny was on his side.

CHAPTER

65

Posing as Cindy Brehmer, Daphne dressed in Ferragamo flats, a cream linen sleeveless shift and a simple string of pearls with matching stud earrings. She wore a light blush, pale red lipstick, mascara, a hint of eye shadow and a bead of penciled eyeliner.

Boldt's wrinkled khakis and blue Oxford button-down did not live up to his wife's appearance. His pale, gaunt face with its prominent cheekbones and sunken eyes lent him the look of a man struggling with disease. Little more than his wife's escort, a man to carry the empty child seat, he took to opening doors for her, arranging transportation for her and carrying on a one-sided conversation, playing the doting husband perfectly, caught in his wife's wake like a piece of flotsam rising and falling beneath her mood swings.

He took the wheel of the Volvo rental, chauffeuring her out of the Quarter, through downtown and into a mixed neighborhood that bordered the Garden District. He drove several blocks out of their way to arrive heading south so that the Volvo could pause briefly immediately below the burned-out shell of a structure that LaMoia had described to him.

"Lou—" Daphne began.

"I know," he answered.

"You wait for chances like this, you work toward them, and then suddenly they're upon you and—"

"I know."

"This is going to be a mess to untangle, Lou."

"Chevalier's phone records and the paperwork filed at Vital Statistics will give us all these kids back. It may take awhile to sort it all out, but it'll happen. These kids are going home: Trudy Kittridge first."

"How do we live with ourselves if something goes wrong?"

"Trudy's going home," he repeated defiantly. There was no mention made of Sarah. LaMoia had to stay with Lisa Crowley at all costs, providing Lisa Crowley showed.

Boldt pulled the Volvo into the back lot. He shut off the engine, but neither passenger nor driver moved, frozen in concentration and second thought. Boldt's hands remained on the wheel; Daphne's sat folded in her lap.

"Kiss me," said the psychologist. "The Brehmers would kiss before going inside. And remember: We're excited, Lou. We've never felt so in love. This is a moment we've been awaiting a long time."

"Tell me about it."

"Kiss me."

"For them. Okay."

He kissed her quickly for the benefit of any surveillance, LaMoia included.

"Good luck," she said.

"Brad Brehmer," Boldt introduced himself.

"Vincent Chevalier."

"My wife, Cindy."

Daphne smiled at the man, studying his cheap suit, his eye movement, his posture, his stubby fingers with their manicured nails. His tongue teased his bottom lip before each word spoken.

"Come in," he said, staring at Daphne's chest and smiling through wet lips.

The office suited him: mobile-home wood paneling, a ragged couch facing a low table that offered a half-full ashtray and dog-eared magazines. A giveaway girlie calendar from Pennzoil. Chevalier's early-generation computer did not belong to a man surfing the Internet for victims' credit cards. Classical "hits" played from a thin-sounding radio.

What would the Brehmers have thought? she wondered. How would they have reacted? It did not strike Daphne as a place to start a family. Friday-night poker perhaps. A place to annul a Las Vegas chapel marriage. "Oh, my," Daphne remarked with just a hint of the Carolinas. "How authentic looking," she said to her husband.

Chevalier said, "The paperwork will go pretty fast. You'll see." He checked his watch. "Have a seat."

Chevalier snatched the ashtray, dumped its contents into a wastebasket and then lit a cigarette without asking and without offering one. "Been busy around here," he offered.

Chevalier was smaller and more pitiful than Daphne had pictured him in her mind's eye, a sluggish little creature who overate and gambled with people's lives. She didn't doubt his resolve—he was in bed with a pair of con artists that had pulled in nearly a million dollars as baby brokers. She pasted a smile onto her face and asked, "When do we get to meet our little darling?"

"City services lady should be here soon," he acknowledged. "Let's take pen to paper, roll up the sleeves and get down to brass tacks, whataya say?"

"There's *more* paperwork?" Boldt complained.

"Hell, you pick up a package, you sign for it." The troll winked at her. She felt numb, capable of anything.

Chevalier transferred documents from his desk to the coffee table, and placed pens down in front of them.

"Full signature here and here, and again," he said, flipping pages manically, "well, initials there, again here, and then signature there. That last one you wait on so that it can be witnessed by two parties—that's me and the social worker, the two parties. Whataya say?"

Boldt had Brehmer's scrawl down pat, an indistinguishable mass of loops with a few vertical lines thrown in for the sake of the B's and the H. Give a first-grader an hour with a #2 pencil, and he or she could be forging Brehmer's checks. Daphne faced the greater challenge. Cindy Brehmer's signature was controlled and pretty. Not that Chevalier would think to check. The paperwork was a masquerade for the buyer's benefit. Chevalier was not the brains of the operation; he was, at best, a facilitator.

The attorney nervously checked his watch, offered them both coffee and then edged over to the window, parted the blinds and looked down at the street. "Should be here any minute," he said.

"I just can't wait!" Daphne cried out. "How about a cup of that coffee?" asked a woman who, like Boldt, drank nothing but tea. She reached over and took her husband's hand lovingly in hers.

Chevalier complied with her request and turned to address Mr. Coffee.

Daphne squeezed Boldt's hand hard, signaling him and directing his attention away from the attorney and onto Boldt's open sport coat where his handgun and holster showed. He buttoned up.

"How many of these adoptions do you arrange in a year?" Boldt asked conversationally.

Chevalier spun around and glared, fixing onto him like an attack dog on an intruder. "We agreed previously never to discuss *anything* to do with my business, Mr. Brehmer." The man behind the invective did not share much of anything with the gawking attorney of a few moments earlier. This new man, at once dangerous and unpredictable, intrigued the psychologist. Chevalier, wound up like a venomous snake ready to strike, threatened, "I suggest we stick to our agreement."

"Bradley!" Daphne barked at her husband, "don't you dare mess this up." To the attorney she said, "He didn't mean a thing by it, Mr. Chevalier. Not a thing. Bradley just likes to talk, that's all." She added teasingly, "Whataya say?"

"Bradley?" Chevalier questioned suspiciously, throwing the name into the air with great disdain. "Bradley?" he repeated.

Boldt blanched the moment Daphne barked at him. He had practiced the signature enough times to recognize her mistake.

Printed in capital letters on the documents in process of being signed—documents that shouted up at him from the low table where they lay open to the last page—was the name she should have called him: Bradford, not Bradley, as his make-believe wife had misspoken.

Attorneys caught such details. Chevalier had drawn up the documents, likely without the word processing abilities of an assistant: Why involve anyone else? He had typed them, printed them and proofed them. He certainly knew Brehmer's first name. He had to be wondering why the man's wife did not.

Tension hung in the air as thick as the smell of smoke and burned coffee.

Chevalier's head snapped toward the street; he had heard something only a resident of the building could discern. He eyed Boldt cautiously, crossed to the window and peered down into the street. When he looked back into the room his eyes flashed angrily between his two guests, and though Boldt scrambled for an alternate plan, his mind wouldn't function, clouded by thoughts of his daughter.

Smoke caught in the man's throat, burning it dry as Chevalier said, "She has arrived."

CHAPTER

66

People were creatures of habit, LaMoia thought, as he watched a Ford Taurus pull into the postage-stamp parking lot behind Chevalier's office. Such habits were a detective's bread and butter; they offered behavioral links to the past and future alike. People chose to dress the same, eat the same food at the same places, travel in the same circle of friends, frequent the same bars—drive the same cars.

Lisa Crowley had a thing for the Ford Taurus.

She parked in the first open spot in the lot, the one immediately adjacent to the street, providing LaMoia a good look and the driver a quick exit.

As the driver's door came open, LaMoia prepared himself for the ready, putting away the .38 Boldt had loaned him and the stun stick he routinely carried tucked into his right boot, a handheld, less powerful version of the Pied Piper's air TASER. He confirmed the pick gun's location in the pocket of his windbreaker. No cuffs, no ID wallet. His life had changed, no doubt about it.

He did not recognize Lisa Crowley from the mug shot provided Daphne by NOPD's Detective Broole. Dressed in a professional style in keeping with a job of such responsibility, and yet a state employee, this woman wore a starched white cotton top and a pair of crisp, pleated khaki pants. He assumed the hair was not hers, but one of many wigs, and yet it seemed perfectly in keeping, fitting her face and complementing her looks remarkably. She wore a colorful scarf on her head and a pair of shades. She might have been anybody.

LaMoia wondered if the scarf and glasses concealed head injuries sustained in the Boise pileup. If so, there was little she could do to fully hide herself. Body markings, regardless of how small, were an investigator's God-given gift.

Confidence artists were fully versed in identity changes. LaMoia was prepared for Lisa Crowley to enter a building with one look and, moments later, leave as an entirely different person. The woman who climbed back in the Taurus and drove it away might not be the same woman who had arrived and now climbed out. Opening the car's rear door, Crowley leaned inside and retrieved the baby seat.

LaMoia headed for the burned-out tenement's fire escape and the blistering heat of another hazy morning. His assignment was simple in word, difficult in practice, and yet critical to Sarah's rescue: to place Lisa Crowley under surveillance and never lose track of her. Boldt had entrusted him with nothing less than his daughter's life. He had no intention of letting anyone down.

CHAPTER

"B̶radley?" a suspicious Chevalier repeated curiously, stepping away from the window.

"Cindy's way of putting me in my place," Boldt told the man, vamping. "One of those husband and wife things, that goes back to a childhood story I wish I'd never told." Looking at Daphne, Boldt said for the benefit of the attorney, "No one but the teachers ever got my name right in school. It was always 'Bradley' this and 'Bradley' that. It really got on my nerves after a while. I came to hate the name. Still do. No one ever seems to get Brad*ford*."

"Bradley gets your attention, sweetheart," she said without hesitation, picking up the ruse beautifully. "And you know how I just love to have your full attention." She tugged on the hem of her shift, lifting it a little more open than necessary, well aware of how to win Chevalier's attention as well.

Chevalier sucked on the cigarette, his small eyes flitting between his two clients.

Boldt felt a tear of sweat charge down his ribs. He knew that Trudy Kittridge's keeper had arrived when footfalls in the hall drew Chevalier to his office door.

Daphne jumped up, ran an open hand down her shift and
headed straight for the car seat—the baby!—catching herself at
the very last moment and thinking to introduce herself to the
woman. The woman responded, "Susan Chambers."

The woman who called herself Chambers passed the baby seat
to Daphne, set down a baby bag slung over her shoulder and
gingerly removed her sunglasses. Her left eye was badly blackened
and considerably swollen.

She preempted any questions. "Slipped, standing up out of the
tub." She touched the scarf. "Pretty stupid, you ask me."

"You've seen a doctor, I hope," Boldt said, stepping closer,
studying every line in her features, every bump, blemish and
bone. He would never forget that face; he made sure of it.

"I'm fine."

Boldt couldn't help himself. "A blow to the head like that can
give you real trouble," Boldt said. "Headaches?" With an eye like
that she would be living on pain killers—aspirin at the very least.

Chevalier agreed with Boldt, nodding. He said pointedly, "*You
should have it looked at.*" He added strongly, "Hear?"

The woman clearly didn't like the conversation aimed onto her.
Maintaining her composure, looking down at the child, she asked
them all, "She's beautiful, isn't she?"

Daphne repeated her introduction. She spoke in a breathy,
slightly hysterical voice, slipping at once into baby talk as she
dropped to one knee to greet the baby girl. Daphne's performance, the use of the altered voices, was essential because the social
worker—in all likelihood, Lisa Crowley—had spent the most
amount of time in phone conversations with Cindy Brehmer.
With only the few calls made over a protracted period, it was
doubtful Lisa Crowley would identify the voice as that of another
woman, but Daphne was taking no chances. She focused her attention on the child and left the documentation, paperwork and
chitchat to Boldt.

"May I?" Daphne said in a girlish voice, indicating the baby
seat.

"Please," Lisa Crowley answered, "and I'm here to answer any questions you or Mr. Brehmer may have about parenting the child."

Boldt felt a sudden fit of rage unlike anything he had ever experienced. Triggered initially by simply the woman's presence—his daughter's kidnapper in the same room with him, for there was no mistaking Lisa Crowley—it struck to his core as she spoke so evenly, so controlled, so generously. She *was* a social worker, not a woman playing a role. Her professional calm and authority were an affront to his own professionalism and authority. He could picture her in a police uniform at the door to Millie Wiggins' day care. This woman had physically touched Sarah, had trained a video camera onto her while she screamed for her daddy. Boldt wanted desperately to hurt this woman.

"Sir?" she asked.

"Yes?" Boldt returned.

"I asked if you have any questions on the caring and feeding of the child."

"No, I don't think so. We've been through the parenting classes as you know," he said, pointing to the documents. The Brehmers had briefed them on the requirements they had fulfilled in order to take possession of the child. The nationally sanctioned parenting classes, offered by a Houston hospital, included a certification diploma that accompanied the Brehmer paperwork. After two kids of his own, Boldt could have given the parenting classes himself.

Something in him stirred, and Boldt couldn't avoid confronting her. He looked directly into her eyes and said, "Do you have children of your own, Ms. Chambers?"

All color drained from Lisa Crowley's face.

Daphne looked up sharply from the baby. "Bradley!" she chastised. "What possible business is that of ours? Please excuse my husband, Ms. Chambers. He can be impertinent and obnoxious in the most unexpected situations. And I assure you our little angel will learn nothing of the kind from her daddy. I nearly have him trained for the dinner table, after all, don't I, Bradley?"

"None," Crowley whispered. Regaining herself quickly, she added, "Which is one reason this work is so rewarding, so fulfilling for me." She met eyes with Boldt; for a moment he believed she might have seen through their ruse. Her subsequent smile, patronizing though it was, relieved him of this fear.

"Of course it is," Daphne said, supporting him. "I'll bet you want to go home with every one of the children you and Mr. Chevalier place."

"Mr. Chevalier places them, Mrs. Brehmer," she corrected. "I merely oversee the transfer for the benefit of the children and the state. Though, yes, every child is precious and a wonder under God."

Boldt felt a knot in his throat. He fought against it but broke into tears. They spilled down his cheeks.

"Well, looky there!" Daphne said sarcastically. "I don't think I've seen my husband cry since the Rockets lost the finals."

Chevalier smirked as he busily sorted through the remaining paperwork, a cigarette pinched tightly between his moist lips.

Daphne approached Boldt, kissed him gently and said, "We're a family now, sweetheart."

Boldt nodded, recovering quickly.

Daphne said, "We're so eager to get her home."

"Yes," Crowley replied, "you're very lucky." She glanced at Chevalier.

"A few signatures is all," Chevalier piped up anxiously. "Now that Miss Susan is here, she can witness for us."

A thunderous rain crashed down on the roof of the building without warning, sounding more like a small explosion. The baby cried out.

Daphne reached down, unfastened the seat's restraints and scooped Trudy Kittridge into the safety of her arms.

The first of the children had been recovered.

CHAPTER

LaMoia cursed the rain from behind the steering wheel of his rental. It wasn't simply rain; rain he could handle; rain he was used to. Anyone who had lived in Seattle for fifteen years knew rain on a first-name basis. But this? The sky blackened like someone had thrown a switch and water fell in sheets, like a fire hose aimed at the ground, fell so hard that when it struck the hot pavement, droplets bounced up a foot or more before falling again and converting to a layer of steam.

Water pounded the roof of the car so loudly that LaMoia could not hear the radio.

The downpour cleared the sidewalks. Umbrellas made vain attempts to withhold the deluge; the roadway flooded as gutters roared like rivers. LaMoia saw only a blurred silver film. To turn on the wipers of a parked car was to give his position away.

Through the blur, he saw Boldt running toward his Volvo. He pulled the wagon up close to the building, and the woman he assumed to be Crowley braved the downpour to help Boldt and Daphne get the child seat into the car. Crowley then sprinted to the Taurus, opened the trunk and withdrew a dark overnight bag before scrambling into the front seat.

The only movement on the street came from the windshield wipers of a pair of cars that had double-parked to allow the rain to let up. These double-parked cars in turn blocked others parked legally.

Boldt's rental edged forward out onto the flooded street, one of the only cars moving.

LaMoia caught another set of wipers moving—this from one of the blocked cars.

Crowley's Taurus backed up, but then paused as the rain fell even harder.

LaMoia snagged the cell phone as he saw a man wearing a trench coat hurry from the blocked car and pound on the window of the car that was blocking him. This man motioned frantically for the double-parked car to move so he could pull out from his own parking space.

The driver took the hint. The double-parked car rolled.

So did the Taurus.

LaMoia fired up his engine as Crowley's Taurus backed up and pulled out into the street.

The phone rang through and Boldt's voice answered, "Brehmer."

"Can you talk?" LaMoia followed out into the street. Cars that had pulled over were moving again. The cell phone reception was awful.

"She's smacked up pretty badly," Boldt told him, attempting to supply identifying features. "Her left eye . . ." Static sparked loudly in LaMoia's ear. "A scarf . . ."

LaMoia interrupted, "We got ourselves a problem, a visitor. You copy that? We've got ourselves a stick in the spokes. You there?"

"I'm here."

"It's Hale."

An enormous flash of lightning occurred simultaneously with a crack of thunder that shook the car. The cell phone went dead.

LaMoia turned the wipers to high. Couldn't see a damn thing.

CHAPTER

69

LaMoia and Hale followed the Taurus in tandem, Hale in the lead in a dark green Jeep Cherokee. The rainstorm remained so strong that LaMoia wouldn't have recognized his own mother crossing the street, forcing bumper-to-bumper traffic. For LaMoia, the slower the better—both the Jeep and the Taurus stayed close.

Based on nothing concrete, he decided Hale had not noticed him, assuming he would be consumed with following the Taurus and paying little attention to other traffic.

He tried the cell phone again, its red NO SERVICE light pulsing in warning. His attention fixed on the Taurus through a series of turns and one red light he was forced to run, LaMoia tried to figure Hale.

There seemed to him at least two explanations for Hale's behavior. Either Broole had alerted Hale to SPD's presence, or Hale had made the same connection to Vincent Chevalier. Unaware of the Pied Piper's identity, Hale had attached himself to Chevalier like a tic. In turn, he had stumbled onto Crowley.

LaMoia tried the cellular again. The network remained down.

The highway signs suggested Lisa Crowley's destination was the airport. If Hale so much as attempted an arrest, he would blow Sarah's chances.

He considered his options and made a difficult decision. Crowley would be alert for anyone entering the airport terminal *behind* her, but if he arrived *ahead* of her, he might stay with her.

He asked himself, *When the hell have I ever been wrong?* He pulled out of his lane and passed both Hale and Crowley. The international airport was the next exit.

CHAPTER

70

Boldt drove to the airport, wife and child in the car, exactly as the Brehmers had planned. His eyes remained divided between the rearview mirror and the traffic in front of them, believing it a good possibility they were being followed. They would make the flight to Houston together for the sake of appearance. From Houston, it was on to Seattle for Daphne and Trudy Kittridge. Boldt intended to return to New Orleans to assist LaMoia in the surveillance of Lisa Crowley, the only link to his daughter.

The recovery of Trudy Kittridge filled him with hope.

Daphne said from the backseat where she held a bottle of formula for the child, "Those injuries are severe, Lou."

"I know."

"You hear Chevalier trying to get her to see a doctor? He saw it too. That eye . . ."

"I know."

"We need her healthy. If she's going to lead you back to Sarah—"

"She'll survive. It's Hale I'm worried about. A couple phone calls from Hale and we're either talking a federal invasion led by Flemming, or the Crowleys blowing to Singapore."

Daphne considered this. "Are you saying Hale's working for *them*?" she called out loudly from the backseat, sending the baby into a volley of cries. She settled her down.

"It would explain him playing this solo. It doesn't fit with Bureau policy, Daffy. He has carried this too far. It has to be explained. If he's not down here to investigate these people, he's down here to protect them."

"He came onto Flemming's team late in the game."

"The two have known each other for a long time, have worked together before. Hale could have easily monitored Flemming's progress in each city and told the Crowleys when to bail out. It would explain their perfect timing."

Daphne played along. "She gets involved in an injury car accident. That changes things. Flemming is warming to her. I see what you're saying: At that point either the Crowleys or Chevalier could demand protection. Hale would respond."

"Which explains his being down here alone. He tells Flemming he's chasing leads. Flemming buys into it, it's how he runs things. Flemming's not sending in the troops before he's absolutely sure they have the collar."

"The tattoo shop?" she asked him.

"Hale removes that evidence ahead of us. They go ahead with the Kittridge adoption, thinking they're okay. That's the best sign of all as far as Sarah's concerned: They haven't pulled the plug."

"But Hale?" She sounded incredulous.

"He knows better than anyone Flemming's determination and his resources. He knows what's coming. Lisa Crowley is injured. Their credit card identities have been made. For all they know, Spitting Image as well. It's coming apart on them."

"So they blow off Seattle."

"So they blow," Boldt agreed. "And poor Sarah is suddenly a liability."

CHAPTER

71

LaMoia pulled into short-term parking and snagged an automated ticket.

He stowed the handgun and cuffs under the front seat but kept the stun stick wedged between his calf and his right boot. It would have to be removed before he passed through security, but the idea of going naked was beyond him—he'd spent fifteen years with some form of self-defense pressed against his skin. The loading areas outside the terminal were crowded with travelers avoiding the storm. LaMoia shoved his way through the crowd and rode an escalator to obtain a view of the entrance ramps, crowded with cabs, vehicles and buses. He could just make out the entrances to the short- and long-term parking lots.

The combination of rain and traffic limited his chance of identifying Crowley's Taurus. He waited there for less than a minute, abandoned the effort and headed inside.

LaMoia snagged an abandoned *USA Today*—McPaper—and took a seat with a view of the ticket counters, a set of escalators and the terminal's central security station. He expected Boldt and Daphne, who had left ahead of him, to be checking in for their flight to Houston, but he didn't see them, which meant they were probably already at their gate.

According to the video monitors, the next flight to Houston didn't leave for an hour and a half—gate 14. Flights to Dallas–Fort Worth, a hub for several major carriers, left regularly. He suspected Crowley would ticket one of those flights, knowing firsthand that American flew several nonstops between Dallas and Seattle.

Five minutes lapsed. LaMoia nervously checked his watch and then tried the cell phone. NO SERVICE. Hovering on the edge of panic, he took up position, the paper held as a prop as he scanned the terminal. Two bus groups crowded the Delta ticket line, filling the area with chatter and too much luggage.

A moment later, a woman arrived in the terminal via the baggage claim escalator. Outwardly, this was not the same woman he had watched climb into the Taurus, but he took a mental snapshot of her just the same. She wore a blue skirt, not khakis, as Crowley had; a white cotton T-shirt, small black boots that laced up over her ankles and a French beret pulled down on her head. She carried herself in a fluid feminine walk that shared nothing with the woman outside Chevalier's office. But the dark wraparound sunglasses *were* the same, as was the general shape and size of the overnight bag slung from her shoulder. That bag caught La-Moia's eye.

He lowered his head back into the sports pages, the presence of that bag suggesting she was there not to observe the Brehmers but, indeed, for a flight of her own. The change in disguise, accomplished in the rental's front seat or in a baggage claim washroom, contributed to her confidence. She walked with her back straight, her chin held high, and yet she failed to disguise the pain that each step cost her. He could sense her measuring the remaining distance to the security check, like an exhausted boxer heading to his corner.

The sunglasses not only obscured her injuries but prevented others from knowing where she was looking. For this reason, La-Moia remained slouched in his seat, his long legs crossed straight in front of him, his casual attention alternately divided between

the terminal and the newspaper. He sized up every skirt that
passed by. *In character*, he told himself. Some things came easily.

Hale appeared in the center of the ticket terminal, wet and be-
draggled. LaMoia, distracted by Crowley, had missed his entrance, though he had expected him. Looking like a businessman
in a hurry, Hale checked the departure monitors, his wristwatch,
and then the monitors a second time. LaMoia looked left to
Crowley, right to Hale, encouraging Crowley to get through the
security check.

When Hale made for a bank of pay phones across the terminal,
LaMoia knew instinctively the man had to be stopped, knew what
had to be done.

Boldt, Daphne and Trudy Kittridge waited amid a clutter of
people and carry-on luggage, their flight more than an hour away.
The public address announced a white courtesy phone call for
"Scott Hamilton."

"That's for me," Boldt informed her.

"You know how many Scott Hamiltons there are?" she asked.

"The cell phones are out. How else is LaMoia going to reach
me? He can't page me by my name."

"And what if it's Hale?" she asked, stunning him. "What if
Hale recognized us?"

"Not in that rain."

"What if he did? He probably knows everything about you,
including your love of jazz, even Scott Hamilton. What if all he
wants is to flush us?"

Boldt stood, eyes searching for the nearest white phone. "Then
I guess I let the caller speak first," he said.

"Don't do this. It's what he wants. He's a federal agent. He can
arrest us for kidnapping, don't forget—we haven't reported this
to anyone. If he's part of this, if he's trying to buy time, that's
exactly what he'll do. Don't play into that." She added, "For Sarah's sake, please don't play into that."

Boldt hesitated. Daphne was right more often than not. He met eyes with her—the public address repeated the page—and he hurried toward the white phone on the far wall.

LaMoia's talk with Boldt lasted all of twenty seconds, at which time he hung up and hurried toward Hale, whose back was to him as he approached the pay phones.

Panic stole through him as he realized he had spent too much time trying to contact Boldt. Hale could not be allowed to reach Flemming! LaMoia, midstride, stopped abruptly, as if to adjust his pant leg, and slipped the stun stick out of his boot and up into his shirt sleeve.

One didn't step lightly into assaulting an FBI agent. It wasn't the best career move. LaMoia reached up his right sleeve and twisted the round cap on the butt end of the stun stick, two clicks to LO.

Hale reached the phones, picked up the receiver and dialed.

He might have been calling Roger Crowley, Chevalier, Judge Adams, Flemming or Kalidja—it didn't matter; he had to be stopped.

LaMoia rarely submitted to panic; he had been given the gift of cool. As situations became more frantic, John LaMoia became more relaxed. There was no wasted effort, no wasted time in his movements. No regrets or indecision. Hale was talking into the phone—he could not turn back the clock, he could only take action.

Over a few beers, cops talked about time standing still, of an eerie slow motion that overcame their situation. LaMoia experienced no such distortions. Time neither slowed nor sped up as he crossed the terminal. He glanced back to see Boldt approaching at a jog.

Hale was apparently focused on his conversation, the receiver held to his ear.

LaMoia took in his surroundings, aware of two couples and a family walking through the terminal to his left; a teenager at the next kiosk of phones, with her back to him; a newsstand agent, a woman, twenty yards ahead, manning a cash register with a view of the pay phones. LaMoia slipped the stun stick from his sleeve and reversed it, aiming it at Hale's spine. At that same moment, Hale sensed someone approaching and glanced back in time to identify LaMoia's face. His startled eyes went white with surprise.

LaMoia needed a clean shot with the stun stick. He bought himself a diversion with a left-handed palm slap to the phone receiver, crushing the agent's ear and focusing the man's attention on that pain. With his right hand, he jabbed forward strongly to insure the stun stick's probes made contact. It fired off its jolt of voltage, but Hale remained unfazed and standing—LaMoia had hit the leather strap of the man's shoulder holster.

The stun stick required fifteen seconds to reset its charge. La-Moia thumped the outside of the man's knee with his own, staggering him; rabbit-punched him low under the rib cage with his left, bending him; and threw his right elbow into the base of the agent's skull, numbing him. LaMoia caught the man as he slumped, wrenched Hale's arm behind his back as the phone's receiver dangled and swung like the pendulum.

. . . *twelve* . . . *thirteen* . . . *fourteen* . . . he counted silently in his head.

He released the agent at the count of fifteen and Hale grabbed for support, latching onto the phone box. Without looking behind him, LaMoia warned Boldt, "Clear!" swinging his left arm out like a gate and stopping Boldt. He delivered the stun stick again, this time finding the man's skin through his clothes. The pulse of high voltage caused the phone to ring despite the receiver being off-hook—one long peal of bells echoing into the terminal. Hale stiffened with the initial jolt, tight as steel. LaMoia pulled back the stick, and he and Boldt caught the man as he sagged.

"You certainly have a knack for timing," LaMoia told Boldt, who, looking around, replied calmly, "His wallet." LaMoia slipped the billfold out of Hale's rear pocket and into his own.

Boldt found the man's FBI ID wallet, opened it and then kept it in his left hand.

LaMoia asked, "What now?"

"Security," Boldt said.

"You fucking nuts?"

"By now they're already on their way," Boldt advised him.

"Cameras," LaMoia realized aloud.

"Exactly."

"But—"

"For once, let me do the talking. And stay with the game, damn it all."

"Me?"

"Here they come," he said, indicating two men in gray pants and blue blazers.

Boldt held Hale's ID wallet open from a distance, his thumb conveniently curled around the wallet and covering Hale's photo. He knew the psychology of rent-a-cops: overly self-important but with an urge to play with the big boys. Daphne would have played to that urge, and so Boldt did. "FBI!" He snapped the wallet shut with a flip of his wrist and stuffed it into his inside breast pocket alongside his SPD ID. "This bozo's involved in a kidnapping. Been posing as one of us," he said in a low voice, because the sagging Hale was already drawing the attention of the curious like moths to a light. "No ID on him, but he's carrying." Boldt slipped the man's sport coat open just enough to reveal the holstered semiautomatic. "Take that for me, would you?" Daphne would have fed their egos by giving them responsibility immediately, making certain they felt included.

"Son of a bitch," the one who looked like a surfer gasped. He stepped forward and slipped the weapon out of the shoulder holster.

"You mind cuffing him and giving him a hand?" Boldt said. "We're gonna need a little privacy here."

LaMoia asked, "You got four walls and a door?"

The two glanced at each other. "Conference room?" Surfer asked. "It isn't very big," he apologized. "It's upstairs."

Boldt said, "Where this guy's going, the rooms are a hell of a lot smaller, I guarantee you that."

The two security guards cuffed Hale and took him under both arms. The man was not unconscious, but severely dazed and incapable of walking or speaking.

He tried to get words out, but gibberish and a trickle of drool took their place. His feet dragged heavily. Boldt and LaMoia followed the two security guards to an elevator and up one floor.

Hale was assisted down the long hallway to an unmarked door that Surfer's assistant keyed open. "This okay, sir?" he asked Boldt.

"Do just fine." Hale was deposited into a chair. Boldt eyed both men. "Now listen," he said. "News like this travels fast, and that's exactly what we don't need. A little girl's life is at stake here. You understand that? A human life," he said, choking on the expression. "It's imperative that we do this quick and dirty. After that, we turn him over to you. Your story is this: You saw the piece, you asked for ID, he didn't have any. You took him in."

LaMoia said, "He'll blow smoke up your skirt about being a Fed. That's his cover."

Boldt added, "This girl has a chance if you lose him for a day or so until he gets his phone call. Someplace no one can find him, you know? That way, no news leaks, no inside information, and this little girl has a fighting chance. If this guy surfaces within the system—"

Surfer said, "We got a drunk and disorderly tank right here on airport. It's run by NOPD, but we know all those boys."

"Thanks," LaMoia said.

The two men insisted on shaking hands all around, as if the four of them had just won a touch football game. They left the room and pulled the door shut securely. LaMoia locked it. Looking at Hale, Boldt said, "Time to have a little chat."

CHAPTER

72

Hale's level of awareness and responsiveness reminded Boldt of a man with a bad hangover. "Jesus!" the man choked out, coughing. His eyes floated in his head like an ice cube in a glass of milk. Discovering his hands cuffed, he struggled briefly to get free, then peered out like a man half blinded.

"It's Boldt and LaMoia," Boldt informed him.

"Shit."

LaMoia patted him on the shoulder from behind, leaned in close to his ear and said, "Welcome to New Orleans."

"What the hell?" He struggled again and protested, "Do you realize what you're getting yourself into here? You want to think about this a minute?"

"We have thought about it," Boldt said frankly. "We've wondered what a federal agent would be doing down here solo."

"The field office doesn't even know you're here," LaMoia said. "Are you aware of that? Is that standard operating procedure, Hale?"

"You're outta your minds."

LaMoia told him, "You've been watching Chevalier."

"You ought to think about what you're doing." He struggled with the cuffs.

"You were on the phone just now. With whom? Flemming or the Pied Piper?"

"Is *that* what you think?"

LaMoia leaned in from behind and whispered hotly, "Don't jack us around."

"You are interfering with a federal investigation," Hale warned. "Undo the cuffs. I'm outta here. All is forgotten."

"I don't think so," LaMoia said.

Boldt asked, "Why would a federal agent not check in with his local field office?"

"You are interfering with a federal investigation," Hale repeated, this time more calmly.

"Tommy Thompson tells you about the tattoo," Boldt told him, winning a look of surprise. "You do a little quick footwork. If we've got the tattoo, then maybe we can run down your boy. The tattoo leads to New Orleans—of course, you already know that."

"So you get your ass down here," LaMoia filled in, "to see if anyone can follow the tattoo anywhere. Damage assessment. You decide it doesn't look so bad, but it's bad enough that someone—"

"You've got this way wrong," Hale bleated. "Don't screw this up, Goddamn it!"

"Enlighten us," Boldt repeated.

Hale wrestled with the handcuffs again, working himself into a frenzy. LaMoia and Boldt simply stood back and waited.

"Time's a wasting," LaMoia said, when the man calmed. He and Boldt moved toward the door.

Boldt said, "Enjoy New Orleans."

LaMoia added, "What little you'll see of it."

"Okay, okay!" The man shouted in disgust. "I came aboard in Portland."

"We know that," Boldt told him.

"Yeah? Well did you know that I was working the Vegas field office? The AFIDs at the crime scenes identified TASER car-

tridges that were purchased by a valid credit card. The purchase
was made in Vegas, so indirectly I had an active involvement with
the investigation from the very start. Flemming and I were in
nearly constant contact. The credit card led nowhere. We tore the
residence of the cardholder to pieces—lived in Kansas. Nothing.
But there were no other fraudulent charges on the card. None. So
why's somebody bother to steal a credit card and only charge one
item? Right? So we work this cardholder into the ground: known
associates, business relationships, family. We had an army looking
into him. And it's my lead on account of the Vegas connection to
start with, and because Flemming asks me to take it for him. Then
the Pied Piper moves his act to LA out of the blue, and I get a call
from the Hoover Building telling me—ordering me—to maintain
contact with Flemming. His girlfriend has vanished. There are
some inappropriate deposits in his account."

"Flemming?" Boldt barked.

"That's what I'm saying. Same reaction I had. Gary Flemming? You gotta be kidding me! But an order's an order."

"Flemming?" Boldt repeated.

"By San Francisco, things are going really bad with the case.
And when they suddenly look a little better, Flemming fires the
whole team, claiming incompetence. Maybe he asks for me,
maybe the Hoover Building helped the decision, but suddenly I'm
on the team. I get to see things firsthand. Evidence that goes east
to the lab and seems never to come back. Little stuff, but important. He's not returning some calls. He's not paying attention to
certain witnesses, certain evidence. The local cops in Portland do
some good police work. I pass it along. Suddenly the Pied Piper's
on the run again. Then you guys, even better police work I might
add. The holes are a little more apparent. And then Andy Anderson. Flemming is fixated on Anderson, can't let it go. Has the
place under surveillance. Has us pulling evidence without warrants—messing up everything—and I'm getting nervous."

"You're reporting back to Washington this whole time?"

"I'm supposed to be. But Gary Flemming? Am I going to sink
a career like that based on a bunch of nothing? It's all little stuff.
A lot of it doesn't add up. Mostly because I get this feeling—it's a

feeling, right?—that Flemming wants this asshole more than me, more than anybody."

"I've felt that too," LaMoia confessed.

"Right? And then this tattoo you guys surfaced—and come to find out the task force knows squat about some tattoo, and now I'm really scratching my head. I gotta get down here and see for myself."

"The phone?" Boldt asked. "Just now? You got through?"

He nodded. "To Hill. You know Captain Hill," he told LaMoia, "better than the rest of us."

LaMoia bristled.

"Flemming knew you were dicking her. Had me follow you more than once. Nice hotels."

Boldt called out sharply to LaMoia, preventing him from delivering the blow he intended.

"He's been saving it as his ace. Push comes to shove, the task force is his. All his. And he would'a played that ace, believe me. Was all set to. Only now you've gone and gotten yourself suspended, and that messed up everything. He doesn't have the leverage he might have had."

LaMoia's face flamed red.

"Hill?" Boldt asked.

"Gave her the flight number. Described the suspect." He said, "There's a nonstop from DFW to Seattle, arrives early tonight."

"Hill?" Boldt asked.

"Better than giving the suspect over to Flemming," Hale complained. "He'd screw up the surveillance. He'd do it intentionally."

"He'll find out," Boldt said. "Once Hill deploys Special Ops—Mulwright and that mouth of his—everyone in law enforcement in that town will know."

Boldt said, "If it checks out, we'll call down and free you. As it is, we've got to know before we risk the Kittridge girl. Maybe you understand that, maybe you don't."

"Get back here!" Dunkin Hale demanded loudly.

LaMoia pulled the door shut with a thud. The two security guards stood sentry.

"Nothing rough," Boldt demanded. "Just give us overnight."

"We got you covered." Surfer added, "Pleased to help out."

Lisa Crowley was about to get caught in a squeeze play between SPD and FBI surveillance. Sarah required that Boldt prevent that from happening, even to the point that he come to Lisa Crowley's rescue. Crowley remained his only chance of locating his daughter.

Big & Easy Charter wanted seven thousand dollars to charter a private jet to Seattle. Boldt split it between three credit cards, maxing out two of them.

Daphne and Trudy Kittridge headed to Houston and on to Seattle as planned, scheduled for a late-night arrival.

Within the hour, Boldt and LaMoia were airborne, with crab and avocado salads and every drink on the face of the earth available to them. An Airphone. A choice of fifteen videos. LaMoia watched *Jurassic Park*.

Boldt made calls.

CHAPTER

73

"Listen up, people!" Sheila Hill shouted over the heads of the crew assembled in the Public Safety Building's second-floor squad room. Boldt stood leaning against the back wall. "The suspect, traveling under an assumed alias of Julie De-Champs, is scheduled to arrive at Sea-Tac airport in less than an hour from now—at 7:07 P.M." She stood balanced precariously on a chair in front of a large white board that carried team names in a variety of colors. Of the twenty people collected in the room, only a few were qualified for surveillance, the rest were patrol personnel dressed in civvies. To her benefit, the group included Patrick Mulwright and a six-man Special Ops unit—highly trained in both surveillance and hostage situations—already on their way to Sea-Tac, along with one of the department's three mobile command vehicles. Hill noted that Bobbie Gaynes was not in attendance.

She shouted to be heard. The excitement had infected the group, rumor running rampant. "Listen up!" she repeated. "Remember, we don't have much of a description. She's traveling alone as Julie DeChamps. Dark hair. Five feet six. We know the

Bureau has established surveillance at the airport, but that's about all we know.

"Flemming wants this collar for the Bureau and federal prosecution. Obviously, that does not perfectly match our picture of things."

A few derisive boos rose from the gathering.

"We suspect the FBI will move to arrest the suspect once she has made contact—either physically or through communications—with her male accomplice. We've established that the Feds have trap-and-traced all pay phones at Sea-Tac. We assume they will apprehend and arrest the suspect somewhere outside of baggage claim once she is either picked up by her accomplice or makes for public transportation—sooner, if she makes a phone call.

"Teams Bravo, Charlie and Zulu, you have your respective assignments. The Bureau is, without a doubt, able to monitor our open communications. Possibly even our secure frequencies. We will not have their radio traffic, but they may have ours. That means we use our radios as little as possible. Remember this: They may have the gear, but we know the city.

"We are following a plan conceived by Lieutenant Boldt," she said, pointing.

Boldt was working not one plan, but two. He had no intention of either the FBI or SPD arresting Crowley, although his role at the moment was to convince otherwise. He said, "We've worked closely with Matthews as to the psychology of both the suspect and the FBI. We aim to give the Bureau a decoy while we stay with the real suspect. It's going to get confusing, so stay alert; team leaders will brief you on your assignments." He looked them over and reminded, "At the troop level, the Bureau's people are just doing their jobs. We don't begrudge them that. If any of you are put into a position to put your life on the line, you can trust that their agents will be there to back us up. Likewise for us. Copy that? This woman is the only bad guy out there. Questions? No? Good." His voice cracked as he said, "There are children counting on us." It took him a moment to collect himself.

He looked over at Sheila Hill, who cleared her throat and said loudly, "Let's go."

Gary Flemming used his considerable clout to delay American Airlines flight #199, buying his surveillance team twenty-seven minutes. By that hour, Flemming had over two dozen FBI field operatives stationed at key locations inside Sea-Tac airport's concourse B. Eleven of these agents—an elite FBI Hostage Rescue Unit—had been flown up from Sacramento that same evening, accounting for Flemming's delay of the aircraft.

Eleven minutes before the delayed flight 199 was scheduled to touch down, Boldt and a woman named Teibold from Special Ops met with Peter Kramer, a former SPD sergeant who had retired and taken an executive security post with Field Security Corporation, which held the contract for Sea-Tac. Kramer had survived a triple bypass ten months earlier, and had the fresh look of a man in full appreciation of life. He had lost nearly forty pounds since the operation, with another twenty to go. The cigarettes that had forever been a fixture in his jovial face were nowhere to be seen.

By agreement, the three met in the recovered baggage office of concourse C.

Boldt introduced Teibold. She wore blue jeans and a cream-colored T-shirt and carried a large handbag. She had brown hair down to her shoulders. Inside the handbag was a multicolored scarf and a pair of large sunglasses. "We need Teibold in the jetway for American one-nine-nine as the plane lands," Boldt stated.

"One-nine-nine?"

"Gate 11. B concourse."

"I know the concourse. But there's the small problem of an FBI team working this same flight."

Boldt explained, "Task force is crumbling, Krames. We're here to protect SPD's interests."

"Special Agent in Charge is the name of Flemming."

"That's the guy."

Kramer winced. "How'd I end up on the wrong side of this? He's in our control room hooked up to a mobile command unit parked outside. You know what you're up against?"

Boldt checked his watch. Nine minutes. "We need to get Teibold in that jetway."

"*No problemo*," Kramer replied. "Door code on B concourse is three-five-one-three. I'll see to it that none of my people stop her."

"Can't use the concourse," Boldt explained. "Flemming's people will be all over it." He asked, "Have they put any of their people field side?" He checked his watch again.

"One on each field gate. Nothing near the jetways. I got one of my people at the bottom of the jetway stairs. And you're right about the concourse. It's sewn up like a gnat's ass. How many people in your show?"

Avoiding an answer, avoiding any chance that Flemming might get the information, Boldt told the man, "We need to hurry, Krames. Let's get Teibold into the jetway from the field side. All she's going to do is exit the jetway with the other passengers."

"Unarmed?"

"Unarmed, you bet," Boldt answered.

"What the hell are you up to, Boldt?" the man asked, eyeing Teibold in the process. "What kind of angle you working?"

"We've only got seven minutes, Krames."

"Seven 'til they land. At least another five on the ramp. Okay," he said, glaring at Boldt for not answering his question. Addressing Teibold, he instructed her, "You come with me. We'll cross over to B, field side, beneath the restaurant." Anticipating Boldt's objection, he added, "There are no field side cameras in that location. Flemming is monitoring the cameras. It's the best way." Handing a business card to Boldt, he said, "My pager and cellular are on there. You guys on radios or cellulars?"

Boldt gave him his cellular number and Kramer wrote it down onto his greasy palm. "What I'll do," Kramer told him, "is monitor what the hell they're up to and try to keep you posted. You know they're working with some serious radios."

"Yes, we do."

"They're scanning cellular frequencies as well."

"We are expecting that."

"They've got the pay phones covered."

"We know."

"You using any kind of radio code?" Kramer asked.

"The suspect is 'the truck.' Tiebold here is 'the Toyota.' Direction is by compass, with east as baggage claim. Inside, 'one mile' is a hundred feet. Outside, a mile is a mile."

"They'll think they're picking up some vehicular surveillance that Special Ops is running. Pretty damn clever."

Boldt tapped his watch. "Krames."

Kramer grinned. Opening the door he confided in Teibold, "He hasn't changed one bit, has he?"

For Boldt, Sarah's safety demanded he sabotage both attempts at surveillance. At the same time *he* had to maintain continual surveillance of Lisa Crowley if he hoped to follow her to Sarah.

"The bird is down," Boldt heard through his earpiece. A flesh-colored wire ran into his coat to the walkie-talkie strapped to his side. SPD's Special Ops communication center, a black panel truck crowded with video surveillance and radio equipment—SOCC-EYE—was parked downstream from baggage claim outside concourse D. Boldt wore a Mariners' baseball cap pulled down tightly to shield him from airport surveillance cameras, no tie, his blue blazer and badly wrinkled khakis. The concourse teemed with travelers, family and friends.

Boldt reached for a paperback book in the newsstand rack. He spoke into a tiny microphone clipped inside his coat sleeve. "Report." His full duplex radio was the property of Special Ops and did not require him to trip a transmission button, although a transmission button did exist; when depressed it sent an ID slug to command.

A flurry of clicks filled his ear—other SPD operatives checking in sequentially.

"That's a great read," a woman's voice said. She stood alongside Boldt dressed in a dark blue business suit and carrying a leather briefcase. "I've read everything by her."

Boldt grimaced and returned the novel. He didn't need a chatty-Cathy.

"I didn't mean to scare you," the woman fired off quickly, as Boldt returned the novel to the rack.

"No, no." Boldt glanced around looking for a way out. The newsstand's layout floor plan trapped him. A suit by the newsstand caught his eye, one of Flemming's?

"This is a good read as well," she said, indicating a legal thriller.

"Is it?" Boldt said, trying to sound as uninterested as possible. The suit at the front of the store spent a little too much time studying the pedestrians. Flemming had his people checking for SPD operatives. A chess game.

In his ear he heard, "Two minutes."

Again, a series of clicks filled his head as operatives acknowledged. Two minutes until the plane reached the gate and the jetway beyond where Teibold waited at the bottom of the steps. Like Boldt's, each handheld radio transmitted a digital identification slug. Logged by computer in the command vehicle, the Incident Command Officer—Mulwright—could immediately identify who was transmitting and speaking without any name or code ever being uttered. The computer also kept a running count for the ICO, who, on that night, expected twenty hits for each acknowledgment.

"LA," the woman next to Boldt said, unprovoked. "Just for the night. Business. How about you?"

"Actually, I'm meeting someone," Boldt said.

"Lucky her." She added, "Is it a her?"

He didn't want any small talk, and yet perhaps it made him less conspicuous. He glanced over her head into a convex mirror that produced a distorted, fish-eye view of the newsstand, keeping his eye on the man out front and willing him to go away. His woman friend chose that moment to tussle her hair. In the process she exposed a tiny clear wire leading up her neck and into her hair. Boldt's chest knotted tightly.

Flemming's people had IDed him.

He took a step forward to pass by her, but she was too quick. She seized his forearm with considerable strength and in an all-business voice said, "The S-A-C would like to have a few words with you, Lieutenant." Controlled, professional. "Now," she added.

Boldt needed a clear view of the concourse to run both SPD's team and his own team. He didn't have time for a visit.

In his ear, "One minute." Boldt did not acknowledge, hoping Mulwright would interpret his lack of a signal as indicating that he had problems.

Again, Boldt eyed both the woman and the agent out front. Would they risk a scene one minute before the suspect's arrival? "I'll take a rain check," he said.

"I don't think so."

"You two are going to manhandle me out of here? You want to check with the S-A-C about that?"

She asked, "You're going to put this surveillance at risk?"

"Oh, very good," Boldt said. "You're very good."

"Thirty seconds," the voice in his ear announced. After a series of clicks the dispatcher called, "Bravo One, report please." Boldt's call sign. He did not report.

Boldt stepped back from the woman and called out loudly, "Hey! You can't put that book in your purse! You have to pay for it!"

She stiffened and offered him a confused look.

In the convex mirror Boldt saw the clerk turn the register key, pocket it and step out from behind the counter—smoothly and quickly; he had done this before. The clerk's actions blocked the outside agent from Boldt's aisle. Boldt knocked loose the woman's grip, spun her around and gently shoved her toward the approaching clerk. "That's shoplifting!" he said.

Boldt cut around a rack, took two steps toward the front agent, seized a hardback off the shelf, and said loudly, "Have you read this one?" He delivered the book into the side of the agent's face, driving the man's flesh-colored earpiece in deeply and bending him over in pain. Boldt hurried down the concourse knowing that Flemming could not afford a scene.

Defiant, and charged with adrenaline, Boldt spotted a mirrored panel in the suspended ceiling and knew that it hid a security camera. He offered the panel his middle finger, immediately thinking about LaMoia. He felt better than he had in ages.

CHAPTER

74

As passengers disembarked from gate 11 Boldt stood at a bank of pay phones, reminded of Dunkin Hale. Holding the phone's receiver, his eyes trained not on the gate but on the person in front of him, Boldt listened to the commentary through his earpiece. Bravo Five, a plainclothes Narco cop, sat facing gate 11, a hot dog in one hand, the sports page open on his lap like a giant napkin. Atop the sports page was a Camcorder aimed directly toward gate 11. A well-hidden wire ran from the Camcorder into a small duffel bag in the adjacent chair. The duffel bag contained a transmitter. In the control van, Mulwright had a view of the gate.

A husband-and-wife team cheered as camera flashes strobed blindingly into the mix of arriving passengers—Flemming's people, without a doubt.

Behind him the two agents from the newsstand stood waiting for phones by the bathrooms, their attention divided between Boldt and the arriving passengers. Flemming's presence was formidable. Boldt had expected nothing less.

BRAVO 5: "The Toyota is just leaving." Teibold was the *Toyota*.

COMMAND: "Command copies."

BRAVO-5: "Toyota is heading toward Bravo One."

Boldt reported in with a single click.

BRAVO 5: "I've got a vehicle approaching the Toyota."

Bravo Five believed an undercover FBI agent had taken the bait and was focusing his or her attention onto Teibold instead of Crowley. Another of SPD's team reported, "Two more vehicles."

BRAVO 5: "Okay. I'm looking right into the headlights of the truck." The *truck* was Crowley.

BRAVO 7: "I copy that. I've got the taillights."

Bravo Seven, a woman police officer in plainclothes, was in the throng directly behind Crowley.

COMMAND: "Toyota and the truck have hit the street. All report."

The frequency sparked with two dozen quick clicks. All of the SPD team knew that Teibold and Crowley had left the jetway and that at least a few of Flemming's people had picked up the wrong scent.

Anger filled Boldt—how dare he be put into a position to protect this woman who had kidnapped his child! His stomach twisted.

BRAVO 5: "Toyota is rolling."

Teibold, wearing a brown scarf and sunglasses, passed within a few feet of Boldt.

COMMAND: "Bravo Five: rotate left please." (Pause.) "Your *other* left."

From within the Special Ops command van, Mulwright and the others watched the video shot from Bravo Five's lap. The camera's images were SPD's only look at the situation, unlike Flemming, who had all the airport's security cameras at his disposal.

BRAVO 5: "I've got the truck's taillights."

Boldt spotted Crowley then: She wore a wig of short blonde hair, a bandanna around her forehead covering her wound, a brightly colored African skullcap on top. She had used eye shadow to blacken *both* eyes, giving her a haunting, brooding look—urban sheik mixed with biker girl. The blue bag doubled as a backpack, and she wore it as such. A different woman.

Boldt feigned annoyance with the caller in front of him—all an act for Flemming's cameras. He turned and glanced down the hall following Crowley, who kept pace with other passengers.

Teibold dropped her purse, bent to retrieve it, and stepped out of the surging pedestrian traffic. She dealt with a shoelace as she appraised her surroundings, doing a convincing job of playing a paranoid person looking for tails.

The male agent from the newsstand, halfway down the concourse, took notice of Teibold and entered the men's room, out of sight. Boldt marveled at the professionalism of the FBI undercover unit. He had spotted the couple with the flash camera, now headed toward baggage claim. But other than those two, and the two agents from the newsstand, he couldn't identify any others. Flemming was probably relying on the security cameras for gate area surveillance and saving his manpower for the street.

Pros in every regard. Boldt worried Flemming's people would not sucker onto Teibold for long.

His cell phone vibrated in his pocket. Kramer whispered in his smoker's voice, "Our friends are following the Toyota. You copy that?"

"Got it." They were following Teibold, just as Boldt had hoped. "How many on foot?" Boldt asked.

"At least seven near you."

Boldt had missed three or more of Flemming's agents.

"That truck's working a flat tire," Kramer said, referring to Teibold's toying with her shoes.

"Affirmative."

"Back at you in a minute." The line went dead. Warm sweat drizzled down his ribs. Above all, in case *he* was being watched, he had to avoid looking at Crowley—his full attention on Teibold. Only the radio kept him in touch with Crowley's movements, and his one human link to his little girl.

Daphne, on her way to Houston with the child, and eventually to Seattle, had spoken to Boldt twice since their separation and had correctly predicted Crowley's change of disguise on the plane. She had also suggested that Crowley would head directly to the women's room upon arrival for another change. "She will take a stall. Close herself in, sit down and settle herself. She won't take her pants down, even if she might have to pee, because you can't run with your pants down and she is in a defensive mode. She's been here before. Every con artist has been in a bad situation. They survive by staying cool, and this is one cool woman. She will change her looks again. It'll be a fast change. Something simple but effective. We won't know until we see it. Something unexpected. Who knows? If she's really good, she crawls between stalls, leaving hers closed. All I know for certain is that she'll enter one woman, and leave another."

For this reason, the housecleaner polishing the mirror in the women's washroom, concourse B, was a Sex Crimes detective by the name of Morgan Blakely. Her call sign was Bravo Three.

Crowley was reported entering the women's room, as Officer Blakely removed her earpiece so that it would not show. In doing so, she isolated herself.

COMMAND: "No vehicles seen entering the car wash. Only the truck."

The resulting radio silence filled Boldt with anticipation. If no FBI agent followed Crowley into the washroom, then using Teibold as bait had worked. On the other hand, Flemming might have thought to cover the lavatories with someone inside, just as Boldt had. Time crawled. Women came and went from the lavatory's open entrance. With no signal from Blakely, Boldt assumed Crowley remained inside.

Within a few seconds of this thought, chaos broke out at the bathroom's entrance. Women poured out into the terminal—several in the midst of zipping and buttoning themselves. A waft of gray smoke appeared. Officer Morgan Blakely appeared in the cluster, looked frantically in all directions, caught sight of Boldt, and vehemently shook her head no.

They had lost the suspect.

CHAPTER

75

Lou Boldt's hopes for finding Sarah disappeared with Lisa Crowley. Rather than storm into the women's bathroom, which was his temptation, he casually lifted his right hand as if to scratch his head and spoke into the mic clipped there. "All units in the vicinity of the car wash, adopt one-on-one surveillance."

Boldt, knowing that he had been made by the FBI, could not participate in the one-on-one surveillance for fear of giving Crowley away. Fulfilling his ruse, he charged off after Teibold, who was just reaching the far end of the concourse.

Every available SPD operative, including Blakely, was to follow one of the women leaving the bathroom. Command assigned four agents from Charlie—the baggage claim and car rental team—to head toward the concourse and join the one-on-one.

Boldt stayed with Teibold, radio traffic blurring in his ear, the next few minutes crucial. He knew that Flemming could not overlook the commotion at the bathroom, a fire there was certain to raise the man's suspicions. Forced to divide his efforts, he would reconsider Teibold as a suspect; she had gone nowhere near that bathroom. Flemming would, out of necessity, move to arrest their prime suspect: Teibold. Before that happened, Boldt and his team needed to find Crowley, because once Flemming discovered he had arrested an SPD operative, all hell would break loose.

Teibold passed the security checkpoint on her way to baggage claim, both agents from the newsstand not far behind, Boldt, twenty yards back.

Teibold slowed as she approached the escalators leading down to baggage claim, making a point of taking note of an empty bank of pay phones to her right. Boldt stepped up to a Marie Callender's cookie counter, keeping her in sight as Flemming would expect of him.

His earpiece sang with radio traffic, as a young Asian girl with bangs requested his order.

"Chocolate chip," Boldt told the girl. He pulled out two dollars and set them on the counter. Teibold picked up the pay phone's receiver, searched her purse for a quarter and dropped it into the slot. As she did this, she glanced over her shoulder cautiously and spotted the agent from the newsstand. Her face twitched as she hung up the phone and quickly made for the escalator. At the last possible second, she joined a family moving toward the elevator.

Boldt left the cookie and the money on the counter. The FBI agent took the stairs between the escalators. Boldt increased his stride as a series of radio transmissions confirmed that Crowley had once again been spotted.

BRAVO 7: "We have the truck in sight. Moving east. Bravo Five and I are in pursuit."

COMMAND: "State location, Seven."

BRAVO 7: "Approaching traffic light." The security checkpoint.

COMMAND: "Charlie Three, do you have the truck in sight?"

CHARLIE 3: "The purple truck?"

BRAVO 7: "Affirmative."

CHARLIE 3: "Roger that."

CHARLIE 6: "We have a potential pileup at the freight dock. Advise."

The message was that the FBI agents were rushing Teibold's elevator. Behind everyone, Crowley made her way slowly toward baggage claim. It was the worst of all possible scenarios for Boldt: By busting Teibold, the FBI would make Crowley aware of their presence.

At the bottom of the escalator Boldt turned around to see a woman who wore a long purple dress. The purple truck: Crowley. Her hair now a curly brunette, she carried a gray tote bag, not the blue Boldt expected. She looked nothing like the short-haired blonde woman of a few minutes earlier.

Boldt could not afford to be seen; to Crowley he was Brad Brehmer. Only a stubborn refusal to allow his daughter's fate being put in the hands of others had put him on the concourse in the first place. He hurried to a white courtesy phone and turned to face the wall, his right hand coming up toward his lips.

BOLDT: "Toyota, *hold your position*. Do not move! Do you copy?"

A beige cinder block wall separated the elevator from the automatic doors at baggage claim. Boldt stood only feet from the group of FBI agents intent on busting Teibold.

A purple blur passed by. Boldt kept his face turned. Crowley stopped, no more than ten feet from him. The phone went damp in his hand, as he willed her to move on. In his ear, SPD tracked her movements, Command passing her from one agent to another. A commotion erupted on the far side of the cinder block wall. Boldt could not—*would not*—look back at Crowley. As it turned out, he didn't have to. The purple dress entered the ascending escalator, heading back up to ticketing. Again, Boldt adjusted himself, turning right. The commotion grew louder, though the agents did an impressive job of keeping Teibold's detention from becoming an all-out scene.

Sea-Tac used a sky bridge to reach rentals and parking. Crowley had first headed down to baggage claim in error, before reversing herself.

Boldt waited for her to clear the top of the escalator and then jumped on for the ride, only seconds behind her.

Crowley followed signs to the sky bridge. Boldt followed her, Sarah's life relying on his every footstep.

One story below, outside the elevator, FBI agents were dis-

covering that for the last ten minutes they had been following an
SPD undercover cop. Flemming would panic, his attention certain to fall onto Boldt. Boldt walked quickly, despite the fact that
it drew him closer to Crowley. He needed to clear the terminal's
security cameras.

They crossed the sky bridge, he and his daughter's kidnapper,
fleeing the FBI, she in disguise, he with his head down, mixing in
with dozens of other impatient travelers.

He glanced out of the sky bridge windows, down to the taxi
stand, where FBI agents in blue suits hurried about, checking
taxis, jumping onto various buses—bees in a disturbed hive.
Their blatant disregard for covert techniques informed Boldt that
Flemming had indeed panicked. Two dozen FBI operatives were
scrambling to salvage their operation. Boldt realized that he was
his own worst enemy; he had to break away from Crowley to
avoid alerting Flemming. And yet he had to stay with her.

At the end of the sky bridge, he stopped and fished the cell
phone from his pocket, using it as a prop. Crowley continued
straight ahead into the parking area, *not* downstairs to rentals, just
as Boldt had expected.

It was Gaynes who had put him onto this over the phone; she
had followed the Taurus from the Park and Ride to Sea-Tac,
where the driver, a male, had parked it on the sky bridge level and
then lost her. Boldt took the male to be Roger Crowley, the car
having been left for his wife. Boldt had ordered Gaynes to drill
the Taurus's taillight.

Drilling taillights was something Boldt had learned from an
ATF agent named Reisnick twelve years earlier. Vehicular surveillance, even with a team of three or four tails, had less than a thirty
percent success rate, contrary to its representation in film and on
television. Improved technology, namely Global Positioning, had
permanently changed things, but that required the surveillance
team to place a transmitter on the suspect vehicle—SPD's
planned course of action. In the right hands, a drilled taillight was
nearly as good as GPS. The tiny hole in the taillight emitted an
unexpectedly brilliant spike of white light, laserlike in its quality,
that could be seen clearly at a distance of several blocks, or from

a helicopter. It singled out a vehicle from all others. Though less effective, the technique even worked in daylight hours as the brakes were applied; at nighttime it was foolproof.

Boldt's challenge was to double-cross SPD's attempts to follow Lisa Crowley and to get the suspect safely out of the airport, while still keeping her under surveillance himself.

To accomplish this, Gaynes had drilled the taillight. He and LaMoia had assembled a motley crew that included a variety of snitches hungry for a hundred-dollar hit and waiting for orders.

The question remained: Would it work?

CHAPTER

76

The Taurus backed out of its parking space just as Boldt reached Gus Griswold on his cellular. Griswold had been an SPD informer for seven years. He worked part-time as a butcher for one of the supermarket chains. He lived out of the back of a Ford Country Squire, which he referred to as his mobile home.

"You on top of this?" Boldt asked the man.

"You want me on top of her? I thought you just wanted me to follow." All snitches were wise-asses. The headlights from the Taurus threw long shadows across the concrete. Boldt spotted the drilled taillight without any problem. Gus Griswold's rusted Ford pulled out of a parking space right behind that tiny white light.

"You see that taillight?" Boldt asked.

"Later," Griswold said. The line went dead. The two cars disappeared into the guts of the parking garage, their engine noise fading.

While Special Ops' identification of Crowley played out in his right ear, Boldt cut through a tangle of parked vehicles in the darkened garage. He caught a last glimpse of Griswold's taillights as the snitch followed Crowley down the spiral exit ramp. Boldt broke into a run heading for the fire stairs, aware that Special Ops had closed two of the three exit lanes and had placed an SPD undercover cop behind the garage's only open cash register window. The SPD plan was to fix a GPS transmitter to whatever vehicle the suspect drove out of the garage, rental or not. The cashier was to intentionally drop the rental contract or the parking receipt as it was being passed to the driver. The cashier would then quickly leave the booth as if to retrieve it and, in the process, slip the magnetized GPS transmitter onto the undercarriage of the car. From then on, Special Ops would be able to track the vehicle's movement and location electronically, either from the command van or the Public Safety Building, as long as the transmitter remained within the cellular telephone network.

Special Ops—"Zulu"—also had four surveillance vehicles in place. These vehicles, called trailers, were to rotate line-of-sight surveillance, keeping the suspect in view at all times. A dozen SPD patrol cars were established along the more commonly used routes awaiting instructions.

It was the reliance on the GPS technology that Boldt intended to exploit. A few years earlier, a similar surveillance operation might have used six or more trailers, but trailers were cops being paid overtime in city-owned vehicles burning fuel and requiring maintenance. A GPS, once installed, required one technician sitting at a computer terminal studying a moving map and directing dispatch.

Boldt raced down the cement stairs to ground level and cracked open the steel door, gaining a view of the exit booths, their red-and-white striped barrier arms blocking lanes. With several flights having arrived within minutes of one another, and only one booth open, seven cars were lined up awaiting the cashier. The third car back was a brown Taurus, followed immediately by Griswold's Country Squire.

The first car paid and left, then the second. The Taurus pulled up to the booth. An exchange of radio traffic confirmed this. Boldt understood the level of tension inside that command van. SPD's success relied entirely on their ability to place the GPS. He understood this well, because the success of his operation relied on preventing it.

Boldt looked on anxiously as the cashier reached out for the parking stub, intentionally lost hold of it and then shoved his head out the booth announcing to Crowley, "I'll get it!"

But Gus Griswold beat him to it. Having left his vehicle, ostensibly to fix a wiper, he lunged for the fallen parking stub like a good Samaritan, blocking the cashier from exiting the booth.

"Back in your car," the undercover cashier ordered somewhat desperately. "I've got it."

"No sweat," the snitch answered, passing the stub to the cashier and making eyes at Crowley. The GPS transmitter remained inside the booth. The red-and-white arm lifted and the Taurus motored ahead.

Boldt hurried past the booths, the cashier's back to him, and out into the dark and the drizzle. The Country Squire passed a moment later, and Boldt climbed inside.

"How'd you like that shit?" Griswold asked.

"You're a natural," Boldt said, strapping in, the Taurus's drilled taillight shining as brightly as an evening star, calling him, tugging at his heart, leading him toward his child and her abductor.

"The bird is not in place," Boldt heard in his right ear. "Repeat: The bird is not in place."

The dispatcher's professional calm never ceased to amaze him. Command ordered Zulu's mobile surveillance units to be on the lookout for the brown Taurus.

Boldt winced at mention of the Taurus. Without realizing the mistake, Command had more than likely just handed Flemming everything he needed to know.

CHAPTER

77

Lisa Crowley's Taurus followed signs to Seattle via 509 North; Griswold and Boldt were fifty yards back and following. Her one stunt had been to drive around the block in an effort to spot any surveillance, but Boldt picked up the ruse before her second turn, instructing Griswold to drive past, take two lefts and wait at the intersection. Moments later the Taurus sped past, silencing Griswold who was, at the time, exercising his right of free speech. They reentered traffic and followed, allowing several cars to come between, Boldt monitoring the steady flow of radio traffic as SPD attempted to keep watch on Lisa Crowley.

"They're two cars back," Boldt informed the Griz.

"Cops?"

"Yes."

"So we're fucked."

"We're challenged," Boldt corrected.

"It's that taillight. Can see the fucking thing for miles, I'm telling ya. I never knew how bright."

"That's the idea," Boldt said. And as he did so, another idea took its place. "You just earned yourself a bonus, Griz."

"No shit?" Griswold sat up a little higher in the seat. Squared his shoulders. "This cop shit's okay," he said. Regarding his filthy dash, littered with candy wrappers, he added, "Wish like hell this thing had a siren."

Bernie Lofgrin had used his considerable clout as director of the Scientific Identification Division to trick the motor pool into giving him another of SPD's surveillance vans, a steam-cleaning van confiscated in a drug bust and presently outfitted with surveillance hardware.

Acting as the Gang of Five dispatcher, Lofgrin monitored SPD's progress at Sea-Tac from an I-5 Park and Ride five miles north of the airport. The step van had full radio capabilities, a cellular phone "switchboard" that allowed real-time conferencing between up to six separate cellular numbers, digitized video surveillance and four separate computer terminals, two of which were specialized for law enforcement. Lofgrin was like a bear in a honey jar, enjoying his chance to work the high-tech gadgets to where he had nearly every major component of the van's electronic arsenal working in some regard. He even had the video camera trained out the back at the on-ramp's approaching traffic, a color SONY playing to his left.

Boldt called Lofgrin a few minutes before eight o'clock and requested he reposition the van at the intersection of 99 and South Lander in a parking lot on the southeast corner facing the traffic light. Boldt paged Raymond, his snitch who spent a majority of his time at the Air Strip but was on that night driving a lime green Corvair with whitewalls. The page went through; he would be hearing back from the man within minutes, in however long it took Raymond to leave the Corvair and walk to the pay phone. LaMoia was given specific instructions and told to rendezvous in the same parking lot on South Lander, as soon as he had switched cars with Gaynes, who was parked on South Jackson, a block from the Kingdome. With quick access to either I-5 or 99, Gaynes remained on standby; Boldt's wildcard, placed well north of Sea-Tac, Bobbie Gaynes was his last line of defense.

"What the hell are you planning on doing?" Griz asked, having overheard the series of calls.

Boldt didn't feel like explaining himself, nor was he sure he could. He finally mumbled, "I'm pulling an end run on my own people," voicing his own realization of what he was doing. It didn't sound right to him; he wished he hadn't said it.

Griswold knew to let well enough alone. He said, "You ever want a quarter of beef real cheap, I'm your man."

"Freezer's full," Boldt said. Pointing, he said, "Change lanes."

Griswold pulled out from behind the truck and accelerated past it. Boldt pointed back into the right lane; Griswold obliged him. "Pork bellies are cheap right now."

"My locker freezer needs defrosting. If I get around to it . . ."

"Yeah, okay." He reached for the car's radio. "You mind I listen to the Sonics? It's the fourth quarter."

"I mind," Boldt answered.

Griswold debated turning on the radio anyway, but he caught Boldt's eye and withdrew his hand and placed it firmly on the wheel.

"Hang back a little," Boldt instructed.

"That same truck's gonna come right up my butt."

"Hang back," Boldt repeated firmly.

"Sweet mood you're in," the driver muttered.

"And put a sock in it," Boldt added.

He didn't know the whereabouts of Flemming's surveillance crews, but he doubted they were far off; in the panic of briefly losing Crowley, both the Taurus and the drilled taillight had been mentioned over the airwaves. Minutes later, SPD's mobile surveillance had reacquainted themselves with Crowley; two cars unmarked were currently trading the tail back and forth. Boldt could only hope that what was good for the goose was good for the gander, and that if SPD took the bait he offered, Flemming might too. He had little doubt of the FBI's participation in the tail, although unlike SPD he had yet to identify the offenders. As in so many on-the-fly, real-time operations, it all came down to a matter of timing and coordination, and of luck, good or bad.

Another truck passed them—SYSCO Food Services—blocking Boldt's view of the pinprick taillight, followed by another surge of adrenaline that swarmed his system in a flood of heat and anxiety, a kind of mock flu with which he lived for weeks on end. He chastised Griswold not to lose the taillight, not to allow himself to be passed, and so the Country Squire pulled out and struggled to regain its position. "Seattle drivers suck," Griswold said, swerving and confirming his statement. The SYSCO truck sped up, preventing them from passing it. Boldt wondered if it was FBI and if they had made the Country Squire. "Faster," he said, as if this might help.

The Country Squire grumbled and complained and then sounded as if a rocket had been ignited beneath it. It lurched forward, throwing their heads back in unison, and roared ahead. Griswold smiled warmly and said, "The old girl has got it when you want it."

They traveled another ten minutes this way, blocked by a vehicle, passing it, blocked again, passing again. Car tag. Boldt used the cell phone to check on his troops. He felt grateful for the Seattle drool, the light drizzle that leaked from the sky, for it delivered extreme darkness and low visibility, and yet was hardly the kind of weather to keep Seattle's homeless off the streets. The closer they drew to the city, the more abundant and apparent the city's nomads. One or two clung to hand-scrawled signs proclaiming "I'll Take Any Job." One man sold flowers at a stoplight.

Boldt bought a bouquet of daffodils for three bucks. If anyone had been considering the Country Squire as a possible surveillance vehicle, Boldt had just shattered that image. He rolled up his window, confident he and Griz were now off any such list for consideration.

"What the hell you do that for, Big Spender?"

Boldt set the flowers down gently onto the trash-strewn dashboard. "Try to get the stink out of this thing," Boldt answered. The car crashed through a set of potholes. It felt like an amusement ride.

"We're what, two, three miles from the light at Lander? You want I do anything special when we get there?"

Boldt heard the man, but only as a distant hum, his words indistinguishable, his attention riveted instead on the dash, where with each bounce of the poorly sprung car the bouquet of flowers shook additional yellow dust—pollen—onto the candy wrappers. He wetted the tip of his thick finger and touched it into the pile and returned it to arm's length where his tired eyes could focus upon it. "Daffodils," he said softly.

"Hey, you gotta give it a rest, man," the driver suggested.

"Arrest?" Boldt replied, mishearing. "They grow daffodils in Skagit, don't they?"

"Every damn flower there is, far as I know."

"Bulb flowers," Boldt said.

"Whatever. Flowers is flowers."

"No," Boldt said, grabbing up the bouquet and shaking it violently, his hand open beneath it catching the fine mist of yellow dust that fell. "It's tulips mostly in Skagit, and tulips produce all kinds of pollen, but none of it's yellow, not this kind of vibrant yellow. You see? There can't be that many daffodil farms." It made the FedEx vehicle manifests all the more important.

"One mile, maybe."

"Stay with it."

Boldt called Liz and asked if Theresa Russo had dropped any papers by, and before he finished with the woman's name, Liz confirmed that she held an envelope for him. A long thoughtful pause hovered between husband and wife, all the unspeakable questions lingering between them, unintentionally driving Boldt's sense of guilt to higher places. "We're making some progress," he said. It was all he could think to say.

"I'm praying."

He wasn't sure if he should thank her or not. He was going to have to learn more about his wife's faith and how to respond to it. The idea of a strong faith nibbled at his conscience, tempting him. With all he had seen, all he saw in the line of duty, he wondered if he could bring himself to such a place. Others had. It worked for some. As the Country Squire closed that last mile to

South Lander, Boldt caught himself in a state of silent vengeance; not the pure faith required of him, but an attempt to make a connection with something, someone, greater than himself and to seek partnership and to gain confidence in what he had planned. Not exactly prayer, but he was trying.

"Is that Lander?" Boldt asked his driver, indicating a traffic light in the distance.

"That's the one."

He dialed Lofgrin in the surveillance van. As he did so, he instructed Griz to negotiate the Country Squire immediately behind the Taurus. Griz was beyond questioning him; he accelerated past several cars and then pulled in behind the drilled taillight.

"Okay?"

"We're all set," Boldt said.

He looked ahead to the right and the mostly empty parking lot that included a lime green Corvair and SPD's steam-cleaning van, the command van, the destination of his phone call.

"Yeah?" Lofgrin answered from inside that van.

"Do it," Boldt said. In the next minute or two he hoped to throw both SPD and Flemming off Crowley's scent. He sat back and watched, reduced to spectator, frustrated, tired and angry.

Mounted to the dashboard of the steam-cleaning van was a small gray box that might have been mistaken for a radar detector. All fire trucks, ambulances and certain police vehicles—including all command vans—carried such boxes, the function of which was to transmit radio signals to upcoming traffic lights, switching and holding the lights to green. Aimed as Boldt had directed, Lofgrin engaged the box and stopped traffic on 99, including Crowley and Boldt directly behind her, a half mile and closing.

The moment the traffic stopped, a good-looking black man stepped into the street and approached the stopped traffic carrying a spray bottle in hand and several more hooked in his waist. The light rain continued to fall. Raymond sprayed a part of the windshield of the first car and wiped it quickly. He hurried around the front of the car and clearly delivered a sales pitch into the driver's window, holding up the bottle for the driver to see. The driver motioned him away.

Ten seconds had passed since the light had turned red, no cross-traffic in the intersection. Boldt willed Raymond on. Seattle drivers were notorious for running red lights.

Before Raymond raised his rag, the second driver waved him off. The street person worked the windshield to the third car and the driver passed him some money. Boldt had been approached this same way, also during a light rain—the fluid Raymond was selling repelled water off the glass windshield, making it far easier to see. The stuff actually worked.

Thirty seconds . . .

"Hurry up," Boldt mumbled.

Crowley waved, refusing the service, but Raymond went at her windshield anyway. Her window came open and he gave up, shouting, "No charge! No charge!" He crossed in front of her, walked along the curb, and patted her car on the rear fender to let her know he was there. In a sleight of hand worthy of a magic show, Raymond stuck a piece of chewing gum over the drilled hole in the taillight.

At this same moment, across the intersection, the hood of a car stuck its nose out onto 99.

Lofgrin allowed the light to go green, and the first cars surged forward.

"Go ahead," Boldt told Griswold, "but allow this car up here— you see it?—to cut in ahead of us."

"I got it."

A car horn sounded impatiently from behind. The Country Squire rolled but allowed Crowley to gain a car's length that was quickly filled by the car pulling out. It was a dark car, a Nissan, its shape similar to a Taurus. They nearly rear-ended the car.

Griswold honked before Boldt could stop him. "Turn your fucking lights on!" Griswold roared.

As if hearing him, the car in front did just that, and as the taillights flashed red a white pinprick hole appeared.

Griswold understood the switch then and said to Boldt, "You

sneaky bastard." He added, "He got us close like that so we'd block him—"

"Screen him," Boldt supplied.

"So like the others don't see the lights come on." The driver grinned. "They just see the hole in the same taillight." He added, "What's all this about, anyway?"

"It's about a little girl," Boldt said. He held his breath awaiting radio traffic to confirm the ruse.

"Anything?" he heard over the radio.

"Nothing yet . . . check that . . . Affirmative, I've got the target up ahead."

Boldt heaved a sigh of relief: Surveillance had bought the switch.

As instructed, LaMoia waited a mile before turning off, making a right onto Royal Brougham and immediately speeding up. At 4th he would make a left and then would join the long on-ramp to 90, with each turn going faster, making sure to keep enough distance to use the darkness to hide the make of the car.

Crowley, and Boldt with her, climbed the viaduct, the traffic thickening. Behind them, three vehicles turned right in pursuit of the drilled taillight.

Griz, checking the rearview mirror, said, "I don't get it. Aren't those *your* guys?"

"In a matter of speaking," Boldt replied.

"I suppose that's the part I don't get," he said.

Boldt gloated at his success. Through the rain, the skyscrapers shimmered to his right. Viaduct traffic was clocking sixty. It was fast for wet highway, fast for Boldt, but there were no more drilled taillights to follow. They had to stay close to the Taurus.

"She sure is checking her mirror a lot," Griz reported.

"Back off," Boldt ordered.

"We could lose her."

"Back off!" Boldt saw the nervous head movement in silhouette.

"She's changing lanes—"

"Get over!"

Griswold dropped back further and slipped in behind a limousine. "Can't see her."

"Shut up!" Boldt barked nervously, his stomach a knot.

"Tunnel," Griswold said, as the limousine slowed for the short tunnel further separating them.

"This is not good," Boldt said, "*not* good." The Country Squire flowed with traffic into the tunnel.

Boldt caught a faint glimpse of taillights.

"Exit!" Boldt shouted at the driver.

Griswold jerked the wheel and negotiated a sharp right immediately at the tunnel's end. He slammed on the brakes. Every street, every intersection, was jammed with bumper-to-bumper traffic.

Griswold said, "I told you we should'a listened to the Sonics game. At least we would'a known when it was getting out. Who needs this shit?"

"She does," Boldt answered. "She knows exactly what she's doing."

CHAPTER

78

Boldt took off on foot through the drizzle, slamming the car door while telling Griswold to park somewhere within a few blocks and pointing to a corner where he wanted Griswold to wait for him.

Boldt now believed that the Crowleys had timed Lisa's flight for an arrival to coincide with the end of the basketball game and the guaranteed mass confusion that always resulted around the Seattle Center. Slip a car into any one of dozens of emptying parking garages, and it would not be spotted for hours, perhaps days. Grab a bus, or go on foot with the thousands of people crowding the sidewalks; it was a place and time of night to get lost.

Crowley had been less than a hundred yards in front of the Country Squire when it had entered the tunnel. Boldt knew that if he had any chance of locating her, it was now—immediately— while she, like them, was still crushed and hemmed in by the traffic. With traffic barely moving, she couldn't have made it far—on one of three or four streets, or inside one of the two parking garages that were in plain sight.

The rain fell as a cold mist, a gray swirling curtain that seemed to go unnoticed by all but a few of the hundreds of pedestrians.

Boldt cut across the moving traffic, horns firing off at him in volleys of protest. He wished like hell that they had never plugged up that drilled taillight; it would have stuck out like a searchlight. He looked left, right: endless lines of cars. Every possible direction. But with eastbound traffic the worst—the traffic moving toward I-5—and with westbound traffic aimed directly at the Seattle Center, into the lion's mouth, Boldt chose straight ahead.

The sidewalks were more packed with pedestrians than the streets with cars. He threaded his way through and around groups, couples, families, all gabbing about the game and a great shot at the buzzer that had won it for the Sonics. The mood of the crowd was festive, even carnival-like. Although he was polite at first, Boldt's patience wore thin quickly, and he began to bump and claw his way through the melee, his efforts unappreciated. He craned over shoulders, stole his way to the curb, hoping for sight of the Taurus. Whereas the teeming horde walked, Boldt ran, faster and faster, driven at first by curiosity and finally out of desperation; he would not see Sarah's chances swallowed by a crowd, would not write her off. He charged through the elbows, the bumps and the complaints, a man driven by love and a fear of the future. He had spent over twenty years in the company of victims—he knew their fate. He would not become one.

At the intersection, he looked right, straight, left, and then started the process again; right, straight ahead, left, searching shapes and colors. The cars all looked the same, he realized. In shape and styling, so little difference existed. LaMoia, a gearhead, might have spotted the Taurus, might have singled it out from the Lexus, the Toyota, the Nissan, but to Boldt they blended homogeneously into a moving parking lot of identical vehicles. The light changed and, driven at the front of the pack, Boldt found himself caught in the current of pedestrians, carried across the street like a pile of snow in front of a plow.

He would later think that prayers are often answered in strange ways. There is no voice from heaven, no finger pointing the way, only unexplained coincidences that, coincidentally, happen to follow moments of prayer. Pushed across the street by the throng, Boldt stepped up onto the curb and saw the Taurus in traffic, five cars away. He could even make out a small black blob, Raymond's patch of chewing gum on the taillight. Crowley.

Behind him and to his left he heard a car door open and shut. A group of teenagers formed a knot in the sidewalk in front of him.

He took avoidance maneuvers and ran smack into another man, like hitting a brick wall. He apologized, but the brick wall remained firmly in his way. He stepped back to untangle himself and looked up into the eyes—they were dead eyes—of Special Agent in Charge Gary Flemming.

They wrestled briefly, locking forearms with matched grips, Flemming the larger, more powerful man. The crowds flowed around them, barely paying them any mind.

"Fight!" a kid shouted.

"Forget about it," Boldt said, struggling, glancing around furiously through the mist for Flemming's backup.

"It's *my* investigation now," Flemming announced, shaking him like an angry parent. "It's my task force, not Hill's. I took over in Boise."

"It's irrelevant," Boldt conceded. He wondered about what Hale had told him. If true, he was looking into the eyes of the Pied Piper's insider, his accomplice, a traitor.

Hundreds of people streamed past, most oblivious to the weather. The Taurus inched forward in gridlocked traffic, the rain in the headlights swirling like oil in water.

"You're within my jurisdiction," Boldt reminded. "This is my city." It seemed possible that Flemming might have gained control of the task force, and if so the investigation was indeed his, its outcome his to bend, break or detour. But Boldt remained proud of Seattle and his own place within it.

"You'll follow orders, Lieutenant. You've run investigations. You know the importance of—"

Boldt managed to yank his right arm free, reached in for his ID wallet and pressed it into Flemming's huge open hand. "Wrong."

Flemming glanced down at the ID wallet. "Nice try." He attempted to pass it back.

Boldt threw his arms in the air and said, "No harm, no foul. The investigation is all yours." He inched his way to Flemming's left and into an area of clear sidewalk that had formed around them like an eddy behind a rock in a stream. He turned his back on the man and took a tentative step forward.

Flemming roared over the noise of the passing crowd, "She celebrated her birthday in captivity."

The words froze Boldt. He turned, and said, "Not yet she hasn't."

"Stephanie," Flemming told him, eyes shifting nervously among the passers-by. "I'm talking about *my* daughter."

"You aren't married," Boldt said. "Have never been married," he corrected. Drawn to the Taurus, he couldn't keep his eyes off it. Flemming was not one to look away from. Following Sarah's abduction Boldt had looked into the private lives of the various members of the FBI team; only Hale was married and a father, only Hale had made sense as a candidate for the Pied Piper's insider. Everything was turned around. He backed off, taking another step toward the Taurus, which had crept even further down the street. He wasn't going to lose that car. Again, he threw his hands in the air and said, "You've got to shoot me, Flemming, you want to stop me."

That comment won him some extra room from the pedestrians.

"Gun!" a shrill voice called out. The pace of the crowd picked up, but it did not scatter as Boldt expected.

Flemming's hand was indeed stuck inside his sport coat.

Flemming explained loudly, "She's white, Boldt—my woman. We never married, no. We thought it a bad idea for both of us. Our daughter was two-and-a-half when this monster took her." He said clearly, "I know about Sarah. That is, I suspected. I didn't exactly know until right now."

Boldt's knees felt weak. He sagged. *Sarah* . . . Flemming knew. "Not possible," he mumbled to himself, the Taurus slipping away. The ransom demands were violated. He felt comfortable with Flemming as a traitor; Flemming the victim was all too unreal for him. Six months of abduction? Impossible to survive such a thing. Flemming? he wondered. Had Hale lied to protect his own interests? Or was this a smoke screen to allow Crowley to escape?

"Kiss and make up," some punk kid with green hair shouted at them.

Flemming said, "They sent you a video clip on CD-ROM. Hell, I didn't even know how to work with one of those things. Saw it for the first time in a computer store." He insisted, "How would I know that? Think about it!"

An insider would know this as well as a victim. By posing as a victim, Flemming had frozen Boldt—exactly what he would want to do. The Taurus eased ahead in traffic. Boldt's hand found the butt of his sidearm, his index finger pried loose the Velcro tab that secured the weapon. He glanced over his shoulder.

"Do you know her name?" Flemming asked. "The driver? Who is she?"

Nice try, Boldt thought. Convincing as all hell. The powerful man with a small federal army assigned to him playing the naive victim.

Flemming stepped closer. Boldt looked around for the man's agents then, late in doing so, expecting they might be closing in on him. Too many people to tell. Flemming said, "You want to follow her, I'm with you. But you know the rules: No suspects in custody, or I never see my daughter again."

"I know the rules," Boldt answered, out of energy, out of time. He could still reach the Taurus if he ran. "I even played by them for a few days." It seemed like a month ago.

"We follow and we see if our kids are there," Flemming proposed. "Follow only."

For the first time, Boldt heard the man's calm, penetrating baritone break, riddled with grief and uncertainty. For a moment he actually allowed himself to believe the man, which was, no doubt, exactly what Flemming wanted.

Flemming said, "My team is chasing the car you substituted,

same as your people. But you? I followed you and that piece of shit Ford."

Boldt searched the area again. Still no sign of agents. Could Flemming possibly be telling the truth?

Boldt said confidently, "I have one stop to make, and I'll know where she's going. Some paperwork was left with my wife. I can find the place."

"Bullshit." The man was unnerved.

"No bullshit. Anderson could have told you, if you hadn't killed him."

Flemming's jaw quivered, his eyes hardened and went cold. He looked into the stream of pedestrians as if debating to shoot Boldt right there and then. His eyes flashed darkly toward Boldt, who explained, "The choke hold you put on Weinstein. Left-handed. Same thing killed Anderson. I should have made the connection right then."

"I . . . It . . ."

Boldt wished the man's hand out from inside the coat, but it remained. He said, "You want to shoot a cop in the back in front of a couple hundred witnesses, that's your choice." He turned and ran for the Taurus—for Lisa Crowley, stuck in traffic—the rain beginning in earnest.

Flemming caught up to Boldt a few yards from the Taurus, both men at a run. "I'll take the driver's door. You take the passenger," Flemming said.

"We need her alive."

"I know that."

As the traffic surged forward again, the two split up. Boldt cut behind the Taurus and hurried to the passenger door. "Locked!" he called out to Flemming just prior to the agent presenting his gun and shield to the driver's window.

"FBI! Open the door!" The car lurched forward, but only a matter of feet before slamming bumpers with a Mazda. Flemming shot the rear tire. Screams errupted from the sidewalk.

Boldt stayed with the passenger door. He pounded on the side window with the butt of his gun. The safety glass cracked, but held.

An enraged Flemming reached across the front windshield and aimed his weapon directly at the driver's head.

"No!" Boldt shouted, understanding the temptation. "We *need* her!"

"Out!" Flemming shouted to the driver.

Lisa Crowley popped open the door.

"Hands where I can see 'em," Flemming hollered. He said to Boldt, "I'll cover. You cuff. We'll take my car."

Boldt came around the vehicle. He tugged the woman's arms behind her with more force than was necessary. He squeezed the metal around her wrists, an incredible anger burning through him. It felt incredibly good to feel the metal click into metal. "Lisa Crowley, you are under arrest for the kidnapping of Trudy Kittridge, Stephanie Flemming and Sarah Boldt. You have the right—" The words caught in his throat. Tears stung his eyes.

"—to remain silent. You have the right to an attorney. If you cannot afford an attorney—" Flemming ran through the Miranda effortlessly. Together the two men led the handcuffed woman down the sidewalk, against the flow of pedestrians. Horns sounded behind them, frustrated at the parked Taurus. Flemming finished the rehearsed piece and then said, "Now let me tell you something, Crowley: Where you're going those rights won't do you a damn bit of good, because you're going with us." He met eyes with Boldt, and the two men understood each other perfectly.

Boldt said, "It's over." But his words fell flat. For he and Flemming, it was only just beginning.

CHAPTER

79

LaMoia drove east on I-90, well over the speed limit, maintaining a decent lead on the surveillance cars that trailed behind him. He cringed as the rain lessened to sheets of gray mist, for he feared the Nissan would be seen to have taken the place of the Taurus, at which point the surveillance net was certain to collapse upon him *en force*.

Dividing his attention between the road ahead of him and the cars behind, he thought for a moment about the road of life he traveled, and how little time he spent thinking about the future. His affair with Sheila Hill had awakened him to wanting more than raw physical relations, and he considered putting some distance between that relationship and his next, to solidify his notion of John LaMoia. In the past, it had been one bed to the next, one pretty face to the next in a long chain of women that rarely went broken by more than a week or two. The damn kidnapping case was getting to him, he decided at last. He wanted children. A family. A future outside of himself. He was, for the first time in his adult life, tired of John LaMoia. He didn't like himself.

The red flashing lights appeared in his rearview mirror simulta-

neously, one vehicle directly behind him, the other partially blocking the highway's center lane. It felt as if they had gained on him
in a matter of seconds, pedal to the floor. He stretched it out for
half a mile, letting them sweat whether or not they faced a high-
speed chase. Then he signaled and pulled over.

He thought the signal a nice touch. *Just wait,* he thought, *until
they find out who they've pulled over.* He wanted to see their faces.
He could hardly wait.

CHAPTER

The contents of the envelope left for him by Theresa Russo lay scattered across the front seat of Flemming's Town Car along with a map of Skagit County. Liz had passed them through the passenger's window with a simple kiss to Boldt's cheek, a suspicious glance at the driver and a look of hatred aimed at Lisa Crowley, handcuffed in the backseat. They drove with the windows partially down, delivering a wet, heavy air. Little more remained to be said. They had decided on a course of action. They intended to see it through, regardless of the outcome.

Millie Wiggins' address in Haller, near Bitter Lake, proved difficult to find. After several incorrect guesses on Boldt's part, the Town Car drove into the paved driveway in the Pinnacle Point subdivision. Flemming locked the parking brake and kept the car running. A moment later the front curtains parted, an expectant face peered out into the dark and the front door opened.

The detour, while not costly in time, offered the unlikely partners substantial long-term risks that, if taken to their limit, included imprisonment. But the cop in Boldt had overruled the father for the first time in weeks, and he accepted that as progress.

In blue jeans and a green flannel shirt, Millie Wiggins looked nothing like she did while running her day care preschool. She hurried down the brick walkway carrying an umbrella open over her head and called hello from a distance. Boldt signaled her around to his side of the car.

As she stepped up to Boldt's window, she bent over and studied Flemming. Boldt said calmly, "Just a yes or no is all we need. You must be definite. There must be no doubt whatsoever. Even a hint of doubt and I'd rather you say no." He hesitated. They needed probable cause to ever hope for criminal charges. Without the chance of criminal charges, Boldt feared it would, quite possibly, come down to killing this woman. Strangely, he felt no remorse at the idea. He told Wiggins, "You know you don't need to do this. No one is forcing you to do this."

"I understand."

"I'm sorry, but we can't open the back door. You'll have to look from here."

"That's fine."

Flemming switched on the car's interior light, illuminating the woman in the backseat. Boldt rocked his head to the side, affording her a better view, and Millie Wiggins stared long and hard, unknowingly in the act of determining Boldt's future. She blinked repeatedly, nervous and under the strain of his requirement to be definite. He appreciated the difficulty of her task, having been through countless lineups himself.

"You've taped her mouth shut."

"She was a little noisy," Boldt said.

"It isn't easy without the mouth."

"Do your best."

"The hair's a different color," Wiggins said, close enough to Boldt that he could smell wine on her breath.

He said nothing, waiting patiently for her to remember the rules. Flemming had yet to speak.

"Yes," she said strongly, delivering Boldt a jolt to his system. He hadn't realized how good it could feel, how different for the father than the cop.

"You're positive?"

"She was in her uniform, of course," Wiggins said, assuming Boldt's passenger to be a cop. "But that's her." She looked directly into Boldt's eyes. "That's the woman who picked up Sarah. That's her." She asked, "What has she done?"

Crowley protested from behind the duct tape. She squirmed and writhed and then settled down.

"Do you always tape their mouths?"

"You won't see that on TV," Flemming said. He popped off the brake and put the car in reverse. He had not wanted this stop, had agreed to it only in negotiation for Boldt's sharing the contents of the FedEx delivery manifests.

Boldt leaned his head out as the car backed up and addressed a stunned Millie Wiggins, standing in her driveway beneath an umbrella with rain cascading from its rim. "Only our most difficult suspects," he informed her. He thanked her and got the window up. The headlights spilled over her, throwing an enormous shadow against the garage door.

"You see? We didn't need her," Flemming protested, repeating an argument he had beaten to death. "You knew you had the right woman."

Flemming's silent rage terrified Boldt; he was glad to have the man talking. By his own admission, for six months Flemming had attempted to piece together any evidence that might lead him to the Pied Piper, while at the same time continually compromising the public investigation. Now that Boldt had done his job for him, the man seemed hell-bent on handling the Crowleys in the same manner he had handled Anderson. The end justified the means. Boldt, who understood such reactions, who empathized with them, found himself defending the suspect's rights and wondering how far Flemming might go—if he too might end up a victim if he crossed the man.

In the name of probable cause, Boldt had just tricked Flemming into buying himself a second witness, and both men knew it, perhaps Flemming even understood it, though he was difficult to judge. Millie Wiggins, and Liz along with her, could place Crowley and Boldt in that car. Both women had taken good long looks at Flemming.

"Cross over to I-5 on 145th," Boldt said. "There's an on-ramp off Fifth Avenue."

"It doesn't change anything," Flemming warned, letting Boldt know that he understood everything. "If you fuck this up, if you can't find this place, I'll pull her eyelids off and drip battery acid in them until she talks, until she tells me where I can find my daughter. And if you even *think* about trying to stop me—" He didn't bother finishing the threat. Flemming was played out, any ability to reason in him long since exhausted. He had waited for this day for six months, and Boldt or no Boldt, he knew what had to be done. Boldt had tried to use Anderson as a bargaining chip, reminding Flemming that no evidence linked him to the man's murder—implying Boldt would not make a case of it if Flemming played this right. But Flemming was numb from the neck up, lacking any concept of prison terms or punishment. He simply didn't care. He wanted his daughter back. Nothing—no one— would come between him and that end.

Pressured into an alliance of which he wanted no part, Boldt found himself an unwilling passenger. He might as well have been handcuffed and in the backseat himself.

The interminable drive north on I-5 left Boldt referencing the FedEx manifests and plotting delivery routes for March 25 on or about twelve noon, creating small boxes on the map with arrows to the appropriate location. Darkness outside, darkness inside, the rain obscuring the windshield, his own fears obscuring his efforts.

Boldt decided to speak directly to the issue. There were questions to answer and he had no way of knowing if he might be around to hear them later. Without backup, anything could happen. He said to the driver, "According to Hale, the Hoover Building thinks you may be working for the Pied Piper."

"Hale knows?"

"He's been spying on you ever since your girlfriend disappeared and your bank account grew."

The big man nodded, a man defeated. "The money—cash— was deposited in five-thousand-dollar amounts into my account. She," he said, pointing toward the backseat and their prisoner, "knew it would appear that I had misplaced loyalties, that I wouldn't be able to explain the deposits. And of course I wouldn't have been able to. So they had my child, and my career. I sent Gwen away the minute they got our child. Told her not to surface. Believe me," he added, "she's under so deep no one will ever find her unless I'm involved."

"She could support your story. You just might get yourself out of this."

"It's Stephanie I care about, not me. Stephanie first. The rest comes later. The rest hardly matters."

"Yes, I know," Boldt replied.

"You?"

"No money. Just my child."

Flemming confessed, "They had me use E-mail to supply the information they requested. I tried to trace it back to a source, but they knew their stuff: bogus accounts, bogus credit cards paying for those accounts."

"So they knew when to pick up and leave."

Flemming nodded again, though reluctantly and with a heavy heart. "I misled and delayed the investigations as best I could. When it got away from me, I sent off a warning and they packed it up."

"Me?" Boldt asked. "Did you give them me? Was it you who IDed the local cop to go after?"

"It was."

The road whined, the wipers lapped at the water. "I'd like to apologize for that, but I can't," Flemming said. "I did what I thought I had to do." He admitted softly, "I worked constantly to ID them. If I had managed, it would have stopped right there. I would have seen to that, as we will see to that tonight," he said, stealing a glimpse at the prisoner in the rearview mirror. "You're a better cop than me, Boldt. Is that what you want to hear?"

"I want to hear how you could volunteer another person's child," Boldt whispered hoarsely.

Flemming said nothing.

"You gave them my daughter."

"And I'd do it again in a heartbeat," he admitted. He switched the wipers to high. The rain was too loud to think.

Boldt knew intuitively that following Anderson's murder Flemming had settled on killing the Crowleys as the only form of justice. Perhaps it was only by seeing such a thing in another that Boldt could exorcise it from his own thoughts, but he wanted no part in it. Death was too easy for the Crowleys and Chevalier. A life sentence in a maximum facility where the inmates would not tolerate any crime to do with children seemed a far more appropriate sentence. Boldt wanted this done legally, correctly. He wanted Millie Wiggins on the stand, and Chevalier in manacles; he wanted Daphne called as an eyewitness to Lisa Crowley's baby-selling. He could see the logical steps toward conviction. He continued to plot delivery times onto the map.

"So?" Flemming asked, a while later, shattering the monotonous grind of the wipers and interrupting a bass solo on the radio.

"Four delivery trucks servicing Skagit the twenty-fifth. At noon, two were on lunch break, two still delivering. I have one truck delivering at 11:37 and again at 12:12. The second truck made drops at 11:51 and 12:19. Two stretches of road to search for a house that sits up a slight knoll, a tree directly outside."

"How many miles of road?" Flemming asked.

Boldt took rough measurements. "Twenty to thirty, all together."

"It's too much." Flemming told their hostage, "You could simplify this," studying her in the rearview mirror. But as did Boldt, Lisa Crowley assumed the driver intended to kill her no matter what she did; Flemming had played his cards far too early, not thinking anything of it. She had only her husband to sacrifice by cooperating. She would not talk, unless Flemming resorted to torture. Perhaps not even then. In a way difficult for Boldt to grasp, he felt sympathy for this woman, his daughter's abductor. After weeks of wanting her dead himself, he had agonized for the better part of the last hour over his strange association with her, an us-against-them mentality directed at Flemming and including Lisa Crowley. Nothing surprised him any longer; there was no room left for such luxury.

CHAPTER

The small brick town of Mount Vernon, Washington, spread out almost entirely on the eastern banks of the Skagit River, had served as a timber course for the better part of half a century, until every stand of old-growth forest had been cut to the ground, stripped of its branches and skidded and floated to the mills. Throughout the winter the river pushed against its banks, swelled by weeks of rain or unseasonable snowmelt from the east, sometimes jumping and driving the residents to band together in a pitched and fevered battle, lacing together lives in a way only shared disaster can. For millennia, those same seasonal floods had driven silt and topsoil out across the surrounding plains, fertilizing and enriching the soil. Combined with the mild season offered up by the Pineapple Express ocean currents, it made for thousands and thousands of acres ideally suited for the cultivation of bulb flowers. Little Holland, the area was called. More tulips were produced here than in any spot on earth.

Boldt tracked the second hand of his wristwatch. Flemming drove Boldt's selection for the most likely route between the two deliveries, drove five miles an hour over the 35 mph speed limit, knowing FedEx's tough policy for its drivers, drove from a point marked on Boldt's map as 11:37 A.M. following a southerly arrow and a line finally joining a box indicating 12:12 P.M. Flemming drove the entire route, although Boldt was guessing the delivery van had driven a minimum of five miles before the noon hour, and therefore restricted their area of intensive search to a four-mile stretch roughly three-quarters of the way along the route, believing that, in order to have been captured on video, the delivery truck had passed the Crowley safe house somewhere along that same four-mile stretch.

Given the direction of the delivery route, and the direction of the FedEx truck in the video, the safe house had to be on their left. Boldt impatiently studied the homes they passed, annoyed and frustrated that the farmhouses were few and far between. Along the four-mile stretch that Boldt had highlighted, they passed only six homes, not one of which was close enough to the road to explain the FedEx truck's presence in the video; nor did any of the six houses sit up on a slight rise, also apparent in the ransom.

"It's a strikeout," Boldt said, checking his watch.

Flemming drove the same route back toward Mount Vernon, his eyes divided between the road, the houses and Crowley in the backseat. The tension in the car built as Boldt sensed Flemming's desire to beat the truth out of Crowley. He double-checked the route of the second delivery truck, measuring and approximating the timing. "It's about a three-mile stretch," he said.

"We drive the whole route."

The rain let up and the swiftly moving clouds raced east as if a curtain had been drawn. Moonlight streamed down onto the surrounding tulip fields bleeding lush colors into the black of night. Every available strip of asphalt, gravel patch and turnout was occupied to overflowing with RVs and Westfalias. The annual tulip festival under way, Mount Vernon swelled with thousands upon thousands of tourists. With only a few hundred beds available between Bed and Breakfasts and motels, most of the visitors slept in, and lived out of, their vehicles. During daylight hours, travel by car bordered on impossible. Given the location, the bumper-to-bumper traffic often moved less than five miles an hour. The fields of color spread out like quilt patches a quarter mile square. Even in moonlight, the sight was breathtaking: yellow, reds, deep violet.

Noticing all the traffic pulled off for the night along the road's shoulders, Flemming said to the woman in his rearview mirror, "Planned it this way, didn't you? Mount Vernon. The festival. The crowds and all. Who would notice a couple of renters this time of year?"

With her lips taped shut, the hostage said nothing. Caught in the faint glow of ambient light, her eyes seemed heavy and sad. Fatigue caught up to her and dragged her down. Depression set in. Boldt realized it was all but over for her. He wondered silently if the safe house was better off left undiscovered. He was debating intentionally misleading Flemming, when the man tugged the map off Boldt's lap and struggled with the wheel and the map light. A moment later he said, "Okay, a left up here. Then another left at the tracks. Then across the bridge and we're basically at the first delivery: 11:51. Twelve minutes later your daughter is on the video as this truck passes behind her. Have I got this right?" he asked aloud. "We're approximately twelve minutes from finding this safe house?" He drove faster. "Let's shave a little off of that, shall we?" He said to the mirror, "You better say your prayers that we find it. If my friend here is wrong about all this, then it's my turn. And believe me, I've been waiting for this." He said, "I've got a cattle prod in the trunk. A couple other little toys: phosphorus, stun grenades. All courtesy of the U.S. Government. You ever had a stun stick light up your private parts while you're half blind and completely deaf? I'd be thinking about that, if I were you. You can save yourself a lot of grief. Boldt here gives me thirty minutes with you in one of these barns? You won't know what hit you, sweetheart, and you'll be talking a blue streak, believe me."

Mention of the weapons brought Boldt a step closer to realizing the task before them. Of primary importance was to keep Flemming screwed into his socket. But of equal concern was that their daughters were in that house under the watch and care of Roger

Crowley. Besides his sidearm and the stun stick, Flemming had pressure and phosphorus grenades, but the latter were useless with kids in the picture. Stun grenades could rupture a victim's sinuses and eardrums if detonated too close. Phosphorus grenades occasionally did permanent eye damage in the process of "momentarily" blinding a suspect; they were also on record as having set a great many structural fires. Flemming sounded eager to use his toys. Boldt would not allow that. The man was a greater liability than their passenger.

"There," Flemming said, pointing out a white house to their right. "That's the 11:51 delivery. That house, right there. By 12:19 he's made—"

"She's made twelve miles," Boldt answered, correcting the driver's gender.

"So *she* was going at a decent clip."

"Highway 536," Boldt reminded, naming the state highway. "It's probably posted at fifty-five."

Flemming picked up the speed, and Boldt's heart rate right along with it. Sarah was somewhere within a few miles, he felt certain of it. His palms sweating, he took back the map, measured distances and checked street names.

Flemming glanced at his watch. "Somewhere past here, isn't it?"

"Yes. Within the next five miles."

"On our left again," the driver said.

"Correct." Boldt checked the hostage, hoping to see some faint recognition in the woman's eyes, but she was either in shock or in complete control of herself. He saw nothing at all, a smug vacancy that made him fear they were nowhere near the safe house.

The miles ticked on. Not one of the houses had a decent size tree planted close enough to a central window to qualify. Again, the property lining the roadway was dead flat, not elevated as had clearly been the case in Sarah's video.

"I'm not liking this," Flemming said.

"No," Boldt agreed.

"I got a hunch your little theory stinks," the driver said. He glanced into the rearview mirror. "I think we're wasting our time." He added, "We've got all the answers we need right there. You may be too weak to stomach it, but I'm not. I've waited six months for this."

"Drive it again," Boldt said.

"What for? Those houses weren't even close."

"Maybe another route," Boldt said, vamping for time. "Maybe I got the route wrong. Turn around."

Flemming hung a U-turn, but drove fast. "And make that kind of time? No. You picked the right route. That delivery truck had to be doing forty or fifty to make it to that next drop by twenty after twelve. It's your theory that's wrong. Fuck the FedEx truck—she's a *witness*, Goddamn it. An accomplice! We've got an accomplice in the backseat, and there is no way under heaven I won't get her to talk. She'll be telling me her life story if I want her to."

"And any chance of conviction—"

"Oh, bullshit! Does Sarah care about conviction? Do you? Are you honestly going to go Boy Scout on me here? You gonna explain that to your wife, to Sarah? Forget about it. Nice try. No sell. You want this as badly as I do. Admit it. You don't give a shit about this scumbag in the backseat, about conviction. You want justice, same as me. Believe me, justice will be served." He stopped the car. In the distance, in the moonlight, a barn shimmered in a dark field of cut-flower stems that without their blossoms reminded Boldt of long rows of thin soldiers.

"Looks good to me," Flemming said. He rocked his head to look at Crowley. He looked half mad. "How 'bout to you?"

CHAPTER

Flemming took the car keys as he climbed out, and Boldt lost any hope of stealing the car and the hostage while Flemming walked back to the trunk. The FedEx truck was not *theory*, he reminded himself, but evidence. It had appeared on that video clip and was, as such, irrefutable evidence. The video included a piece of a noontime CNN program, and the cable carrier had been identified as serving this community. With only four trucks delivering on the twenty-fifth, two of which were down for lunch break, Boldt had set his sights on locating the safe house and recovering Sarah. By dawn Seattle time Hale would be released—if he hadn't been already—and the Chevalier-Crowley connection exposed, and Sarah's ransom demands failed. He glanced at his watch, then at the trunk coming open, and finally back to the FedEx manifest, at which point it hit him.

He came out of the car in a hurry.

"I knew you'd come around," Flemming said, collecting pieces of his traveling arsenal from the trunk, including a shotgun.

"The driver took his lunch hour," Boldt said, offering the map.

Flemming slapped the open map away. "Eliminating two of the four trucks."

"No," Boldt contradicted, "that's where I had it wrong. Look at this manifest: The first drop *after* the lunch break is south of La Conner." He paused. Flemming wasn't interested. He explained, "The driver took his lunch in La Conner, not Mount Vernon." Flemming looked up from the trunk. Now it was indeed all theory, but Boldt was loathe to admit it. "He drove from Mount Vernon to La Conner right at lunchtime. We ruled him out when we shouldn't have: That fourth truck was on the road at the same time."

"More theories. Enough theories. We're running out of time here, you know that. You pissed off Dunkin and he's going to fuck this up for all of us without knowing it. There's no more time."

He jabbed the map, his index finger nearly poking a hole through it. "It's within this six-mile stretch. Has to be. How long for you to walk her out to that barn and get down to it? Why bother?"

He slammed the trunk, handed Boldt the car keys and said, "You don't get it, do you? It's no bother." He wore an armored vest, neck to groin. He looked like a killer there in the moonlight, pockets bulging, the shotgun in his right hand. "Happy hunting," he said. "First man to find Crowley and the kids wins."

Boldt toyed with the keys between his fingers. "Think this through."

"I have." The low sonorous voice carried so much authority it was difficult for Boldt to argue.

"When I find it?" Boldt asked.

"*If* you find it, you know where to find me." He looked out across the expanse of harvested flowers toward the distant barn. "I'm not a monster, Boldt," he said, reading his thoughts. "I'm not after her." He indicated the backseat. "I'm after my kid. But unlike you, I'm not afraid of how to get there." He pushed past Boldt and opened the door to the backseat, took Lisa Crowley by the hair and dragged her from the car, standing her up.

Her injuries lent her a defeated look. Her empty eyes found Boldt and he warned Flemming, "You push her too hard in that condition and you'll kill her."

"More's the pity," Flemming said. He took Lisa Crowley by the arm and led her into the field. She offered no resistance, willing to sacrifice herself for her husband. Boldt stood there frozen by the sight of the two ghostly figures shrinking into the enormous field of black that gladly swallowed them.

A moment later, the Town Car sped away.

His imagination impossible to contain, Boldt spent the drive envisioning the activity in the barn, knowing full well that Flemming had every intention of following through with his threats, and that the man would enjoy it far more than he had been willing to admit perhaps even to himself. Flemming would kill her without meaning to. He would be left with a second murder—this one with a witness and too much evidence to overcome. How he would then choose to deal with Boldt remained uncertain to all concerned.

The enormous number of cars parked along the roads gave the night an eerie feeling, as if scores of people had deserted the area in a mass exodus. Boldt took a dirt road shortcut, saving himself five minutes and coming up to his suspect stretch of road from the backside. As he approached the paved intersection, another dark field of headless flowers enveloped the landscape to his left, several feet of which had not been harvested. He slowed and rolled down his window. Drooping dead daffodils, their heads slumped toward the pungent earth in silent prayer, kept vigil by the side of the road. It told Boldt that the entire forty-acre parcel had, quite recently, been a sea of daffodils in bloom. Yellow daffodils, he thought. Yellow, with yellow pollen. Knee height.

In the distance, a cluster of small sheds and the western slant of a metal farmhouse roof glowed a wet pale gray in the moonlight. The dead field rose slowly toward the outbuildings, and Boldt recognized immediately that the rise would elevate the farmhouse above the paved road.

Boldt steered the Town Car through a left turn and drove at a decent speed to avoid arousing suspicion. A large sycamore standing surprisingly close to the upcoming farmhouse spread its branches luxuriously over and down the small knoll toward the paved roadbed. Still a hundred yards off, Boldt knew intuitively that a large window would exist immediately behind that tree, that the living room walls inside would be painted a cream yellow. He knew the positioning of the furniture inside and the name of the man who had locked and now guarded its door, and that this same man ached to see a brown Taurus pull into the driveway and a woman climb from behind the wheel. He was to be disappointed that night, this man who stood sentry. The Taurus was never to come.

Boldt drove past, the dash lights dimmed, his eyes fixed on the road, not allowed to wander or stray toward the farmhouse to his left. He had seen all there was to see from the outside.

He needed inside now, and he needed Lisa Crowley in one piece.

Boldt ran through the moonswept field toward the distant barn, the cut stems of the headless flowers slapping at his pants legs, his shoes engorged with wet, sticky mud so that his legs weighed ten times their normal. The faster he tried to run, the heavier the mud, the slower he moved. He stopped and scraped the rich-smelling earth from his shoes, soiling his hands in the process.

As he came upon the barn, he listened into the stillness for her voice, hoping for any such sound at all. Greeted only by the silence, he sank into a pit of despair, confident that the only card they held was the life of Lisa Crowley, that her husband would cut any bargain to save his accomplice from torture and death. Flemming had jumped the gun.

Boldt checked the three doors he could find and finally knocked on the huge barn's wood door, gray from decades of weather. Flemming must have had a peephole, for he removed the wooden bar and opened the door without a word spoken. Boldt stepped inside and stopped cold.

A pale flashlight beam stretched from a tractor's tire across the barn's aisle to a large square post that helped support the hayloft above. Lisa Crowley's bare back and naked buttocks caught the light looking like a side of beef hung in a freezer. Her clothes were strewn in the dust and dirt of the aisle. Flemming had looped the cuffs over a rusty spike pounded into the cedar post well above head height, stretching her so that her toes just barely touched the dirt floor. Her head sideways, Boldt could see the left side of her face, smashed and swollen from the car accident. He walked toward her slowly. Flemming had removed the tape from her mouth and had stuffed her underwear there so she could make noise if she so chose, and he could evaluate her information by simply removing the underwear, restuffing her, if he went unsatisfied. The bright red blotches from the stun stick glowed violently red near her breasts and across her buttocks and the backs of her thighs. A dozen or more.

"Dress her," Boldt said, disgusted with the man.

"We're just getting warmed up."

"I'll do it then," Boldt said, approaching her. "I found the house. It was exactly as I said. The driver took his lunch hour in La Conner. He drove past the farmhouse shortly after noon, on no particular route, unlisted on the manifest."

Removing the woman's underwear from her mouth, he told her, "I'm going to help you get dressed. I'm going to lift you now." He stepped behind her and reached his hands up under her sweating armpits.

"Leave her." Flemming had hold of the shotgun in his right hand, its barrel hanging toward the dirt floor, but its presence very much felt by all. His eyes revealed a man void of thought or reason. Revenge had sunk its teeth into him, and he had tasted its blood. He wanted more.

"I found the farmhouse," Boldt repeated.

"Then we don't need her," Flemming said. "Step away."

Her damp back pressed to his face, Boldt still supported her. "I'm taking her down," he said.

Flemming engaged the shotgun in a sound all too familiar to the cop he faced.

Boldt gave another heave and Crowley's bound hands came

free of the spike. She crossed her arms in front of her bare chest in modesty, her breasts riddled with stun gun burns, and sagged to the dirt, cowering under the threat of the shotgun. Boldt pushed the underwear into her hands, crouched close to her, placing himself between her and Flemming and said gently, "Dress yourself. Hurry."

She struggled with the underwear. Boldt snagged the purple dress. Flemming had torn the arms out to get it off her. Boldt helped her into it, the black hole at the end of the shotgun barrel boring down on him, and tied a ripped length of fabric behind her neck to cover her chest.

He turned to Flemming and said, "We're going. The three of us. We're going to get our daughters."

"No."

"She's our bargaining chip. If you're going to kill her, at least wait until we've used her to get our girls back. Don't throw them away for the sake of some score that can never be settled." Boldt wondered how Daphne would have handled the situation. She understood the Flemmings of this world, he thought. And then Boldt realized that with Flemming being a cop, he understood him as well. Knowing the answer, Boldt asked, "How many years do you have?"

Flemming looked confused.

"With the Bureau. How long?"

The man's expression sobered.

"How many agents, black or white, look up to you? Model themselves after you?"

"Save it *and* the violins. Let her go, and step away."

"You discharge that weapon and we'll never make it to that farmhouse. A community like this? Forget it. Sheriff'll be all over us before we make it to the car." This appeared to register on the man's face. Boldt held Crowley ever closer. Indicating the variety of weaponry that Flemming had laid out on a hay bale, Boldt said, "Collect that stuff. We may need it." Crowley leaned her weight into him, weak, her stretched and cramping legs unable to support her. Boldt turned his back to Flemming and walked her out of the barn.

CHAPTER

Boldt cut through the field of headless daffodils, bent at the waist, staying as low as possible, hoping to avoid the glare of the moonlight. The investigator in him knew that he was, in some form or another, retracing footsteps taken by Andy Anderson some weeks before. Mindful of Anderson's fate, Boldt paused randomly and sank down into a crouch, like a swimmer ducking into a wave. His decision to leave Crowley alone in the car with Flemming had come with great difficulty, but better that, he had decided, than leave it to Flemming to approach the farmhouse. Gun happy, and crazed with the thirst of revenge, Flemming felt more like a time bomb than an ally. Boldt hurried—the fuse to that time bomb was lit and burning.

The warm night air carried the promise of summer and the faint scent of the millions of tulips that ran for mile after mile. On a different night, the two-story farmhouse would have looked picturesque to him, glazed in moonlight, clustered in a nest of outbuildings. As Boldt drew near he used those sheds as a screen, abandoning his crouch and running fully erect.

He and Flemming held many advantages, not the least of which was Roger Crowley's expectation and anticipation of his wife's arrival. Although not a Taurus, the Town Car would work to that end with proper timing; it was for this reason that Boldt's cell phone was already dialed to call Flemming, awaiting the simple touch of the SEND button.

His chest pounding from a combination of nerves and the run up the slope, Boldt ducked around one shed and then another. He carried two stun grenades and a phosphorus bomb in his sport coat. Flemming had retained the stun stick and the shotgun.

The downstairs of the farmhouse was lit up like the Fourth of July, every window ablaze. Boldt stood in the lee of a shed carefully studying what lay behind each window. Toward the back, a kitchen: empty. Toward the front, a living room: empty. The upstairs remained dark, and Boldt knew from his own exploration of the Pied Piper's surveillance points that the man preferred the higher ground, the darkness and seclusion of a pair of curtains partially drawn.

In the end it came down to a string of decisions for Boldt and Flemming, none of which held any guarantees, all of which carried tremendous risk for their two daughters. They lacked a Taurus. They lacked manpower. Time. Their one hostage was weakened to the point of near unconsciousness. Their adversary held a farmhouse, elevated for good security, no doubt fortified, and containing two of the most precious people on earth.

Boldt considered Special Ops and SPD's Emergency Response Team, wondering if he would have dared put Sarah's life into their hands.

If he attempted to sneak inside but gave himself away, Sarah would go from kidnap victim to hostage. Of primary importance was knowing Crowley's exact location. All else was secondary, as the man's location represented the degree of threat to their daughters. Boldt moved around the shed in shadow, reemerging on the structure's other side with a different, and improved, view of both the kitchen's interior and that of the living room. Both still appeared empty.

Roger Crowley, the Pied Piper, was somewhere upstairs in the dark.

Boldt pulled out his cell phone and pressed the SEND button, initiating the signal. He waited to hear it ring through and hung up.

Seconds later, a pair of headlights rounded the far corner of the forty-acre field and motored slowly toward the farmhouse. Boldt pressed himself flat against the damp wood and waited.

CHAPTER

Flemming pulled the Town Car into the gravel driveway and quickly shut off the engine and headlights. Boldt realized an unexpected advantage they held: The sycamore's grandeur obscured any view of the driveway from the farmhouse's second story. For all Crowley knew, the Taurus and his injured wife had finally arrived.

Boldt heard the man's descending footfalls through the wall of the house as Crowley hurried down a set of back stairs—he had taken the bait. He appeared fleetingly in the kitchen, then passed into the living room. Boldt stepped farther into the light, straining for a better view and winning sight of him by a far window. Then gone. Crowley reappeared at the front door, as he opened it a crack and craned his neck to get a view of a Taurus that wasn't there.

The kids were being kept on the second story, away from a random sighting by a curious tourist, within reach of Crowley as he played sentry in the dark. By exploding toward a reunion with his wife, he had left his flank open.

Boldt hurried to close it.

He cut to his left, crouched and ran across the damp, recently mowed lawn, the smell of which wafted up and overwhelmed his senses. He delicately climbed three steps at the rear of the house and slid an eye to the window: He was watching Crowley, who in turn was focused on the driveway and the car parked there. His heart beat frantically. Sarah's face floated in his vision. He could feel Liz there with him, like a warm coat. He wanted to kick the door and run upstairs. His weapon in hand, he stayed frozen in place, one eye glued to the window's dirty glass.

Thump! he heard the car door shut. He switched the gun to his left hand and dried his right palm on his pants leg, returning the weapon to the proper hand. He heard another car door shut, followed by Flemming's deep voice, and Crowley let the front door swing open as Flemming demanded. There, just beyond the front door and slightly to the left, bathed in the spread of lamplight from inside the house, Boldt saw Flemming leading Lisa Crowley up the lawn, under the tree, holding her by the hair, his sidearm aimed into her right ear.

Boldt kicked the back door, dove to the kitchen floor and aimed his weapon onto Roger Crowley. "Hands in plain sight!" Boldt shouted. Crowley froze. Boldt repeated the command even louder, hoping the sound of his voice might call his daughter to him.

Crowley's arms jumped and his fingers laced on top of his head.

"You got him?" Boldt shouted.

"Got him," Flemming answered. "Face down, motherfucker, arms out straight ahead."

Roger Crowley, the Pied Piper, collapsed to the floor.

Boldt came to his feet and charged the man. Flemming held the sidearm aimed into the front door, the handcuffed Lisa Crowley on her knees, gripped by her hair.

No cars coming from either direction.

Boldt checked the man and found no weapon on him, not even a penknife. Daphne had been right about that: Con artists by trade, the Crowleys abhorred violence. "Clear!" Boldt shouted.

"Go!"

Boldt hurried through the ground floor of the house checking every room, every closet, every hiding place large enough to hold a two-year-old girl. "Downstairs is clear," he reported out the door. "Basement and upstairs to go."

"There's no one here," Roger Crowley complained, his face pressed into the plank flooring. "Who are you? What do you want?" A convincing performance. Ever the con man.

"Shut up!" Flemming bellowed. "Upstairs!" he shouted to Boldt, ever the commanding officer.

Boldt ran back into a kitchen he had already searched, located the narrow stairway and took it two treads at a time. The dormered roof held two cramped bedrooms and a shared bath. Three closets, a chest of drawers, a green metal steamer trunk. He checked the closets first, no longer breathing despite a heart attempting to rip from his chest. He held to the doorknob, unable to turn it, to open it, for fear of what he would see inside.

"Anything?" he heard Flemming shout.

He twisted the doorknob and pulled. Empty.

The next room, the same.

He stood then over the steamer trunk. He had worked crime scenes before with bodies in steamer trunks. Women usually. Folded up. Molested. Dead. He couldn't see his daughter that way; he couldn't find her like that. It was not something a father could live through. He kneeled and sniffed the seams of the trunk. Cedar—like a breath of fresh air. He threw the trunk open: blankets.

"Clear," he shouted, heading directly into the basement.

The small cellar, lit by a single bare bulb, held a washer and dryer that had seen better days, tools, a workbench and a clutter of broken bicycles, lawn chairs and a doll collection. Boldt stopped, held in a trance by the shelves of dusty dolls. If the girls had spent much time there, the dolls would have been put to good use. His heart fluttered and he became conscious of his breathing again—slow, like a man dying.

He struggled up the stairs, one heavy foot after another, his gun hanging lifelessly at his side, walked into the living room to the front door and trained the gun at Crowley's head. "Where's my daughter?" he asked, his voice breaking, his eyes stinging.

Crowley cowered under the threat of the gun.

"Boldt," he said dryly. "I'm Boldt. Sarah's my daughter." He glanced up into the room, the gun still aimed at the man's head. "She sat in that chair," he said, "while your wife shot the video."

"We can make a deal," Crowley offered. "A trade," he proposed.

"A trade?" Flemming shouted in a bloodcurdling tirade.

"My wife . . . Our freedom for the girls."

"Your wife?" Flemming bellowed. "I'll give you a fucking trade." He let go of her hair, stepped in close to his hostage, trained the gun at her head and pulled the trigger. Lisa Crowley slumped back and fell into the grass.

"Nooo!" Crowley shouted, raising up onto his arms and met there by Flemming's weapon. His body shook as he wept, bawling on the floor.

It wasn't enough for Boldt, to see this man grovel. He squeezed the trigger, putting a round into the floor inches from the man's head. "Where . . . is . . . my . . . daughter?"

Flemming occupied the entire door, a gargantuan, his weapon aimed directly at Crowley's head. "You want a trade? Your life for our daughters. But time's up, fella." He hesitated. "You got a god, you better say good-bye—or hello—whichever it is."

"A home!" Crowley shouted. "Jesus Christ, you killed her!"

"Home?" Boldt and Flemming said nearly in unison.

Flemming added, "Say good night, motherfucker." He stepped closer to the downed man.

"Yours," he said to Flemming, "is in San Diego!" he sniveled. "A home for abandoned children." He met eyes with Boldt. "Yours is in Seattle. Capitol Hill. Homeless children. We put them into the system—your system. We knew you'd never look."

Boldt raised the gun to where the bead settled on the man's right ear. His weak arm began trembling, the bead dancing across the man's head— temple, ear, cranium. Sarah had been available to him all along, a few blocks from Public Safety. The Crowleys had used the very system that had refused them an adoption.

"You had better kill me too," Crowley said to Flemming, suddenly much calmer, "because so help me God, I'll testify you did that in cold blood."

Boldt laughed aloud and Flemming followed, the two men with their guns still aimed at the Pied Piper's head. They laughed and suddenly sobered nearly at the same moment.

"You stupid shit," Flemming said to the man. "I'm a cop," he looked up at Boldt, "I'm not allowed to go around killing people, much as I'd like to sometimes."

Crowley's face contorted.

"I stunned her—left-handed, I might add. Aimed the piece clear of her head. She'll be awake in twenty minutes."

Crowley muttered, finally making sense of it. "You conned me?"

"Takes one to know one," Lou Boldt said.

CHAPTER

85

Daphne circled the interrogation table in Room A—the Box—like a hawk after a snake. Boldt had brokered a deal with Hale, who won Chevalier's arrest in New Orleans as an FBI collar in return for his silence concerning his overnight in an airport drunk tank.

With Chevalier under federal lockup, Crowley had been appointed a little pencil of an attorney, a man who looked about eighteen years old, a man who did not know how to handle a woman like Daphne, intimidated by both her looks and her powerful sense of control. Crowley dismissed him, electing to take Daphne on alone. He chose to do this in front of her, to make a statement about control. She continued to circle, changing strategies, attempting to find a jumping-off point. She lived for such moments.

Her concentration ever intense, she nonetheless found herself required to push away thought of Owen Adler's invitation to dinner in the Georgian Room at the Four Seasons Olympic. He had said it was a celebration dinner, but she intuitively expected more. The Presidential Suite perhaps. A ring on her left hand—the same ring she had returned to him a year earlier. Her life moved in arcs, and she felt certain that arc was to rejoin her with Owen. *But not now*, she willed, finding her way back to the dismal room and the sad excuse of a man handcuffed at the table.

"If you are pacing out of nerves," Crowley said calmly, "pray continue. When you feel up to it, we'll have ourselves a talk. If you are trying to make a statement—you're free to move around, I have my ankles shackled—save it. Been there, done that. I know where I'm going, do you? You're good-looking but you're single. You have a body and a face that men fall for, but something keeps you out of serious relationships, and I bet that something is you. You are your own worst enemy, aren't you? They are never good enough for you, are they? Never quite live up to dear old dad, do they? Afraid to take them home, are we?"

She should have expected this from a con artist of his accomplishments—he could see into his marks and knew which nerve to strike without second thought; it was an instinct with him. She had prepared herself for a kidnapper, not the man Crowley turned out to be. She chastised herself for this. She wanted a confession; she didn't want the trial left only to evidence, some of which had been compromised through the behavior of the Gang of Five.

She said, "The Pied Piper of Hamelin was caught. You knew in advance that you and your wife would be caught if you continued. You could have stopped, but you didn't. That fascinates me."

"Of course I fascinate you. You're what, the staff shrink? Not a detective, are we? You don't have the attitude, you see? You're curious. The detectives think they know it all. Of course I'm fascinating to you. We both make our living by looking inside people. Hmm? The only difference is that I see what's really there. You? You're a phony."

She grinned at him, though it didn't come naturally. She guessed at people's secrets; this man seemed to know them in advance. He made no reference to the kidnappings or his crimes, steering the topic back to Daphne. She wanted that confession. "You put Lieutenant Boldt's child into a home. What made you think that would work?"

"I see you more as a mistress, someone's mistress. It leaves the door open, doesn't it? Always open, easy to walk out. Get your jollies—you're a hell of a ride, aren't you?—but sleep in your own bed, thank you very much."

The attack struck home, and Daphne's only defense was an immediate rebuttal—focus his attention away from her. She had played the role of mistress with Owen Adler; she owed him more than that. She countered, "I think I would pose as a social worker. Your wife too; a team is more effective, more believable. I deliver little Sarah to the institution saying that her parents are dead, a cop and his wife—what? a car accident?—that the child hasn't been told yet, that I'm looking for closest living relatives. I need her taken care of for a week or two, maybe a month or more. Something like that. If the child is capable of communicating her surname or that her father is a cop or an FBI agent, her comments will not draw reactions from her keepers because they know she hasn't been told about her parents—that's the key to the deception I would think: the child is still in the dark about all this. They will placate her, patronize her, but ultimately she's a victim of the system, which was just what you wanted. She'll be looked after, treated well, and in the case of Bowler in Portland, and who knows how many others like him, when all is said and done, once you've packed your bags, you can return as the same pair of social workers, pick up the child and deliver him or her back to the parents. Nice and clean. How am I doing?" She saw perfectly well that she had guessed accurately. Crowley's complexion went the milky white of the acoustical tiles overhead.

"Or maybe not a social worker. A cop? A pair of cops? You used that at the day care center. I don't know that it matters."

"You didn't answer me, about your being a mistress. I was right about that, wasn't I? You're the Teflon woman. You never stick to anyone you get close to."

She fired back, "You want to discuss relationships? Good. Glad you brought it up. Your inability to have children. It's *your* problem, isn't it, not your wife's? Lisa is fertile, isn't she? And yet no kids. I bet a man like you made her go through a dozen tests while all the time knowing that your seed was at cause. Your seed is dead, isn't it. Like you. You can't admit that, can you? Dead seed, dead man."

"Shut up!"

Knowing she had scored a direct hit, she withheld any self-congratulations. She wanted him on record as confessing the crimes.

She hurried, "You don't want kids anyway. It's Lisa who wanted them, not you. They would only get in the way of your brilliant career. Tie you down. Take your wife off the team, leave you working alone. What fun is that? The fun is showing off for her, isn't that right? For Lisa. Showing her how good you are. What a liar you can be. No audience, what's the fun? It's not the money. You spend any money you win because you want her to need you again, you want to keep up the game. It's all about the game. The confidence game. It owns you—that thrill of deception. Or maybe she's the one with the brains. I bet that's hard for a man like you, a man with dead seed, to accept that your wife is more clever than you. She came to you with the plan, didn't she? She wanted to kidnap a baby and keep it."

"Absurd," he protested.

"It was her plan," she fired off.

"That's bullshit."

"She wanted a child badly enough to steal one, and you saw your life in flames if she pulled it off—"

"We *both* wanted that child, but you people took him away from us. Why? Because we'd served some time? So what?"

"So you got back at the system."

"Damn right!"

She knew that to beat him she had to con him, exactly as Boldt and Flemming had done. She saw only the one area of vulnerability and decided to exploit it, making assumptions that were only that. "She wanted the baby, but you couldn't live with that. It was you who suggested to give other women what the two of you had been denied. I don't see you as the compassionate type, but I have a hunch it was your idea nonetheless. Why? Because it was another game. You didn't want a baby underfoot; you didn't want your precious team broken up. Give your wife children to take care of, but keep the game alive." She leaned her hands onto the table and said confidently, as if every word was knowledge not guesswork. "What if I go next door and tell your wife that all those tests she did were for nothing? All that equipment up inside her. All those doctors, the drugs, the grief. That very early on you lied to her about the results of your own fertility test because you couldn't live with the dead seed inside of you. That you're shooting blanks now and that you always were, and that everything she did was for nothing? Maybe we should test you. How about that? How do you think she's going to feel about that level of betrayal? You think she won't give you up?"

"That's lies!"

"Maybe it is, maybe it isn't." She added, "It makes a hell of a story, doesn't it? One I'm sure she'd pay particular attention to."

"You . . . You can't do that!"

"I can do anything I want," she corrected. She waved her hands in the air—his were manacled. "Why else would you talk her out of keeping the first baby? You made her think it was her idea, didn't you—selling them to women like her? You conned your own wife. You never stop, do you? How often did she ask you to end the kidnappings and keep one of the babies? To make a life with her? And you always had a reason for her, didn't you? Always a reason waiting on the end of your lying tongue."

"She wanted the money just as much as I did," Crowley objected, confessing for the first time their involvement in the kidnappings. Daphne felt a triumphant surge of adrenaline. He shouted angrily, "She wanted the kid to have all the chances, all the opportunities. The schools, the clothes, the whole nine yards. Bank a million bucks for ourselves and then keep a kid of our own. And you're wrong about me not wanting our own—" He caught himself. If he could have rewound the tape and erased the last few sentences he would have, but instead he stared at Daphne and a grin slowly stole over his thin lips and his sweaty face rose into a smile that gave way to laughter. He tried to communicate something to her through eye contact, but the message was lost on the volume of his laughter and the keen concentration in his eyes. He stopped laughing, maintained the eye contact, and said, "I think I'll take that attorney now."

"So noted," she said. The comments were as good as a confession.

As she placed her hand on the doorknob, Roger Crowley conceded, "Well done."

Daphne hesitated there a moment, knowing that Boldt and Flemming had had the chance to kill this man, to bury him in a tulip field never to be found.

She looked back at the man in the orange coveralls and steel handcuffs. "They should have killed you," she said.

"Opportunity is the name of the game," Roger Crowley said back to her.

CHAPTER

86

"How's my hair?"

"What hair?" Boldt answered.

"The wig, stupid."

"It's fine."

Miles held tightly to his father's neck, clutching to him like a drowning man to a lifeboat.

After only a few yards of controlled walking, Liz and Boldt broke into a run at the same time, their speed having little or nothing to do with the rain as it began falling, and everything to do with a parent's excitement.

Liz laughed into that rain, part primal scream, part cry, chin up, mouth catching the drops. It was not the voice of a dying woman, her husband noted. This woman alongside of him was very much alive. "I can't stand it!" she shouted in glee.

Boldt endeavored to speak, to say something, to answer his wife, to acknowledge her, but his tears mixed with the rain and his eyes blurred and he reached out for her arm like a blind person wanting guidance. This woman had guided him through so much. Reluctantly, he left her disease to her and her god; willingly, he turned over his soul and heart, abandoning the isolation he had felt since her hospitalization. If she died, he would come to terms with that. In the meantime, he would hold no part of himself in reserve, would seek no shelter in moods or in his work. He gave himself back to her freely, and of his own will.

Miles shouted his sister's name, for the small girl stood in the gothic doorway of the institution's entrance, jumping up and down on both feet, a black social worker at her side.

They hurried up the stone steps, splashing puddles of rainwater like small explosions at their feet, Miles calling her name, Liz reaching, straining forward to touch her daughter.

They came together then, a family, a rich embrace that for Boldt defied time or description. The moment—a single moment in time he had been living for. Not a bit like anything he had dreamed or imagined. Something else entirely better.

Little Sarah cried for days off and on—months, if measured in fear—and Boldt would listen painfully as his wife attempted to soothe the child with that calming voice of hers. Each sob stabbed his heart viciously and unforgivably. Up and down the West Coast, a dozen other children sobbed this same way, clutched tightly in their parent's embrace, most too young to know the source of their tears, too young to ever remember clearly the days, weeks or months of separation they had endured.

But Lou Boldt remembered. In the darkness of a room without lights, a haunting tenor wailing from the stereo, he sat in the corner blinded by a consuming guilt that would not pass. He picked up the phone and called LaMoia to his house.

Thirty minutes later the reinstated sergeant stood in Boldt's music room, not a wrinkle in his jeans, not a dull spot on his steel gray ostrich boots.

"You rang?" LaMoia said. He had regained some of the weight the suspension had cost him. He looked good. Nothing new there. "You hear the engagement is back on?"

"I heard."

"Surprised?"

"Happy for her."

"Will we lose her?" LaMoia asked, genuinely concerned—he, the man who often battled with her.

"It's possible. But not forever. She can't leave this forever. It's in her, same as you and me."

"The Anderson case is still not cleared," LaMoia reminded. "We can't get a confession out of him."

"Crowley didn't do Anderson," Boldt informed him, "Flemming did."

LaMoia stood perfectly still. "Jesus."

"Crowley spotted Anderson while out on that run. He got a message to Flemming telling him Anderson was taking pictures, that something had to be done. Flemming knew that for his daughter's sake Anderson had to be shut up. Flemming used his FBI ID to get him through the front door—I've got to admit that fooled me, threw me off. I thought it had to be someone who knew Anderson or had a relationship with him. He claims he went there to convince Anderson that he had it all wrong, arrest him if necessary, but that Anderson knew he was onto the Pied Piper, and that he got arrogant about it. Things went bad. Anderson's neck ended up snapped. Flemming covered himself."

"And he just walks?"

"It's your investigation. Yours and Gaynes's. You have any evidence linking Flemming to that kill? You want to prosecute it?"

"You've changed, Sarge."

"Yes. I'm a lieutenant now," Boldt said. But he was a father most of all, and he knew what Flemming had endured for those six months. The man had announced his retirement. He would go into security work somewhere, ride out the next fifteen years being bored behind a desk. How much more did society require of him?

Boldt rose out of the chair and switched some buttons on the stereo. He pushed PLAY on his cassette deck. A series of familiar tones filled the room, not quite music.

"Know what that is?" Boldt asked his former detective.

"Telephone tones."

"Move to the front of the class."

"So what?" LaMoia asked.

"Umm," Boldt muttered. Guilt was a difficult cross to bear, but more difficult to break. "I needed you," he explained. Or he thought he did. "I trusted you. I needed you."

"You need a Valium is what you need. Word is, you're coming back to the shop next week."

"Tech Services wiretapped every member of the task force—their phones—for me. I ordered it."

"When?"

"After Sarah." He hesitated. "But before your suspension."

Boldt rewound and replayed the telephone tones—a long string of tones with a few, equally long pauses. "It took me forever to figure out the code. I broke it when I realized the first numbers were your pager. Tech Services, actually. They're the ones that filled in that blank."

"You tapped Hill's line?" LaMoia barked in astonishment, not listening clearly. "You tapped a fucking captain's phone line?" A touch of reverence. He glanced around, embarrassed by the loose tongue. "You're outta your gourd," he whispered. Then the realization Boldt had awaited finally cascaded over LaMoia's face as he added the information together. His brow tightened and his mustache and mouth sagged into concern.

"You?" the sergeant asked, incredulous.

"She told me that she was going to assign you the accident in Boise."

"You?" Outright astonishment.

"I couldn't allow that. I needed to short-circuit Flemming's plan to steal the task force and preserve you for my team. For New Orleans. For Sarah."

"You bastard."

"Yeah, I know."

Silence hung between them, and with it, Boldt feared their friendship as well. LaMoia's record would forever be blemished; it was an unspoken rule that a suspension, even though cleared by review, affected an officer's rate of advancement forever.

Miles cried out LaMoia's name from the other room—a child's

shrill peal of pure pleasure. A moment later, Sarah's tiny voice echoed the same delight.

John LaMoia grinned, lifted his head, shut his eyes and drank in the sounds like sweet perfume. "You bastard," he said, offering Boldt his back and hurrying into the room to play with the kids.